The Ghost in the Corner and Other Stories

For Dylan —
best wishes

LORD DUNSANY

THE GHOST IN THE CORNER AND OTHER STORIES

Edited by S. T. Joshi and
Martin Andersson

Hippocampus Press

New York

CONTENTS

INTRODUCTION

It is only in recent years that we are coming to understand the full scope and extent of the writings of the Anglo-Irish fantaisiste Lord Dunsany (1878–1957). Hailed as a pioneer of fantasy literature, he is best known for the exquisite tales and plays he wrote during the first decade and a half of his literary career, from *The Gods of Pegāna* (1905) to *Tales of Three Hemispheres* (1919), and including such memorable volumes as *A Dreamer's Tales* (1910) and *The Book of Wonder* (1912), not to mention such plays as *The Gods of the Mountain* (1911) and *The Queen's Enemies* (1916). The work that Dunsany wrote in the remaining four decades of his long life are just as distinctive, ranging from the novel-length prose-poem known as *The King of Elfland's Daughter* (1924) to such a poignant novel of Irish life and character as *The Curse of the Wise Woman* (1933).

But the totality of Dunsany's writings—novels, stories, plays, essays, poetry, and miscellany—is far greater than this. Among his published work we find fourteen novels (including his final one, *The Pleasures of a Futuroscope*, published in 2003 by Hippocampus Press), nearly 600 stories, 550 poems, nearly 50 plays, and much else besides. Hundreds of works remain uncollected, and among his papers at Dunsany Castle in County Meath can be found manuscripts of dozens of unpublished works. This volume offers a representative selection of some of the best of these unpublished and uncollected writings, especially those produced during the final three decades of his career, when Dunsany was generating material with the speed and efficiency of a journalist for all manner of magazines and newspapers—each item, however, still infused with a modicum of the ineffable charm and otherworldly aura that characterize his best work.

H. P. Lovecraft, among others, lamented the apparent diminution of the fantasy element in Dunsany's later work; and it is true that the "real" world enters more concretely in his novels, tales, and plays of the 1920s and thereafter; but even those works that appear to be purely realistic still manage, in some inscrutable manner, to retain an element of the strange and the whimsical. Dunsany never became a Hemingway. Consider such a late story as "The Romance of His Life" (1952), which is nothing more than an account of a famous actress who, insulted that a

man on a train seems impervious to her beauty, exercises all her feminine skills to make the man her "abject slave." Once the train arrives at
its destination, she walks away from him and forgets all about him. To
be sure, a satirist such as Evelyn Waugh would have turned a scenario of
this sort into a pungent satire on feminine wiles; but in Dunsany there
remains a hint of the fantastic that in some strange way allies it with the
romance of Lirazel and Alveric in *The King of Elfland's Daughter.*

Humor and satire, indeed, were at the forefront of Dunsany's writing during this entire period, as the story "The Use of Man" (1931) re-
veals. This story—later rewritten into an even more effective play of
the same title, found in *Plays for Earth and Air* (1937)—asks us to believe that the spirit of a somewhat foolish man is summoned to a con-
clave of the spirits of all earthly creatures and is pointedly asked to
justify the "use" of man on earth. The man has trouble coming up
with a plausible case for why the human race is of any use at all to the
animal kingdom. This is one of several tales ("A Witch in the Balkans,"
"A Goat in Trousers," and "As It Seems to the Blackbird" are others)
in which Dunsany—a pioneering environmentalist and champion of
animal rights—compels us to look at the world from the perspective
of the creatures who cohabit the earth with humans. This motif
reached its pinnacle in the novel *The Strange Journeys of Colonel Polders*
(1950), a forgotten classic of fantasy.

Another major theme in the stories in this book is Dunsany's con-
flicted view of Ireland and his fellow Irishmen. In spite of the fact that
he wrote several poignant novels about Ireland—not only *The Curse of
the Wise Woman* but also *Up in the Hills* (1935), *Rory and Bran* (1936), and
The Story of Mona Sheehy (1939)—he was long looked upon with suspicion by his countrymen, perhaps because of their lingering resentment
of his title and background. Dunsany himself remained definitely Anglo-Irish and was opposed to the cause of Irish independence. He only
wrote *The Curse of the Wise Woman* because he appeared to be offended
that W. B. Yeats neglected to make him a full member of the Irish
Academy of Letters because he had not written extensively of his native land. (Dunsany was actually born in England, but his family had
resided in Dunsany Castle since the fifteenth century and in Ireland
since possibly as early as the eleventh.)

As a result, Dunsany's tales of Ireland and Irish life, almost always comical and satirical, do not shy away from tartness and pungency. Some of them tell of amusing incidents of Irish chicanery ("The Rations of Murdoch Finucan," "Little Tim Brannehan"); others mock Irish credulity in regard to the supernatural ("The Burrahoola," "A Tale of the Irish Countryside"). Perhaps the most pungent of all is "Helping the Fairies," a story whose humor is decidedly black. On the strength of stories like this, to say nothing of his having taken the "wrong" side on the questions of home rule and independence, it is not surprising that Irish readers and critics long felt the need to write Dunsany out of the literary history of Ireland; but with the passing of time and because of the high regard that Dunsany continues to claim in fantasy literature, Irish prejudice against him seems finally to be on the wane.

Dunsany's life in the 1930s and 1940s was an adventurous one. Aside from his frequent trips to Africa and Asia in quest of big game, he participated as much as he could in the struggle against the Axis powers during World War I. Sent to Athens as Byron Professor of English Literature at Athens University in 1940, he was forced to evacuate when the Germans invaded, taking an incredibly circuitous trip down through Africa before sailing back to Ireland by boat. His sense of the doom that might overtake the human race when the United States dropped the atomic bomb on Japan in 1945 is searingly etched in a series of papers he was writing at the time, *A Glimpse from a Watch Tower* (1945); and the threat of nuclear catastrophe is the basis of several grim tales, from "The Stolen Power" to "The Price of the World."

To Dunsany, the atomic bomb was just the most visible symbol of humanity's self-destructiveness. Civilization was, in his view, threatened from many other directions, and not the least of them was the fundamental irrationality and absurdity of much of what passes as modern art, poetry, and architecture. Many of Dunsany's screeds against these things may come off sounding like the crotchety intolerance of a Philistine, but his tales on the subject are among his most piquant and amusing. "The Awakening," "A Theory of Evolution," and "A Modern Portrait" effectively skewer their targets with a satirical flourish that Evelyn Waugh himself (whom Dunsany admired) could not have improved upon.

Remarkably for one who seemed so attuned to the fantastic, Dunsany excelled in the detective story, whose keynotes are realism and rationality. Ellery Queen considered the late collection *The Little Tales of Smethers* (1952) to be one of the cornerstone volumes in the literature of detection, so it is no surprise that "The Old Detective's Story" appeared in *Ellery Queen's Mystery Magazine,* albeit under a different title and apparently heavily rewritten. (Our text is a restored version based on Dunsany's manuscript.)

But in Dunsany the need for fantasy as an antidote to the prosiness of modern life was unremitting, and in such tales as "The Traveller to Thundercliff" and "A Breeze at Rest" we find hints of the Dunsany whose early tales set at "the edge of the world" inspired such adulation among their first readers—and continue to do so today. "The Dwarf Holóbolos and the Sword Hogbiter," written for his young grandson Edward, enhances Dunsany's claim to being a pioneer in the subgenre of sword and sorcery, a mode he may have pioneered with the story "The Fortress Unvanquishable, Save for Sacnoth" (1908).

Dunsany's continuing vigor even as he entered his eighth decade of life is remarkable. One must consult his scrapbooks—in which he wrote the first (and oftentimes the only) drafts of his tales, poems, and essays, frequently using crayon—to see how productive he remained to the end of his life. *The Pleasures of a Futuroscope* probably dates to 1955; around that time he also compiled a final volume of stories focusing on the clubman Joseph Jorkens (this volume, unpublished in Dunsany's lifetime, has now appeared as *The Last Book of Jorkens*). In 1956 he assembled an untitled story collection to follow *The Man Who Ate the Phoenix* (1949) and *The Little Tales of Smethers;* but it too was never published. We are happy to present the complete contents of this volume herewith, featuring both uncollected and unpublished stories.

Lord Dunsany's immensely prolific output is difficult for readers to grasp, both because of its diversity of mode (novel, story, play, essay, poem) but also of literary genre (fantasy, supernatural horror, detection and mystery, humor, satire, mainstream). But every one of his works is imbued with his distinctive vision as an Irishman, a nobleman, a devotee of Nature and simple living, a scorner of technology and industrialization, and a keen observer of the foibles of the human race. The sum total of his work stands as an imperishable contribution to the literature of the imagination.

—S. T. JOSHI AND MARTIN ANDERSSON

A Note on the Texts

The editors have consulted Dunsany's manuscripts and typescripts in establishing the texts of the stories presented in this volume. In several instances, the manuscript versions differ substantially from the published version, and in every instance we have chosen to follow the former. We are grateful to Maria Alice, the Dowager Lady Dunsany, for allowing us access to these documents.

Tales and Sketches, 1931–1957

The Use of Man

If ever a man slept with a good conscience Pelby did. He was the master of the Beldale and Annersham, and a few friends, all members of the Committee, had been dining with him. They had had some very good port, but not too much of it, and after the port they had all talked at some length in answer to Pelby's question, "What is the use of badgers?" And on this conversation and good port he had gone to bed. Surely, nothing to disturb any man's conscience in that. Of course all masters of hounds hate badgers.

Pelby got to sleep very soon. He always did in the hunting season, and it was now November. Sometimes he fretted a little in the summer, so that idle rambling thoughts kept him awhile awake; but all through the autumn and winter the content of a simple life entirely enveloped him. For spiritual things he cared little enough, and of spirits he knew nothing at all, having never even read of them; so that he was all the more surprised on waking suddenly to see one all erect at the foot of his bed.

"You, you wanted me?" he said to the thing of lines and shadows. The deep and musical tones of its answer filled the room.

"I have a question to ask," it replied.

So stern were its tones, so strange the sweep of its outlines, that awe of the proud dim thing troubled the M. F. H.

"Nothing serious?" he asked.

"Come," said the Spirit.

"But where?" said the M. F. H.

"Come," it said, its arm sweeping away and pointing like a great weathercock at a change of the wind. Pelby rose at once, the Spirit turned and he followed, having no choice but to do as he was bid, and together they passed through his wall and drifted swiftly away.

The whole incident and the speed at which they were moving stimulated his thoughts at first to a greater rapidity than he had ever known: the past flashed by, while his guesses illumined the future; and then the great speed of the journey bewildered him altogether and his thoughts were either numb or incoherent.

After a while their speed seemed to have gone, and neither they nor anything round them seemed moving. Only the Earth was dwindling rapidly, a ball behind them with ever narrowing sides. When Earth was out of sight they came to a level space that appeared to suffice to hold up the feet of spirits, a sward of air or ether that seemed to slide softly into the stillness about them. And it was there that they saw the great gathering that was their journey's end. Spirit on spirit flashed in that place all round them. Then the Spirit that led Pelby turned round and faced him, and the Master of Fox Hounds knew he was going to put his question.

And the Spirit said to him, "What is the use of Man?"

The hundreds of spirits all round him turned their faces towards Pelby. And Pelby was conscious at first only of a difficulty in finding words to express what everyone knew and agreed on. Precise definitions never came easy to him. Nothing troubled him at first but that. And he turned to the Spirit and said, "Man, as everyone knows, civilizes, builds cities, makes roads."

"That is only for Man," said the Spirit.

"For whom else?" said Pelby.

"What use is he?" said the Spirit.

"Really," said Pelby, "these will explain it better than I can. Everyone knows, even if I can't find words for it." And he pointed to the hundreds of human figures about him that all stood silently watching.

"Who'll speak for Man?" said the Spirit.

"I will, I will, I will," said one. But all the rest were silent.

"I will, I will, I will," went on that one spirit, till the Spirit that guided Pelby turned to it and called out sharply: "The use of Man."

"Man is Man," the vociferous spirit answered. "He is Man. That is enough."

"That's his view," said the first Spirit. "Will any other speak for Man?"

In the silence Pelby turned to them and said, "I say, you fellows, speak up for the lot of us. Words aren't in my line, you know; but speak up for us all."

"They are not men," said the Spirit.

"Why, what are they?" asked Pelby.

"The spirits of all the others," came the answer. "The beasts, the birds, the insects, and the fishes. They are in human form so that you can perceive them, you would understand no other. But these are visible to you, so that you are not judged in the darkness."

"All a lot of animals?" said Pelby.

"Even so," said the Spirit.

"And you?"

"A spirit of air, born of the morning. A messenger, carrying errands from orbit to orbit."

Then Pelby began to consider more deeply than ever he had before. No man to help him out; all alone to explain what everybody knew, and yet what was not so easy to define, especially to those whose unpleasant silence showed them to be wilfully ignorant.

But, though verbal definitions did not come easily to him, he was none the less shrewd, few shrewder in all the area hunted by the Beldale and Annersham; and he saw that he must approach the matter from the point of view of others. He began to see who they were. That cheerful fellow who had Man's point of view so pat, and was continually repeating it, was the dog: it showed in all his movements. Then there was a comfortable spirit at ease, with eyes that were never at ease, being far too intense for rest. That would be the cat, thought Pelby. And a great solemn spirit that was absurdly nimble with a sort of misplaced jocosity. He recognized him for the horse. And a sober, friendly spirit dressed in black, he knew at once for the rook. He seemed to know every one as soon as he caught its eye. In a while he knew them all, the lion with streaming golden hair and eyes that seemed nursing an injury, the sly fox, the merry squirrel; he knew them all. But still none spoke for Man, except that one.

"Another must speak for you," said the Spirit of Air.

"And if they won't?" said Pelby.

The Spirit was silent.

"It will be the end of me, I suppose," Pelby continued.

"The end of your race," said the Spirit.

"The whole race!" exclaimed Pelby.

"Why not, if they're no use?" asked the Spirit.

Then Pelby saw that, having lived his whole life judging all things in terms of Man, he must not fail now to explain his creed, however hard logic might be to him; and he must make it clear to the most ignorant. Arguments that only the dog would agree with he abandoned; and presently several little points occurred to him and he began to argue neatly, not for the first time, for he had often argued successfully with farmers who had raised objections to hounds coming their way, or even (in extreme cases) the survival of foxes. He began with the rook, who was walking near to him.

"We turn the furrow," he said, "not for our own benefit only, but so that the rooks may get their food."

The rook put his head down a little sideways, and thought of the long furrows all damp and odorous and full of worms. Then he turned it a little the other way and thought deeply of other things. In the end he was silent and gave no voice for Man.

Then he thought of the cat, who shares men's houses. She should speak for Man, he thought. Yet he did not trust her. And just then there went dancing by him, swift as wind, light as a shadow, with all the grace of a fairy, a spirit he knew for the mouse. Pelby was no fool: to appeal to the one he knew was to lose the vote of the other. To whom should he make his appeal, the cat or the mouse? A score of reasons pointed to the cat; but he did not trust her; and in the end he made his appeal to the mouse.

"Neighbour," he said, "we have lived for a long while side by side. Will you not speak for us now if our crumbs were good? There would have been no wainscotes but for Man."

But the mouse's spirit answered: "The traps of steel. The beautiful cheese that none could resist and the cruel traps of steel. I do not speak for Man."

Too late then Pelby spoke of cushions, of deep soft rugs, of the fireside, of sure shelter from rain. The comfortable spirit with the intense, deep eyes gave him but one look of scorn. Too late he appealed to the cat.

Then, as one householder to another, he appealed to the pig, and to all that dwell in houses, the cow, the horse, and the poultry; and found, as he might have known, that the pig was thinking of the acornwoods, the cow and the horse of the prairie, the hen of the jungle, and none of them all had the feeling of Man for a house. He spoke of the storm, the snow, the coming of winter from which Man's houses protect them, and it seemed that they loved these things. None of them spoke for him. And when he appealed to the horse as his oldest friend, the equine spirit only tittered and wore a foolish expression. Pelby began to grow desperate. He was driven to appeal to the hippopotamus, reminding him of cabbages Man had planted in Africa here and there, near enough to the banks of rivers. But the hippopotamus cares more for being left alone in his river than he does for rolling in cabbages, and would give no voice for Man. And now the spirits of all the birds began to soar up rejoicing, believing the end was come to the race of Man. Futile appeals the man uttered to them as they went; black currants, raspberries, and strawberries that Man grew with such care, the birds got as many as Man.

"Nets, nets," said the birds. And one said, "Cages." And they all took up that cry after him.

The dog cried out and abused them and still spoke for Man. All was for Man, he said. Man was Man. That was enough. What other argument needed?

"Does no other speak for Man?" cried the Spirit of Air.

And the hush that fell on the spirits froze Pelby silent. And in the hush there came the sound of a horn, a far faint horn that was coming nearer and nearer. And then above the assembly, on a pinnacle of the air, there halted a slender figure holding a radiant horn, a silver trumpet that he lifted and blew. And when he had blown he spoke, saying: "I will speak for Man."

"Of what use is Man?" enquired the Spirit of Air. "Tell this assembly."

It was the spirit of the mosquito. He raised his silver horn and blew again, and lowered it and answered: "He is my food."

When the mosquito spoke for Man the Spirit of Air turned round; and, guiding the Master of Fox Hounds with one sweep of his arm, they moved thence so swiftly that all the place of that assembly seemed to slide away from them like an avalanche in full flight. Earth appeared, and grew rapidly larger, till it turned from a glittering orb, wandering in emptiness, to the dales and the fields we know. And very soon Pelby was back again in his bed.

So few believed his story that as time went by he came himself to think it was merely a dream, and so he does to this day. And yet, while firmly believing it only a dream, if anyone asks what is the use of badgers, or even of wasps, he is silent. While, if somebody raises a single point in their favour, you are certain to hear him say, "There's a lot in that."

THE GHOST IN THE CORNER

When I dined with Medleigh the other day in the country, it was pleasant to dine by candlelight, as he always does. To me there always seems to be so much more in a room when the light is rather dim, and lights and shadows are able to run about and change places among the curtains. Besides, we had plenty of light all along the table, which was where we required it; it was only at the ends of the room, and here and there among corners, that there was any dimness at all. And in that dimness at the far end of the room, in the left-hand corner, I saw, for the first time in my life, a ghost. I was not sure that it was a ghost; but you may see far solider things than ghosts, even a rabbit, for instance, and not always be sure that you saw what you thought you saw. Yet not only did I see it myself, but I had corroboration, so rare in ghost stories, from Medleigh. He saw it too, and had often seen it. There were three or four others of us dining with him, but they were not so sure. I first noticed the white of it among the shadows, standing out rather unmistakably. And the shadows all round it seemed rather blacker than the rest of the shadows were. And I saw that it was the ghost, if it was a ghost, of a man in evening dress. It was then that Medleigh turned to me and said: "You are looking at the shadows."

"Well, yes," I said, "I was rather."

"Do you see anything?" he said.

"Well," I said, "I almost thought I did."

"What is it?" he asked.

"Well, I thought almost a man," I said.

"Do any of you see him?" he said, turning to the others.

And some said they thought they did, and others said not.

"It's my butler," said Medleigh.

"Your butler?" I said. "Why, yes, it looks quite like a butler."

And some of the others said then that they thought so too.

"Yes," said Medleigh sadly, "he is always there; very nearly every night for the last ten weeks."

It was a long room and we all stared silently at that further end and could not be quite certain, but it looked like a large white shirt-front and a black tail-coat, waiting there in the corner and sometimes moving slightly. Looking back on it all, and remembering that I never saw the face clearly, it seems to me now that in the rather unusual circumstances which Medleigh revealed to me, unusual, that is to say, in a ghost-story, it may have been merely the ghost of a tail-coat or a shirt-front, but that is only a speculation. We all of us gazed for quite a long while, except Medleigh, who seemed to be used to it. And the longer we gazed the clearer the thing became, till I definitely saw a shirt-stud. Sometimes the ghost moved back further among the shadows and grew dimmer awhile, and once it came a few paces towards us, but deferentially, as though it knew that a certain space should be kept between shadows and flesh-and-blood. None of us spoke a word, and the silence was growing heavy, and even the shadows in that far corner seemed to be heavy too, if it were not an absurd thing to say of shadows. And then one of us spoke.

"Poor fellow," he said. "Was he killed by something? Was it anything sudden?"

"Oh, no," said Medleigh. "Nothing like that. He is alive and perfectly well. I heard from him only yesterday. But I had to get rid of him as a war-economy."

It is that that makes me think it was more the ghost of a shirt-front. For the man was alive and well, and had no grim wrong to resent; but *look* at the things that they do to shirts in a laundry.

VERY SECRET

The man who told me this story may have been pulling my leg: you never know in these days: or he may have had an even wider purpose and, by spreading a tale which should deceive the public, may have hoped for the assistance of the public's whole weight in pulling the leg of Hitler. For this purpose false information must have a certain value in these times, and the truth is always of value; so that I feel, as any writer always does in any case, that the tale may be worth passing on, in whichever category it is. A message had come by wireless to a divisional Headquarters in Africa, of course in code. I was not told what part of Africa, but it is evident that it was in the North. It was in the ordinary Playfair code, and was soon decoded; but when decoded all that they got was *"Very Secret. It might have been elapse. Kate evidently upset, your sport returning with nothing inside it to disordered units."*

The first two words were clear enough, but they were the cause of the whole trouble, for the rest of the message was protected not only by code but by this sort of double lock, which still made nonsense even when decoded. What Intelligence decided was that, as it must have been intended to be read, Corps, who had sent it, must have counted on Division having a cipher-expert to whom it would be clear; and experts there were, but they could make nothing of it. That was the mistake that they made and stuck to: the meaning was clear enough to the right kind of man, but not to the cipher-expert. To wireless back to Corps to ask what it meant was not one of the things that could be done; just as banks do not take their safes out into the street to be opened by chance passers-by. And I doubt if they'd have sent to Corps to ask for the clue, even if they could have done so without letting the Germans know, for nobody on the staff of Division wanted to admit that they couldn't read something that Corps had obviously credited them with being able to understand. So there they were. There was a lot of talk about it, but it led nowhere. "He's getting too clever," Intelligence said, and tried to be clever too, but that only led him further and further away. He worked a lot on the word *sport,* fancying that the message was told in terms that Englishmen would understand, and that the Germans knew nothing about. But the word sport only misled him. I certainly could make nothing of it myself when the message was shown me.

Well, what happened in the end was that the message, decoded but not reduced to sense, was left lying on a table in an orderly-room tent, and an orderly-room corporal came along and saw it, partly obscured by another sheet of paper which lay over the top of it and hid the words "Very Secret." Happening to have a piece of pencil either in his hand or in his mouth this corporal sat down and began using it. And within a minute or two the staff officer returned, having just got a new and even deeper theory to work on.

"Where's that secret paper, Corporal Glubb?" he asked.

"Secret, sir?" gasped Corporal Glubb.

"Yes, very secret," said the officer.

"I am sorry, sir. I didn't know it was secret," said Corporal Glubb. And he lifted it up and saw the words "Very Secret" written at the head of the message.

"Thanks," said the staff officer, and took it from him.

"I am sorry, sir," said Corporal Glubb. "I did not see the words Very Secret, there was a bit of paper over the top. I am afraid I read it."

"Oh, there's no harm in that," said the staff officer. "It isn't fully decoded yet."

"I mean I solved it, sir," said the corporal.

"You solved it?" said the officer. "What do you mean?"

"I mean I read it off, sir," said the corporal. "It goes: 'Please take your troops to Tunis.' I didn't know it was secret."

"But are you a cipher-expert in private life?" asked the officer.

"No, sir," said the corporal. "I just read it off. You see, sir, 'Might be elapse' is obviously 'please.'"

"Please?" said the staff officer. "But why?"

"Perhaps you don't do crosswords, sir?" said the corporal.

"Well, no. I don't quite have time for them," said the officer. "Then what's all that nonsense about disordered units? Whose units are disordered?"

"Oh, that means Tunis, sir," said the corporal.

"But how do you know?" asked the officer. "It seems all non-sense."

"Well, I'd just been doing a crossword," said Corporal Glubb, "and I sat down to it, not knowing it was secret, and I got it straight off. That thing about nothing inside it, that always means adding an O, in a crossword."

"Does it?" said the officer. "But why?"

"I don't know, sir," said the corporal. "It's just the way crosswords go."

"Well, I don't understand it," said the staff officer. "But it's quite clear that Corps must have thought it would make sense to somebody here; and, as it makes sense to you, that must have been the message that they intended. Perhaps you can write out our acknowledgment of the receipt of the order, in the same language."

For a moment the corporal bit an end of his pencil. Then he wrote down: *"Your alternative red returning. The deceiver appears confused."*

"Well, thank you," I said to my informant. "I like to hear what's going on about the war. And of course you can trust me not to write a word about the order, that you tell me was sent to this Division. I realize that an order like that cannot be published."

"Oh, that's all right," he said. "I expect they'll have acted on it long before it gets into print."

Tales for the Dark Continent

Just where the last houses of London look out over turnips and cabbages, and pavement ends and lanes and paths begin, lived Smithkin with his dream, which he once explained to me like this. "If all the money I've saved in four years on bananas and oranges, and other things we can't get, will run to it, I'm going to Central Africa for a couple of weeks when this war is over."

"What will you do when you get there?" I asked.

"Well, that's the point," he said, "and it may sound rather a silly one; but the fact is when I was a boy I always loved tales of adventure."

"Yes," I agreed, "most boys do."

"But I was desperate keen on them," said Smithkin; "so keen that I never really shook the taste for them off. And that's the trouble; I have got that taste still. It may seem silly, but I expect you had it yourself once: well, I've got it still, that's all."

"Yes, I see," I said. "I don't see anything silly in it. Any way, travel is a good thing, if you can afford it."

"Yes," he said. "You see, I've lived all my life in a suburb of London and I would like a bit of travel. But it is not that that I am going for. It is this silly craze of mine, and somehow I can't shake it off."

"And what kind of adventures are you going to look for in Africa?" I asked. "Big game?"

"No adventures," he said. "Tales of adventure."

"Oh, I see," I said, as one very often does when conversation takes a turn that is a bit obscure. "I see."

"Yes, tales of adventure," he said.

"Well, I hope you'll hear some good ones," I said, perhaps a little doubtfully.

"Oh, it isn't to hear them that I'm going," he said.

And, oddly enough at the moment it didn't strike me what you could do with a tale if you didn't hear it, except read it, and that could be more easily done with the help of the post.

"No, I'm going to tell them," he said.

"But why do you have to go to Central Africa for that?" I asked.

"It's no good here," he said. "No, I've tried it. They've all had their own and won't listen, especially on this south-eastern side of London. No, I'm going to tell them in Central Africa. And I think I shall make them sit up."

Advance Regulations

As soon as the Tube Extension to New Zealand is in operation, the following arrangements will come into force, and are printed now so that intending travellers may become familiar with them. The coaches will be air-conditioned, and well-lit with daylight bulbs. As the motive power employed is solely the force of gravity, except for a fraction of the journey, and as the engines will not run till the last half-hour, the journey will be found to be smoother and quieter than any other upon the Company's system, and will indeed compare more than favourably in those respects with any railway company in the world. Four meals will be served during the run: breakfast, luncheon, afternoon tea and dinner. It is most important that intending travellers should make themselves thoroughly acquainted with the following regulations. All loose articles, including magazines and even newspapers, should be stored in the lockers provided for that purpose. Any that are not so stored will be collected by an attendant shortly before reaching the centre of the earth, and handed back to their owners on arriving at the other side, but a fee of sixpence will be charged for each article so collected. No drinks will be served within half an hour of reaching the centre of the earth. Two minutes before reaching the centre all lights will turn green. On seeing the green light, passengers should at once get on to the floor beneath their benches and lie face downwards, pressing their backs as much as possible against the under side of the seats, which they will find to be comfortably upholstered. On the floor at either end of each bench they will find two leather straps, and, as soon as they see the red light, if not before, they should grip one of these firmly in each hand. The red lights will be turned on, in place of green, five seconds before reaching the centre of the earth. The more firmly passengers press themselves against the under side of the benches, the more comfortably they will find themselves lying on them as soon as the centre of the earth has been passed. The benches will then immediately be lowered until they are one and a half feet from what will then be the floor, and passengers are requested to remain still until this has been done. Drinks will again be served whenever required, and any loose articles needed may be taken from the lockers. We hope eventually to install an automatic system whereby the benches will be rotated without inconvenience to passengers, and without our having to request them to leave the side on which they are sitting, but owing to our inventor being now on his holiday we are unable to give the details of this at present. For the further convenience of passengers there will be a revolving cocktail bar, which, occupying a position exactly half-way between the floor and the roof, will be rotated on reaching the centre of the earth, and will then be found to provide precisely the same amenities as were enjoyed on the hither side. When the coaches are connected with the rails in the tunnel towards the end of the journey and the engines are turned on, there will necessarily be some noise, but we have done all we can to reduce it and believe that it will compare very favourably with the noise in any of the tunnels through which the Company's coaches travel at present. It will, however, be advisable for passengers who may be having dinner to give any orders for anything they may require to the Company's waiters during the perfect quiet of the rest of the journey, before the rails are connected.

On emerging from the tunnel passengers will be met by one of the Company's reception commissionaires, who will help them in every way, and who may be recognized by the Company's badge, worn on the front of his cap, a rabbit in gold lace.

A Modern Portrait

Going to see an exhibition of pictures the other day, I went straight up to one of them, ignoring a hundred and forty-two, for the rather inadequate reason that I had heard several people talking about it. Well, it would not have been an inadequate reason if they had greatly praised it; but, as it was, they had all been doing the opposite. And I am glad I went, for I might otherwise have accepted their hasty opinions. I must say that, at first sight, I agreed with them, and the picture seemed to me to be all they had said of it. It was a picture of a woman, if you could call her such, standing in a very smooth fawn-coloured landscape that went right to a pale-green sky beside a thin ruined tower full of odd angles. Looking at it close, the picture seemed quite impossible, so I stepped back four or five paces and sat on a bench to look at it, so as to give it every chance, and was just about to decide that it could be no likeness of anybody on earth, when I glanced at a lady who was sitting on the same bench. Then I saw how wrong I had been. The likeness was astonishing, and she was obviously sitting in front of her own portrait. So perfectly had the artist got her likeness that I could not help turning away from her portrait to gaze at her. This of course she saw, but did not resent, as she showed by saying at once, "Do you think it is like me?"

"It is marvellous," I said. "A speaking likeness. How did you come to be like that?"

My last remark sounds so rude, that I should like to take up a little space in explaining it. To begin with, it was wrung from me by surprise, the surprise of finding myself so completely wrong, and all my friends wrong who had told me about this picture, believing it to be unnatural; and there she was beside me, with the same long Victorian dress right to the ground, that there was in the picture, the same forehead of steel, or bright metal, with a wisp of rusted iron above it in the form of a query mark, and one of those small horns sometimes carried on bicycles, in place of a nose, with one eye just below it. And I noticed that one of her hands was a lobster's pair of claws, while the other one was a spanner, with a gold wedding-ring on one of the horns of the implement, neat and well-fitting as it was in the picture. Her only other ornament was an oval brooch in gold, framing a miniature of a gentleman wearing whiskers, and a few jet buttons down the front of the black dress. As I have said, my words were wrung from me. But she took no exception to them, and answered at once: "My mother was a late-Victorian lady," she said, "and my father was a bicycle; a lady's bicycle, you know."

I glanced at her again and saw it all in a flash, the long dress, the cameo, and then the bright drops of rain on her metal forehead, and a few faint stains of rust, marking some earlier drops.

"Yes, yes, of course," I said, and I could not at first think of anything more to say to her, till I remembered something that had puzzled me, at first sight, over the tower. "That tower," I said, "the one you were standing by. Was it quite safe? I was wondering if it might not have fallen."

"But why?" she asked.

And all I could find to say was "The force of gravity."

"Oh, that's quite superseded now," she said.

And again I said, "Yes, of course."

And with her next remark we luckily got away from modern science, of which I really know nothing; for she looked up at her portrait again, and said to me: "Do you think I take more after my mother?"

But as I was beginning to get a little bit bewildered, I hurriedly spoke of the artist, instead of answering her question, and said what a wonderful likeness he had got. And this could not be denied, and somehow left little to talk about; so little that she soon got up from the bench and hurried away. And it was not till I saw the swift gliding movement with which she went down the gallery, that I noticed, what her long skirts had prevented my seeing before, that she had wheels instead of feet. One snort through the bicycle-horn may have been some sort of farewell.

It only shows that one should not say of any portrait that it is like nothing on earth, as a good many people are too ready to do, until one is quite sure.

The Rations of Murdoch Finucan

Sergeant Macinerny walked up to the whitewashed porch of Mick Heraghty's house and knocked, and Mrs. Heraghty came to the door. It was an ordinary enough Irish farm-house in front, with a kitchen to the left as you entered and a little parlour to the right, with a large mahogany table in the middle, and a photograph on the wall of Mr. and Mrs. Heraghty on their wedding day, and a holy picture and a print of one by Landseer. But leading out of the kitchen was a door that opened upon a spiral staircase of stone that wound up a tower many centuries old, that was all covered with ivy. There was only one room in the tower, now used as a store-room. There had been three other towers once, it was said, but this was the only one that remained of a castle of bygone days, whose story was still remembered, a story that, true or not, was somewhat bloodcurdling. The tower rose up behind the house and loomed strangely above it.

"I was wondering, Mam," said Sergeant Macinerny, "would himself be indoors at present."

"Sure, he is," said Mrs. Heraghty. "He's after coming in. Didn't you see him?"

"Sure, I saw somebody entering," said the sergeant. "But I couldn't be sure was it Mr. Heraghty."

"It was so," said Mrs. Heraghty. "Won't you come in?"

"Ah, it's very kind of you," said Macinerny. "Sure, I will, if it's not troubling you."

"Sure, it's no trouble at all," said Mrs. Heraghty.

So the sergeant went in, and there was Mick Heraghty sitting by the big fireplace in the kitchen. They shook hands. "Won't you sit down?" said Heraghty.

"It's very kind of you," said the sergeant.

"Was there anything you were wanting?" asked Heraghty.

"Ah, nothing at all," said the sergeant; "sure, nothing at all. There was only one thing I wanted, but it will do any time."

"And what was that?" asked Heraghty.

"It was only that I wanted to see Murdoch Finucan, to speak a few words with him about his ration-card."

"Sure, you can do that any time," replied Heraghty, "any time that he comes to my old tower."

"I know," said the sergeant, "I know. But maybe, as it's only a little formality about his ration-card that they were asking about in Dublin, I might have a word with him before that."

"Sure, you might," said the farmer. "I'd go and call him for you now, if I knew where he was."

"I know you would," said Sergeant Macinerny. "But maybe you could tell me about it yourself, without putting Mr. Finucan to any trouble."

"I'd be glad to help you," said Heraghty. "What was it you wanted to know?"

"Hasn't Murdoch Finucan been dead three hundred years?" asked the sergeant.

"He's been *buried* three hundred years," corrected Heraghty.

"Isn't it the same thing?" asked the sergeant.

"Not in the case of Murdoch Finucan," replied Heraghty.

"May be not," said the sergeant, "and I'm not saying it is. But what I was getting at is—does a man want a ration-card when he's been buried all that time?"

"Sure, I got the card for him from Sergeant O'Phelan before you came here," said Heraghty.

"May be you did," said Macinerny. "But Sergeant O'Phelan has left the force, and he was too easy-going any way."

"Sure, it was only for the tea and sugar I wanted it. I wouldn't give a damn for the rest," said the farmer.

"I know," said Sergeant Macinerny. "But the point I was making was—what good would that be to a man who's been dead three hundred years?"

"Buried," said Heraghty.

"Well, buried, then," said the sergeant.

"Ah, would you grudge a cup of tea to a ghost?" complained Heraghty.

"They might in Dublin," said Sergeant Macinerny.

"Ah, what do they know in Dublin of the way things should be done?" asked Heraghty. "Or in any town, for that matter. Sure, they're out of touch with things there. They know nothing."

"Maybe," said the sergeant. "But they're very sharp with us if we don't keep to their rules. And what they are asking now is— Who signed Murdoch Finucan's ration-card?"

"Sure, he signed it by proxy," said Heraghty.

"I understand all that," said the sergeant. "But there's ways and ways of signing by proxy. And did he do it in a way that would satisfy them in Dublin?"

"Ah, maybe he didn't," said Heraghty. "But wasn't Murdoch Finucan a terrible man any way?"

"Sure, he was, by all accounts," said the sergeant.

"Was he the sort of man you're wishing to pick a quarrel with?" asked Heraghty.

"Maybe one mightn't believe in him at all," said the sergeant.

"Don't the people believe in him?" asked Heraghty.

"Sure, they do, seemingly," said the sergeant.

"And are you going to set yourself against the people?" said Heraghty. "Sure, you'll never go down here if that's what you do."

"I only wanted to see Murdoch Finucan," said the sergeant, "and to ask him about his ration-card."

"Then you may come to my old tower at the full of the moon," said Heraghty, "and you may say to his face the things that you have been saying to me about him. And tell him to his face, his white face in the moonlight, that you grudge him a cup of tea. And you may tell the people what you've done."

"Ah, sure, I wouldn't go to those lengths," said the sergeant. "Sure, I don't want to annoy you. I'll tell them in Dublin that Murdoch Finucan signed by proxy; and that he'll look in on them and verify it next time that he is in Dublin. Won't that be the best way?"

"Sure, that will do grand," said Heraghty.

A Day on the Bog

There was gentlemen in Ireland in the old days, said Mickey Tuohey, such as you very seldom see now. Severals of them there were, and all of them great gentlemen. And I'll tell you what they used to do: when they'd go out shooting grouse on the bog they'd take silver flasks with them that held as much as a quart of whiskey. A quart of whiskey in one flask. Sure, you never see anything like that nowadays. The old stock are nearly all gone, more's the pity. I mind the time when Mr. Fitzcharles (the light of Heaven to him, for he is dead long ago) went out on the red bog one day, and he takes me with him to mind the dog. And the bog went right to the horizon and over the other side of it. And we walked all day, and when it got near to one o'clock, and we had a fine bag of snipe and a few grouse, he says to me, "What about a bit of lunch, Tuohey?"

And I says to him, "Sir, it was the very thing I was thinking myself."

And we sits down on the heather and eats a few sandwiches, and that sort of stuff, that I had in the game-bag. And then he says to me, "Did you happen to remember to bring my flask, Tuohey?"

Remember it! Sure I remember it to this day.

And I says, "I did, sir."

And I brings out the great silver flask that used to hold a quart.

"Then shall we have a little whiskey," he says, "to keep our throats from getting dry?"

And I had two tumblers in the game-bag, made of horn, the way that they wouldn't break. And our throats never got dry that morning. It was the best of old whiskey that Mr. Fitzcharles used to have in those days, mild as milk, and did you no more harm nor milk, and a great deal more good. And Mr. Fitzcharles gave me half of it for myself, and he drinks his half straight off, without taking a breath. That's the kind of grand old gentleman that he was. We sat there in the sun resting and feeling the good that the whiskey was doing us, and the red bog round us as far as they eye could see. And a leprechaun comes over the bog and he runs straight up to us, the only time in my life I ever seen a leprechaun close, though I'd often heard tell of them; a little brown lad not half the height of a man. And he stands there on a patch of bright red moss and looks at us. And he says to us, "You are the two grandest men ever I seen."

And Mr. Fitzcharles says to him, "Is there anything I can do for you?"

And the leprechaun says, "Sure, there is. Would your Honour give me your soul, that I may become a mortal and go about on the dry land, and see towns and wear boots and a fine glossy hat?"

And I was terrified for the sake of Mr. Fitzcharles, for he was the most generous-hearted man in the world, one of the great gentlemen, and he would never refuse anyone anything; and I was afraid that he would give up his soul and be damned. But he thinks for a moment before he answers, as a man should. And then he says to the leprechaun, "I'm afraid I'm only a Protestant."

"Ah, well," says the leprechaun, "what matter? But never mind now. Sure, I'll ask you for it some other time."

And then I was more frightened than ever, for I was afraid he would ask me for mine. And I couldn't refuse him, if he did, in the presence of Mr. Fitzcharles, on account of him being one of the most generous-hearted men in the world, as I'm just after telling you. I couldn't refuse anybody anything when I was out with him, whatever I might do at another time. So I sat there trying to look the other way. But the leprechaun hops round in front of the way I was looking, quicker nor I could turn my eyes away from him. And he says to me, "Will you lend me your soul?"

Well, you know the way it is when anyone asks you to lend him something: it is harder to refuse nor when he asks you to give it. But the result is the same either way. And I thought for a moment or two, the same as Mr. Fitzcharles had done; and then I says to him, "I'll lend you my soul for so long as you like, if you'll give me your crock of gold."

And, mind you, it isn't that I valued the crock of gold more nor my soul. Sure, it would be a great mistake to do that. But I knew that he'd never part with his crock. And, sure, he wouldn't. And what he says is, "Sure, I wouldn't pay you all that for it."

"You and your crock of gold," I says to him. "Sure, you've not enough in it to buy a pig, let alone a good Catholic soul."

"Begob," he says to me, "I've enough in it to buy a herd of cattle, and your soul as well, and another one like it thrown in for luck. And you'll not find my crock, for I'm going to run away in the opposite direction from where it is, so as not to lead you to it."

Well, we hunted most of the evening for that crock in the opposite direction from the one in which he had run. But after a bit I says to Mr. Fitzcharles, "Maybe he's not so simple as he appeared. What if the little devil has been telling a lie to us?"

"And so he might," says Mr. Fitzcharles. "I would never trust a leprechaun."

And that was perfectly right, for there was nothing Mr. Fitzcharles didn't know.

So we hunted in the other direction, the one in which he *had* run. But very soon the good that the whiskey had done us seemed to begin to run out of us, and there was no more left in the flask to keep us going, and it was like looking for a snipe, without a dog, that has fallen a long way off. Sure, the red bog has a great knack of hiding things. So we give it up. The cheek of him, saying that he wouldn't make the exchange! Ah, but those were the good days. You can't get enough for two shillings to moisten your lips now.

LittlE Tim BrannEhan

Either to deceive the Germans in case they should come, or some more local enemy, the people of Sheehanstown had twisted sideways the arms of the signpost that there is a mile from their village; and as some years later, when I came that way in a car, the arms had not yet been put straight, I asked the way of an old man who chanced to be walking by. And one thing leading to another, we got into conversation, and I asked him how things were in those parts. "Terrible. Terrible," said the old man. "Sure, they're terrible. And it's the same in the whole world, too. It's all going to ruin."

"As bad as that?" I said.

"Aye," he answered. "And worse."

"And what do you think is the cause of it?" I asked.

"It's all those inventions that they make," he replied. "Sure, I can remember when bicycles were new. But that wasn't enough for them, and they must go on till they invented aeroplanes and wireless, and I don't know what all. And no good came of it, and the hearts of men has corrupted. Listen now, and I'll tell you. Did you ever hear of the house and family of Blackcastle? No. Well, I was thinking you came from a very long way away. And once there was no country in the world that hadn't heard of them; but they're all ruined now. And it happened like this: the estates fell into the hands of a young Lord Blackcastle, that had a hard, dry, withered heart. So that was the end of their greatness, for no man can be great with a hard heart. Aye, that was the end of them. God be with the old days."

"What did he do?" I asked.

"Do, is it?" he said. "Sure, he had a hard, withered heart. What could he do?"

"Did he commit a crime?" I asked.

"Begob, it was worse nor a crime," he said. "Sure, you wouldn't mind a bit of crime in a man. He grudged a sup of milk to a child."

"He shouldn't have done that," I said.

"It's what he did," said the old man.

"How did it happen?" I asked.

"Sure, the good Lady Blackcastle, that had been his mother, died," he said, "and there was nobody to look after him then. And he went abroad, and he went from bad to worse; and he comes home, and that's what he did. Mustn't a man have a black heart in him indeed to grudge a glass of milk to an ailing child?"

"Are you sure he did it?" I asked. "And did he mean to?"

"Did it!" he said. "And mean to! Sure the whole thing's down in writing. Look now. It's in my pocket. I have it there night and day. Can you read that?"

And he pulled out an envelope holding a half-sheet of notepaper, with writing in faded ink; and, crumpled and thumbed though it was, I could still read the old writing. "Let a pint of milk a day," it said, "be given to little Tim Brannehan, since he is weakly. Moira Blackcastle."

He gave me time to read it and time for the import of the note to sink in, as he stood before me, a tall, white-bearded, reproachful figure, looking at the evidence which I held in my hand, of the ruin that was coming to the world.

"He comes home from abroad," he said, "and goes into his dairy, and he stops that pint of milk being given out any more. And I shows him that very letter. And it has no more effect on him than a snow-flake in the face of a charging bull or a wild lion. And you have seen the letter yourself, and a man must have a hard, black heart to go against a letter like that, written by such a lady as was Lady Blackcastle, now in Heaven among the blessed saints. Sure, the world's going to ruin."

"But when did all this happen?" I asked. "And who is little Tim Brannehan?"

"Sure, it happened only the other day," he said. And the old man drew himself up to his full height, straightening for a moment the limbs that the years had bent. "And do you think I don't know what I'm talking about? Sure, I'm Tim Brannehan. And I was never refused that milk for seventy years."

The Burrahoola

All the pigeons were home to their spruces in the woods along the valley that lay under Gurtnamore, and the rooks had long gone by to the elms on the high ground, when a man came through the village down the wide white road alone. And to the first man that he saw, one Michael O'Leary, who stood by the edge of the road in the glow of a lamp-lit room, that streamed out behind him through an open door and mixed with the fading daylight, he said, lifting a warning finger, "The burrahoola is in the woods."

"Ah, and what is the burrahoola?" asked Michael O'Leary.

"It's well for you that you don't know," said the stranger and passed on.

And next he met an old woman hurrying home to her tea. And as she came up to him he stopped, and said, "Excuse me, madam, but I thought you had better know that the burrahoola is loose, and is in them woods now."

"Ah, sure," said the old woman, "I never bothered with them things."

"And indeed you're right," said the stranger. "It's well to avoid them."

And he passed on. And the old woman crossed herself, and was soon safe in her house beside her kettle and her cup of tea.

And next the stranger met a young man driving a cow up the road to its shed at the end of the village of Gurtnamore; and to him he repeated, "Hist! The burrahoola is in them woods."

"Ah," said the young fellow, "there's none of them things nowadays."

"And it would be well for you if there weren't," said the stranger.

And so he passed through the village and just outside it he met with a small girl, a child of about eleven. "Be getting home with you," he said. "And don't go near them woods." The child stared at him with round eyes. "Do you understand now?" he went on. "There might be things in them woods that you know nothing about." Still the child said nothing. "Get home with you quick," the tall man said and went on. And next he came to a young man riding a bicycle, a lad no older than the one that was driving a cow, a very few years from his school-days. But, though he was of the same age and held the same views, the evening was some minutes older and its shadows a little darker than those among which the stranger had met the lad with the cow, and slight though the difference and trivial the cause, the boy on the bicy-cle was more impressed by the news than the boy with the cow had been. For he stepped from his bicycle and asked, "Where is she?"

"It is a he," said the stranger, "as much as it is anything. And it's in them woods near the far end."

Now the far end was thickest and darkest, and though the boy with the bicycle had no evidence that the burrahoola was there, or that it existed, he had at least this much particle of evidence, that if the bur-rahoola should be in the woods at all, that was the end to which it would be most likely to go. He did not on that account believe in the burrahoola, but it was a trifle worth remembering which he often turned over in his mind as he considered the pros and cons of a bur-rahoola being in the woods.

"Ah, well," he said. "Maybe it will not trouble me."

"And I hope it will not," said the stranger. And the boy rode away.

And the next man the stranger met was the parish priest going home to Gurtnamore from a visit to some cottage beyond the village.

"The burrahoola is in the woods, Father," he said.

And the priest merely nodded his head. If there were wonders, they were not new to him. No more words were uttered between them, and both passed on.

The stranger had never before been seen in Gurtnamore, and I be-lieve that he was never seen there again. More lights were lit in windows, and soon they shone brighter than any light in the West; and men began to drop in to Murragher's public house, about the time that ducks were coming down dark through the night to a pond, that lay between Gurtnamore and the woods. There was no talk of the burrahoola. Many topics were talked of in turn; and not until all had been well dis-cussed and silences fell, and longer silences and more often, not until then did an old farmer call out, "And what is all this talk about a bur-rahoola?" He looked from face to face, and no-one answered, till he fixed one man with his eye, and seemed to draw the words from him; which were, "Ah, sure I heard some talk of one. But I never knew anything about burrahoolas."

And the silence about them was broken, and at last they were all discussing the burrahoola. And when I say they discussed it I need hardly say that there were men that denied the burrahoola and ridiculed all mention of it as an absurdity, and as superstition and ignorance; while others, as must always be the case with any discussion, said there was more in the burrahoola than young men might suppose who had never seen one, and who had never seen a great many other things either. So the discussion went on, and warmed as the night grew later, and to give the details of it would take me many pages. And, as at the beginning, so it was at the end, and men walked homeward from Murragher's muttering, "Silly nonsense," while others said, "There may be more in it than that." And the next night the same discussion started earlier and went on longer, and the burrahoola had gained more supporters.

And on the third day a man came into the village at nightfall, a smallish man with a sandy moustache, unlike the tall dark man who had spoken first of the burrahoola. "Excuse me," he said to the first man he met in the street. "Would you care for a charm? For I have a few for sale, that I got from a wise woman."

"How do you know she was a wise woman?" asked the man of Gurtnamore.

"Sure, she was my mother," said the sandy-haired man.

"Is that so?" said the other. "And are they good charms?"

"Sure, the very best," said the stranger.

"And what are they for?" asked the villager.

"They're charms against the burrahoola," said the small man. And he brought out some little packets.

"And what's the burrahoola?" asked the man of Gurtnamore.

"Sure, I wouldn't know that," said the stranger. "But these things keep him off."

"And how do they do that?"

"Sure, it's very simple," said the wise woman's son. "All you have to do is to take a pinch of these powders; for it's powders they are; and sprinkle it before your front door, and some more by your back door, and another pinch under your windows. And it will keep off the burrahoola. Sure, they're grand powders."

"Sure, I don't believe in the burrahoola at all," said the man of Gurtnamore. "What class of beast is it at all?"

"Sure it's a terrible class."

"I don't believe it."

"At the same time," said the stranger, "wouldn't you care to have a charm to make sure, for fear you might be mistaken? And the powders is very cheap."

"And what's the price of them?" he was asked.

"Only two shillings a piece," said the wise woman's son.

And the man of Gurtnamore had bought many a packet of different things that had cost him more than that, so that comparatively they were cheap, as he had to admit.

"I'll take one packet," he said.

And the man with the sandy moustache persuaded him to take two. And he passed on, and the next man he met by the side of the road was Michael O'Leary, who had been the first man in Gurtnamore to hear of the burrahoola.

"It's a fine evening," said the son of the wise woman.

"It is, sure," said Michael O'Leary.

"Would you like to buy a charm to keep off the burrahoola?"

"Sure no-one's seen one hereabouts yet," said Michael O'Leary.

"And is that to say you'll never see him?" asked the other. "And what will you do when you do?"

"Sure, I'll wait till I do," said Michael O'Leary.

"Sure, it would be too late then," said the vendor of charms.

"I don't know about that," said Michael O'Leary.

"Better be sure," said the stranger.

Well, the ways of selling things are fairly well known, and I needn't describe every device by which the wise woman's son with the sandy moustache sold every one of his powders. But every one he sold. And that was all that was ever heard of the burrahoola in Gurtnamore, or anywhere else. A short sandy man and a tall thin one were seen afterwards in a bohereen some distance from Gurtnamore, and I rather think they were dividing some spoils on a basis of fifty fifty. But that is a matter of business, such as business men keep to themselves. So I can tell my reader no more.

Kind Pagan Lights

In the little Irish town of Clonadaly there had been a market all day, and now with the early evening of December beginning to darken the fields and to bring an orange glow to gleam on the one street, as window after window winked out from houses preparing against the night, a group of farmers in a room at an inn were getting a few last drinks before long and lonely journeys. Their remarks were few and were concerned with the most material of all things, as they briefly discussed the prices given for sheep and cattle, while bottles were being brought in from the bar and corks were drawn, and the cold of that winter's evening seemed to be in their blood. Only an idle curiosity had lured me into that room, a curiosity that had perhaps led me to think that among so many men something interesting might be said of the country they knew so well, but all they talked about was the price of cattle. I was just about to leave, when I saw that all the drinks had been served and were now in tumblers and being drunk, and I began soon after that to detect a certain change in the conversation. It was not merely that more men spoke, and at greater length and more openly, but the subject of their reminiscences had become changed and they spoke of material things no more. And so I stayed and listened. Where that town stood with its hundred white-washed houses, fields sloped for only a little way from their doors and ended then, and there were no more houses. Wild and untamed by man the bog came then. So that what I heard the farmers discuss in that inn was not so remote as trees would be to people talking in any other town, for the bog was little more than three hundred yards away. They spoke of will-o'-the-wisps, or, as they were all calling them, jack-o'-lanterns. "Whatever you may say of politicians or foxes," one farmer was saying, "I'd say there was nothing craftier, nor slyer, nor more deceptive than a jack-o'-lantern."

"Did you ever see one?" asked the cattle-jobber who had come over from Liverpool.

"Where is it you come from?" asked the farmer, a man named O'Reilly.

"From London," said the Liverpool man, thinking to awe the room with a larger address than his real one.

"Begob, you'd see no jack-o'-lanterns there," said O'Reilly.

"Why not?" asked the cattle-jobber.

"Sure, it's all pavement," O'Reilly said, "and it would be too hard for their feet. Sure, there are hundreds of them about here."

And other men nodded their heads.

"Are there such things?" asked the man from Liverpool.

"Haven't I seen them myself," said O'Reilly, "many a time? And my old grandfather, God rest his soul, had spoken with some of them."

"And have you spoken with one?" asked the Liverpool man.

"Ah," said O'Reilly, "they don't talk any more, these days, with all this wireless in the air and one thing and another. Sure they are dumb now. But I seen them."

"Ah," said others, "we all seen them, and O'Reilly is right; they are the slyest and deceptivest and craftiest of things."

And then from a dim corner of the room up spoke a man named O'Kinahan, saying, "I'll hear no word said against jack-o'-lanterns."

Everyone turned to him, and O'Reilly said, "They have a bad name hereabouts."

And many heads nodded.

"May be," said O'Kinahan. "But I'll hear no word against them."

"Did they do you e'er a good turn?" said someone.

"They did," said O'Kinahan.

And so resolute he appeared that no-one abused the jack-o'-lanterns any more, and a brief silence fell, and then we got his story.

"I was out one night on Tullaghooley bog," said O'Kinahan, "to see could I get a goose for my poor old mother. For it was about the time of year that it is now, and I had heard tell that the geese were in. And I went out into the middle of it where the bilberries grow and the geese do come at night. I took my gun and went out about sunset, and there was a sheet of ice all over the bog; nothing that you would no-tice, no thicker than paper. But it was cold. It made walking a little slower than usual, because of course each footstep went down through the ice. And it was getting darker when I came to the bilberries. The little clump of bushes weren't high enough to give cover during the day, but they were good enough at night, for they and I were a dark patch all together. On the patches of moss that the ice had not covered there were droppings of geese. So I had come to the right place. All the rest was ice. Sure, you all know the Tullaghooley bog. So I needn't tell you what it's like if you get off that one safe pathway that takes you into the middle."

"What is it like?" asked the Liverpool man.

"Sure, there's no bottom to it," said O'Kinahan. "None at all."

"There must be a bottom to it somewhere," said the stranger.

"None at all," said O'Kinahan. "It goes right down to where Satan sits alone. Isn't that so?" And he turned his head to the other farmers there.

"It is, sure," several replied.

"Well, then," said O'Kinahan, "I had gone by the pathway, and I knew it well. And I knew how things alter at night. It's as though the night had enchanted them, or a spell had been laid by a witch. And I've heard tell of such things. But I thought I could find my way out of it even at night, for I knew all the small things that grow beside it, and could recognize them at any time. But the ice altered all that. A big change it made, though you wouldn't think it. And, what was worse, it froze all the time I was there, and the ice grew harder and harder while I waited there for the geese, that never came that night at all, knowing how hard the ice was going to be. And with that knowledge that they have, they would have gone away to some stream.

"Well, there I was in the bog, with the last of the colours gone from the sunset, and no geese came, and it was time to find my way out. There was no moon, and not even a star, and the ice hid my landmarks, such as they were. But that didn't trouble me at first, for I had only to follow my foot-tracks. So I looked about me and found one, and then another. But, searching for each one in the dark was like looking for something you've dropped, and I think my tracks were smaller than they had been, for it was freezing hard by then, and the ice seemed to be closing in on them from the edges. Still, I found two holes in the ice that I had made on my way in; yet from the time I took to find them I realized clearly enough that if I were to search like that for each footstep, I should not find many of them before I froze, as they were doing. Little patches of sedge one had scarcely noticed by daylight hid some of them, and the others seemed to be hiding themselves. A nasty wind had got up, blowing from where the snow comes from, and it was getting in under my clothes and under my skin and chilling my bones. There must have been black clouds in it, for I suddenly saw one star, which winked at me and went away in a hurry. To my left was shaky bog, quite bottomless, going down to where I said; and to my right was bog that I did not know at all, but no better than what lay on my left. There was only the pathway, the narrow solid track by which I had come, but there was no finding it. I began to wonder what would happen if I could not get out, and I searched for my footsteps again, but could only find one. And by that time I had broken large sheets of the thin ice, so that there were no more tracks to be found at all and I had to give it up. And then the knowledge came to me that, with that wind and that ice and my toes freezing already, I could not last that night out on the bog, and all the Saints seemed very far away. Maybe I should have given more attention to them before. But that's how it was now. And then it was that I saw the jack-o'-lanterns rising up before me as if they were beckoning to me, and moving slowly away towards the dry land, a procession of them one behind the other, all going the same way. Well, I took no notice of them, because they were only pagan things, and I asked help of the Saints instead. But no help came. And the wind grew stronger and stronger, with more cold in it, and then it began to snow. And then I said to myself, Those silly jack-o'-lanterns seem to be going about the way I wanted to go, and it would be no harm following them, pagan or not, if it was my way they were going. Sure I would be only going my own way; and anyway, I said to myself, if I don't follow them now I'll not be able to see them at all when this snow gets any thicker, and it's thickening already. And, sure, it wouldn't be following them, I said, when I was only going my own way. Well, rightly or wrongly, when no other help came near me, I followed them things. God help me if I did wrong. And they led me along the very pathway by which I had come, not more than two yards wide, or three at the most, and sometimes I splashed right into one of my old footsteps, that I could not find by searching; and the jack-o'-lanterns went dancing before me all the way.

And what I ever done for them I don't know, nor why they wished to save me. But wish it they did. For they went before me all the way to the dry land, which is no place that a jack-o'-lantern would wish to go to, if he consulted his own whims; and a very whimsical folk they are, and every whim of them is for the deepest part of the bog, and the shakiest and most dangerous. And of all the jack-o'-lanterns that do be in the bog not one rose up that night anywhere except to guide me. And they all danced down that path till I came to the dry land and no more were flickering before me and the snow came down behind thick as a curtain. I was a cold man when I got out of the bog, but a live one; and I owe it all to the kindness of them jack-o'-lanterns. And for that reason I'll have no word said against them by any man. Maybe they've led some men to the deeps of the bog. Maybe some men have deserved it. But they saved me. And let you account for that, if you can, before you say anything against jack-o'-lanterns."

"I've read," said the cattle-jobber from Liverpool, "that what you call jack-o'-lanterns are luminous gases from decomposing matter that decays under the water."

"Whatever they were," said O'Kinahan, "they led me to land by the only safe way there was."

"The scientific explanation of that," said the cattle-jobber, "might be that the only outlets that night for all the gas in the bog were the holes that you made in the ice when you walked in."

"Scientific explanation!" exclaimed O'Kinahan. "Science may be all very well in your towns. But the bog is a wild place, and I never heard of any science out on the bog on a winter's night in the snow. Did any of you ever hear tell of it there?"

But the farmers shook their heads, and all agreed in silence to the words of the eldest of them, uttering the verdict of Clonadaly, "No science ever got as far as the bog."

A Witch in the Balkans

It was Christmas eve at a country house, in which the house-party were gathered in armchairs before a fireplace that had never been modernized and still had room for big logs, which were now quietly burning. Ghost-stories had been told, while one of the guests, one named Frederick Parnet, who in his time had wandered about the world a good deal, sat silent. As a tale ended, his hostess turned to him, and said, "Won't you tell us a ghost-story now, Mr. Parnet?"

"I have never seen a ghost," said Parnet.

"It needn't be a true one," said his hostess.

"I shouldn't tell it if it were not," said he.

"Don't you know any tale of banshees, goblins or witches?" she asked.

"O, witches," he said. "That is a different matter."

"Then tell us a tale of a witch," she entreated.

"Well," he said, "in the Balkans they all believe in witches. At any rate in the parts of the Balkans I know. And it's very hard on the people they think are witches. They don't give them a chance."

"What country are you speaking of?" he was asked.

"I was among the Vlachs," said Parnet. "They don't quite belong to any particular country in the way that we do. They come South out of Macedonia to the hills of Greece in the winter, and when it gets warm they go back to their mountains in Macedonia and Bulgaria. They bring their flocks with them and build reed-huts and go north again when the violets are over. There was an old woman who lived in a cottage near their huts, and they said she was working witchcraft against them. She had frightened their children somehow, and they had run with some story to their parents, and they had got as frightened as the children and wanted to kill the witch. That is how things were when I happened to come along and, seeing a crowd and hearing a noise, I asked what was the matter. And the Vlachs told me that the old woman was a witch and that they were going to kill her. Well, I was young and had no experience with such things, and I told them that it was all nonsense. I told them I was English and didn't mind witchcraft, and that I would go into her cottage and she could practise her witchcraft on me, and then she wouldn't want to be bothered with them and they would be all right. Their children gazed at me all the time with big round eyes, and their elders talked with each other for a while; and then they said, if I would do that, they would leave the witch alone. And so I saved her life. Well, I walked into her cottage then and found her seated in front of her fire, and I said, 'Look here, those silly devils think you're a witch. But I told them that is all nonsense.'

"And she looked at me and did not say thankyou.

"'All nonsense,' I said again.

"'I make spells,' she said then.

"'Yes, I know,' I said. 'All nonsense.'

"'I make them out of this book,' she said. There was a great book beside her bound in black leather.

"'Well, you can make them at me if you like,' I said.

"And then she opened the book. I really don't think she understood what was going on. She had heard the Vlachs shouting all round her cottage, and probably thought I was in with them. My Greek wasn't her kind, and she can't have understood me very well. Any way she opened her book and began to read aloud out of it.

"'Look here,' I said. 'I'm English. You needn't read at me. Spells don't impress me. I'm not a Vlach.'

"And she smiled a very curious smile, and as I looked at her the spell worked. I never dreamt it was possible. She made me into a cat.

"It was so utterly astonishing, I did not know what to do. And gradually the instincts of a cat went surging through me, and I walked to the fire and lay down. It was a fine big fireplace, as big as this one, and I lay looking into the fire and began to think. And the more I thought, the more awful my predicament seemed to be. I couldn't speak; I couldn't explain; and the Vlachs had gone away. They couldn't have helped me even if they had stayed. There was I in the old woman's cottage, and she evidently thought that I was in with the Vlachs. I thought and thought, and the only thing I could think was that I had better be a good cat. But even that didn't promise any chance of escape, since the better the cat I was, the more she would want to keep me. It was an awful predicament. She gave me one look, as much as to say, 'that is what comes of meddling with witches,' and then went on with her work, which seemed to be chiefly muttering into the fire, whether spells or old memories I can't say. I was never in a situation I liked less. Never."

"And do you mean that you were actually a cat?" said our hostess.

"I was actually a cat," said Parnet. "There was no doubt about it. A black cat covered with fur. And I was gazing into the fire. That would have been pleasant if I could have thought of any way of escaping doing it for the rest of my life. I had other things to do. But for the moment it was pleasant. You have no idea how pleasant. It seemed to supply all that we get from a whisky and soda and a good book to read, and a comfortable chair. However, I didn't want to go on doing it all my life, and I could see no way of avoiding it. The witch sat there perfectly content. She wasn't going to do any more. I heard the Vlachs call to their children a long way off. They weren't going to do any more either. What on earth was I to do? After a while she gave me a saucer of milk, which I accepted gratefully. There was no use in making a fuss. The milk tasted extremely good. Better, in fact, than anything I had ever tasted before. I don't like milk as a rule. But I did then. The windows of the room began to grow blue and dim. Then it got quite dark, and not till then the old woman lit a candle. Time went by more pleasantly than what it does here, in spite of my awful predicament: it went by more cosily and without impatience, and somehow there seemed more in the fire than there is in our newspapers and our talk, and all the things with which we concern ourselves. It seemed to have more interest in it and to be more full of change. It's difficult quite to explain, especially as none of you have studied it as I had to do. I had nothing else to occupy me for weeks; except plans of escape; and none of them turned out to be any good. Soon after the old witch lit the candle she picked it up, and without a word to me went out of her kitchen and into her other room, and I heard the creak of her bed as she lay down for the night. I was up on to the table, where lay her old black book, in a moment. I realized that was the key; but could I turn it? I opened it with a paw, and it was all full of black spells. But they were in Chinese. That was no use to me. So I closed the book and went back to the fire and looked into its red and golden and orange deeps; a very pleasant occupation, if you had nothing more serious to worry about."

"I shouldn't have thought . . ." began one of us.

"No," said Parnet, "nor would I. It wasn't until this unfortunate thing occurred to me that I realized how much interest there can be in the glow of a fire. I can't get it now. But at the time it supplied nearly everything. Everything except what I wanted most, a plan of escape. I had no hope from the Vlachs. What they ought to have done was to go in and rescue me, and, when they saw what had happened, demanded my release. But they were evidently content with things as they were. The witch was working her witchcraft on me, and that suited them, and they felt their children were safe. Soon they would go back to their mountains, for the great carpets of violets that grow in those lands were nearly over. Then I should be all alone with the witch, and no-one would know what had happened to me, for the Vlachs wouldn't bother to tell anyone. What was to be done? I pondered for some time. And then I turned to watch the glow of the witch's fire and the little flames that jumped up every now and then, and the grey ash that covered more and more of the glow. And watching the embers I must have fallen asleep. And morning came, and I was still a cat. First the dim light came into the room through the windows. And then came the witch. She took no notice of me at first, but boiled an egg in a great pot over her fire. Then she went to the cupboard and took out a piece of meat and threw it down beside me. I looked at her gratefully and purred, which was all I could do. It was no use resenting her offhand way, as my only chance seemed to be that she might disenchant me, though it didn't seem very likely. As soon as I began to eat the meat, another black cat walked in from the other room, and came up and looked at me. I looked back at it, and it lay down and went on looking with pale-yellow eyes with dark slits down the centre. I suppose my eyes looked the same. I wondered what it would do. Then it shut its eyes, and opened them no more for an hour. I never knew whether it had been a cat always, or whether it had been enchanted like myself. I thought for a long while of how to communicate with it, in the hope of planning some sort of escape; but then I gave it up, because I didn't trust that black cat. It did not do anything that I could complain of; I only went by its looks, which is often a good thing to go by. Somehow I felt I would sooner have trusted the witch. There was no sound now from the Vlachs, and I fancied they must have gone. I was quite alone with this witch and her other cat. That black book on her table was the only hope that I had. But what good I could get out of it I did not know. I could tell you a great deal of those days in the witch's cottage, if I thought that you would be interested; but I spent so much of the time looking into the fire, and in spite of its mystery and wonderful beauty I am afraid that that is a thing to which you have given so little attention that you would scarcely care to listen to me, were I to describe to you all those caves of colour and golden valleys and mountains that I saw for many weeks in that witch's fire. Yes, I was there for weeks. And all that time the old witch never allowed her fire to go out. She used to drag in large logs and throw them down on her fire and then sit in front of it muttering; spells or old memories; I never knew what she muttered. Sometimes she boiled meat in her cauldron, sometimes tea, and that was about all the housekeeping that she did. Where she got her meat or her tea I never found out. Easily enough, I should say, considering what she could do. All day I sat and looked at the fire, and the other cat did the same. It was a lovely thing to look at. As evening came on and the light of the witch's window grew less and less, the dark part of the eyes of the other black cat grew larger and rounder, and I suppose mine did too. Then we were each of us given a saucer of milk, and the old witch went to bed. Many days passed like that, and then one day it struck me that, pleasant although it was to look in the fire, I should think of no plan of escape if I did that, but would just grow like the other cat and stay there all my life, as he appeared to be going to do, whatever he may have been before. Perhaps he had been a cat all his life, but never by the slightest hint did he let me see whether he had been or not. And the spring was coming on well, which is like summer here, so I lay outside the door in the sun. The old witch did not mind. There was a path that went by close to the door, and sometimes as many as ten people would go by in a day, sometimes nobody went by at all. I watched them all, even though I knew that none of them could help me. And I thought. But I could never think of a plan that would disenchant me. One thing I knew at once; and that was who was friendly and who was hostile. All cats know that. But it was no use going away with a friendly old woman. She couldn't disenchant me. The other cat knew that I was up to some game, though that was more than I knew myself, for the problem beat me. What depressed me more than anything was that that black tom-cat did nothing to interfere with me, but merely sat there with a supercilious look that seemed to show it was hopeless. People of every race in the Balkans went by in a fortnight, as well as some that looked like Arabs, and all kinds of Turks, not only Balkan Turks but some that looked almost Mongol. I watched them all going by, and the other black cat looked at me every now and then with the look that seemed to show I was doing no good, and never would do any, either. And then one day a Chinaman came by. I wasn't surprised: I had seen so many different kinds of men and women go by as I lay there in the sun. The old witch had gone away to milk her cow, and the other black cat had followed her, and I was quite alone. And all of a sudden I remembered the old black book. I ran up to the Chinaman. He would be able to read the book, whose spells were all in Chinese. You know how appealing a cat can be. I was all appeal. I had to be. I knew that this was my only chance. I rubbed against his legs, I stretched out a paw, I miaowed, I did everything I had ever seen a cat do to attract attention; and when I had got it I ran a little way and looked round till at last he followed, and I led him right into the old witch's kitchen. If I could get him to read from that book, he might hit on the right spell. It was pure chance, but the only chance. I jumped upon the table and opened the book with my paw. He was a very intelligent Chinaman. He saw at once that I wasn't an ordinary cat. I think a European would have been surprised, but he was evidently not that. That saved a lot of time. I pointed to the book and looked up. Then I put my paw to my ear, the ear that was turned towards him, and sat in a listening attitude. The Chinaman understood at once, and began to read aloud. Queer things happened in the room as he read, for of course the spells that he read were chosen purely at random. A pair of tongs, for instance, got up and walked out of the room. That too would have surprised a European; but the Chinaman read on. Then for a long time came nothing but little spells; flies, for instance, fell dead; and mice ran out of the room backwards, and dust got up in little eddies and whirled away out of the door like dust-devils in Africa. It was evident that it was by spells that the old woman did most of her housekeeping, though I had not seen her using them. These little spells soothed me, for I had been rather afraid of some big spell, and did not know what might come into the room, though I comforted myself with the thought that a cat can generally look after itself, whatever comes. I looked up to the low rafters, and saw that I could easily get up there and hide between them and the thatch. But nothing bad came. Still nothing useful appeared among the spells, and I remained a cat. I watched the Chinaman continually, fearing that he might grow tired of reading. But he seemed to understand, and read on. Of course I did not know a word of his language, but I could tell what he was reading by what happened. There were for instance several cockroaches running about the floor, and, as the Chinaman read one of the spells, they all fell dead at once; and another spell swept them out of the door like a broom. Then the other cat walked into the room. It seemed to know what was going on and looked unpleasantly at the Chinaman and at me; but, then, it always looked unpleasant. For a moment I thought it would attack the Chinaman, but then it lost interest and sat down and looked at the fire. The Chinaman read on. I feared now that the witch might return. Her cat was never very far away from her. If she came in, she would snatch her book and drive the Chinaman out, either with her old broomstick or with some spell, and my only chance would be gone. Still she did not come. A small imp ran into the doorway, called from a wood by one of the spells, and looked enquiringly at us and saw that he was not wanted and ran away. An owl flew by and swept two or three times round the room on his great white wings, and hooted something that witches would have understood, and sailed out again. Then a great number of bats appeared, and they fluttered away too, when they found that they were not wanted. And I saw a great many lizards. Of course I never knew what was coming next. And all of a sudden the Chinaman, who had just turned a page, stopped reading straight on, and seemed to pick out a spell, and looked at me with what almost seemed like a smile, but you couldn't tell. And then he read it. It was the right spell, a spell to turn cats back into men. When I say back, I do not know if it only turned back cats that had once been men, or whether it would turn any cat into a man. I felt a very odd change at once and the room swam in a mist, and when it cleared the first thing that I saw was that other cat getting up from the fire and hurrying out of the room, no longer a cat, but a man, the kind of man I don't greatly like, a sharp, slick sort of fellow; but not sharp enough for the witch, for he had not escaped being turned into a cat, unless of course he had been a cat all the time. Any way I was glad to see the last of him. And the next thing I noticed was that I was a man again. Well, I thanked the Chinaman in English, and such Greek as I knew. But he didn't know any English and could make nothing of my Greek, and I tried a little French with the same result. But he understood I was grateful. Then he smiled and he went away. What he was doing in the Balkans I never found out, and I never saw him again. Then I thought the best thing to do was to follow the example of the other cat and clear out as fast as I could before the witch should return. So I cleared out. And I was only just in time, for I caught a glimpse of her coming back with a pail of milk, but fortunately she did not see me. It was a lovely summer's day, and the Vlachs were all gone with their straw huts from that part of the country, and I thought I had better go, too."

I wondered what our hostess and the rest of the party would say of that story. So I said nothing, and listened. But the story had been long, and it was late in front of that lovely hot fireplace, and all but I and the man who told that strange tale were asleep.

A Talk in the Dark

It was very early spring in a suburb of London, and late evening, where a garden ran down from the back door of a house to the curves of a small stream. And a child at the hour of its lawful bedtime had escaped not only to the end of the garden, but over the stream and up the embankment that rose beyond it, and was seated now on one of the shining rails that crowned the embankment. And there in the dusk she heard the sigh of a wind in trees. But there were no trees there nor any in sight, except three lilacs that along the garden behind her flashed green with the spring, and the saplings that had strayed upon the embankment and that no-one had tidied up. And so she knew that the sound must come from a spirit. And so it did. For it was the spirit of the forest that was haunting the twilight there, so far away from its home. Gradually the sound of the sigh among trees that were not there grew to almost the sound of words, and then was unmistakably saying "Hush. Hush."

"Who are you?" the child said then.

And now the words came clear through the stillness of evening. "I am the spirit of the forest," they said.

And so like to the language of such a spirit the dim words had been sounding from the first, that the child felt no surprise.

"But what are you doing here?" asked she.

"Looking at my dominion," said the forest.

"But here?" said the child. "It is all houses here."

"My rightful dominion," answered the forest.

"Used you to own all this?" asked the child.

"Certainly," said the forest.

"How many years ago?" she asked.

"What are years?" asked the forest.

"I don't quite know," said the child.

"Nor do I," said the forest.

From further away than the child could hear, there came the mur-

mur of an approaching train. But the forest could hear it, for all im-
mortal things know their friends and their enemies and know the approach of both from great distances.

"Go back. Go back," he said to the child.

"But why?" said she. For she had never been allowed on the railway before, and it gave her a great sense of freedom to be there.

"Because these things," he said, "are my enemies. Do not touch
them."

"Have they harmed you?" the child asked.

"Go back," he repeated. "They have driven me into exile."

"Are they stronger than you?" she asked.

"For a while," he said. "But go back."

And the murmur of the train having risen now to a deep hum, and
the earth vibrating with it, the voice of the spirit seemed fainter, as though
he feared this power that had driven him into exile, and his words sank
low into muttering, yet still were audible to a childish ear.

I have said little enough to give any clue as to what kind of spirit it
was, but the child was young enough to be a perfect judge of character,
and saw that it was a good spirit. So she did as it said and got up from
the shining rails. Nearer still came the train, and the hum rose to a
roar. "Is that one of your enemies?" asked the child.

But no answer came now from the spirit. So she climbed down the
embankment through the little ash-saplings, and turned round at the
edge of the stream to call back to her friend. But at that moment lights
burst on the evening, and then the train roared by, with its row of luminous windows pouring beauty into the dusk, but scattering from
shadowy places where they lurked such little mysteries as a child and a
spirit love; and leaves of last autumn awoke from their sleep and hurried after. And when the last of the leaves was tired, the child spoke to
the spirit again. "It has gone now," she said.

"Ah," said the spirit of the forest.

"Are you afraid of it?" asked the child.

"Not really," the forest said.

"But you said it is stronger than you," she went on, though she
had been taught not to argue.

"For a while," the forest said. "Just for a while."

"I am sorry it has driven you into exile," she said.

"I will come back," said the forest.

"When?" asked the child.

"Hush," said the forest. "Hush. That is a secret."

And the whole air rang with the sound of the forest's Hush, and even the little saplings took it up and it spread far through the evening.

"When?" asked the child again.

And again came that great "Hush."

Whether the spirit of the forest would have relented and ever revealed the secret I cannot say, for at that moment the child was caught and brought back to the house, and I regret to say smacked.

Mid Snow and Ice

Chalder's was a hard life. As he worked for his living his fingers were blue with cold. But numb though they were, he never dropped his pen, and went on with a dogged determination, writing line after line, though the paper on which he wrote was damp with icy water. His livelihood was to write stories, and he was writing one now, a grim and ghostly story that would be read by warm firesides by men who would know nothing of the cold drip that soaked Chalder's head as he wrote, and ran chillingly down his face, nor the sough of the wind as it drove those frozen drops against his right cheek and against his hand as it worked. "The grey form," he wrote, "that had been following Nickthorp noiselessly, now drew so close that it was as clearly visible as anything could be in that desperate night, till a sudden sheet of snow riding past on a bitter wind hid its monstrous form completely." Chalder shuddered as he put down those words, not through any horror in the scene that would haply make others shudder, but because of the frozen air that shrilled round the ice that was chilling him. What he wrote was, after all, no more than his own invention, and, however those words might later affect his readers, they had no effect upon him; but the bitter cold was real. Most of us might perhaps have endured as much while at work on our own jobs, whatever our jobs may be, but any of us whose fingers were numb as his might well have said that they could do no more work, especially if they were trying to hold a pen. Not that Chalder worked with a pen; his paper was too damp with the icy drip for that, and he had to use a pencil. How his fingers held it and used it I do not know, for they really were blue when I saw them. Blue with cold. "The sleet that lashed the side of the lonely traveller's face was sheer from the North," wrote Chalder, "and chilled him with all its might." He was merely describing his own sensations then, and using them for fiction. There was always reality in Chalder's fiction; but few, if any, knew how intimately he explored the very atmosphere of the stories he wrote. He wore a cap that was pulled down over his eyes so that he was able to see to write, but it had long been soaked through and was too sodden now to give any other protection. Chalder wrote on. "Nickthorp's right hand," he wrote, "was now too cold to feel the hilt of his sword, and yet he contrived to draw it, vain though his better judgement knew it must be against the ghostly thing that so grimly pursued him. He shivered bitterly, and all his body felt as cold as his sword."

Chalder's reputation as an imaginative writer is probably unassailable, but barely half of what he wrote came from imagination. The mere ghost was imagined, but the bitter cold of the storm, all the ice and the wet, and even the chill in the traveller's heart when he glimpsed the apparition, were all sheer fact from Chalder's actual experience that he lifted out of what was raging around him. "There was now ice on his saddle," Chalder continued, "and Nickthorp feared that his horse could soon endure no more and that he would be left dismounted amongst the snow, a prey at last to the grim grey thing that followed. The shrill of the wind rose now to a taunting hoot, as though the storm knew he was doomed. The cold of the frozen saddle was no worse than the cold of the wind, and Nickthorp still rode on."

The corners of the page upon which he wrote fluttered now and then drearily, but the page was too damp for it to flutter away, and Chalder's pencil still went to and fro in fingers that were no longer able to feel it. Nor could he feel his toes, for they were frozen too, ten numb lumps in his boots. "The ghost drew up to the rider's elbow now," wrote Chalder, "and walked beside him looking level from its dark sockets right into Nickthorp's eyes. And now he found that his arm was too cold to strike. 'Alas!' said Nickthorp."

Not till then did Chalder cease for a moment to drive his scurrying pencil and lifted and bent his arm, in the hope of waking the circulation that the cold seemed to have stopped. An iced drip fell from his fingers.

All this I saw when, happening to be near Chalder's house, I looked in to see him one sweltering day in June. They had been carting hay in a meadow before his windows, but as the very hottest hour of that parched day seemed to have come, the men were resting against uncarted haycocks drinking beer and fanning themselves with handfuls of hay, or fallen dog-daisies mixed with bunches of tottie-grass. It was of course the time of year when stories for Christmas numbers have to be written, and, as we have all noticed, they are not about hay. He was writing one for a Christmas number now. They would pay him forty guineas for it. And so they should, for it had the very sting of the snow in it, the very bite of the sleet. I saw him sitting on a block of ice as I came into the room, actually sitting on it. And close beside him chilling his right hand and the right side of his face, he had an electric fan going at full blast, while a drip from some sort of a cistern that he had rigged above his head, and that was full of chopped ice, came just where it was caught by the electric fan and was driven against the face and fingers of Chalder. His feet were in a footbath that broken ice filled up to the top.

"Just local colour," said Chalder to me. "One must have local colour." And indeed Chalder always has it.

And then he said, "For a Christmas number, you know. They want it in three days. You'll excuse me."

And of course my visit could not halt the hurrying pencil that the icy draught and the drip had been unable to check. I took in the whole outfit, and Chalder's grim endurance, at a single glance. And then I apologized and left him in the cold.

I read the story afterwards in one of the Christmas numbers. The ghost got Nickthorp, biting into his brains with teeth that turned out to be icicles, and his horse froze to death. It induced a warm appreciation of the good fire before which others read the story, and when they shuddered they only drew in closer. And then they praised the imagination of Chalder, praise that perhaps he deserved for the sake of his endurance, however false his claim to imagination may be. But to me the story always brings back the memory of that burning day towards the end of June, and the exhausted men that were leaning against the haycocks with bare glistening arms, drinking beer from tumblers that flashed with a blinding light, as one by one they caught a blazing ray of the sun, and Chalder sitting there on his block of ice.

A Treasure of India

I was always keen on shooting, whether at snipe or at larger things, and I was on my way to India to look for some of the larger ones. I had a light and very handy .275 Mauser and a double .450, and a .360 magazine rifle which will do for anything, if the .450 is not at hand. And in the smoking-room of a ship one night in the Red Sea, when it was too hot to sleep, and talk rippled on lazily, I heard a story which, West of Suez, one would have been disinclined to believe. It was a tale of bowls of jewels in a cellar of a long-deserted city in a jungle, all overgrown with greenery, the capital of an emperor who seems to have forgotten about it, and been in his turn forgotten. What is perhaps unusual in such stories was that the man who told it, lolling in shirtsleeves before a long cold drink, gave the name of the actual jungle and the exact site of the city. Where the cellar lay, of course he did not know. All who listened with me to the story seemed as much interested in it as the heat would permit, though nobody seemed to have enough belief in it to show any sign of an intention to do anything about it, or even to trouble to go to look for the city when they arrived in India, where all of them had other things to do. But to me there came all of a sudden the idea that what would be incredible in England, or in any land to which our civilization had penetrated, might be perfectly true in India. A good friend in England, all of whose working days had been given to India, had written for me some letters of introduction, and one of them was to the ruler of the very State in which this jungle lay, and which indeed covered most of it. So there I went first, and there I found the kind of hospitality of which I had read in the Arabian Nights, a splendour of lavish benevolence. That I was keen on shooting my kind host soon found out, and all arrangements were made for me, including many elephants; but my request to see the ruins in the jungle was harder to explain, and my wish to go there alone hardest of all; for the hospitality of that land never allowed me to go anywhere without someone walking behind me, either to protect me from something or to supply any need; I never knew which. Only when I asked His Highness as a direct favour did I get that permission. So a motor was provided to take me to the part of the jungle in which the old city lay hidden. But I left the car a mile from the jungle and asked the driver, and a man who had been sent to attend me, to wait there on the road until I returned. We had driven for miles through plains of ochre-coloured grasses brilliantly shining in sunlight, and had seen no drop of water all the way. Many beds of streams, and even of rivers, we passed, but no water, for a great drought had been raging for many weeks. The jungle, when it came into sight, was a great relief after that arid plain, with pools of cobalt-blue air lying in all the hollows of the branches. They did not like my going on alone, but I thought that I could not take anyone with me without the whole of India knowing it, if I were to find the treasure. How much they knew already I never guessed, nor why they did not all of them go and search for it. Something they must have known, for the rumour to have reached so far as the smoking-room of the ship in which I had heard it. For a mile I walked down the road with a .275 Mauser, rather light for anything really big; but I was not expecting anything big. I suppose I was too preoccupied with the thought of those bowls of jewels to think of anything else. And the rumour told too of one huge diamond which the forgotten emperor used to lay on a pedestal on his terrace and look at in the late sunlight when the rays were nearly level. They said that was still there too. The jungle came down to the very edge of the road, the mighty trunks of the peepul trees standing there like the legs of elephants halted just where the wild lands ended. And there I met what seemed to me for a moment a most extraordinary man, until I realized that it was I who was extraordinary there, with my European clothes and my rifle, and a water-bottle slung over a shoulder. He with his brass bowl, long stick and a loin-cloth, and no other possession at all, seemed perfectly ordinary to everyone else in this land. He was a tall figure neither lean nor fat, with a beard turning grey. As soon as I came near he opened his mouth and pointed at it, and I saw that his tongue was swollen: he was indeed terribly thirsty. I handed him my water-bottle without a word, and he gratefully drank from it and handed it back. But I knew that there was no water for twenty miles by the way that I had come, and doubted if there was any more for that distance in any direction, so I gave him the whole bottle. Then he began to speak, and I found he could talk English of a sort, and I knew a few words of Urdu, and one way and another we were able to understand each other. And he said that as I had given him this he was bound to do something for me; and what would I like? It suddenly struck me then that my chances of finding that cellar were very small, let alone the treasure it hid, and that here in India, talking to a fakir, I might be at the source of the rumour whose treasure I sought. And there and then I gave up my hope of finding the treasure alone and decided to try my luck with the fakir. It was no use being mysterious, and I told him straight out what I wanted.

"Certainly," he said. He would show it to me.

Well, I asked the question that anybody would ask: if he knew where the treasure was, why had he not gone and got it himself? It seemed a hard question to answer. But he answered it pat.

"I seek content," he said. "Not the things you seek."

And the odd thing is that one glance at his face showed me he had found it. I hadn't.

So we went under the great trees into the jungle, I seeking for all that wealth, he content with his brass bowl and his stick. Sometimes from the branches of those towering trees hung little prayers, written on paper in some jungle language to some gods of whom I knew nothing, praying for other needs, while my need was for bowls of gems, and he had climbed above all needs. Something in the great calm of the jungle and the serene calm of my guide and the little prayers on the peepul trees set me contemplating, as one says one has not time to contemplate here, though that of course is nonsense. Once another Indian said to me, "You do not give us credit for centuries of contemplation." I reflected now that that was perfectly true. What contemplation, I wondered, had lifted this man's desires above all the things that we seek, such as I was seeking now, and all the things that we own and which in reality own us, holding us all our lives with a grip of iron? As I was trying to make head or tail of all this, a panther sprang, a black and gold creature of infinite grace. It was not a single spring, it bounded towards us more like a tennis-ball bouncing with its long tail rippling as it floated on air; and the third bound was coming straight at the fakir. He did not dodge or flinch, and just seemed resigned. I do not know what good his resignation would have done him, if it hadn't been for my rifle. I threw up the light Mauser and fired as I would at a woodcock, remembering to aim in front, and pure luck made a perfect shot of it, and the panther dropped with his head on the fakir's feet. The fakir stepped quietly backwards. "He is not dead," he said. And I fired one more shot, and that was the end of this brief episode. Looking up at the fakir then, I saw real gratitude shining in his eyes, and a friendliness that he evidently could not feel before for anyone foolish enough to seek for material treasure.

"You have saved my life," he said. "Now I will save yours."

And he turned round and led me back, away from the treasure, and all the way to the road, and I had the sense to go with him.

He never told me why.

Two Young Officers

"There's such a thing as being too sharp," I heard a man pronounce one day at a club.

It was a wintry day near Christmas, and a fire was burning well in a cosy room, and a bunch of members was gathered before it, of whom I was one. They had been talking about journalism, when this remark was made that has so often been made before. And yet, stale as it was, and far from any profundity even when it was new, it served to start a story which sufficiently caught my interest to give me the idea of wanting to share it with my readers.

"Not in journalism," replied another of the men in front of the fire.

"Yes," said the first speaker. "There was a journalist who had that very fault. I knew him well, a man keen on making a name for himself, but going at it too hard. You may care to hear about him."

Just then a gust blew past our outer door, full of snow as a gust could be, as we all knew very well; and, with no inducement whatever to go outside, I think we all of us felt that we might just as well listen to any story as do anything else. And so we listened, and we heard this story. "He was a young man called Clayacre. I don't know if any of you knew him. He wasn't a member here. But he probably would have been, for he had the most brilliant abilities."

"Why wasn't he?" asked one of us.

"I'll tell you," said the first speaker, standing before the fire with a glass in his hand. Now he put down the glass and went on with his story. "Clayacre was his name. Ah, I told you that. A name no-one has heard of. And yet he was one of those men who had all the qualities but one for making a big name. That one was moderation. He was too sharp. Well, he was a journalist, one of those men whose job it is to get news. And he got it. There are people who will tell you that there is no news today, nothing much happening. But not Clayacre; there was always news where he was, and he knew how to get it. It is the same everywhere: one man will tell you that there are no foxes in a country, but another will hunt them. Or a man may say that there is nothing of interest to see wherever he may be; while another man will find such fascination there that life is a perpetual thrill to him. It was like that with Clayacre wherever he was; and so he was able to thrill others. A born journalist with a wonderful future. Well, it was during the war, and Clayacre was a little bit old for it, and they had not yet got to his age-group, as they called it, and he was still free to go on with his job of getting news, which to him was probably as important as the war. Some men found news difficult to get in those days, on account of the rigorous censorship; but the difficulty thrilled Clayacre and he went at it harder than ever. Of course a great many things that he found out couldn't be printed; but that didn't stop Clayacre, any more than you could stop a keen foxhunter by telling him that foxes were inedible. It's the sport that the foxhunter cares for, and that's what news was to Clayacre. I remember meeting him one day in the Strand a little before D day. 'What are you doing now?' I asked.

"'I am on to a big thing,' he said. 'I am going to find out when D day is, and where the landing will be.'

"'Good Lord,' I said. 'You can't print that.'

"'Print it?' he said. 'I'm not going to.'

"'Then what do you want to find out a thing like that for?' I asked.

"'For the excitement of it,' he said. 'To keep my hand in. It's my job.'

"'Better leave it alone,' I advised.

"But a light flashed out of his eyes, and I saw that news was to him all that a gazelle is to a lion, and that nothing would stop him.

"'How are you going to do it?' I asked him then.

"'I know two young officers at the War Office,' he said.

"'But I don't suppose all of them know, even there,' I told him.

"'They are in a department that does,' he answered.

"'But they aren't going to answer a single one of your questions about a thing like that,' I said.

"'Questions?' he said. 'But I shan't ask them questions.'

"'Then how are you going to get any information?' I asked.

"And he was silent while we walked ten or twenty yards. And then he said, 'I have had talks with them already. They are really very stupid.

I do the talking, and I notice the moment that anything I have said makes them at all embarrassed.'

"'How do you notice that?' I asked.

"'Well, I just have a flair for it,' he said. 'That's how I do my work.'

"'And then?' I asked.

"'Then,' he said, 'I just go right away from the subject and come back at it again from quite a different point, but remembering what I have already noticed. And when I get near the mark once more, I put two and two together. It is just a matter of feeling, or like seeing in the dark. I can't explain it.'

"'They'll get into awful trouble, if you do find anything out,' I told him.

"'I won't give them away,' he said.

"So cocksure he seemed that his intellect could ferret anything out of two young officers, that he gradually persuaded me that he could do what he said. And this alarmed me; for, though he had neither the intention nor the power to print it, it would be a shocking thing for the biggest secret that England had to be in the possession of a civilian with no responsibility to anybody not to blurt it out. I had to decide on the spur of the moment what line to take to dissuade him, and what I hurriedly decided on, whether it was the best line or not, was to try and persuade him that he could never do what he thought he could, and that for that reason he should abandon the whole idea. I think, now, that I took a wrong line; for it only made him more pig-headed, and he told me that nobody with any news worth having was able to hold it back from expert investigation; by which he meant methods such as his; and, as for two young army officers, he would very soon get from them all the information he wanted. Then he spoke more of his methods, and more of the intellect of the two young officers at the War Office whose acquaintance he had made; rather giving one the impression of a skilled fencer comparing his rapier to some rustic cudgel. And this put me more at my ease, for I thought that so much vanity as what he was now revealing could not accomplish anything serious, and that the great secret was safe. But I underrated him; and I think he saw that I did. 'I've asked them to dine with me at the Griltz,' he said.

"'And are they coming?' I asked.

"'Certainly they are,' he replied.

"I could hardly believe it; yet, after all, why shouldn't they eat a good dinner when it was offered? And the Griltz could give a good dinner even in those days.

"'And what are you going to do then?' I asked.

"'I shall give them champagne and let them talk,' he replied.

"'And what do you think they'll tell you?' I asked.

"'Come and see,' he said.

"When I saw that he really meant it, I accepted, not only out of curiosity, but so as to check him if there was really anything in his boastful claim that, when they had an experienced journalist to deal with, these young officers would be quite unable to keep from him any secret, however vital. I accepted, and we were all to meet at the Griltz in two days' time. So we parted. And, when the day came, I went early, hoping to find the host arrived first, as I did, and to reason with him again in case there should, after all, be anything dangerous in his boast. And reason with him I did; but I might as well have tried to reason with a wild horse to stop it galloping with its herd on a grassy plain, when all the rest were galloping down a mild wind in the morning, for all the good that I did. Chasing news was his avocation, and he followed it furiously; and not only could I never have held him back from it, but he couldn't hold back himself. Perhaps no man inspired to do any job cares much for anything but the work for which he has been inspired. And Clayacre was inspired to do the work he had chosen, if ever a man was. I did my best, but I might as well never have spoken. And then the two young officers arrived, and I was introduced to them, Captain Smith and Mr. Lokner, and we went into a small room that Clayacre had had reserved for us. Clayacre glanced at me, as we walked in behind his other two guests, with a confident air of assurance. And then as he gave me one more triumphant glance while we sat down, my old opinion returned to comfort me, that Clayacre was altogether too cocksure. We had a very good dinner, a very good dinner indeed, and good champagne with it. Clayacre was a well-paid journalist, and evidently spared nothing in the one pursuit of his life, which was that of news. And most people are probably prepared to spend all they can spare from their earnings for that one aim in life that almost every man has, and a different aim with nearly every one. With the champagne conversation began, and it was remarkable to notice how little Clayacre spoke, and yet how deftly he turned the conversation this way and that. Again I was enthralled at seeing an expert at work, and forgot for a while the danger of the game that was being played, and then, as I admired the skill with which he directed the chatter, the thought came to me that a man who knew his job as well as Clayacre evidently did, would probably know the sources of his information as well as he knew how to draw it out of those sources, and that he would be right in thinking that these two officers possessed the secret he sought. Once more by trying to turn the conversation to innocent channels I tried to restrain him. But my clumsy efforts were futile beside his skill. The younger officer, Lokner, seemed reasonably cautious, even at the high tide of the champagne; but Captain Smith seemed to be saying whatever Clayacre wanted him to; and gradually, like a boat approaching Niagara, his babbling tongue seemed nearing the deadly secret. But there it seemed to hover; and, to my very great relief, it would not go over. I could see Clayacre trying again and again, and I fancy he must have seen the relief in my face and known that I thought he was beaten. For he actually said to me in a low voice, 'Do you think I can be beaten at my own job by . . .?' And there he stopped, but a smiling contemptuous glance showed me clearly enough whom he meant. And, as he turned from me to talk again with Captain Smith, he had an expression that conveyed as clear as an expression can, 'Now watch me.' And that look was enough to have warned anybody. But the young officers took no notice, and went on sipping their champagne, and Captain Smith was talking almost as Clayacre wanted him to, and even Lokner now. Clayacre's methods were really remarkable. What he did was to mention casually names of towns or capes or bays on the coast of France, beginning with Calais, and watching to see if he caused any embarrassment, and getting right away from the subject when he hadn't, and covering it up with words, as well as a place can be covered up by such means. And then he got with one of his remarks right on to the coast of Normandy, and evidently noted a sudden calm in the talk of both the young officers and saw them steer away at once from that subject. And then Clayacre talked of it as though he knew all about it, and I think they believed that he did. That was his mistake.

"Well, this was too much for me. I had had some champagne myself, but I had wits enough awake to see that Clayacre knew his job and was hell-bent to find out what he should not, and that I could not stop him unaided. But, as for aid, the whole armed forces of the Empire would aid me as soon as I explained to any of them what the peril was. And it was a peril; for Clayacre was floating triumphantly in on tides of champagne to his damnable harbour. I made a last clumsy effort to divert him. But what can any amateur do against an expert employing his skill at his life's work? He glanced contemptuously at the young officers, and turned back to me with a superior and triumphant smile. The elder one looked uneasy. But that only intensified my fears, for it showed that he corroborated them; and although I thought that he might be at last on his guard, it looked to be too late, and I feared that both of them were wax in Clayacre's hands.

"Did I tell you that there was one waiter listening all the time? Which only made matters worse. Clayacre actually spoke to me about what he was doing, though only two words. 'You see,' he said.

"And then he started talking about the South coast of England. I rose hurriedly then. On the spur of the moment I could think of no excuse. I said, 'I have enjoyed the dinner immensely; but I told you I had promised to take my aunt to a theatre, and I find it is time now.'

"Clayacre tried to stop me, but I shook hands with the two young officers, saying goodbye. He tried to stop me again, but I muttered, 'Poor old lady,' and was gone.

"I got a taxi and drove straight to the War Office. I said that I had very important information; and I will say that they showed me in very quickly, and evidently to the right room. There were two majors sitting there, and I told them at once that there were two young and inexperienced officers being pumped by a journalist at the Griltz about the secret of D day. And I told him their names.

"'O, Smith,' said one of the majors. 'He is not so inexperienced as all that.'

"'No,' said the other.

"'But the secret is probably out by now,' I exclaimed.

"'Really?' said the major before whose desk I was standing.

"'Well, any way there is a waiter in the room,' I said, 'listening to every word.'

"'That would be . . .' said the other major in a low voice.

"I didn't hear the name. They seemed quite uninterested.

"'But it might get all over London,' I said to rouse them.

"'Not till your friend leaves the hotel,' said the major before me.

"I didn't know what he meant by that. I turned to the other major then, and tried to get him interested. But it was no good.

"'Well, I thought I would just tell you,' I said to the major at the desk.

"'Thank you very much,' he said.

"And there was nothing more for me to do but go. I seemed to be able to make no more headway there than I had been able to make at the Griltz. I left in a very depressed mood and I don't think I got to sleep till 2, thinking of all the frightful harm that would come if Clayacre ever blurted out the news he was obviously getting, and which, as I look back on it all, I feel sure he actually got.

"I never saw Clayacre again. Nobody ever has. Of course I made enquiries. I went back to the hotel and asked to see the head-waiter and the reception-clerk, and finally the manager himself. And all I met was a perfect blend of two things; ignorance and politeness, which simply got me nowhere. I liked Clayacre, fool though he was. I asked to see the waiter who had been all the time in that room. Do you know, I might just as well have asked for the late Shah of Persia. They were merely mystified, though always polite. I called again at the War Office, fearing that they would be even far less helpful there than the Griltz; but somewhat to my surprise I was shown in, and allowed to see both Captain Smith and Lokner. They were charming, and said what a nice dinner it had been and how sorry they were that I had had to leave early. But, when I asked of Clayacre, they were merely amused. He had gone away rather hilarious, they said; and they both laughed a little.

"'How did he go away?' I asked.

"'In a taxi,' said Smith.

"'In what direction?' I asked.

"'We don't remember,' said Lokner. 'Nor, I think, does he.'

"Getting no more information there, nor seeing much likelihood of it, I went and told the police. But they quite evidently suspected me. So I left them and went back to the Griltz, and, finding them still polite, I made enquiries of anyone that I saw; not directly about Clayacre, because I saw that information about him was not to be had, but about any unusual thing whatever that had occurred there that night or the following morning. For I decided to do a bit of detective work, guided by all the detective fiction that I had ever read; and I decided that something very odd having occurred, any clue to it could only be found amongst unusual events. So I hunted for news of any unusual events, in order to rummage among them and see if I could find a trace there of the missing man. Nearly a week had gone by before I started on these enquiries, for I had not missed him at first. This of course made it still more difficult. Nothing unusual that I could get hold of was too trivial for me, for I knew that clues are not often written large. I learned that one of the waiters about that time had bought a new suit, and that another had got hold of two bottles of champagne; but of course that led nowhere.

"And then I learned that the chef, who had a great cauldron in the kitchen, that he called his stockpot, had got a lot more meat about that time for his stockpot. But of course that led nowhere either."

The Unforgivable Choice

"And you are Mr. Hulton?" said the reporter in the little village of Mereham.

"Yes, I am," said Mr. Hulton.

"And you live in this village?"

"Have done so all my life."

"And you saw the body."

"Yes."

"And I understand," the reporter went on, "that his dog was watching over him?"

"Yes, there was a dog there."

"And he stayed by the body, and would not come away?"

"Yes, that is so."

"There should be quite a story in that."

"Well, yes, in a way."

"Perhaps you would come inside and sit down," said the reporter. "And then you could tell me the story."

"I don't mind if I do," said Hulton.

For they were standing outside the Long Dragon, and they went into a room at the back of the bar, to which two words seemed to gain them entrance and to cause drinks to be brought and put on the table beside them. The two magic words were The Press. And there while Hulton sometimes sipped at a glass of stout and talked on, and sometimes answered questions, he told this story, which when coherently put together by the reporter, went like this.

There arrived one day in the village of Mereham a total stranger, who had just bought a villa at the edge of it, with gardens and pleasant lawns running down to a little lake, from which the village was said to have got its name. So quiet and inconspicuous he was, that one would not dream there was any mystery about him. And yet one mystery there was, which there was not about any other man or any woman in that village or in either of the villages on each side of it, and that was that, after gossip had said its last word throughout Mereham, and that took several weeks, nobody could tell anything of his origin, either who he was, what he did, or where he had come from. He was quiet and friendly, he was in the early forties, he wore a beard; nobody had much more than that to say about him, except that they all summed him up as being a very respectable man. He seemed interested in respectability, to be really fond of it, as other men were fond of their various hobbies. It showed in what he did, what he said, what he liked, a wistful yearning, almost, for respectability. And one thing the simple rustics of that village found out very quickly, and that was that he was sincere in his likings, sincere in his dislike of gambling, however mild, in his dislike of more than two glasses of beer, in his attendance at church, and in such philosophy as appeared from his conversation, or, if philosophy be too big a word for it, his attitude towards life. He would often have a glass of beer with others in the Long Dragon at evening and was soon friends with everybody he knew, and got to know more and more as the weeks went by. Only one thing they felt a little sore about at the Long Dragon, and indeed throughout the village, and that was that he should grudge them one thing that they all would have relished. For here was obviously a man with a mystery, and yet he would not share it with anyone. Drinks he would stand to any of them, but when the very air of the Long Dragon seemed mellow, and when the time had come to enjoy the full savour of whatever mystery so completely concealed his origin—not a hint from him, not a word. Had they liked him less they would almost have called him greedy, for keeping a mystery all to himself. The guesses of gossip supplied substitute mysteries, telling the story of his life in their own way, but there was nothing to corroborate any guess. One guess, based upon nothing more than a certain look which someone once saw in the eyes of the stranger as he heard the sound of a distant train coming towards Mereham, was that he had done some work on one of the great railways that cross America and made his money in that, but that was a guess that led to no more than the rest, and they all led to nothing. In his quiet way he was hail-fellow-well-met with everyone, and many came to his house at evening to play draughts with him, and sometimes dominoes, though never any game of cards, for any means of gambling, however low the stakes, he quite honestly disliked. And often he would throw darts with them in the inn. He was the greatest help to the vicar, subscribing to any good cause about which the vicar approached him, and on a scale that nobody else in the parish could afford. To a raffle in aid of a charity he would not subscribe, anxiously apologizing to the vicar for his inherent distaste for anything even so remotely connected with gambling. No-one ever heard him swear, or use any word that men used for the purpose of swearing. He was never sanctimonious, merely feeling a mild dislike for any form of riotousness, trickery or dishonesty. And, as this story mentions before, one thing those villagers could detect with absolute certainty in all men, even in those far better educated than themselves, was sincerity. He was a respectable man; he chose respectability for himself and he liked it in others: they soon found that out in Mereham. About such a man there may seem little to tell; no-one could call him dull for leading a quiet life and a good one, but a story about him might have been dull but for one thing, and that was that this quiet friendly man seemed to carry a fear about with him. A sudden noise, even somebody ringing his doorbell, or anything unexpected, would bring a swift look of alertness to his eyes, and from playing a game of dominoes with a glass of beer on the table beside him he would suddenly look like a hunter, or like a soldier suspecting an ambush, or a scout in a hostile country; then he would smile slightly, utter a little sigh and become all engrossed in the dominoes again. This did not happen only once, and Mr. Hulton among others, who used often to have supper at his house and play draughts or dominoes after, felt quite sure of that fear. Once Hulton even tested him by dropping a pebble from his pocket, and always there came the sudden change from that quiet easy man to one with the eyes and poise of a leader of armed men in a difficult country. The face altered strangely little, but the eyes and the attitude did. Soon that alertness would always give way to the dominoes player or the kindly host over his supper, as though a danger had passed. Hulton was a farmer of two or three hundred acres all along one side of the village, only just across the mere that lapped at the edge of Jack Smith's lawns. That was the name he had, a name as inconspicuous as himself and revealing as little to anyone of his origin. He lived with a cook, and a maid to look after the whole house, and often got in a charwoman, whom he paid very well, to save the maid too much work.

And he kept a cat, which had one day strolled into his house and, seeing no dog there, settled down and was soon encouraged by Jack Smith to stay. He seemed to want something, Hulton thought, on which to expend his friendliness, and the cat seemed to answer that purpose. It was not that he preferred a cat to a dog, Hulton thought, but rather that he had left a dog behind in the country that he had come from, and he gathered that he had been fond of the dog and did not like to supplant him, or felt that no other dog could fill his place. That was what Hulton thought. And then Hulton remembers somebody's chance remark, as chance remarks do get remembered, just as one speck of soot will stick on one's nose while a thousand others float by. They were talking of Mr. Jack Smith, as they often did, one evening at the Long Dragon, and someone, hunting the mystery of him still, wondered if it was his own beard, when one man made the remark: "Yes it is. But it isn't his own nose." And that remark had stuck in Hulton's memory. And one scrap of plausibility helped to keep it there, and that was that the extraordinary remark at least explained why Jack Smith's face remained so immobile even when his eyes flashed and they and his whole attitude showed him to be all alert. If there was anything artificial about his face, that might account for this strange look of alertness and somnolence that sometimes came down on the same man. Hulton got to know him very well and became his friend and would have liked to help him to oppose that fear; yet no remark of Hulton's would ever draw the least hint from Jack Smith of what it was that he feared, until one day when it all poured out and he told Hulton the story. And that day Hulton remembers very well, with every vivid detail. He had gone up to Jack Smith's house to have supper with him, and had found Jack Smith standing before him with his hands drooped at his sides, instead of the welcoming handshake which he had always had from Jack Smith, and his mouth was slightly open and he looked utterly helpless; and when he spoke, as he did by way of apology for giving no welcome, all he said was, "I am a dead man." And Hulton tried to cheer him and could not do it, and then he got him to sit down, and they both sat at the table at which they used to play dominoes, and Jack Smith began to talk. He began to talk about the law, and how murderers, both in England and the United States, though sentenced to death, were often reprieved before they went to the gallows or chair; and from that he went on to tell that one thing was never forgiven and one death sentence never reprieved, and that was where any man had belonged to a gang in the country that Jack Smith came from and, having made a few hundred thousand dollars by wicked means, gave up his bad ways and chose a respectable life. In fact, "murder may often be pardoned by the law," said Jack Smith, "but respectability by gangsters never." And he had been one of such a gang and he had made at least a hundred thousand pounds out of it, and it was not just because he had made his pile that he wished to desert his pals, but because he had come to hate murder and robbery, and the money had given him the opportunity to lead a respectable life for which he had always longed. For in spite of his past, which he admitted was black as could be, he liked respectability now, and that was the one thing of all things that a gang never forgave. The penalty for turning respectable was always death. "And now," said Jack Smith, "I am a dead man."

"No, no," said Hulton. "They'll never find you, once you have crossed the Atlantic."

"Let me tell you," said Jack Smith. And Hulton was silent and listened. And Jack Smith said, "Never mind what my name was or where we worked. Our headquarters were near Chicago, but we worked as far as the Coast, I mean California. We robbed trains. You needn't tell me how wrong that was. I know that well. I have lain awake through long nights over it, thinking how bad it was and wanting to be respectable. I resolved to give it up and to leave the gang. That would not have been possible in the ordinary way; the gang saw to that. But I had heard of a man who could alter faces, alter them thoroughly, a man who had given handsome faces after the war to airmen who had had their own faces burned away. I went to that man and stayed with him for some time, and it hurt a lot every day, but not so much as thinking by night over my past life. And when I had paid him ten thousand dollars and left him nobody in the world could have recognized Jack Smith for a member of that gang of train-robbers. My own face had gone like my name."

"Why, then, you're safe," said Hulton. "They could never recognize you, even if they came here."

"They have come here," said Jack Smith.

"Here?" gasped Hulton.

"One of them has," said Jack Smith. "He is at the Long Dragon now."

"But you said no man can recognize you," said Hulton cheerily.

"No man can," said Jack Smith.

"Then you have nothing to worry about, old fellow," said Hulton.

"Let me tell you," said Jack Smith. "They would have sent a man to every country in Europe, and to South America too. Your Scotland Yard seem pretty keen on hunting down murder, but they are nothing to one of those gangs if they have any reason to suspect respectability. That is a choice they will never forgive.

"They would have known I should clear out of the States. I had slipped away at once, not even waiting to take my dog with me. But they soon knew. One of them came to England. He would have searched every village, carefully making enquiries about every stranger who had arrived about the time I did."

"But that would take a long time," said Hulton.

"They don't grudge time," said Jack Smith. "And they have all the money they need, and can get plenty more, but they won't have one of the gang turning respectable. It took him a long time, but he got here at last, and now he is in Mereham, talking to them all in the Long Dragon."

"But he'll get nothing from that," said Hulton. "No-one knows anything here of who you are or where you came from, no-one at all." And again Hulton tried to cheer him, quoting his own words to him, that he could not be recognized, and telling him that the gangster would soon pass on, if he was going to search every village. But there was in Jack Smith's attitude and his voice and in all except his immobile face, the expression of a rabbit that, however far behind him it be, knows there is a stoat on his tracks. Hulton suggested staying locked up in his house, going for a while to the seaside, and many other things, but Jack Smith seemed helpless and hopeless. To cure that dreadful depression Hulton suggested his going for a walk, partly for the sake of the open air, but chiefly so that Jack Smith might learn how safe it was to walk abroad with his altered face. For it was clear to Hulton that, if he had got away from the United States with that face, it really was unrecognizable, as Jack Smith had said. Well, Jack Smith gave a sigh and went for a walk over the fields alone on the other side of the mere, still with that air of a doomed rabbit knowing that there is a stoat on his tracks. He seemed bent on going alone, so Hulton stood by the door of the house and watched him go, and that is the last that he saw of Jack Smith alive. His face was unrecognizable by any man, as he said. But he had left his dog behind him when he had fled from Chicago, and the gangster had his dog with him now. And the dog must have come gambolling up to Jack Smith, wagging a welcoming tail. Hulton heard one shot, and knew what that would have been, and he went over the fields the way that Jack Smith had gone, and found him lying dead with his old dog guarding him and not letting Hulton come near.

The Old Detective's Story

When I feel like reading a detective story, as I suppose most of us often do, I usually read it in the ordinary way, in an evening paper or in a book; but sometimes I get a taste for having the story raw, uncooked by any printer, as it were. And then I take a walk along a road that I know, which brings me past a garden in Surrey, in which if I choose the right time of day, preferably on a summer's evening, I am likely to find an old detective of my acquaintance, working among his bean-rows, of which he is very fond, or doing a little digging, or hacking away his weeds. Then I have only to lean over his wooden paling awhile, and, if he is not too busy, he will lean on his spade or whatever it may be, and begin to talk reminiscently. If he just says, "Good evening," to me I will know by the nod of his head as he says it that he has too much work to do among his weeds, or with his digging, to spare much breath for more than politeness; and then with a greeting and a nod of my head I go on my way. But if I find him among his bean-rows, where the work seems lighter, and if it is a nice warm golden evening, he will be pretty sure to talk, and so I get my detective story raw. Very likely it will come out of years long past, so that it will be a tale that has long been forgotten, and so all the fresher to me. One evening, leaning over his paling, I said after I had admired his beans, "What is the strangest case you ever knew?"

"The strangest?" he said almost at once. "Well, the strangest was when they found a body in a garden in what was then called, I think, the Irish Free State, and it had puzzled them a good deal over there, and they asked if one of us would go over and lend a hand; and that was me. It was a lovely little garden in the suburbs of Dublin, all full of crocuses, for it was Spring, and they had found this body lying on the lawn among the clumps of crocuses, shot through the heart."

Of course he began at the end, when he first saw the garden, and then told me bits of evidence by which he pieced it all together, and so got back to the beginning, which is not a very good way to tell a story. So I will tell it as it was finally unfolded to me. And this is the story.

Television was pretty new at the time that these things happened, and the TV company that was run by the man Straeger was a very little thing then, nothing like what it has grown to now; in fact I think he was working then for the ordinary screen, though his ambitions were towards TV. And one day he went over to Ireland from the United States with his eyes blazing with his new idea, and went to see a certain James Moloney, to whom he had some sort of letter of introduction; rang his bell, went in, and told him about his project at once. And his project was that Moloney should play in a film or television, whichever it was. And Moloney said that he had never acted in his life.

"All the better," said Straeger. "You'll be absolutely fresh."

And apparently little details like whether a man could act or not didn't trouble Straeger.

All he thought about was his wonderful new and absolutely original idea. There has been something like it since, a native being killed by a lion in East Africa, and perhaps one or two other things, but it was absolutely new then.

"You needn't be able to act, my boy," he said to James Moloney. "It is only the wonderful thing you have to do, which has never been done on the films before."

"And what's that?" said Moloney.

"Shoot a man," said Straeger.

"Nothing so new in that," said Moloney. "I have seen it dozens of times on the films myself."

"Pooh," said Straeger. "You mean pretending to shoot a man—only a pinch of powder in the gun, and no bullet, and somebody hitting the floor with a big hammer, and the shot man falls back gracefully on to a sofa. But my stunt is the real thing."

"Shoot him dead?" said Moloney.

"Quite dead," said Straeger.

"But I wouldn't like to do that to any man," says Moloney.

"Now, see here," says Straeger. "I've got all this taped out. He'll be a man that doesn't much matter any way. And we'll compensate all concerned, the whole of his family. And we'll compensate them well. Everything will be on us. Don't you worry about that."

"But that would be murder," says Moloney. "And I should be hanged."

"Now, don't go running away with fancy ideas," says Straeger. "We have everything worked out in detail. To begin with, they don't hang in the country in whose territory the thing is going to be filmed."

"But I don't want to leave Ireland," says Moloney. "I've got a bit of farming to do here, and one thing and another, and . . ."

"Now don't you bother about one thing and another," says Straeger, "nor your farming either. Nobody is going to ask you to leave Ireland."

"But I thought you said—" began Moloney.

"And so I did," says Straeger. "But have you ever heard of extraterritoriality and diplomatic immunity?"

"And what are they?" asks Moloney.

Well, that kind of thing was all new to Moloney, as they hadn't had legations in Ireland for very long then, and Mr. Straeger explains it all and tells him that the film is to be shot only half a mile from where they are talking in Moloney's house, which is in the suburbs of Dublin. It is to be filmed, he tells him, in the garden of the Eldoradan legation. I have found out, I may say, since my talk with my friend the old detective that there is no such country as Eldorado now, whatever there may have been once, but he insisted on calling it that all through his story, tactfully concealing its real name. Well, Straeger was a smart business man and he not only explained extraterritoriality to Moloney, but got him to understand it, and added that, there being no extradition treaty between Eldorado and Ireland, the moment he stepped out of that garden he would be free from any legal proceedings whatever, so long as he kept away from Eldorado. I never heard why Straeger chose Moloney to act in a film. Perhaps he may have been the only Irishman Straeger knew. But chiefly he was so excited over his new idea of killing a man in cold blood for the films, that he didn't bother much about whom he got to do it. And when he had talked away the natural decent feelings of Moloney, so that there was no longer too much resistance to his mad scheme, he began to flutter the dollars before his eyes, not the actual dollars, but easy talk about thousands of them; and so he got Moloney. And on the appointed day away they went to this garden, just Straeger and Moloney and the man who was to be shot, a little man named Hennessey, whom they found waiting for them just inside the garden, as Straeger had arranged. Straeger and Moloney went in through a little gate that there was in the side of the

garden and joined Hennessey. Hennessey looked like a man who had
been a bit fond of his drinks for the last few years; and of course he
would have got all of them that he wanted from Straeger. Straeger had
explained to Moloney that Hennessey was married and had two or
three children, but he had repeated when Moloney began to protest,
"Everything will be on us." Moloney was naturally puzzled at seeing
Hennessey there, apparently waiting to be shot, puzzled as he would
have been to see a sheep walking into a butcher's shop all by itself. But
Straeger took him aside and explained that Hennessey was a very simple fellow and thought it was all to be done with a blank cartridge; and
his family knew nothing about it except that he was to be well paid.
"And so he will be," added Straeger.

The house seemed all shut up, and as a matter of fact it was. There
were just these three men in the garden and nobody else was about.

Well, to begin with, it wasn't the garden of a legation at all, Eldorado
or anywhere else. Straeger had just picked a garden whose owners he
knew to be away, and Moloney had taken his word for it. Either Moloney must have been a bit of a mug, or Straeger must have been particularly sharp at salesmanship, or whatever they call it; perhaps a bit of
each. Well, there they were all three in a garden among the crocuses.
And then Straeger set up his camera and pulled out his script and stood
Moloney just where he wanted him, and saying to him again, "The ex-
penses are all on us," he was just handing him the revolver, when Hennessey said, "No. I'll take that." And, before Straeger could make out
what he was doing, he let him have it. And, whether Hennessey was
drunk or sober, his mind seemed illuminated with a clear view of the
whole situation. Probably Straeger had let him have one drink too
many; too many for Straeger, I mean; and it had shown up Straeger's
little game in a flash. And during that flash, at least, he was not the
mug that Straeger must have miscalculated that he was. For without
saying a word he shot Straeger dead. And then he and Moloney, having
the same dominant interest, which was to get away, got into Straeger's
car, which was waiting outside, and drove off as fast as they could. So
it was Straeger's body that they found lying among the crocuses.

"Yes," said the old detective, "that was by far the strangest case I
ever investigated. I never really did understand it."

Tales from the 1956 Collection

HɛlpiNɡ tHɛ FαiRiɛs

The young journalist from London on holiday at Rathgeel was feeling lonely for want of news. There was plenty of fishing and shooting, but no news; for nothing ever seemed to happen in Rathgeel. The weather may have changed a bit at times in Rathgeel, but not while he was there; the wind blew warm and damp from the South West all the time, and all the thorn-trees sloped the same way, as though that one wind had been blowing for ever. And the odd thing was, as it seemed to Draffin, the young journalist I have mentioned, nobody seemed to want anything new to happen; they complained a bit while they were talking, of the weather and the crops, the price of cattle and one or two other things, but they never seemed in their hearts to want anything new. And Draffin was lonely and homesick for want of news, good as the fishing was, and the shooting too. And then one day a man called William Smith was found lying dead in a narrow old sunken lane, where nobody went but an odd tramp once a week, and he had been lying there nearly a week when they found him, and there were some bullet-holes in him. This was like dawn to Draffin after a long night. News at last! And he ran round with his notebook open in his hand to all the acquaintances that he had made during his holiday, to get the details of it. And nothing could he get.

"I thought the Irish were a talkative people," he said to one of them at last, a tall dark thin man called Michael Heggarty.

"And so we are," said Heggarty.

"I think you are the dumbest people in the whole world," said Draffin. "And that's not excepting the people in deaf-and-dumb asylums."

"Is that so?" said Heggarty.

"I am sure it is," replied Draffin.

"Maybe that's because you don't use the right key," said Heggarty. "You would not say there was no money in the Bank of England because you couldn't open the vaults. But there's a key to them."

"What's the key here?" asked Draffin.

"Sure, it's whiskey," said Heggarty, "if you can find the right man for it."

"And who's the right man?" asked Draffin.

"Ah, I'd not like to be telling you," said Heggarty.

"Well, one must make a beginning," said Draffin, "so I'll begin by trying you, if you wouldn't mind coming in here."

For they were standing outside the white wall of Jimmy Doyle's public-house, under its dark thatch.

"Sure, I don't mind if I do," said Heggarty.

And they went inside and whiskey was ordered by Draffin and drunk by them both, sitting together at a table, and the heavy silence continued. And Draffin paid for more whiskey, and that was drunk too. And in the few minutes that went by after that the little room seemed to grow darker in the autumn afternoon, but a light was growing in the eyes of Heggarty. And then Draffin said half to himself and half to the far wall at which he was gazing, "I wonder what happened to William Smith."

"I'll tell you," said Heggarty. "It was like this. He comes over here from England, or from some place where they must be very ignorant, about a year ago, and he buys a bit of land to do some farming, and he settles down all alone in the farmhouse on it. I wouldn't say he didn't understand farming, but he was terrible ignorant of the land and all the ways of it. And there was a lone thorn in a field that he wanted to plough, an old thorn, what was left of it by the ages, and he said it would get in the way of the plough. There was no harm in ploughing the field, but it stands to reason he could have run a plough round the tree, and by bending his head a bit he could have got under the branches, and the horse too, for a horse would have had more sense than what he had. But he couldn't see that, and he must cut down the tree, a lone thorn of the fairies, one that the Little People had danced round for ages. Well, he asks several young men to cut it, but none of them would do anything so foolish and made various excuses. So what does he do but he gets an axe, and he cuts it down himself. And nobody says a word, at first. We was all too horrified. And then some of us goes to old Timmy Maguire, to hear what he will say. And we tells him what William Smith has done, and he had heard already, and old

Timmy Maguire says, 'No matter. You only have to wait. Watch him and wait and see what the Little People will do. For I never knew anybody do anything agin them without they being revenged on him; never yet, and I've lived to be ninety.'

"Well, that satisfied all of us, except one young fellow who must always be asking questions.

"'What'll they do to him?' he says.

"'You have only to watch,' says old Timmy Maguire. 'They will take his luck away. Watch his luck and see what happens to it. I never knew the Little People leave a man's luck when he had offended them, not a shred of it. I never saw them do that in ninety years.'

"'And did you often see them at it?' asks the young fellow.

"'Begob,' says old Timmy Maguire, 'many's the time I seen them take all a man's luck right away to the mountains, nor I never seen it come back.'

"'Sure, that's terrible,' says one of us.

"'It's what they do,' says old Timmy Maguire.

"Well, we all decides to do what old Timmy Maguire says, and to watch the luck of William Smith and to see what happens to it; and what happens is this: it's the most extraordinary part of my story, but it's the truth I'm telling you. William Smith puts five pounds on a horse a few days later, that's running at a hundred to one. Well, that's tempting your luck to leave you; no horse is going to win at a hundred to one, and it's throwing five pounds away, and a man who begins like that will throw everything away. But this horse wins, and the bookie pays, and William Smith gets a cheque for £500, and cashes it, and we all says, 'What about the Little People?'

"And that isn't all. There's a competition next week to guess the number of rabbits that there are in County Meath, with a motor-car for a prize for the man whose guess is nearest. And William Smith guesses the right number within three, and he gets the motor-car. And the Little People says nothing.

"And it doesn't stop there. For a few days later he sells a horse for a thousand pounds, what he had bought out of a cart for £25, either knowing something about a horse, or finding a man that thought he did; but it was luck either way. Aye, out of a cart, and he sells it for a thousand pounds. And that wasn't all, nor nearly all, but I won't weary you with telling you all of it, and maybe you wouldn't believe me if I did; but he had a run of luck such as no-one ever saw, and it went on week after week, and was an insult to those that dance under the moon. And we goes to old Timmy Maguire and says, 'What about it now?' And he says, 'Only wait.' And that man Smith's run of luck went on and on. And then he backs another horse in a race and it was 3 to 1 on, and he puts on six hundred pounds to win two hundred; and he could afford to do that, when he knew that he couldn't lose. And it was just the same as the horse at a hundred to one, and he gets two hundred pounds. Well, that was the limit, and something had to be done. It was no use asking old Timmy Maguire, who would say nothing but 'Wait' or 'Watch him.' We had to do something ourselves. I had nothing to do with it myself, because I have always kept away from religion and politics and all them kind of things, and I says to the rest of the boys, 'I'll have no hand in it'; and they says, 'Sure, we all respect your principles. At the same time, the Little People are being insulted by this man's luck, as though they didn't exist, or as though there were nothing sacred in their old thorns, and we can't allow that kind of thing in a place like Rathgeel, that never permitted any disrespect to be shewn to anybody.' And I had to agree that that was so: what else could I say? Though I took no part in it myself.

"Well, when the boys was gone I goes once more to old Timmy Maguire to tell him that the young lads is getting impatient. 'Sure, they needn't be,' says he. 'For I never knew any man to hold his luck against that people, and they'll be avenged for their thorn.'

"It was no use telling him of all the good luck that was continually coming to William Smith, for he wouldn't listen, but only says to me, 'Wait.'

"Well, the young lads goes that night to the house of William Smith, and they finds him sitting at a table totting up the figures of all the money that had been coming his way ever since he cut down the old thorn; and there was little smiles on his face. That is what the boys told me afterwards, and I only tell you what they told me, but I can't say exactly what happened when I wasn't there myself, but was at home with my poor old mother who had a cold and wanted me to look after her, so I stayed with her as any son would do. But the young lads came to William Smith and say to him, 'Rathgeel was always a quiet place, where no-one takes any part in religion or politics, and never interferes with anyone, whatever his religion is. At the same time,' they says, 'if anyone thinks that he can come here from England and buy a farm and insult those that dance round the thorn, and make money that many a man would be glad of, with an old mother to support, as though his luck hadn't changed and the Little People didn't exist, he is greatly mistaken, as you'll soon find out if you don't give up all the money you made since you desecrated the thorn, and a great deal more besides, till you've given up to fellows that will know how to use it properly, as much as you would have lost if your luck had turned against you weeks ago, as it should; if you know what we mean, and if you don't it's a bullet you'll get, which may help to teach you.' That's what the young lads told me they said to him. And William Smith says nothing, and they sees he is in two minds what to do; and Rathgeel being a quiet place, as I told you and as you've seen for yourself, where no trouble of any sort ever occurred, and they not wanting its name to become a byword from having a man there that was insulting the Little People and growing fat on it, and interfering with their dancing at night, for a lone thorn is their ballroom, they asks him to step outside with them, before he can make up his mind for fear he would make it up wrong. And they takes him to that bohereen where the body was found, and what happened there they none of them told me, so there's no knowing, and it's no use any man saying there is. But they goes to old Timmy Maguire and tells him that William Smith is dead, and what ought they to do now? And old Timmy Maguire says, 'Sure, there's nothing more for anybody to do. Didn't I tell you that all you had to do was wait?'"

THE STORY OF TSE GAH

I know, now, that there are other lands than our land. I know that there are lands beyond the mountains. One of them is Tibet, another is China, and then there is Nepal. I know this, because I have seen the ambassadors from China and Tibet to our land, and an envoy came from Nepal. They came and stood in front of me. And I know many things besides these. I am going to write down all the things that I know, which were in the past, for they are all gone now, and all things are changing, so that I fear that the old things will come no more. The future I cannot see as I can see the past; yet it will come, and it will be just as much what was ordained as the past; but it is all strange and uncertain and I wish to think of it no more. The monks can write of it, but I will write of the past. Some things I remember separately from other things. I remember them clearly, but I do not remember when they occurred. Other things I remember being followed by others, and they by others again, so that I know when they were. I remember a garden with some very bright flowers, taller than I; and I remember a great white-and-green butterfly coming to one of them. But I do not remember when this was. I was with the women then. They had taken me to the garden of the palace. And they used to be with me in the palace too. Sometimes I saw the monks, but they never came very close. Afterwards I was taken away from the women, and I never saw them any more, only the monks. The women told me a little about Tse Gah, the god of the mountains; just that he was the god of the mountains, and that his name was Tse Gah, and that he ruled over our land, and had made it, and spoke by the thunder. But the monks taught me a great deal about Tse Gah. And the monks taught me to remember things, things much longer ago than what I am writing of now, hundreds of years ago some of them, and a few so long ago that there is no saying how old these memories were. They taught me to remember a great deal. I was frightened of Tse Gah, who had made the mountains. And one night while he spoke, and the lightning flashed also, I was very much frightened indeed, and the monks smiled. One of them standing quite close to me smiled so curious a smile that, strange though it is to write, it was that smile that taught me what I had never yet guessed. And it was a very strange thing to be taught. Who reads this may think it very strange that I did not know, but I did not. Perhaps I was not taught it, but guessed it from that smile when I was frightened of Tse Gah. But the moment I guessed it I knew it was true. I was Tse Gah. I was five years old when I learned this. When I knew this, it accounted for everything. I knew now why the women were afraid of me. I had always known that they were, though I never knew why. All the monks frightened me; and they used to puzzle me too, because I saw that they were a little more frightened of me. Now I knew why. It accounted, too, for the long memories that the monks had taught me to have. I was an earthly incarnation of Tse Gah, and so I could remember everything for ever, even the making of the mountains.

The palace was all of wood, and very dark. I used to sit nearly all day among many great pillars; some were gold and some were red, but they were all of wood. I had never been allowed any toys. But when I found out that I was Tse Gah, I asked for toys. They looked at me and I think they knew that I knew, for toys were brought. I asked for clay to play with, and I was brought clay. When it came before me, I played with it, and the monks watched me playing. I remembered what the women had told me about Tse Gah making the mountains. So I made little mountains. And the monks watched and nodded their heads.

After they brought me clay I asked for more toys; and more toys were brought, lovely ones. When I saw that they brought me toys whenever I asked for them, I asked for a horse. But they would not give me a horse, though I was Tse Gah. They never would let me walk far from the palace, and I very seldom left the palace at all. If I asked to go out to pick flowers they brought me armfuls of flowers, and strewed them before me, but they would not let me go and play in the garden myself. When I did go to the garden there were always three monks with me, sometimes four or five. It was very dark in the palace, particularly my part of it. My part of the palace was the temple. That is where all the big pillars were. And it was full of gongs. Whenever I spoke, a monk would beat a gong, and then call out loudly what I had said. He used to call it in a ringing tone, and it seemed very grand. But he did not always call what I had said, just as I said it. Sometimes he would add things of his own, and often leave out things I said, or alter them. If I complained of this, the gong would be beaten again, and I would hear my complaint being chanted, but not as I had said it. I asked again for a horse, and the monk who beat the gong said I had asked for a dragon, on which to ride over the land. When I saw that the monks would never give me a horse, I said that I would be Tse Gah no more, and that I would remember nothing that happened hundreds of years ago, and would make no more prophecies; for they used to make me make prophecies, and the monks always fulfilled them. And I said I would leave the thunder alone, and it could do what it liked. Then all the monks in the temple looked at one another in a way that frightened me, but they said nothing. And one of them went away into a dark part of the temple where I had never been; and presently an old monk came out of the darkness, one I had never seen before. And all the monks, except him, went away. Then, when we were all alone, the old monk prostrated himself before me, but I was still very frightened. I did not know who he was, or why he had come. I raised my hand, as I had been taught to do, to give him the blessing of Tse Gah. Then he seized my hand, and I found he had chains under his great dark robe, and he fastened an iron band round my wrist, and a chain went from the band and he hooked the other end of the chain to a hook that there was on one of the pillars. Then he did the same with one of my ankles, fastening that chain to a hook on another pillar. Then he stripped off my clothing and brought out a thick bamboo, which was also hidden under his robes, and was as long as I, even longer. And then he began to beat me. He beat me with all his might. I cried out, but no one came. Then I screamed louder, but nothing stirred in the temple; not even the gongs were sounded. At first I cried out that I would curse him, and then I threatened him with thunder. But he still beat on. I have never known such pain. And then I cried so hard that I could not speak. When the pain grew so great that I could bear nothing more, I said that I would never again say I would not be Tse Gah, and that I would do whatever the monks told me, and remember my memories, and prophesy just as they said. Even then he still beat me. At last he stopped. And then he prostrated himself before me once more, and I gave him the blessing of Tse Gah and he went away into the dark and I never saw him again. Then the monks that had left me came back. I was still crying. I told them that I had been cruelly beaten. They said none could have beaten me. I said I had been chained up. They could see the chains. Then they unfastened the bands from my wrist and ankle, and said that I must have been chained by some god from Tibet or China. No man, they said, could have done it. And they asked me to prophesy against the god that had chained me; and I did as they said. I always did as the monks said, after that. They never gave me a horse.

The monks had great horns, longer than a man, that they used to blow to keep away devils. I used to hear them at night whenever I was awake, or it may have been the devils I heard, or perhaps both, the horns and the devils hooting against each other. They used to hoot if I went for a walk in the garden, and the further away I walked, the more they hooted. There used to be incense in the temple: they often burned it before me in brass bowls; it smelt very sweet and it made me sleepy. When I woke from the sleep that I had slept because of the incense, any words that I uttered before I was quite awake were written down in a book. These were prophecies. Gongs were beaten and they were read out. I never remembered what I said just as I was waking up after the incense, so I do not know if the prophecies that were read out were what I had said or not. I used to want to play with other children, but none were allowed near me. No one was allowed to speak to me but the monks. Sometimes they would keep me in the temple for days. Sometimes there were services in the temple from morning till night, and all the time I had to sit on the altar. I grew very tired then. They would never let me go and play. Once there was drought in the valley, and they prayed before me for a week. Then the rain came on the seventh day. I could not have sat on the altar any longer, if the rain had not come. I slept for three days and nights after that.

It was all gongs and horns and the darkness of the temple. One day was just like another. They taught me to read, so that I could remember more easily the things that happened hundreds of years ago. And they taught me to write too. It was very hard to learn, but I am glad now. And then the revolution came. The people came up from the valley and killed the monks. There was great blowing of horns, but they killed them. They would have killed me too, but I easily got away from them. I was accustomed to the monks, but the people from the valley were a simple people, though they had very big knives. I easily got away from them. I slipped from the temple when I saw them killing the monks. It was all over blood. I got out through the door to the garden, and ran down the side of the mountain. I prophesied against the people of the valley as I ran, but it had no effect. I could hear their angry shouts as loud as ever, and the horns of the monks growing fewer.

Now I am going to do more. Am I not Tse Gah? The monks have taught me for years. Now I will do what they have taught. I am going to thunder. I have tried to do it before, and I could not. But now I am going up to the highest peak. I have noticed that lightning strikes often upon the mountain-tops. It will be easier for me to thunder there. Then the people of the valley will know I am Tse Gah. And I shall go back to the palace, and there will be no more monks there, for the people have killed them. And I shall have a horse.

The air is sultry now, and I feel that it will be easy to thunder. It is very sultry, and the sky is growing black. Now I have reached the peak. I will thunder, and the people shall know. I will. I . . .

The Dwarf Holóbolos and the Sword Hogbiter

Now the King of the Bad Countries went to war with the King of the Birch Lands, because of his golden whiskers, which he was wishful to seize. And the army of that first king marched westwards until it came to a forest. And his name was Thlog. A hundred men they were, and they came to the dark of the forest, where night fell early; and when night was come they camped under the beeches. And the stars sailed slowly over the tops of the trees, and the blackbirds sang and it was dawn and the army awoke. "So far so good," said the captains in the morning. "We are well on our way to the Birch Lands. But now we must enquire more particularly of the way, lest we miss the frontiers of the Kingdom of Birchlands and meet with the army of some kingdom with which our master is not at war." And to this they were all agreed, and to that end sent out scouts. Now there was a cottage in that forest in which an old woman dwelt with her son, who was a charcoal-burner. And the scouts came to the door, and knocked thereon, and the young man opened it and saw the soldiers and called out with delight to his mother that soldiers had come; for he had never seen soldiers before. And they asked him to tell them the way to the Kingdom of Birchlands. But he answered that there were no roads through the forest, so that none in the forest knew the way to anywhere, excepting only the witches; so that in order to find the way they must go to the house of a witch. So they asked him where they might find the house of a witch, and he said, "In the deeps of the forest." And they asked him to show them the way to the deeps of the forest, and he took his hat and his staff and away they went. Now the way to the deeps of the forest was easily found, for they only needed to go where the trees grew thicker and thicker, and when they came to where the trunks were so close together that a man could only barely pass between tree and tree, they were there. And they all looked round for a while and could see nothing; and then one of them smelt smoke, and, walking in the direction of the smell, they came on a cottage older and odder than aught they had seen before. The walls were of gnarled trunks, and twisted beams made its door, and the windows were of a dark and bubbly blue through which one could no more see in than one can see to the floor of the ocean. "This," said one of the scouts, "must surely be the house of a witch."

"That is so," came the voice of the witch from inside the cottage.

And the door slowly opened, and an old witch appeared. And one of the scouts asked her respectfully if she were a witch.

"So it is believed by the wise," she said, "and feared by the foolish, and known to the beasts of the forest, who keep their counsel."

"Then will you please tell our army the way to the Kingdom of Birchlands," the scout asked her.

"And for what purpose do you seek the way to that kingdom?" the witch asked him.

"We go to smite off the golden whiskers of the king of that land," he replied. "For our king is at war with him and would have his whiskers, and has promised his eldest daughter's hand in marriage to whomever will bring those golden whiskers back."

"Know you," replied the witch, "that those whiskers can only be severed by the sword Hogbiter, and by no other weapon soever?"

"We knew it not till you told us," the scout replied.

"It is so," said the witch.

"Then be so courteous," they said, "as to tell us the whereabouts of the sword Hogbiter, that we may come by it and strike off the golden whiskers, and that one of us may be given the hand of the King's daughter."

"It lies upright," she said, "in the heart of the oldest oak in the forest."

"And where may that be?" they asked her.

"In the deeps of the forest," she said, "not far from here. You will know it by its size."

Impatiently then the scouts set off through the forest to find the oldest oak. But the young charcoal-burner, whose name was Igdrathion, stayed behind with the witch, for he mused that it was one thing to find the largest oak, and another to cut it down. In the deeps of the forest there were oaks that were fifty paces round, and one that was larger than they would take some cutting. So he said to her as soon as the scouts were gone: "Good Madam Witch, pray tell me how one may cut through that oldest oak."

"Ah-ha," she said. And in the silence that followed her remark they soon heard the sounds of chopping, for the scouts had found the oak and were hewing it with their swords.

"The oak," said the witch, "is thicker than any rich man's house, going through from front to back, and their little swords will not reach the centre thereof in a year."

"And what may reach it sooner?" asked young Igdrathion.

"Only the axe," she replied, "of the dwarf Holóbolos."

"And where does he dwell?" he asked her.

"He dwells where none may find him," she said, "but by calling his name aloud in the deeps of the forest, at dawn when the blackbirds sing."

"And for what will he chop?" said he.

"For the sheer love of chopping," she said; "and for my sake, if you mention my name."

"And your name, Madam Witch?" he asked her.

"The enchantress Lirila," she replied.

And Igdrathion thanked her gratefully, and went back to his mother's cottage. And all that day the sound of the chopping of swords was heard from the trunk of the oldest oak. And early next day Igdrathion went out of the cottage before the blackbirds sang and all was still in the forest, and it appeared yet to be night, and suddenly one wild clear voice rang out, so wild and shrill that Igdrathion knew not what it could be; but before it ceased, and while yet his wonder lived, the chorus of all the blackbirds broke out and joined it, and he knew it was only the voice of the first of the blackbirds. And, standing there while they sang, he called aloud the name of the dwarf Holóbolos. And the dwarf answered with an unearthly grunt, and came waddling towards Igdrathion out of the undergrowth. He was six foot eight, not in height, for he was a dwarf, but across the breadth of his shoulders. And he carried an axe the shape of the moon when it is five days old. And Igdrathion called out to him in the dark of the wood, "For the sake of the enchantress Lirila." And the dwarf answered, "For that I will do all things." And Igdrathion said to him, "I would have you chop." And Holóbolos answered, "Chopping I love above all things."

"Let us haste, then," said Igdrathion, "and we will go to the oldest oak in the forest. For there is an army in the forest and they seek to cut it down."

"They will not cut down that oak," said the dwarf, "for a year."

"How long will you take to cut into the middle of it?" asked Igdrathion.

"Ten minutes," the dwarf replied.

"Then there is time," said Igdrathion. "Shall we go to the oak tonight while the army is sleeping?"

"We will," grunted Holóbolos.

"There is time to spare," repeated Igdrathion. "How shall we spend it?"

"In sleep," said Holóbolos, "the sleep from which you awaked me." And he rolled back among bracken and hazels and saplings, and grunted three times and was asleep again. And faintly there tapped through the forest the sound of the swords on the oak. But Igdrathion went back to his mother's cottage. "What are you going to do with the dwarf Holóbolos?" said his mother, for she had heard the grunts of the dwarf.

"He is going to get me the sword Hogbiter," he replied, "from the heart of the oldest oak."

"And what are you going to do with the sword Hogbiter?" she asked him.

"I am going to smite off the golden whiskers that grow on the King of the Birch Lands," he answered.

"And what do you want with those whiskers?" she said.

"The army want them," he told her, "the army that came to the forest."

And still the old woman would not let the matter drop, but went on with her questions. "And what use has the army," she asked, "for the golden whiskers that grow on the King of the Birch Lands?"

"Much use," he said. "For they take them back to their king, who has promised to whomever shall bring them to him, the hand of his daughter in marriage."

"The hand of his daughter!" she said. "And shall it go to one of them?"

"To whom else?" said Igdrathion.

"Why not to you, if she be worthy of you," his mother replied.

But no such fancy had come to Igdrathion.

"Should I marry the dawn?" he said. "Or one of the stars?"

"Aye," she replied. "If they were worthy of you."

And while he wondered, she spoke to him thus: "See now, the golden whiskers that grow on the King of the Birch Lands are among the seven wonders of the world that are next after the first seven. Moreover they are the prop and pillar of Birchlands, and the envy of the Bad Countries. When therefore they are smitten off from the head of that king, the power of Birchlands will fall and its army will all surrender. But if they go up against Birchlands with weapons that cannot smite away its prop and support they will never overcome Birchlands, but will be overcome by it. Aid them not therefore, but bide your time, and see what may be won by means of the sword Hogbiter."

And Igdrathion said no more, but silently thought of the King of the Bad Countries' daughter. And his mother saw of whom he was thinking, and said, "If she should be worthy of you, let her go to none of that army."

Now the day wore away as other days, and there came the hour when birds are singing and dwarfs awake from sleep and witches come out of their houses. And Igdrathion heard the sound of the chopping of oak grow fainter till it had ceased; and glad he was thereat, for he feared lest any stroke of a soldier's sword should lay bare the blade of Hogbiter. But the soldiers had gone but a little way in from the bark, and now ceased and all fell back on the main body. And as soon as the silence was heavy all round the oak in the distance, Igdrathion went to the undergrowth and awoke the dwarf Holóbolos, and together they went through the forest; and they went quietly, as foxes go, and all that prowl in the night, and so came to the oldest oak.

"There it stands," said Igdrathion.

And the dwarf Holóbolos said nothing, but only took one long breath and lifted the axe that was the shape of the moon on its fifth day. The handle was all of iron, but the great head was of steel and shone like the moon in water. He lifted it and poised it there for an instant, and the whole vast breadth of the dwarf rippled as he brought the axe-head down, and it entered the oak as a shovel enters snow. For the next ten minutes the dwarf shovelled the oak, and the smooth edge of the axe shone still as bright as the moon and no dint or scratch whatever was seen upon it. Sometimes he smote slanting downwards from his full height, such as it was, and sometimes inwards, level with the earth, a little above his ankles. And a great gap appeared in the oak, as though half of a pyramid had been taken out of it. And then at the end of ten minutes, from one of his hail of blows the great axe came back with a gash cut into its shining face, as though it were a slice of melon that had been beaten against a knife. And the dwarf looked at it and knew that he had stricken against the sword Hogbiter, because there was nothing else upon earth that could dint his axe. "Lo!" he said. "We have come on the sword Hogbiter."

"Be careful, I pray you," requested Igdrathion, "not to harm the sword with your axe."

"There is nothing," said the dwarf, "that can harm Hogbiter, but the comet that shall be the end of the world, if it hits the sword fair in the middle; and the time of that comet is not yet."

"And when will that comet come?" asked Igdrathion.

But the dwarf had turned away from him back to his work, and was shovelling the oak away from around the sword Hogbiter. So five more minutes passed; and at the end of that time the sword fell clear of the oak.

"What shall we do now?" said Igdrathion. For, though he had the sword, there was a whole army in the forest, and all looking for that same sword.

"She'll know," said the dwarf Holóbolos, and he pointed to where the house of the witch was hid in the deeps of the forest. So Igdrathion took the sword and went to the witch's house, with Holóbolos ambling behind him. The sword was long and straight, and not gross like the axe, and sapphires were shining dimly in the hilt, and the straight blade shone like a beam of stormy sunlight, and it was a joy to hold. And when they came to the house of the witch among the boles of the beeches, and Igdrathion had knocked on the door and the door opened and the witch appeared in the doorway in her black cloak, the dwarf Holóbolos abased himself kneeling, with his forehead and all his huge breadth to the ground. And Igdrathion bowed and said, "Madam enchantress, I have the sword Hogbiter here. What shall I do with it?"

And she said, "Keep it."

And he said, "What of the army?"

And she turned to the dwarf Holóbolos, still prostrate among the mosses, and said to him, "What are its ways? For I know little of military things."

And he raised his head from the earth and said, "The scouts that work at the oak will be relieved, and others will cut tomorrow."

"Then," said she, "you must hide another sword in the oak and cover it up as well as you may, and let them take it and fight the King of the Birch Lands with that, and not with the sword Hogbiter."

"And where, O enchantress," said the dwarf Holóbolos, "shall we find another sword?"

And the enchantress smiled and said, "There came a knight once to this forest and came to my house, and forgot the world and had no longer any care for its ways, and left his sword here when he went. Here it is, and you may leave this sword in the tree."

So the dwarf and Igdrathion thanked her and went away with the two swords. And she went back into her cottage and shut out the glow of her candlelight from the forest, and Igdrathion and Holóbolos hurried away in the dark, for they wished to hide the sword in the oldest oak before light should come to the forest and the army wake and return to the tree.

"The scouts," said Holóbolos, as he piled in their places again the huge blocks that he had smitten out of the oak, "will boast that they cut in further than they did, and the new ones that will cut on the morrow, when they find their work going easily, will give the credit of it to their own industry."

So he piled up the fallen blocks in the gap in the oldest oak round the sword that the knight had forgotten, and Igdrathion watched him dimly, for it was night, while an owl observed him shrewdly from one of the high branches. And long before the first blackbird knew of the dawn the work was finished, although untidily, and when the scouts marched up to the tree in the morning they set to their work of chopping without observing too closely that it had all been chopped already. And so they came to the sword, and a good sword of its kind, but not magic.

And the first thing that Igdrathion did when he got back to his mother's house was to cut two strips of leather out of a hide the length of the sword, and he laid them together and his mother stitched them, and there was the scabbard. And his mother made him a belt of another strip and fastened the scabbard to it, and he put the belt round him and was ready for travel. Then he said farewell to his mother and to the dwarf Holóbolos, and set out for the Bad Countries, while the army marched off with its sword, going the other way. And going the other way they came to the border of Birchlands, but Igdrathion saw the sunset shine on the spires of the palace of the king that had sent them to war.

Now Igdrathion knew well enough, as he walked over the bright grass of the Bad Lands, that he was only a woodman, dressed in the smoky garb of a charcoal-burner. Yet he knew that he had only to draw the sword Hogbiter for its flash to illuminate him, and so to dazzle the eyes of any regarding him that they would scarce notice his charcoal-burner's clothes. And so, in spite of his garb, he walked with an air, which was noticed by the small creatures that hid in the grass, so that they knew he went on a journey of which great things were to come. But Igdrathion knew not what was to come. He only knew that the hand of the eldest princess of the House of the Bad Countries was to be given to him who should bring to the King of those lands the golden whiskers of the King of the Birch Lands. But what manner of woman she was he did not know, scarce knowing if she were human or divine, or if she were among vast unattainable forces such as precipices, icebergs, or the aurora that shone to the North. Therefore he had determined to go and look, a thing that he dared to do now that he had beside him the sword Hogbiter. And as the sun went under the rim of the Bad Countries, and the light went out of the grass like a smile that has faded, but the spires of the palace shone still, and flashed and rejoiced and twinkled, Igdrathion came to the palace gates, whence the long shadows were gone. Now it so chanced that it was the custom of the eldest princess of that kingdom to sit with her maids in a balcony overlooking the evening, at the hour when moths were about and the odour of flowers arose and birds sang and the west was a glory, for she greatly cared for these things. And sitting among her maids Igdrathion saw her, gazing into the evening. Down in the shadow of the palace he stood, a figure scarce to be noticed, dingily clad in the russet garb that was all the attire of a charcoal-burner. And, feeling this, he slowly drew out Hogbiter from the rustic sheath that enclosed it and laid it on his two hands to look on it. And the light of it beat up and illumined his face, for the sword glowed even when the sunlight was gone from surrounding things. And the princess looking down from her balcony chanced to see him then, a youth untroubled as yet by time, and unfamiliar with cities. And he, looking up, perceived her glowing among her maidens, but had not yet seen her eyes, although a glow came from them along the shades of the evening. And still, though he saw her beauty, he was not sure as yet whether it was all a human beauty, or of things remote though earthly. But at that moment the eldest princess, whose name was Bourodilla, said to her maidens, "He has a sword. Perchance he brings news of the war. Go therefore one of you and ask him what news there be, and if there have been battles yet." So one of her maidens slipped back through the window and through three rooms of the palace and back down the stairs, and came to the door and ran out and found Igdrathion. And to him she said, "The Princess Bourodilla would know what news you have of the war that the army is waging." And he said to the maiden, "I will tell the princess."

And she said to him, "That is not necessary. But tell me what news there be, and I will tell the princess." And he made answer, "The talk of armies is not for maidens. But I will bring to the princess myself the report of the going up of the army and all its doings." And when she found that she could not shake him and that he would not deliver his report to her, the maiden brought him with her to the palace, through the great doorway and up the stairs, and through three rooms and out on to the balcony where the Princess Bourodilla sat, beautiful in the evening, and the moths sailed to and fro. And he saw that she was beautiful, but so were the maidens round her. Then she moved her head and turned her eyes towards him, and all in the full glow of them he knew then what beauty was. And the glow of that beauty flashed in on his mind more suddenly than the glow of dawn through the forest, stealing among still branches over the dew in spring to gleam upon the anemones, but there was the same serenity, waking in him the same wonder, and the light was in them such as came to the forest when he felt that such a light had never come there before, whether dawn brought it every day or not; and he waited for her to speak, as he sometimes waited to hear the chorus of blackbirds before the forest woke. That her eyes were blue he did not so much notice, as that he was held in their light, as the sunlight holds the forest when all its life is awake. And as birds soared up to the sunlight and butterflies woke and flowers opened and shone, so there awoke in him new thoughts and new inspirations, and he dreamed of adventurous quests and of what he would do with the sword. And then she spoke to him musically and low, while he stood there dumb with wonder, and her voice was like the sound of someone singing at evening, heard over the crest of a hill from the other side in a tranquil country at peace.

"Whence are you?" she said to him.

And he said, "From the forest."

"And is the forest fair?" she asked.

"Fair," he said, "as the loveliest shell from which men gather pearls in the deeps of the fairest sea."

"Fair as a pearl?" she said.

"No. Fair as a shell," he said, "from which the pearl has been taken."

And she knew he meant that, though the forest was fair, it lacked the beauty at which he was gazing now. But, turning to left and right, she looked at her maidens as though she sought of them the meaning of his allusion; and they shook their heads and wondered, as though they did not know either.

"And is the army enjoying its war?" she asked.

And he told how the army had marched on through the forest, and how there burned in each man the hope to seize and smite off the golden whiskers that grew on the King of the Birch Lands. But of the sword Hogbiter he said nothing.

"Would you like to seize those whiskers?" she said to him then.

When she said this the sword Hogbiter throbbed in its sheath, for the magic that was in the sword could understand words. But Igdrathion said nothing, not knowing what words could say, and stood there gazing and thought of the sword and dreamed of what it might do. And dreaming still he bowed and turned away, and went from the balcony and through the rooms and down the stairs and away out of the palace, the tips of whose spires were still darting their twinkling rays over Bad Lands.

Now as soon as it was light on that day on which Igdrathion went to the palace of the King that ruled over Bad Lands, the army of that King away in the forest woke early, and twenty of its men were sent to the oldest oak, and there they chopped and found the sword as I said, though it was not the true sword Hogbiter. And it was not yet noon when they got it out of the tree; and they brought it to their captains, who, believing it to be Hogbiter, marched away with it triumphant towards the country of Birchlands. And they marched for the rest of the day and for most of the next day, sleeping two more nights in the forest, but in the light of the third day's morning they found a country beyond the forest, wide and sunny and open, in which white trees were shining. And on the next day after that, whether it was by luck or careful planning who shall say, for none may wholly estimate the part that luck plays in war, they came to the country of Birchlands, fair and bright in the morning. Fair and bright it shone, an open and sunny downland, and afar on a fold of the downs its little capital stood. Then the Chief Captain drew the sword that he deemed was Hogbiter, and all the captains drew their swords and the soldiers lowered their pikes, as the army spread out from its line of march and assumed the line of battle; and in this guise, this stern array, they advanced against the city wherein its king ruled over Birchlands. And, as they advanced, the army of Birchlands gathered along the walls, and flashes gleamed in the city, like the flash of lightning reflected on to the clouds when the storm is far away. These flashes that shone, though dimly, now and then from the city, arose from the activities of the King when he saw his capital threatened, and the magic that began to glow in his whiskers. Some fighting there was at the gates when the army arrived, but it was little more than a skirmish, because the main defence of the city and all that land lay behind the wall of the palace: it was the redoubtable, unbreakable, magical, golden whiskers that grew on the head of the King. There are many heavy tomes of magic lore in the world, bound in dark old leather and locked with hasps, and not all of them have I read; wherefore I cannot say whether those whiskers or the axe of the dwarf Holóbolos were the stronger. I believe that they were of an exactly equal magic, and that, though it was certain that the axe of Holóbolos could not cut them, yet they could never gnash the axe of Holóbolos. But certain it is that no other weapon on earth could equal the hardness of the golden whiskers, and only one could sever them, and that one was not the sword the Chief Captain bore, as he now advanced on the King, who stood before his throne with his magic shining. And on these whiskers now the army of Birchlands had fallen back fighting, as an army falls back on the ramparts of some great defence which is to hold back an enemy for a day and brighten history for ages. And the army of the Bad Countries wavered before those whiskers, but the Chief Captain advanced alone, gripping the sword that he believed to be Hogbiter. And the King of the Birch Lands stood there before him dressed in his suit of armour, hardened by labour of dwarfs through days and nights to make it proof against any blow of a sword. All but his whiskers and mouth and eyes were covered with armour, and even over his mouth and eyes there were bars of steel, forming a grid through which no sword could pass; only his whiskers were completely bare, for them, being harder than any armour in all the world, he left glittering outside the steel; and there they shone, making all the armour bright, and the magic of them, unencumbered by armour, exerted its influence freely over all the ways of the city; and the opposing army could feel the force of it, as a traveller feels the strength of a mighty wind blowing down from a mountain. This the Chief Captain felt, as all the rest, but he raised aloft the sword that he deemed Hogbiter and brought it crashing down on the golden whisker that grew on the left of the King. Though I speak of a wineglass cast to a marble floor, or a flower-pot hurled at a garden-wall in anger, or ice of a lake that is broken by rocks of an avalanche, yet will I not avail to give any picture of how that sword was shivered on touching the golden whisker; for it went asunder like a flash of light, and with the speed of light its fragments vanished, and slowly labouring after them went the crackling sound with which the whole sword was shattered. And the King of the Birch Lands smiled under his armour, and the golden whiskers gleamed. And in the gleam of the golden whiskers the host of the King of the Bad Countries was discomforted, and the power of the magic that blew against them grew stronger, and they drew back and the armies of Birchlands poured after them. Thus was the army defeated which went up against Birchlands, and whether by magic or fighting no historian cares, but only that there was defeat, come how it may, and that victory was with the Birch Lands. Then the army of the Bad Countries retreated, and came again to the forest and marched back through its dimness and home to its barracks, telling all, and truly telling them, that they were only defeated by magic, though how they were defeated no chronicler cares.

Now while this army did half a day's march after finding the false sword, Igdrathion did a day's march in the other direction, and, marching back by night, he was only half a day's march behind them next day at dawn. Round about dawn he rested; then he ate oat-cake that he had in a wallet and drank at a stream and started later than the starting of the army, but travelled more swiftly than they, as a man alone does travel. A glimpse or two he had of birds disturbed and a few cattle running, but no other sign he saw of the routed army. In the early morning of the day after the battle he came to a gate of the city from which their king ruled Birchlands, and flags flew from every tower in honour of victory, and carillons were ringing in every spire. The gate was open and the sentries rejoicing, and Igdrathion went in between them unmolested, and unmolested he walked up the city's widest way. None heeded him in his russet dress, nor heeded Hogbiter hidden in strips of hide. And so unhindered he came to the marble steps of the palace, and up their brightness he walked and came to the main door, which was opened to let the melody of musicians flow from the court and rejoice the popular streets with their music in honour of victory. And while the courtiers danced he marched on alone and came to the King of the Birch Lands, who sat high on his throne, letting the magic of his golden whiskers flow forth to mellow his realm. And the King was still in the armour in which he had won his victory, and the golden whiskers came glittering out through two slits in the helmet, and shone as rivulets in a golden dawn flowing over boulders of iron. And Igdrathion said, "It is war," and stepped up to him, lifting the sword Hogbiter. And the King of the Birch Lands drew his sword at the same time, and lifted it up to parry, but lifted it idly, and smiled as he lifted it, a smile that was hidden in the dark of his helmet; but the golden whiskers glowed, as though they shared to the full with their king his belief that nothing could ever prevail against them. And as they shone like two increasing dawns, brightening the palace and the ways of the city beyond, Igdrathion smote with his sword at the one on the left, and Hogbiter went through the sword which the King held up to par-

ry, as a well-swung scythe will go through the stalk of a daffodil, and
went on and came to the whisker and went through that also, and
stopped on the armour across which the whisker flowed, for no more
force was left in it after the tremendous achievement of severing what
could be severed by no other sword in the world. As the whisker fell
Igdrathion lifted his sword again and with a backhanded stroke smote
off the right-hand whisker, which had no longer even a sword to guard
it, vain though that guarding would be. And as he struck through this
whisker the other one fell to the marble with the clatter as of the fall of
great engines of iron, and the fall of the right-hand whisker resumed
their reverberations; and a glow went out of the palace and out of the
city, and over all the kingdom of Birchlands there came a moment like
the moment at which the sun has gone under the earth and the light
goes out of all things except the sky. Still in the sky shone light over all
the land, for that was the light of the sun; but from the kingdom of
Birchlands itself its own glow was gone, for the magic with which it
shone was gone with the golden whiskers. And with the loss of that
magic a listlessness fell on the army, and the courtiers ceased to dance
and rejoicings died in the streets and all the musicians stopped in the
midst of their music. And Igdrathion gathered up the golden whiskers,
and their magic which had opposed him was now with him, for magic
has no care as to whom it serves. And he walked out of the palace
holding the golden whiskers, and a glow was all about him as he went.
Some there were who might have raised a sword against Hogbiter, but
when they saw the sword rejoicing in Igdrathion's right hand and the
golden whiskers glittering in his left, they knew, and could even feel,
there was too much magic for man. Moreover the magic now in his
left hand was the very magic that had ruled that kingdom for ages, for
the golden whiskers that grew on their king were hereditary. So Igdrathion marched away, and even dogs fled from his coming, fearing the
magic they felt in the golden whiskers, or else in the sword Hogbiter.
More than the golden whiskers he did not take, for he lived a long
while ago, a simple mind, the child of a simple age, waging a simple
war. It was still in the early morning as he marched away from the city,
and when noon was over those lands he was far away, going blithely,
singing a song. So he passed through the country of Birchlands, until
before sunset there darkened the distant horizon the low line of the

forest. It was time already to rest, but he marched on, though tired, so as to sleep in the forest, for its dark glades were as home to him. And night fell and the stars were bright ere he reached the edge of the forest, and he marched but a short way in and lay down and slept on the bracken. When dawn came to the forest and the chorus of birds awoke him, Igdrathion felt a glow in his heart, which shone from his high achievement, before he even saw the rays of the sun. Then he ate a meal from his wallet and, rising up, set off to look for the dwarf Holóbolos. And far he marched to find him, and the sun went under the branches, and again he lay down on the bracken and slept till the blackbird sang. Now this being the hour at which the dwarf might be summoned, he called him many times by his uncouth name, till the monstrous form of Holóbolos crawled out of the bracken.

"What brings you now?" asked Holóbolos.

"Gratitude," answered Igdrathion. "For your axe obtained for me Hogbiter, and with Hogbiter, lo, I have won the golden whiskers."

And he showed those unbendable, unbreakable whiskers to the dwarf, glimmering bright in his hand. And Holóbolos drew a little back with his axe, saying "Let them not touch my axe, lest they blunt its blade."

For though a great gash was in it, from its meeting with Hogbiter, the rest of the edge was sharper than other earthly things, excepting only that sword. And Igdrathion drew back the whiskers as Holóbolos had requested. And now there were met together the four hardest things in the world, which were firstly the sword Hogbiter, then the two golden whiskers that had grown on the King of the Birch Lands, and very close after these the axe of Holóbolos.

"Whither now?" said Holóbolos.

"First to the witch to thank her," Igdrathion replied: "to the great enchantress Lirila. Then to my mother's cottage, and then to the palace of Bad Lands."

"I would stay in the bracken," muttered Holóbolos. "For chopping is sweeter than travelling, and the forest fairer than cities."

But Igdrathion said farewell to him, and set out, and came soon to the house of the witch, and knocked at her door to thank her and to tell her that he had come by the golden whiskers. But this she knew before he knocked at her door, for the glow of them shone through the crannies, and magical things know well all other magical things, and she knew that the glow was that of the golden whiskers.

"Keep them outside," she said as she opened the door, "for there is some magic in my poor house, but none that is able to stand against that of the golden whiskers, and they would but blunt my magic and tarnish its brightness."

So he kept outside with the whiskers and thanked her from there. And then he went to his mother's cottage, and found her there by her fire in an old brown chair carved out of a bole of oak, and showed her the golden whiskers, and for her son's sake she admired them and said they were fine whiskers, although she had no need of magic herself, thinking the simple things of the forest enough. And she gave him a meal of eggs that her hens had laid, and of vegetables grown in her garden under the oaks. And she asked him whither he was going now, and he said to the King of the Bad Lands to give him the golden whiskers, and she warned him against that king. But he took no heed of the warning, for he said, "He has promised the hand of his eldest daughter to whomever shall bring him the golden whiskers that grew on the King of the Birch Lands. So what else can he do?"

But the old woman knew and trusted the ways of the forest and all that went therein, and had little trust in the folk that lived in the lands that lay beyond the frontier of beech and oak. Nevertheless with a high unclouded heart Igdrathion, having said farewell to his mother, set off for those very lands and, travelling all day in the shade of the mighty branches, saw sunset glowing again on the spires of the palace where sat King Thlog on his throne and reigned over Badlands. And it was again the hour when the Princess Bourodilla was wont to sit in her balcony with her maidens about her, looking out on the ways of the city through the mellow glow of the evening; and she saw Igdrathion coming along those ways, with the sword Hogbiter in its sheath beside him, and the golden whiskers glittering in his hand and bringing a brightness to the shade of the ways that had lately lost the sun. And she said farewell in her heart to her father's gleaming spires and to all the ways of his city. And Igdrathion went up to the gate of the palace and the sentries would have stopped him, but he raised the golden whiskers to shine in their faces, and the magic that was in those whiskers troubled them. So he passed through the sentries and entered the palace and strode on, with the glow and the magic going before him, and soon he stood before the King of those lands, King Thlog himself in glory upon his throne. And now he said to the King: "Behold the golden whiskers."

And King Thlog received them graciously. And when the King had received the golden whiskers from Igdrathion kneeling before him, and said no more, Igdrathion reminded him of his eldest daughter and the promise that he had made. But the King of the Bad Lands had forgotten his promise. And, when nothing the young man said could bring it back to his memory, Igdrathion arose and drew out from its rustic sheath the long sword Hogbiter, that no other sword could scratch, and the magic that was in the whiskers was weaker than what there was in that sword. And the King held up the golden whiskers against him, and they glowed, but they glowed in vain against the sword Hogbiter. And the King opened his mouth to speak fiercely, but when he saw that the whiskers glowed in vain he forgot what it was he would say, but kept his mouth open still while he tried to remember, and open it still remained while Igdrathion strode away. He strode away through the rooms that led to the balcony where the Princess Bourodilla was seated among her maidens, looking out on the evening. And as he went he pondered what he would say, but when he came to the balcony, and the princess's eyes were upon him looking into his face, he said nothing, nor did the Princess Bourodilla speak, and her maidens were dumb beside her. And together they went from the palace, he holding the sword Hogbiter aloft in his right hand, she leaning on his left arm, and none who saw the long flash of the bright sword Hogbiter stopped him. Together they went away to the deeps of the forest, to found a kingdom there whereof he and she were king and queen for such long time that no historian uses less than many large pages on which to tell of their happy and glorious reign and the memorable things that the forest saw in their era. Their palace was built for them by the dwarf Holóbolos, partly of standing trees where the beeches grew most close in the deeps of the forest, and partly of the great boles that he cut with his axe near by and placed erect between them, dragging them to their places from where he cut them, alone. And all this he did with inconceivable swiftness, for he cut the oaks and the beeches with his axe as another man cuts poppies and corn with a scythe. And, when he had clamped them together, he laid the planks of the floor, which he cut with his axe from the oaks, as another man with a knife cuts slices out of a cheese. And when the walls and the roofs and the stairways had been all hurled into their places by the might of the dwarf Holóbolos and the power of his swift axe, the enchantress Lirila came out of her cottage and entered the new palace and made the smaller things that a palace needs, by enchantment, either directly by the power of her spells, or by calling up from the forest spirits of which we know nothing, to weave the tapestries and hang the arras, and clothe the floors with carpets of fair design. Certain it is that for the fireplaces and chimneys she called up from the deeps of the forest certain gnomes. And all this building was done by the strength of the dwarf and the magic of the enchantress and the industry of the gnomes, with inconceivable swiftness. Some say that it took days to build this palace, while others write merely of hours. Certain it is that the palace was fair, and that Igdrathion and the Princess Bourodilla lived happily there for as long afterwards as there is any record, and their children and their grandchildren became a dynasty. Of the glories of that palace and its fountains, and the gardens that glowed about it under the oak-trees, of the spring that blessed them and the summer in which they dreamed, and the autumn that touched the beeches with an unearthly glory, of the dawns and the noons and the sunsets that saw these things and the butterflies that rejoiced in them, of the creatures that haunted the forest and left their haunts to wonder at them, and of the mellow years that passed over them and left them lovelier yet, let poets sing. Enough for me to say that between Birchlands and Badlands there arose a kingdom happier than each, at which both of them looked in awe. And the King of the Bad Countries went to war no more with Birchlands, for he dreaded the sword of Igdrathion, the unbreakable sword Hogbiter, which lurked in the forest between them; and the magic that glowed in the whiskers that were won in the war with Birchlands was fading slowly away; every dawn they were weaker, and weaker still in the evening, like an old clock nobody winds, which is running slowly down.

But gradually as the coming out of stars, first one, then three, then hundreds all in a rush, and then millions, the golden whiskers grew again on the head of the King of the Birch Lands.

PROGRESS

"I can see, sir," I said to the figure that appeared late one night in my room, "that you are evidently a ghost."

"That is certainly so," the strange presence replied.

"And your object in visiting me?" I asked.

"Standing room," he replied, "solid ground to walk on, solid, that is to say, compared with the huge emptiness of Space. Your dreams give me foothold, and I would rest on them for a while."

"Have you come from far?" I enquired.

"Nine light-years," he answered.

I saw then that I was dealing with something not at all of this world.

"Then you don't live near here?" I said.

"Neither in space nor time," he answered me.

And let me say here, in defence of my own remark, that I had just awakened from sleep to see an entirely unknown dim figure in an otherwise dark room, and that I have heard remarks no profounder uttered amidst all the comfort and security of a tea-party in broad daylight.

The figure merely shook its grey head, and the faint light that appeared to gleam from it appeared a little less luminous.

I was now wide awake and realized that some more than ordinary remark was called for, with which to address a personality that was so much more than ordinary. Yet on the spur of the moment, as often happens, I could think of no such remark, and I said, "What was it like over there?"

"You could not comprehend," the spirit replied. "Science was so far advanced, that you would not be able to understand if I were to tell you about the progress that we had made."

"We have made certain beginnings here," I said, thinking that if he told me of his scientific achievements I might understand something.

"With the atom alone," he said, "we progressed beyond anything that you have imagined here."

"For peaceful purposes?" I asked him.

"Certainly," said the spirit. "We had harnessed the atom for many peaceful purposes. I was probably our principal scientist, and it was my work to extend the usefulness of the atom further, and I developed its potentialities beyond what you will readily comprehend."

"I will try," I said, "if you will kindly tell me."

"Well," he replied, "I was, as I told you, our principal scientist, and I was at work on the development of the power in the atom, solely for peaceful uses. And so important was my work, and so magnificent the progress that our principal scientists were achieving, that I moved my great laboratory to the slope of a range of mountains in which uranium had been discovered. For, as your people appear to begin to suspect, there are great opportunities in uranium for the development of atomic power. We were far beyond anything you have dreamed of achieving, even when I started. But the progress I made goes so far beyond the understanding of any at your stage of scientific attainment that I could not explain it to anyone on this planet."

"Perhaps I might understand a little," I said.

"Perhaps," he replied. "Well, I moved to a slope of the range of mountains in which uranium was believed to be plentiful. The range was far larger than any upon your earth, because ours was a larger planet and one that revolved round a larger star than yours. The supply of uranium in that range of mountains was found to be beyond our expectation, very greatly beyond it, and the scientific progress I made was enormous. Indeed I doubt if in any planet of any star such progress has yet been made, though of this I cannot be certain, because we were only in touch with the planets of our own system, a system considerably larger than yours."

"Along what lines did your progress chiefly go?" I asked.

"The difficulty of explaining it to one of your low scientific classification," he said, "would take more time than I have to spare, for I am only resting briefly upon your dreams, and must soon go on with my journey beyond your imagination."

"Then, tell me something of your planet," I said, "before you go; something of its scenery, even if it was not so beautiful as ours."

"It was far more so," answered the spirit.

"Then may I ask you before you go," I said, "only why you left it."

"That," said the spirit, "was through no lack of appreciation of its beauty, but was caused by the great progress of our scientific achievements."

"And what was that?" I asked.

"I was releasing the power of an atom," he said, "and there turned out to be more uranium in that range of mountains than our mining engineers had calculated upon, and the power of the atom that I was handling communicated with some neighbouring uranium, which touched off the entire range, which in its turn made the planet radioactive, and its influence reached the star round which we revolved, so that our star and all its planets flared up together, and, to make a long story short, I was the cause of a nova."

It was not so much my astonishment at the magnitude of what he had done, as at the serenity of his contentment with it, that for a little while held me breathless. And before I was able to ask him any more, he said, "I must now go on, for I have further work to do."

"In our system?" I gasped.

"Not yet," he said. "For there is not sufficient progress yet in any of your planets to give adequate scope for a scientist like myself."

One Night in Eldorado

I met the lady in Paris, dark-haired and beautiful though her youth was gone; full of loving memories of her land of Eldorado, yet fitting her ways to the life of Paris as a pearl is fitted into its gleaming shell. And there she told me this story. "You would not think it now, for I am not any longer what I was, and like many another in these troubled times, I have lost my proper place in the world, and what was due to me seems to be due no longer. It is the same everywhere. The poor Duchesse de Longchamps has to drive her own motor as I saw the other day. But you will appreciate that it was not so always. In Eldorado it was different in the days of President Sanhuelvas. Shall I tell you of one night when I dined with him, my sister and I?"

I said, and truly, that it would greatly interest me.

"It was a summer's night," she said, "and we were dining at the Governmental Palace. All down the long table was the beautiful light of candles, and masses of orchids partly hid their glow. Outside was the full moon. It shone so brightly, as it used to in our Eldorado, that in spite of the candles I could see outside. And there came a moment when the man on my right was talking to another lady, and the one on my left wished to talk to the lady upon his other side. He was not doing so, but he wished to. Consequently I had no intention of hindering his wishes. He was in any case a man of no understanding and totally without any merits whatever. I will say no more of him. I forget why I mention him. Ah, I remember. It was because he gave me the opportunity of turning my eyes from the table to look round at the beauty of the night. And it *was* beautiful in our Eldorado. The moths that drifted by were as large as flowers, and when they caught the light from the windows they were lovely as jewels. And then the stars. Oh, they were beautiful. You have nothing like them here. But on this night there was another beauty, the beauty of the full moon that shines on Eldorado. It lay heavy on the flowers in the warm night. A flood of magic. I cannot describe it to you. Well, I looked out of the window, and as soon as I did so I saw two figures. The figures of two men. They were just outside the window and carried, each, a revolver. And then they spoke to each other in low voices, much too low for me to hear the sound of a word. What they said I heard from one of them the next day. They were two captains of el gran revolucion, and one of them said to the other, 'It is the hour. We strike.' They were not the only men there: they had a thousand soldiers hidden amongst the flowers in the gardens of the Palace.

"'No,' said the other, that is to say Captain Alonzo. 'I see two young ladies dining with the vile President. It is not to be said by any that we started a battle in the presence of ladies.'

"It was I and my sister that he saw. There were others and they soon left. But my sister and I stayed on. And the one to whom he spoke, a certain Captain Pedro Caspodar, said, 'The General ordered us to strike now.'

"'The General,' said Captain Alonzo, 'is an Eldoradan gentleman, and commands officers who are the same. Had he known that two ladies would be present so late he would never have given any such order.'

"'That is true,' said Pedro Caspodar. 'At the same time, one cannot move a thousand men into the gardens of the Palace without somebody knowing, and the Governmental forces will be here in half an hour.'

"'That is unfortunate,' said Captain Alonzo. 'Yet we must not compromise the General by letting it be said that he attacked the Palace while two ladies were there. It is past 11 o'clock, and surely they must be gone in half an hour.'

"'Yes, we will wait,' said Pedro. 'Though if they do not leave before the main body reinforces the Palace Guard, we shall be defeated and el gran revolucion will fail.'

"'That will be a loss to humanity,' said Captain Alonzo. 'But we are Eldoradan gentlemen, and cannot be asked to do something that would shame us and our glorious cause.'

"'Indeed not,' said Pedro. 'And surely the ladies must soon take their leave.'

"'At any moment now,' said Captain Alonzo. 'And if we were hasty and should attack before they leave, those dogs, those monkeys of the high woods, would say that we, *we*, were no true Eldoradan gentlemen.'

"That is the way they spoke of the President and our party. But the President was a most enlightened man. He had built 50 miles of railways through the marshes, where, before, there had only been alligators, and had done much else besides for the Republic of Eldorado. But that is how they spoke of him. 'Yes, we will wait,' said Pedro Caspodar. 'And the ladies must soon depart.'

"But we did not depart. The President spoke to me, and my sister was talking with an officer of the Guard, a most perfect horseman and of unusual charm. And the night wore on. And the rest of the party left; wives of functionaries of no great importance. They left with their husbands, and my sister and I stayed on. And the army of the two captains waited amongst the agapanthus under the full moon, and big moths floated by and all the cicalas were chirruping in what otherwise was dead hush, till the reinforcements broke it, arriving even sooner than Captain Alonzo had feared. And in the fighting that night el gran revolucion was broken, and the next morning Captain Alonzo and Captain Pedro Caspodar were sentenced to death, and shut in the Castle gaol. And I visited Captain Alonzo in his cell, and there he told me the story that I have just told you. Curiosity naturally led me to see him again, because I had seen him in the moonlight; and the President gave me a pass. Of course they were our most mortal enemies. At the same time, I had, although quite unwillingly, interfered with their project, and a woman does not like to do that with anything men are doing. It is not one's place. One does not, for example, walk on a polo-ground while a game is in progress, or interfere with men's games in any way; so that, though it was right that they both should be shot, I felt that it was not right that I should have interfered with them in this manner, and that they should be shot on account of me. I am sure you will understand. So I went to the President at once, because they were to be shot next morning. And I, well perhaps I was a little unguarded, even frivolous that evening. It was sunset when I got to the Palace, just before the cicalas sang. And however frivolous I was, the President who was a most impulsive man, went far beyond what the occasion warranted, and seemed to take for granted many things that I had not said at all. In short he ridiculously said that he loved me. And I merely derided him and refused to believe it.

"'Why do you not believe me?' he asked.

"'I don't know,' I said.

"'I swear it upon my sacred honour,' he said.

"Now I should have told you before that the President, who carried no arms of any sort, always had the key of the Castle gaol in one of his waistcoat pockets. 'Have the right men in prison,' he used to say, 'and no arms are necessary. Once let them out, and all is over, though your pockets were stuffed with pistols.'

"And, poor President, how right he was, as subsequent years have shown. 'Well,' I said to him, 'I will believe Your Serene Excellency if you will give me some present as a token that what you say is true.'

"And he swore again upon his sacred honour.

"'But give me some little present,' I said.

"'Certainly,' he said, and rose to look for something.

"'No,' I said. 'Something now. Something you have about you.'

"'Very well,' he said. 'Take my ring.' And he gave me his signet ring.

"'It would never fit me,' I said. 'Give me something else.' And I showed him my hands, on which indeed his great ring would have been absurd. And the foolish man kissed one of my hands, and said, 'Then take my watch.' And he handed me that, a great gold watch with a cumbrous heavy chain.

"'No, no,' I said. 'A woman could never wear that.'

"'I have nothing else on me that I could give you,' he said, 'though I would give you so much.'

"And I pointed to a small bulge in his right waistcoat pocket, the only fault ever found in his perfect dress. 'You have something there,' I said.

"'Only an old key,' he answered.

"'Then give me that,' I said.

"'I cannot do that,' he answered.

"'Never mind,' I said. 'It is of no significance. It is only as I thought. You said by way of a jest that you loved me. Not perhaps very amusing. But Your Serene Excellency may have what jests you will. Then when I ask for a token, it is refused.'

"'But it is true,' said the President. 'Unhappily I cannot give you this, because if any that are now in the Castle gaol escape, our rule would be over, our constitution destroyed, in fact the Republic of Eldorado ruined.'

"'But I will let out no prisoner,' I said.

"'Do you swear it upon your honour?' he said to me.

"'I do,' I said.

"'Well, then,' he said, 'there is the key, since it is your whim to have it. But bring it back to me tomorrow.'

"And this also I swore to do. As soon as I could tear myself away from that impulsive man I ran down to the gaol and, still with my pass, I went in and saw Captain Alonzo and gave him the key, so that he could escape that night, and told him to free Captain Pedro Caspodar also, and to put the key in a place where I should find it, so that I could give it back to the President as I had promised. And I knew he would do as I said. And so it was. And he and the other escaped that night to the high woods, where of course there was no finding them."

"But didn't you promise on your honour not to let anyone loose?" I asked.

"And are men to demand that a woman should never change her mind?" asked the beautiful Eldoradan. "They demand much, these men."

I made some weak sort of apology, and she bore no grudge because of my gauche remark, and we parted as good friends as ever.

The Traveller to Thundercliff

There was a look of thunder about the cliff. It was a clear white granite, but with a menacing darkness about it, a white flash shining in gloom. To the lonely traveller it had the air of a barrier at the end of the world. Well, he said to himself, this must be the end of my journey, the edge of Goblins' Heath that is at the border of Elfland. And so it turned out to be. For the horns of Elfland blew, tinkling faintly; small horns fashioned of silver, or more likely of ice. They blew a challenge from Elfland, that rang over Goblins' Heath, so that all who dwelt on the heath knew that a traveller from Terra Cognita troubled the border of Elfland. And what did not dwell on that heath? All that legend is full of, and much besides. Gnomes were there in abundance, trolls and fairies; and the long coils of dragons slid here and there through the heather. The cliff hung there gleaming but shadowed, across the way of the traveller. Hearing the horns of Elfland blow their challenge, he lifted his war-worn horn of battered copper and blew an answer back. And a hush fell over Elfland, as the echoes died from his horn, and the little horns of silver or ice were silent. The traveller had come far to reach that cliff. Indeed he had travelled for more than half of his lifetime. And here he was at last by the border of Elfland. And now as to why he travelled; not to kill any dragon or to make war upon Elfland, but because of deadlier things than any that Elfland knew, which were spoiling the grace and quiet of Terra Cognita. For he knew that Elfland has different years from ours, being on another level of time from that on which float our fields and the regions of Terra Cognita, and he sought for the old years, or the years of any age that had not yet known machinery, or had outlived it and passed it by. And so he came, not as some knights had done, to the borders of Elfland for the mere sake of conquest, but to rest from all the noises that trouble the years we know. And by jagged difficult ways he climbed the cliff, and came to Goblins' Heath, and drew his sword and passed over it unmolested. For, though his sword was fragile and futile against the spells of Elfland, a mere glittering thing that could have been parried with ease by a shaft of moonlight held in the hand of a gnome, yet they watched him from the heather and scrub and rocks, all they that dwelt on the heath to guard the approach to Elfland. They said never a word to him, nor hoot nor whistle, but watched him every one, and he never saw their eyes. And so he came by the heath to the heart of Elfland; and they never opposed him, they who ruled that land, nor hailed him nor let him see one plume of their crests or a flash of their fairy armour. But he rested long on their heath, knowing where he was come, and knowing that rest thereon was profound and calm and eternal. How long he rested there is no saying nor any way of computing, for the time of Elfland is all different from ours. Beyond the border the buses rumbled on, motors hooted and trains clamoured, but there he rested, perhaps for an afternoon, perhaps for ages and ages.

The Lucky Escape

Mr. Tabbit was standing upon the hearthrug of the drawing-room of his suburban house; his son Jimmy was standing disconsolate before him, and his mother was sitting by the fire. Jimmy had failed, as his father was now reminding him, in one more examination, failed through sheer carelessness; for he had been certainly taught enough, and even remembered much of what he had been taught. "Sheer carelessness," said his father, quite accurately. "Have you no ambition whatever?"

"I should like to do something," said Jimmy lamely.

"Do what?" asked his father.

And Jimmy was silent.

"Do what?" his father repeated.

And Jimmy was silent still.

"Come, Jimmy," said his mother, hoping to dispel the awkward tension that hung in the silent air. "What would you like to do?"

And something in her voice did break down Jimmy's silence, though he had nothing useful to say.

"I dreamt I saved the world, mother," said Jimmy.

"Dreamt," said his father. "Dreamt. It's work you want, not dreams."

"Tell us your dream, Jimmy," said his mother.

But the dream seemed to have been frozen by his father's unsympathetic words. And again the silence fell.

"Work, not dreams," his father repeated. "Look at young Alfred. Well, he may not be young any longer, but he was when he lived near here; and he had no advantages that you did not have. He went to the same school. Look what he has done. Look at the inventions he has made, and had patented. It shows what you might have done, but for your carelessness; carelessness in writing, in spelling, even in reading what the questions were, that you were required to answer. Your grandfather was a civil servant; I have been a clerk all my life in one of the very best banks; and the only job you can get is that of a bus-driver."

He waited, so as to extort from Jimmy some expression of shame. But still that heavy silence. And he went on.

"Why!" Jimmy's father continued. "A driver of one of the old horse-buses, who knew me, used to touch his hat to me when I was only a few years older than what you are now. Now, in spite of all that has been spent on your education, you have no better prospects than to drive a bus, probably all your life."

A more contrite face than Jimmy's would have been hard to find. For driving a motor-bus through the streets of London happened to be, of all the ambitions that come to men, the one that most dominated Jimmy, and knowing how unsuitable rejoicing would be to the present occasion, he did all he could to conceal any. So Jimmy became the drive of a motor-bus, the one that goes up the Strand and turns to its right and goes to the edge of the woods and open country before returning. But this is not the story of Jimmy Tabbit. It is the story of a far more industrious person, of Alfred Arnold. He was the Alfred of whom Jimmy's father had spoken, the young man who had started level with Jimmy, though several years earlier, and who was now so far ahead. It is the story of what was most active about Alfred Arnold, the story of his thoughts. He was walking westwards in the City of London and, as he walked past hundreds of people, none of whom knew him, nor had ever known his name, and to whom the name of Alfred Arnold would mean absolutely nothing, if ever they did see it written, he thought of the immensity of his achievement. For this scientist, who was not yet forty, had made another invention; and, knowing the magnitude of it, it amused him to feel that he walked among people, hurrying by without noticing him, as a man might walk in nailed boots over an antheap. Vain he certainly was, but he did not exaggerate. Indeed exaggeration would have been scarcely possible. For he was right about his last invention. It was not even yet committed to paper, but it was quite complete in the thoughts of which I tell. It was an explosive, founded on work that had been done by others, derived, in fact, from the atomic bomb, but as much deadlier than the bombs that had wrecked Nagasaki and Hiroshima, as those two bombs were deadlier than the bombs of 1940, just as the bombs of 1940 were deadlier than the discharge of the guns of Crécy. For science ever advances. He had only to commit his formula to paper and there would be a weapon in the hand of Man, that someone would very soon use. Who that one would be Alfred Arnold did not very greatly care. He only cared for science and the work that he was able to do. And this work that he had done only that very morning so much elated him, that he felt as he trod those streets, crowded with people, not one of whom knew him, like a giant with one of his feet stamping an antheap. None of them knew him, and yet their lives could all be ended, or the lives of their enemies, whenever he wished; and he could choose which. A moment's reflection showed him that it would be even more than that; for, when this power was loose, both sides would get it, whatever sides they might be, and no cities would be able to stand against that. Probably no houses in all the world. It gave him a feeling of power such as no emperor can ever have felt. Men like Tamerlaine, Genghis Khan, Hitler and many another have longed for power over the whole earth, power preferably destructive, but at any rate power. And this power that emperors had longed for, he had. It was no mad dream, such as some of theirs may have been; for the bomb would certainly work. He was no dilettante in science. He knew. There they came pushing past him, none of them looking at him, none of them taking off their hats, none of them cheering him, none of them acclaiming him as the greatest force in the world. He could afford that neglect. They could not. Henceforth all cities would be so vulnerable, that no-one would dare to build anything above ground any more. And all because of him. What man had ever had such power as this? What brain had ever thought to such purpose? Great achievements of human brains he admitted, but in poetry and drama, or things like that; nothing that would break all the seismographs in the world, like typewriters thrown out of high windows. He was unconcerned with any results. Enough that he, unrecognized by all in the street, was the mightiest power on earth, and would make all streets impossible. Cities would certainly go, rivers would become flooded, even the tides might be altered, and without any exaggeration he clearly saw there would be some effect on the moon. He, Alfred Arnold, would be a planetary influence. And nobody recognized it, as he walked westwards away from the City of London. Nobody thought him any greater than one of themselves. Nobody dreamed of the terror and magnitude of his power. So, he thought, insects might feel about an elephant, deeming themselves as good as it. The fools! He would go home and get the whole thing clearly on paper, but would not release the secret in his lifetime. What would be the good of that? He would be blotted out with all the rest, as soon as the bomb came to be used. A brief recognition would not atone for that. No, he meant to live a long time, getting what recognition he could for other work. It might not be much. But that would not matter, when he was able to cherish the thought, as he did now, that the world was in the grip of his enormous invention. When he died, or very shortly before, he meant to publish his tremendous discovery. And the world would end when he died, or soon after. What remained of it would be something very different from the world that any man knew. And that difference would be all due to him. And the moon too! The moon affected by him! It was a tremendous thought! He was thinking it as he crossed the Strand, head bowed with the weight of the thought, certainly not with humility, as he stepped from the ignorant crowd on the pavement, who had never heard his name. Even the moon, he thought again! A power such as it had not known since its volcanoes ceased to be active, the power of Alfred Arnold. And at that moment Jimmy Tabbit came by, driving his bus. There was some carelessness on both sides, though the driver was afterwards exonerated from blame, a carelessness pardonable in Alfred Arnold on account of the vast magnitude of his thought; and with Jimmy Tabbit any carelessness that he showed was due to his bothering still about that curious dream that Destiny seems to have sent him, in which he dreamed that he had saved the world. Anyhow, he saved it.

How Mickey Paid His Debt

There are two things I can tell you about Michael Mulgraby; one is that he always pays his debts, and the other that he is a very whimsical fellow. I do not for a moment mean that there is anything whimsical in paying one's debts, even in the wilds of Aravara; but he has a whimsical way of doing it, as he has with most things that he does. The man to whom he was most in debt was the one to whom everyone in Aravara owed most, an old fellow in a thatched cottage on the hill, who would lend money to oblige anyone; but in the end they were all obliging *him,* Thady Murragher. What with the interest he asked, and the mortgages of farms that fell in for him, he had enough money and to spare; but he went on lending, for the more money he got, the more he wanted, like a tiger that has tasted blood, as Dickie O'Neil said when he told me this story: And, as it is Dickie O'Neil's story, I had better give it in his own words.

"I saw it all," said Dickie O'Neil. "I saw the beginnings of it when Michael Mulgraby was getting hard up on account of the rain being bad for the oats that the Government made him grow, as it naturally would be in a climate like ours, and I saw the end of it one night when I was up in the big wood looking for a rabbit for my poor old mother." Which meant that Dickie O'Neil was a poacher by profession. "Well, Mickey gets in debt to old Murragher to the tune of £50. And, not having the money handy, or likely to have, the neighbours begin saying to him, 'Go bankrupt and don't pay.' But Mickey Mulgraby always pays. So what does he do but buy an old goat from a tinker for a few shillings, and he says to me that he'll sell the goat for fifty pounds, and will pay old Murragher. Well, I says to him: 'Who will pay £50 for an old goat?' And he says, 'They all will.' And no more will he say. Well, the next thing he does is to go off to a wise woman that lives by herself a little way down the valley, and says to her that it's the way it is that he wants her to turn a man into a goat. And the old woman doesn't say she can do it, nor she doesn't say she can't, for that would be to give away her whole profession. And they fixes something up between them. And there's a lot of talk about this, and it spreads up the valley. But I never says a word about what Mickey tells me, because he says to me, at the time, that there's two classes of people that never gives him away, his friends and dead men, and he hopes I'll always be the one and never be the other. So I said never a word. Then away goes Mickey to a bit of an army that was up in the big wood, lads that he knew. What they were doing up there I couldn't tell you, for I never took any part in religion or politics. But there they was, and Mickey fixes up an arrangement with their general and comes away back to his farm. And he let a day or two go by, during which the story of what the wise woman is going to do to old Murragher spreads all through Aravara. And pretty near everyone partly believes in it; but not old Murragher, having too shrewd a head on him to believe anything that cannot be put into three columns and added up as pounds, shillings and pence. Well, one morning Mickey goes down the valley and brings the old wise woman, Biddy Garraghy, up from her cottage into Aravara, and goes on out of it towards the hill, saying they are going to call on old Thady Murragher; which he needn't have done, for there wasn't a lad or girl in the village, young or old, who didn't know where he was going. And half of them trooped after him. Well, he comes to the old lad's cottage with the old woman, the two of them leading by several perches, for he warns all the young lads that are following not to come too near to Biddy, for fear of any magic of hers that might bounce back from old Thady Murragher. And then he puts his head in at the half-door and calls out, 'Good morning to you, Thady.' And the old woman says: 'Good morning to you, Mr. Murragher. Sure, you look very comfortable there before that nice fire that you have.'

"And Mickey Mulgraby says, 'Sure, I only wished you good morning. And you need not sit there so surly, just because I owe you a bit of money. Sure, I only came to ask you to allow me one more week in which to pay it, and I'll pay you every penny.'

"'Sure, that's a very reasonable request, Mr. Murragher,' says Biddy Garraghy, the old wise woman.

"'Ah, well, Thady,' says Mickey, 'surly or not, I'll take your silence for consent.' And then he turns to old Biddy Garraghy and says to her, 'Doesn't a man that won't answer when you bid him good morning deserve the worst?'

"And the old wise woman says never a word, but waves her hands in a way that I could not imitate, and says words the like of which I never learned at school when I was a gossoon, nor since. And Mickey shouts, 'Shoo.' And a goat runs out of Thady Murragher's back-door, which someone had left open. I don't know who. Mickey runs after it, and so does all the other lads, but Mickey catches it in the end, because he is the only one that has brought a rope with him. And then he gives the old woman two or three pounds, and they all goes back to the village, Mickey leading the goat. And Mickey goes straight home with the goat, without saying a word. But he turns round in the door and says, 'Boys, I am having an auction tomorrow at 12 o'clock.' And then he goes into his house.

"Well, everyone knows what he is going to sell. And there's not one of them doesn't owe money to old Thady Murragher, and they all gets the idea that to be his master, and to give him a hit of a stick whenever they felt like it, would be greater justice than any of us usually sees in this world. So when next day comes and Mickey Mulgraby is out in front of his house with the goat, the bidding is very fierce. And you may believe it or not, but it goes up to fifty guineas. Mind you, all the boys had had more nor twenty-four hours to see if there was any trace left of old Thady Murragher; and there wasn't a trace of him, only the goat.

"It was a big farmer called Jimmy O'Brien who bought the goat, and he had suffered very hard at the hands of old Murragher. And he leads the goat away with a rope. And, sure enough, within the week Mickey Mulgraby pays the fifty pounds to old Murragher. For Biddy Garraghy had never turned him into a goat at all, but had only pretended to do so. For Thady Murragher, you see, was not in that cottage at all, at the time they went up to the door, but only the goat. Thady Murragher was up in the wood with the army, where Mickey Mulgraby had had him taken the night before.

"That's how it was. And when the goat runs out of the cottage, everybody naturally thinks it's old Murragher.

"I don't see that Thady Murragher had anything to complain of. Sure, he got paid all that was owing him, and the army only kept him a few days in the wood. Sure, the thing was only a joke, and everyone saw it, excepting only Jimmy O'Brien, who never could see it at all."

LOST LYRICS

In the nearest village to the university town, in Cranstone vicarage, lived Lydia Marsham, the vicar's daughter, who not only was the best lawn-tennis player of her sex for two or three miles round, but in winter dominated the neighbouring games of hockey. And, although by no means learned, she was bright, so that at tea-parties also she was the principal figure. To Alfred Hoskins, even when the conversation turned to classical themes, of which she knew nothing, she appeared wonderful, and he might often have been seen in rapt attention while she prattled of the glory that was Greece. If anyone is really bi-lingual Hoskins was. Indeed he knew Greek better than English, for he had learned Greek and, though he might conceivably have made some popular error in grammar when talking English, he could never have possibly done so while he was writing Greek. His learning did not awe Lydia: she thought him rather dull. He was a don at the University, and Lydia's father's respect for his classical distinction was perfectly obvious, but that respect never crossed the gap between father and daughter, and it was Alfred Hoskins that respected *her*. I don't quite know why. But that is a thing one can never say of other men's fancies. Partly there was a kind of aura about her of greatness, an aura conferred by all the lawn-tennis players of the neighbourhood, and all the hockey-players, so that the words "Miss Marsham will be coming" were often said in a rather hushed voice, and came to be accepted with a certain awe, even by those who never played lawn-tennis or hockey. And then there was the brightness of her talk. Perhaps a pearl-diver, returning from dim growths far down on the floor of the sea, has a more surprised delight in the glitter of the sun on the myriad ripples laughing upon the surface than those that can sit and watch them all day. Certainly the bright superficialities of Lydia's outlook on life were charming to Hoskins after the profundities of his study. One day in the vicarage garden he proposed to her. Walking beside him under apple-trees all in blossom, she saw, or thought she saw, in a glance the man he was. And then she saw down a vista of the future the kind of life there would be for her with this dull man, and the kind of place she would hold among her neighbours, in a smaller house than the vicarage and among people many of whom would be too much addicted to learned themes to have that respect for her that she now enjoyed so abundantly. Hoskins might have some slight respect accorded to him by those who knew what Greek was, but nothing to what she enjoyed today, and she would be someone who in that circle was of even less importance than Alfred Hoskins, dragged down by his dulness. Often and often she had gone over in her mind the words with which she would accept some man's proposal, but had never practised the words of a refusal, so that they fell now rather clumsily from her lips. But, clumsy or not, they conveyed their meaning all right, and were clearly enough understood. The blow to Alfred Hoskins was enormous. It hardly seemed that a man so dull could feel so intensely, or that a man so immersed in the store of the greatest treasures of the human mind could be so put out. Yet if all his Greek books had been burned, and were out of print for ever, he would not have suffered so much. He scarcely uttered another word as they walked back to the vicarage. Thence he returned at once to his small house in the town, and there he did what he never had done before; he sat down to write a poem. He sat down to write because an inspiration came to him, of such force that he felt no alternative but to do as it bid. All his great sorrow, all his loneliness, all his disappointment, all his vanished ambition, all his learning too, welled up like many streams and poured into one channel, and that channel was poetry. To express such a poem he chose a quill pen, feeling it to be more suitable than another pen for such a purpose, a purpose to which he was about to devote all the energies that had been lashed into life by this blow that he took so hardly. If Destiny records anything before it occurs, this poem, one of the great poems of our time, was to be the first of a book full of melancholy, but full also of a beauty that this age was not to surpass. Alfred Hoskins dipped his pen in the ink, for the poem was already illuminating his mind. But at that moment his telephone bell rang. It rang because the inspiration that had given Alfred Hoskins this poem must have been somehow loose in the ether, and had come to Lydia Marsham too; not as an inspiration to write verse; that would have been impossible; but what it did do was to show her very clearly something she did not know, so that she suddenly heard herself saying to herself, "Well, you are a fool, Lydia, to refuse one of the greatest poets of the day." And she said to herself, "A poet? I never knew he wrote poetry." And the inspiration repeated, "One of the greatest."

That put an entirely different complexion on it. Life as Mrs. Hoskins, if Hoskins was to be that, would not be so obscure a life after all, and when she no longer played hockey, or even lawn-tennis, she might still enjoy that impalpable glory to which she was so well accustomed. The vision remained clear and strong, every bit as clear to her mind as things said on the radio are clear to our ears on days when reception is good. She did not hesitate: athletic people, accustomed to be captains of teams, seldom do. She went at once to the telephone and rang up Alfred Hoskins. This was the bell he now heard, and on answering it he heard her voice with a sense of injustice and anger.

"You seemed to take very seriously what I said just now," said that voice.

"Didn't you mean it seriously?" he said.

"Well" she said, "you hardly gave me time."

"Time!" he exclaimed indignantly.

"I like time to make up my mind," she said.

"How much time do you want?" he answered, scarcely yet beginning to hope.

"Could you give me five minutes?" she asked.

That of course led to their engagement, and the engagement to marriage. As for the poem, it was never written. I have rightly called it one of the great poems of our time, because it shone clear in Alfred Hoskins' mind, although it never appeared upon paper. He threw down the inky quill when he heard Lydia Marsham say that five minutes would do for her, and indeed never picked it up. His housemaid walked on it next morning, after which you can never use a quill any more. Other poems he had in plenty, but he used them for mere prose; and other quills he could have easily got, but never felt the urge any more, let alone the overwhelming compulsion, to write a poem. During the early years of their marriage Lydia Hoskins often said to her husband after tea, as an evening was closing in, "Wouldn't you like to write a little poetry, dear?"

And he usually said, "O poetry. I have other things to attend to."

And so he had. They had two children for one thing; and, what was more important, there were his Greek lectures.

"There's a blackbird singing over there by the lilac," she said once. "That ought to be something that you could make a poem about."

He smiled when he thought of the material for poetry he had at hand already in the open coffers of the treasury of old Greece, if he had a mind to write poetry and the time for it. But he said nothing. She was scarcely disappointed, and she never lost hope; for that vision that she had had when the inspiration was loose in the ether was so clear and strong that she never deserted it. Alfred Hoskins was as dull as she had feared, and the glory of her prowess in the hockey-field and on the lawn-tennis courts faded as she had known it would, and was not replaced by any fame earned by her husband.

They are both old now, and he has never yet written anything, except translations of Homer and Pindar in prose. But she waits and clings to that vision that came to her straight from Destiny, never understanding, any more than I am able to do, how Destiny can allow the captain of the Cranstone Ladies' Hockey Team, or anyone else, to change the course of anything it has planned.

THE DANCE AT WEIRdMOOR CASTLE

It was at an inn by a big road through the flat land of East Anglia. Before a fireplace by which a dozen men could have warmed themselves in comfort seven or eight sat, men upon various businesses who had come in there from journeys in many directions, most to stop for the night, one or two to go on again in the cold after dinner, which all that were gathered before that fire had had. For some while all of them gazed at the orange light of the fire, and watched the slow change of the landscape that seemed to glow there, as though there were significance in it or things to be studied. And whatever calculations they made concerning the scenes in the fire they made in silence, but for the faint sounds that murmured from pipes of those that were smoking. In the warmth of the room in which that good fire was glowing the silence had lasted so long that any remark would have rung in it, and would have held anyone back who was perhaps about to slip through the quiet gateway of dreams.

"Why, I wonder," said one of those before the fire, "do we associate ghosts with Christmas?"

For a moment the silence fell back again after his words. And then from the depths of a chair there came a voice saying, "Everything has its season; butterflies, moths, swallows, cuckoos, and lots of other things. I suppose ghosts have too."

"But why at Christmas?" the first man asked.

"I don't know," said the other and sank back again in his chair.

I was afraid that the conversation was going to be dull. For I was one of those seven or eight before the fire. And I could do nothing to brighten it. And then the man in the deep armchair began to speak again. "At any rate," he said, "I never saw one at any other time."

"Never at any other time?" echoed one of us weakly.

"Never," said the man in the armchair.

"Then you have seen a ghost?" said the one who had spoken first.

"Only once," said the other.

"Would you tell us about it?" I asked.

"Well, if the rest don't object, I don't mind," he said.

Everyone of us leaned forward, and a murmur of syllables arose, all encouraging him to tell his story of ghosts. One or two pipes were tapped out and refilled, and we settled down in our chairs before that warm fire to listen. "It was some years ago now," he said. "Some years. I was a foxhunter in those days. Still am in a way; always will be; though it isn't often I go out now. There was less wire in those days. Well, about the ghosts. We had had a great hunt, and I was riding home alone. A great hunt, and I was out of country I knew. I had heard of the country through which I was riding, but had not been that way before. It was a part of the country called Weirdmoor. It was one Christmas Eve, just as it is now, which is what reminded me of it. Not that I should forget it in any case. It was bitterly cold, colder than what it is tonight. There had been some snow too, and there was a north wind blowing. I had heard of it because of an old castle that there was there; a ruin called Weirdmoor Castle. And I had never been there, because none of us ever did go. There were stories about its being haunted. It wasn't that I was afraid of ghosts; but if there were none there, there was nothing to go for, and, if there were, they are chilly and clammy things and I saw no reason for not keeping away from them.

"Well, there it was, a ruined castle standing by a bleak moor, with bats and owls in it and, there seemed, ghosts. No particular reason for going there, and nobody went.

"But on this particular night, as I came over the moor, the North wind was going by me like a long knife, and I was wet from the snow that had melted on me, and my horse was tired and, ghosts or no ghosts, I wanted shelter, and there was no dwelling anywhere along that bleak road. I might have kept warm if my horse could have trotted, but I couldn't keep him at that without hitting him, and he had carried me well; always did; and I wasn't going to do that. And then an intenser blackness rose beside me out of the dark moor. And it was Weirdmoor Castle. My first impulse was to ride past it, as the members of our Hunt always did, if ever they saw it. It was merely the custom of our Hunt. And that is what I should have done, if there had not come at the same moment a blast from the North that was so especially biting that, cold as I was already and thoroughly wet, I felt that shelter of

any sort was now a sheer necessity. My horse shook me with one great
shiver, and suddenly I saw that the windows of the castle were all shining with what I took to be lamplight. Later I realized that the glimmer,
whatever it was, had not arisen from lamps, and that, for that matter,
there were no windows, but only black gaps in the masonry; but that
was afterwards. At the time I thought that where there was light there
must be warmth. So I rode up to the doorway and hitched my horse to
a rusted iron staple that must have once been a hinge of the door. It
was on the South side, so that my horse was sheltered from that appal-
ling wind. And I walked in. The moment I had gone through the hanging curtains with which ivy half-covered the door I saw that it was true
what had always been said and that the place was haunted, and badly
haunted. One has read of bevies of ladies, and, for all I know, they
should be so described; but here it rather seemed that there were gusts
of them, that floated slightly luminous through the castle's dark interi-
or, while the North wind sighed outside and stirred the air of the cavi-
ties in which there had once been windows, and set dancing the
tendrils of ivy that hung loose from the walls. There was no roof on
the castle, and looking upwards I saw only racing clouds, that rushed
over strips of dim light; but whether such light as there was there came
from any remnant of day, or from the stars or moon, I could not tell.
The ladies that floated through the dark of the castle drifted together
then, and seemed all to look at me, for all of them sharply turned their
luminous faces towards me, then turned away and clustered closer together and were obviously talking of me. I could have no doubt of
that. And what is more, I could feel that they found something wrong
about me. For a while I wondered what it could be. Could it be my wet
hunting coat, or the mud on my stock, or the water from melted snow
that squelched in my boots? And one by one I became sure it was
none of these. And then the idea came to me what it was, a clear feeling, which I corroborated later, that I knew what it was they found
wrong. It was simply that I was alive. And life was something that
these ladies who floated in that dark castle found common and vulgar
and coarse. Then they seemed agreed about something. 'One of us,'
they seemed to have said, 'must receive him.' And at once from the
face of one of them, as far as I could see in the darkness, disappeared
the amused criticism and was replaced by a welcoming smile as she

drifted straight towards me. What she said as she smiled at me with her faintly luminous smiles was said in so tiny a voice that you might have thought I could not have heard it above the howl of the wind through cracks in the walls and the roar of it in the chasms that once had been windows, but it had a clearness like that of the shrill cries of the bats which were also piercing the darkness, and I heard every word.

"'You are from Earth transitory, are you not?' she said.

"And I said Yes, though I had no idea what she meant.

"'Won't you join us?' she said.

"And I said that I should be delighted. And she drifted back to the faintly luminous others, and I followed her, walking in my wet boots over the weeds of the floor. I bowed and said Good evening to that dim cluster of figures, but saw from their vacant expression that evenings and mornings meant nothing to them, and I could not say anything apt about eternity, and did not know what to say. But one of them, a graceful figure that swayed with the sway of her silk skirts in the draughts that were waving the ivy, asked me if I did not come from the transitory ways; and, guessing what she meant, I said that I did. And she turned to the others and they all nodded and smiled, and I heard them muttering again, 'the transitory ways,' and their smiles put me at my ease. I could not trace by their fashions the dates when they had been here, and the graceful lines of their dresses were too mixed up with the tendrils of ivy which hung and swung from the walls. I should have liked to have asked them something about their story, but coming suddenly thus among an assembly of ghosts I was not so composed as they, who had before them only one stranger, and who were in their own home. So it was they that questioned me. And in answer to their questions I told them that I had been hunting and that I had been taken far from home by a great run, and after a splendid fox. 'Is it dead?' they asked eagerly then. And I guessed from the excited eagerness in their faces, and from all that they said later, that they cared only for what was dead; and again and again as they spoke I got the impression that, although they tried to hide it, all living things to them were coarse and vulgar. They closed round me eagerly, asking for news. Had I seen any ghosts by the road, they asked?

"'No,' I replied.

"Any spectres? Any phantoms?

"And I saw from that that there were different kinds of ghosts and that all these were different things. Then the North wind outside appeared to increase in violence, so that all the cracks in the castle and weeds in the windows were singing. And the lady that seemed to be the chief of the ghosts asked if I would dance with her. Well, of course I could not refuse. And we danced, and the wind sang. A graceful figure and a lovely face, so far as I could see by the dim glow of it in the moonless and starless darkness. But no warmth came from her, and no warmth came to me from my dancing, but only an increasing cold that pressed in on me from the darkness and clamminess of the castle, and even from every one of those girls themselves whenever we danced near them. And I saw them looking about as though for partners, as though they wished to dance too, and I wondered what ghosts would come to them. Chillier and chillier I grew as I danced, and the waist and the hand of my beautiful partner were as cold as the leaves of the ivy covered with ice. And as I grew chillier still, I knew it was life that was ebbing. And as the music of the North wind in the crannies sank for a moment, I ceased to dance, and my chilly and lovely partner urged me to go on. And the rest came drifting nearer and were all round us and seemed to be trying to drive me on with the dance, but had not the strength to move my weight, though I could feel them trying. And the girl with whom I had danced looked up at me and said in her tiny voice, 'Will you not dance with me any more?' And when I said that I feared that it was time for me to go, she clung to me still like damp ivy. And something about her then drew the bare truth out of me, and I said, 'The cold is beating me, and my life is ebbing.' And she said 'Life!' full of amused scorn. But, if I was to live, I knew that I must get quickly out of the cold of that castle, even into the wind outside. For somehow I knew that even the North wind would be warmer, if I could only pull clear of the dead. But it wasn't so easy.

"They were not able to move me. They couldn't drive me to dance. But there was an influence about them that, cold as I was now, was growing too strong for me, and they were all round me, and I no longer had the strength that I needed for pulling away. And my partner was fixing me with her glow-worm's eyes. I was growing colder and colder. How could I pull clear? Where could I get some help from something alive? I thought of the ivy, and turned from my partner to clutch at a hanging cascade of it. But there were dead leaves amongst the live ones, and they clutched me and held me back and the live leaves were unable to help me. All the ghosts saw my motive and smiled at my failure. They came in closer still, and I grew much colder. Suddenly I realized that I was too weak for those drifting things, a humiliating discovery for any live body. I grew colder and even weaker, and my partner smiled at me, a welcoming smile, as though I were coming over even then to the dead. And so I was. And at that moment my horse snorted, trying perhaps, poor brute, to drive some cold gust away from him. Life, I thought! Something alive!

"'I must look after my horse,' I said.

"They all of them turned on me the faint gleams of their eyes. And then I heard them exclaiming with all their scorn, 'A horse!' 'A horse!' 'A live horse.' And more than that they had no need to say, in order to show me the indignation with which they knew that I preferred something alive to them. 'A horse!' 'A live horse!' they went on exclaiming and muttering. And then the one that had danced with me said, 'A live horse! Had you wanted a horse the Valkyries would have given you one, or sold it for fairy gold. How far can a live horse carry you over the transitory ways?'

"'Seventy miles in a day,' I said, exaggerating a bit.

"'A day!' she said. 'And one of theirs could carry you a thousand times as far, where there are no days.'

"Her indignation was rising, and the indignation of all of them, while my strength was ebbing away with my warmth and vitality. I struggled against whatever influence the ghosts were exerting, but was only able to move a few very slow steps. I was moving towards the door and feared that I never would get there, for they were all round me now like ivy, and their chill was gripping my heart. And now the door was only four or five yards away, but I felt I could no more reach it than one can run to safety in a nightmare. Their cold and their scorn were all round me, hemming me in. One moment I felt that their bitter cold had got me, and then there was warmth all round me and I suddenly felt I was saved. It was the breath of my horse. In the warmth of that I was able once more to move, able once more to put my weight and my reason against imponderable and ghastly things. I patted my horse, unhitched him from the old hinge and climbed up. As I got to the saddle the dance or whatever it was seemed all to die away. One faint wail of indignation or disappointment remained, hanging in the dark air. And the light, whatever it was, had gone from the windows.

"That was Christmas Eve. I rode on with the North wind, which as I think I told you, was warmer than that dank castle. When I got home it was Christmas. I don't suppose they haunt that place at any other time, or more people would have seen them than have; but I never went back to see."

That is the tale that I heard one Christmas Eve at an inn, and I remember it yet. It was late when the man who told it ceased to speak and leaned back again in his chair, and it was warm and comfortable before that good fire and I noticed that all but he were by then asleep.

As It Seems to the Blackbird

"The transit of thoughts along the cerebral nerves," Professor Bellamere was saying, "can now be transmitted to wires along which they can be electrically propelled with no greater difficulty than what has to be overcome to propel an electric train along its rails; and of course proverbially, I may say, with far greater speed. And, whenever contact is made with another brain, a thought can naturally be shared as soon as it has travelled to the other end of the wire, which, at the speed at which thought travels, is practically instantaneous."

"I don't think I quite understand," I said, for he seemed to be talking to me as well as to two or three other people, after lunch in a club. At least, I was listening, and thought that I might ask at this point for an explanation.

"It is perfectly simple," he said. "The system of wires is put over a cranium, running from the Bellamere battery, as it is called, and connected by a single wire to another small mesh of wires fitted over another cranium. The thought that my battery runs along the wire is then perceived in the second cerebellum; brain, I should say. I don't know if there is anything in that that you don't understand."

"No, no, not at all," I said.

He then turned back to the other two, who had made no interruption, and explained further details to them, and I interrupted no more.

After a while he said, "I don't know if any of you would like to try my system of thought-propulsion."

"I should very much," said one of the men, "though just for the next few weeks I shall be rather taken up with the Club bridge-tournament and may find it rather hard to get away." And the other one said, "I should like it very much, only, being on the committee of the club, I have rather to keep an eye on the catering."

Professor Bellamere had not actually asked me, but he seemed a little disappointed at the lack of interest of the others, and I felt that that was the moment, if any, to make my request, to ask to be allowed

to see this invention of his, which even in an age so full of more important inventions, seemed to me wonderful. And so I asked to be allowed to try on his wires, and, not liking to ask too much, for I did not
know the professor very well, I did not ask to be allowed to overhear
(if that is the right word for it) the thoughts of another man, but merely asked if he could put me into contact with the thoughts of some
small animal, if animals had any. Professor Bellamere smiled at the
triviality of my request, but agreed to do as I asked. Nothing remained
then but to arrange a time and place convenient to both of us, and I
suggested a place a few miles out of London on the North downs, and
was glad to find that the professor did not object to going so far from
London. I gathered from that, and, as it turned out rightly, that he had
recently perfected his invention, and welcomed the opportunity of
showing it, even at the cost of leaving London for some hours. I had
suggested the North downs because I had thought of some small animal like a blackbird, and I knew they abounded there, though I had
not as yet considered how we were going to catch one. But it turned
out that Professor Bellamere knew of a bird-fancier, who used to catch
singing-birds and sell them for caging in the South of Ireland, where
that barbarity is perfectly legal. How he got them into the Free State, as
it was ironically called, he would not say. This man, the professor told
me, would catch a bird in a net; but he did better than that, for it
turned out that he had one in a cage in his shop in London, waiting for
shipment. We saw it when we went to his shop, which was nearly half-
way to Kent and the open downs, when he rather mysteriously took us
to a little dark upper room, where the blackbird was in a cage thinking
of lost woods, and lost thickets of briar-roses in a lost June. We had
gone by bus and tram to the shop; but after we bought the blackbird
we thought it better to take a taxi, on account of the caged bird being
illegal, and by taxi we went all the way, avoiding railways. The blackbird was no more miserable in the taxi than it had been in the dark of
the shop, and sometimes it tried to sing, but only a single bar, and then
stopped at once; as though its song, every time it started to utter it,
brought some memory that was too sad for the bird to bear to continue.

  Well, after a while we came to a valley I knew, and stopped the taxi
under the slope of a hill that went up to woods of beech, which were
just beginning to glitter with their leaves, for it was at the end of April.

It was afternoon, and I thought of going up to the wood at once, helping the professor to carry his rather heavy boxes, and to try the experiment that very day. But the bird seemed so dull and disconsolate that it hardly seemed likely that the experiment would yield anything satisfactory, and we decided that any thoughts of which a blackbird was capable would be more definite if the bird had a night's rest. And so we decided to go next day, at dawn, when the other birds would be singing. So, instead of going up the hill, we got the taxi-driver to take us down to a village that stood below in the valley; and there, at the door of a small inn, we paid him and he went back to London.

At the inn we had supper, and after supper Professor Bellamere talked to me a good deal about electricity, and that other mysterious thing, thought, and tried to explain to me how he got the two of them to run on the same wire, though I did not know quite enough about electricity, or, for that matter, thought, to be able to follow him readily. We were given two comfortable rooms for the night, with low ceilings upheld by large beams that were blackened by time, and were able to arrange with the owner of the inn that an early housemaid should call us before the dawn. And in that bleak hour when the stars are gone, and all the majesty of the night is lost, and there is no glimmer of the splendour of day, we heard a heavy knocking on both our doors; and I, for one, was reluctant to leave my bed. But the professor never saw the chill grey light that was slipping between the curtains, nor felt the dankness of the too early morning, his mind being warmed and lit by the splendour of his invention. I was probably no more to him than the blackbird was to me; we were both of us part of an experiment, though probably an experiment of greater importance to the professor than any other that had ever been. I realized from his haste, and his reluctance to have any more breakfast than a cup of tea from a thermos, that in all probability this would be the first experiment that had ever been carried out with his invention. He was perfectly polite to me, and yet I could not help feeling that our relations were only those of professor and guinea-pig.

The blackbird was sleeping when we started off from the inn, with a dark cloth over his cage. It was a walk of nearly a mile, and hard going with all those boxes, and it was all uphill. When we came to a lane with hazels along one side, that leaned over and met some briars upon the other, night seemed still to be hiding, and we saw grey light but rarely. Gradually I grew warm, carrying two of the professor's boxes up the hill, while he carried one and the blackbird, still asleep. But, though I got some warmth, we got no more light, for when we left the lane we came to the wood, and were still in a hushed darkness. We put the boxes down on as level a bit of ground as we could find on the slope, and the professor unpacked them and began to fit things together. I don't know to what extent his invention may still be secret, but that is of no importance, because I could not in any case give a description of his apparatus that would not seem absurdly inaccurate to a scientist; and, although my description might seem plausible enough to anyone unacquainted with electrical batteries, such a reader would remain as unacquainted as ever, for anything that I could describe. Roughly, there were two batteries, with jars in them containing dark liquids, and very fine wires running from each, and a mesh of wires that was to go over the blackbird's head and a larger mesh that was to fit over mine. The professor fitted together the complicated apparatus with a little electric torch, for day was very slow in coming into the wood. The eagerness to show me what he had to show, which I had noticed overnight, was now greatly increased, as I could see though he said very little.

"What about that bird?" he asked.

I lifted the cloth and looked, and the bird seemed still asleep.

"We shan't get much from it, if it stays like that," he said.

"Perhaps it will wake when dawn comes," I told him.

"Will it?" he asked. For the professor lived wholly in London, and did not know much about the ways of the woods.

"I think it will," I said.

"Not much use to us if it doesn't," he said, and shook the cage a little, but the shaking had no effect, and the professor began to grow uneasy about his experiment, as one could tell by a glance at him. Then he fitted the wires to my head and then opened the cage and caught the blackbird while it was still sleeping, and we fitted the wires to its head, and of course a wire joined up its wire to mine, and other wires ran from the blackbird's head and from mine to each of the two batteries. The blackbird was put back in its cage, but in spite of its handling it seemed only a little more awake, and soon sank back into lethargy. It was cold, standing still in the wood, and I hoped that something of some interest might happen. But, though the professor now switched on his switches, I was aware of nothing that could be called a current of thought; nothing, that is to say, that could be noticed above my own thoughts, which could not help being dull and uninteresting in such a cheerless morning, if morning it yet could be called; for, whatever it was in the open, there in the wood were the dregs of a chilly night. The professor was looking anxiously at me. "Nothing at all," I said.

"I will increase the current," he told me; "which should give the required activity."

And he moved some switch, but it had no effect whatever, unless to give me a kind of boding that something was about to occur. It was perfectly silent and cold in the wood, and the professor and I looked at each other and said nothing, and the blackbird did not move. And all of a sudden a clear cry rang through the wood, and for a moment I did not know what it was, and I am sure the professor did not; and there was silence then for a moment, and suddenly all the blackbirds broke into song. That strange cry in the cold silence was the first blackbird, which on some high twig must have seen the first glint of dawn, though it was dark enough where we were. And the blackbird in the cage began to sing with the rest. It was a wonderful chorus that was singing all through the wood, and a lovely solo that was being sung in the cage beside us. But it was not only the blackbirds that were singing; it was, if I can explain it, the whole of the hills: the great North downs seemed all to have lifted their heads and were looking into the light that they just could see, and were singing to greet the dawn as it came towards them. And all the fossils in their deeps were singing, singing of old oceans forgotten by all but this song. Sea-shells of tribes unknown except to the hills, were singing their old songs there, sea-urchins and sea-anemones, whose bones the hills had held far over a million years. And the merriment of sunlight on waves long dry was dancing now in their song. And the flowers of our own time were singing too, the early purple orchid and the buds of the pyramid orchid; even the buds were singing. And a quiet and solemn song was going up from the violets, distinct from the great chant from the buds of may, which was like an anthem sung by thousands of children. And behind all this their little melody was going quavering up from millions of primroses, a melody as pervasive as sunlight, and all the anemones were singing their strange wild song, and a tinkling like the music of fairy sheep-bells was going up from the cowslips. And though the butterflies must still have been sleeping upon bent stalks of grass, their gentle song seemed rising now and then, as though they sang in their sleep, all the butterflies whose homes are upon the hills of chalk. And all the great trees were singing their solemn song to the dawn, with low murmur of deep voices, and every one of their leaves, which had only lately emerged to the world that was new to them, so that there was a touch of wonder in all their songs, a wonder of which I have only words to tell, but which music can make so clear, the art that seems to begin where the art of words has ended. And the voles in the dead leaves, and squirrels upon pine-branches, that rose dark through the beeches, and badgers in their white corridors that they had dug in the chalk, and foxes in sandy homes on the very tops of the downs, were all singing as well, and all the other birds besides the blackbirds, but gently, no more disturbing that wonderful chorus than the breeze in the trees disturbed it, though that was singing too. And louder and louder, till it even equalled the blackbirds' chorus, another song was rising, answering the song of the hills, a song such as I had never heard before. I looked at the professor in wonder, but he heard nothing. He was busy with his batteries, and only glanced at me to see if his experiment was going all right, and saw by my face that it was indeed, and that was all that he cared about. And all of a sudden I knew what was singing that song, as I had known that the foxes sang and the badgers and voles and squirrels although I never knew how. It was the light that was singing, the light of dawn that was singing its song to the hills.

I have listened with utmost intentness since that day to many a dawn, but never have heard the slightest sound, except the song of the blackbird and a robin or two and a thrush. Human ears cannot do it. It was the blackbird that taught me.

I loosed the blackbird from the cage as soon as the experiment was over, and while the professor was not looking. That seemed to me to be all that mattered. I wish I could greet the dawn as that blackbird is probably greeting it now.

Thε Haunτiɴɢ of Whiτεbεams

It seems hardly credible that the letting of one house, and one outside the village at that, could have so upset the whole village of Woldham. But sure enough it did. It was a small house on a hill, among lawns and beech-trees; with a garden beyond the lawns, and a gardener's cottage at the end of the garden. Had it not been taken by a stranger from London, at a price that to all the village seemed quite exorbitant, the Gibberts would have rented it and given up their big cottage all among yew-trees down in the village, as Albert Gibbert, a senior civil servant, had had a rise at Whitehall. Then Jorrip, the retired blacksmith, would have moved into the Gibberts' cottage, for which he had been saving money all his life. And a man called Chibble, who had no house at all and wanted to get married, would have moved into Jorrip's cottage. And that is by no means the end of it; for Arnet, whose daughter Chibble meant to marry when he could get a house, was interested too. And then there was the gardener's cottage that went with the house on the hill; and further ramifications went all through the village from that, and are more than I can go into. In the village the whole thing was discussed with a thoroughness that the new tenants of White-beams never guessed. And it was vehemently discussed, not only by those who were affected by it in any way, but by all who dropped into the Black Dragon, where the thing was being discussed. For it was felt that the arrival of these strangers, outbidding anything that the Gib-berts could have afforded, was putting a dead stop to such slow trickle of housing as seemed coming the way of the village. At first it was mere discontent that all were expressing, and for well over an hour some pleasure seemed to be found in that expression, which for a while satisfied all. But when everything had been said about the strangers from London in general, and about the principle of strangers coming unwanted like that in particular, or at any rate everything that those present could think of, a new note was brought to the discussion by young Chibble with the words, "What ought we to do?"

All opinions expressed had been strong, but no-one until that moment had made any suggestion of action.

"Well," said one or two.

And one of them said, "Well, it's hard to say."

And there was nobody who had any scheme to suggest; but faces looked thoughtful awhile and the new idea sunk in, the idea that something after all might be done. There was silence awhile. Then one said over his beer, "If I went to a house like that and found that I wasn't wanted, I would go."

But young Chibble was practical. "Maybe you would," he said, "but those people from London with all that money aren't going to bother about us. They'll stay, whether we like them or not."

"What do you think we ought to do yourself?" said Jorrip, the old blacksmith.

"I can't think," said Chibble.

And others shook their heads. It was not an easy problem.

"I tell you what I'd do," said Jorrip.

They all looked up, turning towards the old blacksmith and waiting.

"I'd go to Mulraney," he said.

Mulraney had drifted into the village from Ireland about thirty years ago, with stories of great battles which according to him had raged in and around Dublin, most of which he seemed to have lost; for which reason he had been advised to leave Ireland, and so had arrived at Woldham and travelled no further.

"Mulraney would be likely to have a plan," said Jorrip.

"We can't have any shooting," said one or two of those present.

"O," said Jorrip, "he will have grown out of that. But I don't mind telling him that that's not what we want. You see if Mulraney won't have some little plan for us."

"To move these people out of it?" asked Chibble.

"I shouldn't be surprised," said the blacksmith. "Look at the way those people were able to fool Lloyd George, and to get the whole army and the police out of Ireland. It wouldn't be much to move one stranger out of Whitebeams."

They thought over that for a while. And one said, "We might try."

So they went to Mulraney there and then, a lot of them from the Black Dragon, and found him smoking dark tobacco before his fire.

"Come in, won't you, and sit down," said Mulraney.

So they came in, though there were more of them than Mulraney had chairs for. And Jorrip spoke for the rest and said, "We were wondering if with all the experience you've had, you could think of anything that might induce a reasonable frame of mind in those Chadders, that have got into Whitebeams."

"Sure, nothing would be easier," said Mulraney.

"But no shooting," said Jorrip. "Because we don't do that here."

"Sure, I quite understand," said Mulraney. "And, sure, I never did any of that, only to men that wouldn't listen to reasonable argument. I always tried argument first."

"Argument would be no good with them," said Jorrip. "It's been tried. But there must be no shooting here. It's against the law."

"Ah, sure, it would be quite unnecessary," said Mulraney.

"And can you get them out of it?" exclaimed one or two.

"Sure, nothing would be easier," said Mulraney again. "There's nothing the gentry dislikes more than two things, ghosts and drains. A word on either of them subjects, and give it time to get round, and they're off at once. With all the contraptions that do be in the world today, and all the queer things men are turning their hands to, if you said it was drains they'd only have them tested, and then maybe they'd stay after all, in spite of anything you might say. So it had better be ghosts. And, sure, I know a lot more about them than I know about drains. We'll soon have them moving. Nothing would be easier. Only, when I've done with all my talking and got them out of the place, maybe I'll be a bit thirsty."

"We quite understand," said one or two of the people of Woldham.

And the old blacksmith said, "That would be only natural."

A little quiet conversation took place among the rest, and the upshot of it was that the blacksmith said to Mulraney, "Would half a dozen of whiskey suit you when they were gone?"

"Sure, it would suit me grand," said Mulraney.

Then they all left Mulraney to his pipe, and he sat by his fire thinking, and for some while no more was heard about the Chadders up at Whitebeams, for talk about them at the Black Dragon was restrained,

and any enquiry about them met with a hush and got no further, as
though all were waiting for something.

And then, as quietly as the pale-grey mist that used to rise in autumn evenings from the streams that ran through the valley, the rumour of ghosts arose. Whence the rumour drifted into the village and
up and down its street, lingering awhile in evenings at the Black Dragon and sweeping like the shadow of a storm-driven cloud through the
school, the most careful chronicler could not say. But perhaps one may
say that it reached its climax on the day that the vicar wrote in the parish magazine that a belief in ghosts was an unchristian superstition,
and that there was no ghost of beast or man at Whitebeams. He did
not actually mention Whitebeams by name, but he indicated it clearly
enough for all his parishioners to know what house he meant and what
ghost was believed to haunt it. When the Chadders read this they knew
what it was that men had been talking about, when they suddenly
stopped as one of them came within hearing. They knew that it was
about the ghostly fox that was said to haunt Whitebeams, and that
would utter a weird cry whenever any evil threatened the occupant. After that they listened at night, and they had not listened long when they
heard between their house and the wood that came very close to it that
uncanny cry with which a hungry fox will often break the hush of an
autumn night. It is a cry that is meant to chill the blood of rabbits, or
any small thing that is hiding, out in the night. Human beings, safe in
their houses, are not so susceptible, but after hearing those somewhat
unearthly rumours the family of Chadder were not so immune to what
was weird in that cry as they would have otherwise been, and, while
rabbits heard it and knew their obvious danger, the Chadders wondered what the danger was that that wild cry might perhaps be predict-
ing for them. Next morning they decided that it was only a fox, but by
night it had sounded more like the cry of some spirit prophesying evil
than any earthly thing. The best thing they could have done would
have been to forget it and to shut their windows at night and to listen
to the weird cry of a hunting fox no more. But they did the worst
thing. For after listening attentively for that cry again long after they
should have been asleep, and hearing it thrill through the chill and the
dark of the night again, they went down to the village to make enquiries about that rumour that hung in it now like a mist. And they met a

countryman's reluctance to talk to strangers, and his shyness to speak openly of mysterious beliefs he half held, and sometimes his simple garrulity, and sometimes the guile of those that wished the Chadders far away from Whitebeams. And it is guile that will more easily direct events than will natural and simple causes, for guile is solely concerned with doing so. And so the Chadders were directed to Mulraney, in whose hands the whole plot was, to give them the most accurate information that could be obtained about the ghost that haunted Whitebeams. The family of Chadder were Chadder and his wife, a grown-up son called Albert and a daughter called Marion. It was Chadder himself who, after several enquiries, was directed to Mulraney for information about the ghost. And Mulraney rose up from before his fire and took his pipe out of his mouth and offered a chair to the stranger, and enquired, as though he had no idea of the matter whatever, what he could do for his visitor.

"It's about this nonsense they talk in the village," said Chadder. "They say there's a ghost at Whitebeams, where I live. It's all rubbish, but I am told that you can tell me what they believe about it."

"Sure, I can," said Mulraney. "Sure, I know all about ghosts."

"I don't believe in them," said Chadder.

"Sure, I've known too many of them for me to be able to say that," said Mulraney.

"Well, then," said Chadder, "what's all this nonsense they're talking about there being a ghost up at Whitebeams?"

"Sure, it's a fox," said Mulraney.

"A fox?" said Chadder.

"The ghost of a fox," said Mulraney. "That's all it is."

"And what does it do?" asked Chadder.

"Sure, it only does useful work," replied Mulraney. "It only warns people up at the house when any disaster is coming. It lets out a screech to warn them."

"Useful!" exclaimed Chadder.

"And so it is," said Mulraney. "Sure, it warns them so that they can go away in time. And then the disaster doesn't befall them. That's how it is."

"If anyone thinks I am going away because of a damned fox," said Chadder, "they are much mistaken."

"The ghost of a fox," corrected Mulraney. "And, sure, there's no need to go till it screeches."

"And I'm not going even then," Chadder added.

"Sure, there's no need to," said Mulraney. "It's only a warning for them as don't like disasters."

"It's all nonsense," said Chadder.

"Sure, that fox knows," said Mulraney.

"Well I don't believe it," said Chadder, and left Mulraney sitting before his fire and quietly nodding his head.

But the speaker of those bold sceptical words went out of that house wondering, and all the way to his own haunted house he turned over and over ceaselessly in his mind the pros and cons of unknown spiritual powers having foreknowledge of things to be and revealing that knowledge to the dark of the night in a language one did not know.

"It's all nonsense," he said to his family when he got home, and found them waiting to hear the whole truth about what was haunting Whitebeams, which they felt so sure that Chadder would obtain in the village. "It's only a fox," he said.

"Wouldn't it be better to listen for it again tonight," said his wife, "and then see if it really was a fox?"

And her son said, "Yes, we will sit up and listen."

He was of an age when sitting up late to see anything, especially a ghost, seemed time well spent. And his sister felt entirely the same way, which she showed in her whole face, though all she said was, "O, let's."

So Chadder was committed to listening late for a fox, and then to looking for it on a dark night. At dinner, whenever no servants were in the room, the talk was of ghostly things, till Chadder, who before dinner had only said that it was nonsense once or twice, repeated those words very often, in the effort to drive from his mind the encroaching shadows that seemed to him to be closing in from another world and chilling the house of Whitebeams. After dinner they all moved into the drawing-room and uneasily waited for bedtime, for even the boy and the girl were uneasy by then. And, when at last bedtime came, they all went into a small room, whose large French windows faced to the wood that ran all along the top of the hill on which their house was built lower down, and they waited in silence to hear that cry that is about the weirdest known to an English night. Mrs. Chadder fell asleep, while cold dark hours went by, bringing no sound to the strained ears of the others except the occasional hoot of an owl, which seemed to warn them that something was coming, though nothing came. And it was long past midnight when from the far end of the wood came that wild cry and drifted over the hill-slope faintly towards them, terrifying all small creatures that were out on the hill that night.

"That's it," said Albert.

And Chadder and Marion nodded their heads, and Mrs. Chadder suddenly woke up. That far cry had been too faint to have woken her, and Albert had spoken in quite a low voice and neither of the others had said a word; so it must have been the tension in the room, increasing suddenly at that distant cry, that had somehow woken her up.

"Shall we go and look?" said Albert.

"Wait," said his father.

And they waited; and in the strained hush it seemed a long time before the wild cry rose again, and when it did it was nearer.

"Shall we go now?" said Albert.

And Marion looked eagerly at her father, and said nothing.

And Chadder said, "Yes," and all four went to the French windows, and Mrs. Chadder, whatever she meant, said, "Do be careful."

And the other three opened the window and went out into the wonderful night. For the night is always wonderful. And they went towards the hill, and the fox cried again. And the weird cry made all the night weirder. Of course they saw nothing. Neither ghost nor fox are to be seen in the night, unless very rarely. And this was not one of the nights when either of them was visible. No shadow that those three could see moved over the dark of the hill-side, no wraith was seen by them between the earth and the stars.

"Well, that proves nothing," said Chadder when they got home.

"But it may be a ghost," said his son.

And he said it, stressing the word *may*, as though he were almost on the side of the ghost, and as though he hoped that they had really heard some ghostly warning of approaching disaster. And then an owl hooted from the edge of the wood, with a voice that did not seem like that of a bird, but rather of some small hunter, hunting along the hill, alone and wild in the night. Well enough he seemed to know what it was that had screamed in the night, knowing ghost from fox at a glance; and with one clear syllable he had told which it was, only that none of the Chadders knew his language.

"It was only a fox," said Chadder.

But Albert and Marion said nothing more; for ghosts, and even warnings of disaster, gave to the night a mystery that seemed to them something too delicate to be trod under the ruthless feet of an elder. And then they all went to bed.

Much later that night they all heard the wild cry again; and it sounded ghostlier then.

For the next two nights no sound of a fox was heard. Perhaps he had found some better hunting on the far side of the hill, or he merely changed his hunting-ground from wise policy. Only the owl called out through the night, the owl that seemed to know so much and to be glad to tell it, only that they did not quite know his language and only gathered hints from what he was saying. Gradually the keen and thrilling wonder of Albert and Marion died down and the logic of their father reasserted itself, and Mrs. Chadder agreed with him that it was all nonsense about the ghost. These views of theirs they all supposed to be entirely secret; but, however they may have got out, they were discussed thoroughly at the Black Dragon, and the opinion came to be held that Mulraney was doing no good. So Jorrip and Chibble and one or two others went again to Mulraney's house and told him that the Chadders were still at Whitebeams, and did not look like moving.

"Very well then, very well," said Mulraney, and drew some long puffs at his pipe. "Very well then, you will do this. You will, one of you, go and tell the man that is in that house that there's no harm in the ghost so long as it keeps to the woods, and that it's only warning the people in that house about disaster when it comes to the very door. That's the time it has come to warn them, tell him, and only then, and ask him has he a dog. For tell him that dogs know more of these things than men, and have a subtler sense than we have of the presence of ghosts and of anything at all from beyond this world."

"I don't think he has a dog," said Jorrip.

"Never mind," said Mulraney. "But you will tell him that."

"Won't it be making him easier in his mind," said Chibble, "not uneasier, if you tell him that there's no harm coming to him from the wood? A fox is not likely to come very much nearer."

"We'll see," said Mulraney.

"Is there anything else we can do?" said Jorrip.

"Only for the rest of you just to talk about the ghost," said Mulraney, "and about warnings it gave in the old time and one thing and another."

"We'll do that," said Jorrip. "But what's the use of teaching them about the ghost if we're to tell them not to be afraid of it till it comes up to their door?"

"It will come," said Mulraney.

And no more would Mulraney say. And they all went back to their homes, and talked about the ghost as Mulraney had told them to do.

And the talk went round the village and floated up to Whitebeams vaguely and bit by bit, as the mist came up from the river. But, like the mist, it arrived unmistakably; and Chadder reflected upon it and was comforted, for, though the fox was heard again a few nights later, it never came near the house. And he uttered this dictum to his family, "If there is anything in what they say in the village about this ghost, we need not worry about it, for they all say that it means no harm to the house unless it comes up to the door. And a fox is not going to do that."

"But it's a ghost, not a fox," said Albert.

"I'll believe it's a ghost if it does that," said Chadder. And something in his tone seemed to disenchant the air round Whitebeams and all the hillside up to the wood, and to drive any mystery away, and no more was said of the ghost. But talk of it continued to ripple around them, flooding up from the Black Dragon. And not only at the Black Dragon was there talk of the ghost, for Sam Chickery, the huntsman of the Weald and Wold, who lived five miles away, was seen going into Mulraney's cottage; so that, even if no other entered or left the village, the rumour would have followed the huntsman and spread. For rumour does that more quickly than any infection.

Uneasiness increased in the village during the next few days, and decreased up at Whitebeams. In the village they feared that the Chadders would not go, and at Whitebeams the uncanny cry from the edge of the wood, which they sometimes heard again, brought them little uneasiness now, for any fears which its weirdness awoke were lulled by the information which rumour had brought them that, ghost or fox, it had no warning for them till it came to their very door; and, whenever they heard that cry, it was far away. To make doubly sure, Chadder had bought a dog and kept it in a barrel by his hall-door. And, whatever sense the dog had that was more acute than the fears of the Chadders, stimulated by perpetual ghost-stories and every now and then by the weird cry of the fox, it neither smelt nor saw anything strange, nor detected it by any sense of which we know nothing. Though one night soon after it had got dark they did hear it barking, but only in a routine manner, as a dog barks at a mortal stranger; and soon it suddenly stopped, and they heard it gnawing a bone, or even a bit of meat.

"They aren't going at all," said Jorrip, that evening at the Black Dragon.

"Nothing has come near the house," said Chadder up at Whitebeams. "Nothing like ghosts. That dog would howl if it did."

But that night, as the clock of the church in the village was chiming midnight, all the Chadders, all still awake, who were listening for the cry of the fox, to assure themselves before going to sleep that it was well away from their door, heard, not its almost unearthly cry, but a new sound altogether, a sound that for a moment they thought came from a flock of geese, and was then beyond any mistake the voices of hounds in full cry. Louder and louder it grew. They seemed coming straight for the house. These were no ghosts, but unmistakable hounds. There may be, for all I know, lands where that cry is unknown or can be mistaken, but not in England, and all the Chadders knew it at once for the sound of hounds on a hot scent. But hounds hunting at midnight! Familiar as the sound was, and earthly, it was as strange to hear it then as to meet the ghost they half feared.

"What are they?" asked Mrs. Chadder.

"Hounds," said her husband.

"But are they coming here?" she asked, for their cries grew louder and louder.

"No, of course not," said Chadder.

But they did. They rushed up to the very door and bayed about it, eight couple of foxhounds. Their own dog was baying too. The Chadders never went to the door as they might have been expected to, and as by daylight they would have expected to do themselves. But midnight and that wild clamour and all the rumours of ghosts were too much for them, and they stayed where they were.

It was long before the hounds went away. Chadder said little, but he made up his mind that night, and never altered it. He said he knew nothing about ghosts one way or the other, but he did know that mist was unhealthy and that at any rate in the autumn it came right up to that house from the river, as anybody could see; and so he had decided to sell Whitebeams. The news travelled very rapidly.

"They're going," said Jorrip to Chibble, down at the Black Dragon only two days later.

"Then I suppose we owe Mulraney that half-dozen of whiskey," said someone.

"I suppose we do," said another.

And Jorrip and Chibble and one or two others went over there and then to Mulraney's cottage to tell him that the people at Whitebeams were going and that, however he had arranged it, he should have his half-dozen of whiskey. Mulraney thanked them and then was silent awhile, drawing a few puffs at his pipe. And then he said, "It came a little more expensive than what I thought. Would you give a couple of bottles to Sam Chickery who hunts the Weald and Wold, and the price of a bottle of aniseed?"

THE ROMANCE of His Life

I have a friend who tries to escape from London as soon as his work there is over. Once every three or four years, as his salary increases, he moves further away from it. But London seems to creep after him with new houses, stealing after him as he goes, and slipping streets like tentacles round him and holding him still, though at last he is at the very edge of it. And in that pleasant suburb to which he has come I was walking with him one day after his late tea, to which he is now able to get even on a week-day from his work near the centre of things. And as we walked by a little sandy bank on which a few harebells were growing, I stopped to peer over a small oak paling and between the trunks of a few trees to a lawn on which there were four young children playing. In sunlight that was now slanting out of the west, but was still warm, their parents were sitting at a table out-of-doors, at which they had had their tea. It was the happiness of the children, the calm content of their parents, and the serenity of the whole scene, that tempted my inquisitive prying. My friend stopped beside me when I stopped, and waited for me, not troubling to look, evidently too familiar with all his neighbourhood for there to be any novelty there to attract him as it was luring me.

"There," I said to him as I turned and continued our walk, "is the happy life. Doesn't it show that no great space is needed for it, but that happiness can be found in little grounds round a house of no great size?"

But then I stopped, because I saw that my remarks had got down into one of those grooves worn deep by copybook maxims; although they were true. When I stopped he spoke.

"Well, yes," he said. "Yes, the children of course are happy."

"But aren't they all happy?" I asked. "Does he ill-treat his wife?"

"Oh no, not at all," he said. "She is happy enough."

"And isn't he?" I asked. "He looks pretty cheerful."

"Well, yes, perhaps," he said. "But he had a lost romance, a great brief romance of which nothing came. And I rather think that every-thing after that, even happiness itself, must seem rather flat to him."

"A great romance?" I said. "Really? Who was the lady?"

"Miss Fells."

"What? Not the great Miss Fells?" I exclaimed.

"Yes, she," he said.

"But Miss Lucy Fells," I said, "world-famous, and that little man. No, never."

"But it was so," he said.

"How on earth was such a thing possible?" I asked.

And then he told me the rumour, the collected knowledge that that little suburb had of this small man's story. It was not the story it-self: I gathered that bit by bit with some care from many men. For the astounding contrast between this little bank-clerk in a suburb, and the lady who is perhaps the most famous actress now living in the world, puzzled and interested me. And so I asked my friend if he would be so kind as to introduce me to anybody who, besides himself, might have knowledge of that strange story.

"But everybody knows it round here," he said. "I can introduce you to anybody you like in the neighbourhood. Anybody will do."

And he did introduce me to several. And I pieced the story togeth-er, which they had often heard from the little man's own lips when dining out, when the port had gone round a few times. Or, indeed, he would tell it at any time.

He was very domestic, and dined mostly at home with his wife; but when he did dine out with a neighbour and the men were all talking after dinner, sooner or later he would talk too, and he had told them all his story. It was really the romance of that suburb. They all knew it there, as people in Eddington near Westbury know about Alfred de-feating the Danes, or in Coventry about Lady Godiva. It was their ro-mance, they had made it theirs; and they all told me about it, about their little neighbour's love, not unreciprocated, mind you, for that world-famous lady. Not unreciprocated, but brief as a beautiful mete-or. I pieced it all together from many mouths, and I think I have got it pretty accurate now. It went like this. It was in the 5.15 train from Charing Cross. They all knew that. 5.15 P.M. of course. And this little man was going down to his suburb. Terrup was his name. And in the same carriage, in all her radiance, dazzled Miss Lucy Fells. And Terrup took no notice of her at all. She stirred slightly and looked around; for all her intuitions were aware that any movement is quickly caught by the eye. But still he took no notice. It was not that she was vain, but she had suddenly come upon something that she had not seen for years, sheer apathy in her presence. Was it possible that this little man did not know who she was?

Supposing a tiger striding out of the jungle came on a herd of gazelles, and they all went on quietly feeding; he would naturally be surprised. Lucy Fells's beauty and fame had gripped the heart of the world, and was a power by no means less than that of a tiger: she was surprised too. Terrup sat perfectly still, perfectly uninterested, gazing out of the window. There was nothing to see out of the window either: it was in November and nearly dark. Terrup was nothing to her, but the situation meant a great deal. It might even mean that her grip was failing her, her grip on the heart of the world. It might even mean she was ill. Or was the little man ill? Was he half paralyzed? She must do something for him; she must give him a chance; at least she must let him know who she was. That would help him, and no doubt put everything right. She had bought an evening paper, hurrying to catch her train, and had not yet looked at it. There would be sure to be something in that about her journey. Yes, a large headline on the front page: Lucy Fells Goes to Blackheath. That was where she was going. She leaned forward to Terrup, and in her gracious famous voice said, "Would you care to see a paper?"

"Oh, thank you," he said and took it and looked at it and soon turned the front page.

So he was quite uninterested. Now she must let him know who she was, since he had quite evidently not found out. So she opened her small bag and began to rummage in it holding it quite low near the floor; and as she rummaged her gold cigarette-case fell out. It had her name written clearly on one side, Lucy Fells in small diamonds. Which side up would it fall, she wondered? But it did not matter. As a matter of fact it fell diamond-side upward.

"Oh, I have dropped my cigarette-case," she said.

He picked it up for her.

"Thank you so much," she said. "It was very careless of me. But I can't really lose it, unless it got stolen, because I have my name written fairly large on it, as you see."

And she showed it him. And he said, "Oh, yes."

She saw then unmistakably, though I don't know exactly how, but unmistakably, that he had never heard her name. The evening paper had printed it half an inch high. But he had never heard of it. Aphrodite coming in from the sea, to find all her temples fallen and nobody noticing her, would not have been more shocked.

I used the simile of a tiger among gazelles that paid no attention to him. A tiger in such a situation would not long remain idle. Nor did Miss Lucy Fells. She struck with her full force; with all her beauty and all her charm. She spoke to Albert Terrup about the weather. She said that the days were drawing in fast. She said that the train was slow. She asked what time it got to Blackheath. She asked if he knew the country round there. She asked what it was like. She said that she thought the gardens must be very nice in Spring. She said she was fond of gardens. She asked Albert Terrup if he was fond of gardens too. She asked if he was much troubled with weeds, and what he did to get rid of them. And she asked what kind of weather they usually got at this time of year.

And when all those questions had been asked and lamely answered Albert Terrup was at last at her feet, a tremendously happy, though abjectly conquered, heart. Nor was it to be wondered at. She had won the hearts of big audiences in great cities in far less time. It took her much longer than she felt that it ought to have taken, but she did not grudge a minute of it; for this conquest had to be made. She could not have anyone holding out against her like this, at the height of her glory. What would Alexander have done if some little village of India had ignored him utterly? No, such a thing could not be.

When she had conquered Albert Terrup, he became her abject slave. He made fantastic suggestions: he spoke of flight to the continent, he spoke of settling down in the suburbs. He even suggested that she should marry him.

To none of these suggestions Lucy Fells turned a deaf ear, or definitely refused to accede to any of them. For a conqueror cannot refuse to accept a surrender. And on that short railway journey from Charing

Cross to Blackheath, which was beyond the station at which he should have got out, flowered the romance of Albert Terrup's life.

What I think happened was that in that railway carriage was a brief but idyllic scene, in which the world-famous actress really did become engaged to Albert Terrup. And at Blackheath they embraced and parted with vows of love, which Albert Terrup remembered all through his quiet life, and always will, as Lucy Fells sincerely intended to do on the platform at Blackheath station. But with all her public engagements, and no record of this in writing, it must have slipped her memory, and I believe that quite honestly she forgot all about it.

A Theory of Evolution

Pozzet was a young man well known among cricketers and many others at Oxford; and one day he took his degree and went down, and arrived in London and disappeared. I do not mean that it was a case for the police; he rented a flat and his address was known, but he did not leave it, he did not attend parties, he never dined out, and among his young contemporaries who did these things he was seen no more. At first they were puzzled, and in a while they nearly forgot him; and then one day I met him walking down the Strand. And he remembered me, though with an effort, for his mind seemed to be full of something else, and I asked him what he was doing now. And at first he only said, "Working." But gradually as I walked his way, for I had turned West as we met, I found that he was at work on a theory, and he let out to my great astonishment that he was hoping to leave a name as great as Darwin's.

"Good Lord!" I said. "How are you going to do that?"

"I am at work on my theory," he said.

"Your theory?" said I. "What is it? Can you tell me in a word the kind of thing that it is?"

For of course I did not expect him to expound the whole theory as we walked along the Strand. Nor, as he quite rightly pointed out, can any theory be described in a single word.

"But perhaps mine can," he added. "In a word my theory is about evolution."

"But didn't Darwin discover that?" I asked.

"Ah, but he was going the other way," said Pozzet.

"The other way?" I repeated.

"Yes," replied Pozzet, "upward from the ape. That is what evolution meant to Darwin. But I have been studying modern poetry lately, and modern plays and modern sculpture and painting, and music too; and what my discovery amounts to is that we are on our way back again."

"Good Lord!" I said. "That will be very interesting if you can prove it."

"I think I have proved it," he said. "All I am working at now is to get my proof into clear and simple sentences, so that everyone can see it."

"How far have you got with your proof?" I asked. "Do you think I could see it?"

"Well, to take modern poetry to begin with," he said, "take these four lines,

> 'We are not what we are
> Nor where we are.
> We are none of us here,
> But there.'

They are very well known and very popular. In fact, they have received pretty universal acceptance. That means that our reason finds them reasonable. They are a milestone on our intellectual road, showing just where we are intellectually ourselves. I have been carefully analyzing the lines, and I estimate that, between the intellect of man and that of the ape, they are just about midway. Then I have looked up all manner of references to find how long this acceptance has been going on, and I find that the time is very short, from which it is logical that we are moving back very rapidly. In fact, if my theory is sound, as I feel sure it is, this should bring us back to the trees before the end of this century."

"Wait a moment," I said. "Are you quite sure that those lines are as meaningless as you suppose? May it not possibly be that it is you that are not deep enough to understand them?"

"I have thought of that," said Pozzet. "But, if that is so, and if I cannot understand a perfectly clear meaning, then it is I that am on my way back to the trees, and of course all who, like me, are unable to understand good plain English. I should have to read those lines carefully to a great many people, and watch how they take them. I shall have of course to distinguish very exactly between pretence, that accepts them for fear of being found out to be on the way back to the ape, and sheer honest ignorance, which will show that they *are* on their way back, if these lines are the good plain English that many believe them to be.

But, whichever way it is, a serious proportion of us is on the way back."

"As bad as that?" I said.

"That is my theory," he answered as we walked along the Strand. "And then I have not based my theory only on modern poetry, I have been studying some modern plays as well, though my work has been much interfered with there by the Lord Chamberlain, who cuts out all the obscene bits, which are just the things that would have so much helped my investigations. I got more from modern sculpture. Of course one must allow for every possibility, if one is honestly to build up a theory, and I had to examine the possibility that there might be a race of people at large who are like much modern sculpture one sees, and that all the figures in Battersea Park and elsewhere are faithful portraits. If so, the race is not only well on its way back, but is even beyond the ape already. But no; after very thorough investigations and over a wide area, I have found no such race, merely a pretty wide acceptance of those lines that I quoted from modern verse, both in books and upon the stage. All this acceptance seems to me to point the same way. And then there is the dance-music going back to the negro, and past him on its downward journey to the dances of Harlem, which is a home of the negro depraved by cities. And when you think that only fifty years ago they were dancing the old dances of Vienna, you will see that they and all of us are going back at a pretty great pace, well under fifty years all the way from Vienna to Harlem. And then there is modern painting."

"Yes," I said. "That has sometimes puzzled me."

"Then," he said, "you are not coming along back to the woods so fast as the rest of us. In fact, while it still puzzles you, you will not be coming that way at all. But you will probably stop puzzling after a while and accept it, and then you will be coming along back."

"Do you think so?" I said.

"It is the way we are all going," he answered. "And then look at handwriting. Even that has guided me. I have seen a signature that I have shown to several people, to ask their opinion as to what it was; and one said it was R. Poots, and another A. Umph, and another guessed W. Brown; and so on and so on. But it turned out to be Marmaduke Witherington. It all helped to work out my theory, like sticks building a nest. I know it is presumptuous of me to hope to leave a name like that of Darwin. But I take my work seriously, and, after all, a theory about the evolution of the human race is surely of some importance, provided that I can prove it."

We had come in sight of Charing Cross by now, and were about to leave the Strand.

"Well, that is my theory," he said. "I shall spend another year on it and then give it, all clearly worked out, to the public."

"I wouldn't," I told him.

"You wouldn't?" he said, and stopped dead still on the pavement.

"No," I repeated. "You see, there was resentment for fifty years over Darwin's theory in a great many quarters, and quarters not easy to be ignored. They didn't like the idea of being descended from apes, and it took all that time for people to get over their disgust at it. It is worse to be going back to them. You will have them against you longer than that. They will see you out. No, don't do it."

And I would have said even more, but he would not move and I saw a policeman coming up. It appears you are not allowed to stand still on the pavement and stop the way of those who are walking. So I left him, still standing dejected there. I don't know whether he has got over his dejection or not, or what he is going to do; whether he will take my advice, or whether he has gone back to his work and will show us clearly what we are coming to. Speaking personally, I would rather not know.

The Stolen Power

It is not often that the Ancient Powers permit man or beast to over-hear their private deliberations; and they would never have done so upon this occasion, had not some discussion that was raging among them left them disunited for a part of that dark night, and therefore perhaps weaker, so that by a lucky chance I was able to intrude for a little while on their negligence. Grey shapes of the clustered hills and wind and stars and storm, I had sometimes seen before; but on this night the hills seemed gathered closer together, and there were voices among them that I had not previously heard, where clouds were hurry-ing up to them and stars peering over their shoulders. There is nothing those Ancient Powers are more eager to suppress on the instant than human observation; nothing they are more swift to detect. A single glance in the direction of their mysteries, and they withdraw them at once. So that what a moment before was ominous with some prophetic boding, becomes as you glance towards it mere reaches of common-place pasture. Judge then how lucky I was to meet off their guard those who so rarely, where they sit watching the centuries, permit either man or beast to intrude on their mysteries. And this is what I heard.

"Man is usurping our power. Our power. Man."

Who spoke I do not know; but I think a wind to a valley.

And an answer came through the darkness, "What has he done?"

The words were from one of the hills, which all the hills repeated. For long I heard naught in the night, but "What has he done?" And the question grew gradually fainter, till it faded away in the darkness.

"He has stolen a power from the galaxies," said the first voice.

"He has robbed us," complained a star, looking angrily through a cluster of clouds just over the head of a hill.

"What shall we do? Do? Do?" came a crowd of voices, thridding the night, from the hills. "He has robbed the stars and the earth-quake."

And a great hush fell, through which I could hear the wind running from hill to hill, but saying nothing. And still more clouds came running up with the wind. And in the midst of the hills was sitting a height that had not spoken, a rounded shape like Olympus, or like a seated colossus, cloaked over body and head. Again I heard the hills say, "What shall we do?"

And the great cloaked figure was silent. For as a brooding figure I looked on that silent height. And after the echoes had died away from the hills, they said no more, and clouds and stars seemed expectant and even the wind was hushed. And at last a voice arose from the grand old shape of the height, pouring down deliberate words that rolled on like the echoes of thunder. "For what purpose is he using the stolen power?"

"For the destruction of Man," welled up the words from all of the lesser hills.

And then again I heard them repeating and echoing, "What shall we do, shall we do?"

"Let him alone," said the old grey height. "Do not interfere."

And the lesser hills and the clouds and the wind and the stars must have been satisfied, for I heard no murmur more that night from the Ancient Powers.

The Cook of Santamaria

A summer's evening was shining upon the mountains and on the walls of Santamaria. For the German commandant of Santamaria and for all his staff it was the pleasantest time of the day. Work was over and the hour of dinner approached. They were all billeted in the hotel, the only hotel of Santamaria. The Kommandant sat down in the dining-room and lit a cigar. Work being over for the day, there was no need for his staff to disturb him while he smoked; and yet his adjutant was standing near, and remained there uneasily till the Kommandant spoke. "What? Anything to report?" he asked.

"No, sir," said the adjutant. "Nothing to report."

"What then?" said the Kommandant.

"It's only about dinner, sir," said his adjutant.

"Dinner? What about it?" said the Kommandant.

"It's only that the proprietor of the hotel is to be executed today, sir."

"At what time?"

"The order only says today, sir."

"And he does the cooking himself does he not?" said the Kommandant.

"Entirely, sir," said the adjutant.

"Well," said the Kommandant, "there is still some daylight left at 8 o'clock. We dine at 7. What is your difficulty?"

"Then he is to be executed at 8?" said the adjutant.

"Naturally," answered the Kommandant.

The adjutant lingered. It was the hour when the Kommandant liked to be left alone with his cigar.

"What more do you want?" he asked sharply.

"We could get another cook from Transmontana tomorrow," said the adjutant.

"Naturally," replied the Kommandant.

"But if this man will not cook tonight?" suggested the adjutant.

"But I order him to," the Kommandant replied.

Where an order was given there was no question of argument, and the adjutant left the room. He went to an overlieutenant, and said, "Galpierri is to be executed at 8."

"Yes, sir," said the overlieutenant.

"And he is to cook the dinner as usual," the adjutant added.

"Certainly, sir," said the overlieutenant.

And once more the shade of a doubt stirred in the mind of the adjutant.

"He will obey the order to cook our dinner, you think?" he asked.

"I think so, sir," said the overlieutenant. "They are a simple people. I think he will raise no objection."

"So," said the adjutant.

Signor Galpierri was confined in his own cellar, with a sentry over the door at the top of the steps that led up from it. Thither descended the overlieutenant, and found Galpierri sitting on a box.

"Your execution will be at 8," he said.

Galpierri nodded.

"We dine at 7," said the overlieutenant.

Galpierri nodded again.

"There will be no difficulty about the cooking?" the overlieutenant asked.

"But certainly not," said Signor Galpierri.

The German walked slowly away, meditating. But at the cellar steps he turned, as though slightly puzzled. "That will be all right, then," he said.

"But certainly," said Signor Galpierri. "Why not?"

"I thought you might want to be occupied with perhaps letters," said the overlieutenant, "or with whatever prayers you pray. But you will cook our dinner?"

"Why not?" said Galpierri. "I have cooked all my life, or, at least, for so long as I can remember. It is my art. All artists love to be remembered. Why should not my last hour be spent over my art? It will be, I hope, more exquisite than ever."

The overlieutenant's mouth watered. "So," he said.

At the top of the steps he gave orders to the sentry that the prisoner was to be taken at once to the kitchen, where the sentry was to stand guard over him, till a corporal and a file of men should come to march him away at 5 to 8; and soon Galpierri got to work to cook his last meal. He began upon soup. It was a consommé lightly flavoured by hare, and fainter subtler flavours he added from many different herbs, some of which grew in his garden and others of which he knew where to find on the mountain. This he served with his own hand to eight or nine officers, pouring out for each into a small glass a certain light wine which he implored them to drink with the soup, since this wine, made by monks of great sanctity in an island off the coast, was especially suited to bring out the flavour of the soup and to do justice to it. So insistent was he that the Kommandant suddenly ordered him first to drink a glass of the wine himself; and this he did, drinking it to their healths. Then the officers all drank the wine, which they liked, and as Galpierri went back to his kitchen he heard them eating the soup with evident enjoyment. The sentry with his fixed bayonet, though he did not come into the room with the officers, remained all the while at the door, till he marched Galpierri back to the kitchen. "Be quick with your cooking," said the sentry there.

"No, no," said Galpierri. "It is for the officers and must be perfect. And for me, if I have little time, it is well that I do the best with it."

The German sentry shrugged his shoulders, not understanding the whims of Galpierri, or of any of his countrymen, or of the men of any other land but his own.

The next course was red mullet, over which, while a German orderly removed the soup-plates in the dining-room, he poured a sauce slightly flavoured with one of the wines of his country. And when this was done he carried in the dish and placed it before the Kommandant. He hurried then so fast out of the room that the sentry in the doorway put another hand to his rifle, bringing the bayonet forward. But it was only for two bottles of wine that he hurried, a wine made in the mountains at another monastery, also light, but sweeter than the one that went with the soup. From these bottles he poured out a glass for each officer, imploring them more earnestly than before to drink it with the red mullet; for he assured them that there was a harmony between red mullet and that wine, understood by those who had handed down to him the mysteries of his art, which was cooking. Once more the Kommandant sharply ordered him to drink some first himself, and this he did, drinking this time to the health and long life of the Fuehrer. The officers enjoyed the red mullet.

"It seems almost a pity," said one.

"Not at all," snapped the Kommandant, cutting him short. "This is war, and we can get as good a cook tomorrow from Transmontana."

The next course was loin of mutton, and over this Galpierri took especial pains. "Hurry up," said the sentry. "You've not all that time."

"For that very reason," Galpierri answered, "my work must be at its best."

"I did not mean you," said the sentry. "But officers cannot be kept waiting. Hurry up."

But Galpierri would not be hurried. And when the cooking of the loin of mutton was finished it had the perfection of all those things whose various creations are known as works of art. With the sentry marching behind him he laid the dish before the Kommandant, and went back for the wine. This time he brought four bottles, a darker heavier wine that was another of the mysteries of his country, which his countrymen make from the grapes of a vineyard in a valley of one of the mountains. He drank a small glass of it without being ordered to do so and poured it out for the officers into his large glasses and had little difficulty in urging them to drink it, as soon as they had tasted its heavy sweetness. Twice he returned and replenished their glasses, always followed close by the sentry, and then came back a third time with four more bottles, which he had little difficulty in persuading the officers to finish. Indeed, he merely left them alone, except for one officer who showed some slight reluctance to drink his fifth glass, to whom Galpierri quietly said bending over the officer's shoulder, "Perhaps our wine is a little strong for the officers of the Reich."

And that put the German on his mettle and no more was needed to be said. The Kommandant looked out through the window at the waning light, and then glanced at his watch. It was not a gesture that a guest should have made; but war is war, and its needs override good manners.

The next course was some little bird that the peasants of that land net in their marshes, one for each officer on a piece of toast soaked in some stronger wine. When he had set this before them he went away, and came back with a wicker basket with handles, which he and the sentry carried between them, full of champagne. The small birds were cooked to perfection, and flavoured again with rare herbs that he knew where to find on the mountain. The officers were eating them gladly when he came back with the basket-load of champagne, at which the Kommandant glanced; and Galpierri, with one of those intuitions that so easily visit men in the intensity of a last hour, saw doubt in his eye. Whether or not such a thing was possible, a fear touched Galpierri that the Kommandant might say that the gentlemen at his table had had wine enough. And were the Kommandant to order them to drink no more, his champagne must remain untouched. Galpierri was a man of humour and could tell whimsical stories, and at times had even made a political speech. Pathos was not a weapon often drawn from his armoury, but in politics all weapons are used that the tongue is able to wield, and now he poured out pathos. It was the most beautiful, the most touching, the most poetic speech of his life. He turned to the Kommandant, he said that he was an artist, that he was soon to die, that he was innocent, for he had never gone to the mountain except to pick herbs for his cooking, but that he did not ask for mercy on that account, but only for consideration for his art. Let his last work of art, he said, which was cooking, be perfect. The bird they were eating, flavoured with herbs from the mountain, to which he had only gone for that purpose, could not be supreme unless accompanied by the wine with which it was in so happy a harmony that no two things in the world were so perfectly matched as that bird and this vintage.

"It is not for mercy I ask," he repeated, "but for what to an artist must be even more, a memory on earth of one of his works of art. Let it be perfect, Herr Kommandant. You also will have a memory of one perfect dinner."

War and long preparation for war had so hardened the heart of the Kommandant that it gave no response. But there remained his stomach, and not to that was the appeal uttered in vain. The Kommandant saw the man's sincerity, he saw the tears in his eyes, he had evidence that he was a magnificent cook and took his word that the champagne was in that strange harmony with the little bird from the marshes that he had so ably described. So the Kommandant drank the champagne, and so did all his officers, glass after glass, as they ate that little bird. The Kommandant looked again at his watch, the hands of which were no longer so clear to him as they had been. But what did that matter? "I am afraid it is time," he said, looking up at Galpierri and at the sentry.

"Certainly, Herr Kommandant," said Galpierri, and hurried out of the room with the sentry behind him.

A few minutes passed, during which the Kommandant forgot Galpierri and was surprised to see him and the sentry come in again.

"Just a form for the Herr Kommandant to sign," said the cook, handing out a sheet of paper.

"What? What's it about?" said the Kommandant.

"Only a matter affecting the hotel, Herr Kommandant," said Galpierri.

The Kommandant did not want to be disturbed, but to be left with his memories of that excellent dinner, which he turned over meditatively as he sipped his champagne; and, having forgotten Galpierri, the man came back to him like a new topic, when he did not wish to be bothered with anything new.

"But, but I have no pen," said the Kommandant.

Galpierri handed him a fountain-pen at once. The Kommandant signed the paper and pushed it from him. The sentry stood silent.

"And one thing more," said Galpierri, handing another paper.

"No, no. I'll sign no more. Go away," said the Kommandant.

But the second paper was before him and the cook was still standing there. So he signed it and threw the pen on the floor and turned back to his fine champagne, while an impatient movement of his left hand signed to the sentry and Galpierri to go away to the execution ground.

But the first form was a pardon for Galpierri, stating that he had no complicity with the brigands on the mountain, having only gone there to pick herbs; and the second was a pass over any frontier, of which there were several near. Nobody took any notice as Galpierri walked out of the room with his pardon, except one officer who was well awake and alert. Galpierri caught his eye as he walked past him, and saw that he knew everything. What would he do, the cook wondered? He thought he knew the Germans through and through. But he could not tell. It would not do to hurry. He walked on wondering. The German officer winked. So Galpierri winked too, and walked out of the room with his pardon. And very soon he was back again on the mountain, where he was a leader of those that the Germans called brigands. He never used his pass to cross any frontier, but the possession of it gave him a feeling that his retreat was safeguarded, and that feeling gave to his exploits a new daring, at which the Germans wondered.

The Awakening

A week-end in the country with friends, grass all round him on sandy land on which harebells were swinging while the late summer glowed, was a wonderful change for Alfred Binnet from the hard pavements of London and the work and the crowd and the noise. And yet he was uneasy, for, to sum up the whole situation, he felt that he was a low-brow, while these friends of his, whatever they were, understood things which to him were completely mysterious. For instance the lines,

> Infinity is not infinitude,
> So far as I am able to make out,
> In a manner of speaking,

meant nothing to him at all, whereas to those friends of his, as well as thousands of others, they were deep and rich with great poetry. Those lines had already been so widely accepted, with the whole work of Pornick who wrote them, that it was no use for Alfred Binnet to say that they were not great poetry, and he could only inwardly bewail his own inability to be stirred and exalted by them. He had brought with him on his little visit a book of poetry that he could understand, something that he regarded as a primer, hoping that a careful study of that would lead him to higher things and perhaps ultimately to a proper appreciation of Pornick. The book was the Odes of Keats, and as soon as he was left alone in the smoking-room he pulled it out of his pocket and began to read, and was delighted to find that at least he could be stirred by the beauty of that. But it was a delight that was very short-lived for his host came back to the smoking-room, and, seeing what he was reading, at once said: "No, no, no. Really not that. No, no, my dear fellow. Quite outmoded."

And Binnet slipped the offending book hastily into his pocket.

"No, no," said his host. "It is Pornick who is being read now, and several young fellows inspired by him who are coming on very nicely.

But Keats, no, no. He is as out-of-date as Shakespeare. No, no, Keats won't do."

So mournful an expression came over Binnet's face that his host said: "Never mind, you'll get to like Pornick."

And Binnet could only shake his head mournfully.

"Yes, you will," his host went on. "And luckily you will have an opportunity that may be a great help to you. One of his greatest works, 'Mud on the Mantelpiece', has been set to music, and the musician who did it is coming down here tomorrow to play it over. He is going to play in the drawing-room, and I think that will help you to see the melody that there is in Pornick and may light up, as it were, his deeper profundities, so that you will be able to see them. We have a few friends coming to hear him. I think you will like it."

But Alfred Binnet did not like the prospect, although he did not say so. He knew too well that everybody invited would be someone well able to understand depths that he had never plumbed.

When dinner came that day it was an uneasy meal, the uneasiness that cramped the conversation of Binnet being the natural uneasiness that he felt in the presence of this too-intellectual host and hostess, multiplied by the number of intellectuals that he feared to meet to-morrow. And they, who should have been dissipating that uneasiness, as any host and hostess should, could not easily do so, because of an uneasiness of their own, one that they tried to confine to themselves without troubling their guest. It was a very simple matter for them to make a mystery about, but what was worrying them, what they were taking so much trouble to keep to themselves, was an oppressive doubt as to whether their piano was worthy of the musician they had invited, whether it was in good enough tune, a thing they should have seen to long ago, but had put off until too late, as it seemed it must be now, for Sunday was coming.

In the drawing-room after dinner some cheerier conversation started, but was being constantly interrupted by the departure of the host from the room in order to telephone something about the piano; and, whatever news he got from the telephone, it did not seem to Binnet to have been anything very satisfactory. So they went on worrying about their piano, and, so far as Binnet could tell, nothing much seemed to have been decided. Next morning an air of uncertainty that had seemed to hang over the house appeared to have lifted a little, host and hostess were a little more cheerful now. Not so Binnet, for with every hour the time drew nearer when there would come into the house a large number of people, every one of them on an intellectual plane from which the profundities of modern verse were clearly visible, profundities into which poor Alfred Binnet could see no further than the ordinary eye can see down into mud. Lunch came with a more hopeful expression brightening on the faces of host and hostess, while gloom was settling on Binnet. In the early afternoon, earlier than he had expected it, the purr of the first motor arriving was heard, and Binnet, with the first excuse that he could invent, retired from the drawing-room into the smoking-room, which was next door. He believed that car to be bringing the first guest, but after a while, from where he sat in the smoking-room, he suddenly heard the notes of a piano. And now unembarrassed by the presence of men and women to whom, without anything to be said by them, he knew he was but a lowbrow, he hoped that by giving his whole mind to it, he might quietly learn something of the beauties of Pornick. He listened intently. One long reiterated note uttered its mournful sound, and the piece was begun. Whether the audience had arrived on foot and gone quietly into the drawing-room he did not know, but with all his energies concentrated on the music he did not hear any sound of them; and out of that music he tried to draw the message of Pornick. Pong, pong, pong, went that opening note, and then pook, pook, from a higher one, and then the pong, pong again, lifting its mournful voice. Monotony there was in it certainly and little melody, and yet from the sad notes he did gradually draw a message, that was the reward of his earnest intensity, and he felt that after all Pornick had something to say. His hostess had shown him the opening lines of the poem that the musician had set to music: they went like this:

> Void, void, void.
> My mind in it and my heart in it.
> And the void flowering
> With the voice of thus.

Under the influence of that mournful music he began to see a meaning and as a third note added its monotonous call he began to perceive a message. Another note struck up and then another, till Binnet felt sure at last that Pornick had something to say to him, something he would soon understand, some message that he might yet make his own, so that he could go among those people that were invited that afternoon, not quite the miserable mouse at a cat-show that he had felt himself before. Yes, at last under the influence of that music a meaning appeared and, even though unmelodious, blossomed and grew more clear. Pong, pong, pong, that sad note called out its message, till the moment came of Binnet's awakening, when he felt he so far understood Pornick that now he could dare to mix with a band of his devotees. Stirred by his new hope he rose then on the instant and entered the drawing-room. To his astonishment there was no audience there except him alone. The man at the piano glanced round at him, but continued tapping his monotonous note. Something in the man's air as he glanced at him, something perhaps in his mournful aloof music, made him see that he was not expected in that room, nor expected to stay. Then he heard a voice through the door, that came from the dining-room. So the musician, thought Binnet, must be left alone in the melancholy atmosphere that his reiterated note was building sadly around him. There was much that he did not yet understand in modern poetry, and this must be one of the strange conditions under which it was set to music. He went on without a word and into the dining-room, treading on tiptoe. There were his host and hostess, and not a guest but himself. "I am very sorry I interrupted . . ." began Binnet.

"That's all right," said his hostess. "We are sitting in here till he's finished. James was very lucky to get him last night on the 'phone. He kindly came to help us, although it is Sunday."

"But, but," said Binnet, "I understood you invited him long ago."

"O, the musician," his hostess said. "He won't be here for another half hour. That's the piano-tuner."

A Goat in Trousers

A fog that had been lying over the fields was going away at last along the horizon, with queer weird shapes rising up from it as it went; but for which I might never have troubled with the fancies that what I saw in a field gave rise to, though what I saw was odd in itself. It was a goat wearing trousers. They were good grey trousers with dark stripes in them, and he had a smart black jacket too, and even a hat, jammed down on one of his horns, which came out through the brim. Boys play all kinds of tricks, with most of which one would have no reason to interfere; but, when I looked close and saw the quality of the trousers, it seemed to me that somebody might be put to loss and considerable expense, and that the unsuitable joke, or whatever it was, should be enquired into. So with a view to reporting what I had seen I opened the gate of the field, which was the end of an iron bedstead, so that I need hardly say that this was in Ireland, for this convenient use of old broken-down bedsteads, so far as I know, is scarcely found elsewhere. And indeed the far blue shapes of the Dublin mountains looked serenely over the field and that strangely-apparelled goat, and me going up to it to pursue my enquiries. And the first thing that I saw as I entered the field was a boot of patent leather which I supposed had been kicked off. I don't know where the other one was. And when I got near the goat it turned its head towards me. And I looked into its yellow eyes, and it looked right into mine, and seemed for a moment as if it had something to tell me; and then with a sudden shake it turned its head away, as though neither I nor my enquiries could ever be any use to it. And from all the enquiries I made, not only on the spot, but from many men, this is what seems to have happened. Those pale-blue distant mountains must have looked down also on two statesmen walking along a street in Dublin on one of those days on which their calm grave faces looked clearly all the way down some streets of the city. And, as they went, one statesman said to the other, "It is a shocking thing that, with the great position that Ireland now has, there should be anyone in the country still believing in wise women and witchcraft and all that nonsense, when we should be showing an example to the nations."

"It is indeed," said the other.

"We must frame a bill," said the first statesman, "and get it passed into law as quickly as possible, making it an offence to take any fees for any pretended cures of man or beast, or anything of the sort. I'd like to make it a punishable offence even to talk of such things; but we can't do that. But if we stop those women receiving any fees, we will soon stop the whole nonsense."

And the other statesman was silent awhile, and then he said, "No. We can't do it by laws. The cure for it is education. It's all childish nonsense. But stamp it out in the minds of children, and by the time that they grow up the thing will be done with for ever."

"You're right," said the other. "And it's what we'll do. We'll send down a man, for a start, to give a lecture about it to every school in Leinster, and to explain to them clearly in simple words that wise women are all just nonsense, and witches and all the rest of them, and that they are only helpless old women trying to frighten children."

So a man was sent down from Dublin to go to every school in Leinster, and would lecture for a bit in a school, and go on to another as soon as he had convinced all there. And in the far gaze of the Dublin mountains men were saying, "Isn't it a good thing to have a man down from Dublin teaching the children sense?"

And the answer would come, "Sure it is. Isn't it time they learned?"

And another would say, "It was all very well in the old days, putting horns and tail on a man, or any other queer shape; but a belief in all them things doesn't suit modern ideas, and it is time it was put a stop to."

"It is indeed. Sure, you're right, and it is indeed. At the same time, wouldn't it be a pity to annoy the wise women overmuch? For who is there but they that has any cure for the falling of the palate? Aye, and for other ills and evils. Sure, who would there be to help us in our need, if that man were to incense them so that one night they all went away to wherever such people go? I only ask the question, meaning no harm."

"Isn't there the doctor?" said someone.

"Ah, doctors don't know everything," came the answer.

And heads were nodded at that. And the mood of the men changed, as the mood of the mountains changes, watching from beyond Dublin; and they began to doubt the wisdom of the man who had come to the school of their village to teach the children sense.

But the wise women were troubled. For the rumour ran all through Leinster that all their witchcraft was only to frighten children and that there was nothing in it at all.

The lecturer was a man named Mr. Finnegan; and after speaking to the children of the school of Donnisablane he was put up for the night by Michael Murphy, the young schoolmaster of that village. And the rumour of his coming had run for miles round and told everyone that he would be there. And there it was that Mrs. Garganey, who was a wise woman, had talked with Mrs. Gallagher, who was another, as soon as the rumour had reached her, and said to her, "What is to be done? What is to be done at all?"

And Mrs. Gallagher had brewed a pound of tea only the day before, and it was simmering in the great kettle on her hearth, which, small though her thatched cottage was, had an ampler space than any hearth that you are likely to see in any big house in England. And Mrs. Gallagher said as they drank their tea, darker than brownest chestnut, "I have answered many queer riddles and read strange destinies. And so have you, Mrs. Garganey. But for this we must send for the Wise Woman of Galway. For there is none but she that can deal with this man from Dublin, who is down here putting wrong ideas into the heads of the children, and telling them that we and all our most secret arts are nothing at all, and that what we learned from our great-grandmothers, and that they learned from the old time and from the great witches of those days, is nothing only mere nonsense. And he, what is he but only a little clerk puffed up with his self-importance, and knowing no more of where the big winds rise, or of what news they carry, than he knows of the growth of a buttercup. But he has the authority of them that be in Dublin behind him, and there is no-one able to deal with him but that great witch, the Wise Woman of Galway. So let us send for her, and see what shape she will put on him."

And send for her they did, however their message was carried, and she had harnessed her ass-cart at once and had driven by town and bog and meadow and wood all the way across Ireland, and was now come to Donnisablane. And Mrs. Gallagher said to her whatever such people say when they meet, and made whatever obeisance; and brought her to her house and put her ass in her bit of a stable and gave the great witch a cup of her dark tea. And Mrs. Garganey came to that house too, and the three conferred. And they spoke of strange transformations. And then the Wise Woman of Galway told them what they should do. And about that time a look came over the Dublin mountains, as though they all crept nearer to listen; so that their very hedgerows could be seen below, and their glens and valleys above, as they show when rain is coming. But it was more than the rain that was coming. For the Wise Woman of Galway had bid summon the wise women from all the province of Leinster, and it was they that were drawing nearer. They harnessed their ass-carts at that summons, and came trotting. And those that had no ass for their journey ran. And on the night of which I tell, whatever magic may be, there were more of them that make it in Donnisablane than in any other townland in all Ireland. And they came with a great cauldron, and drew all round the house of Michael Murphy, with Mr. Finnegan inside, and lit a fire under their cauldron among the trees of an orchard, and chanted their incantations and made their spells and did whatever witches do. And Michael Murphy looking out of a little window saw what was going on, and he ran to Mr. Finnegan and said, "Mr. Finnegan, sir, clear out of this and change your name and get to foreign parts. For the witches are after you."

And the man from Dublin said, "Now, you know that is all nonsense. Didn't I tell your children so this afternoon?"

"I know, sir. I know," said Michael Murphy. "And you put it very well. But look out of that window now towards the orchard. Look out; only don't let them see you."

And the man from Dublin looked out. "I see," he said. "I see there is something over there in the orchard."

"And it's all round us," said Michael Murphy. "Only there's a little path that runs along under the hedge of my garden, and you could get away by that. Only go quick, and go to foreign parts; for they're after you."

"I see," said the man from Dublin. "Mind you, it's just as I said; witches and cauldrons and spells and all that kind of thing are just nonsense. At the same time, to avoid any unpleasantness, I will perhaps do as you say."

Then he left the house, and that is the last that was ever seen of him.

I have made very thorough enquiries into the case; too thorough perhaps, for they have established three separate theories. Some believe Mr. Finnegan fled to France, or one of those foreign countries, changing his name and his clothes, however his clothes got on to the goat. And then many believe that the wise women, whose whole profession he threatened, closed round him at the back of the garden and murdered him and put him into the cauldron in the orchard and boiled him, all but his clothes, and then dressed up the goat in the way that I saw. That is a theory that has been put to the police; and it is for them to investigate it, not I. But they seem to have investigated very half-heartedly, and with no sympathy from anyone in the townland, where men were heard to say, "Why can't the gardai get on with their work, and leave the wise women alone?" A sentiment with which the gardai almost seemed to agree. For, from all I hear, they questioned very few of the old women, and those politely and briefly.

The third theory, and the one perhaps the most widely held, though men say little about it, is that Mr. Finnegan is still alive and wearing his own clothes in fields around Donnisablane. But that is a theory of which I need say no more, for my readers would never believe it. Nor could I believe it myself anywhere away from the influence of the South-west wind, full of the scent of turf-smoke, blowing by old gnarled willows away over wastes of bog.

A Breeze at Rest

Of voices that rarely speak, voices of simple and ancient things that sometimes sleep for years, and then wake on some summer evening as birds are going to rest, is poetry mainly made. Or one of those voices may shrill through the night, or call across the dawn to us, or indeed speak at any time or in any place, or be dumb for a whole generation. The one of which I will tell I heard by a Kentish roadside, while the last of a saffron gloaming was lit by the evening star. It was in a hollow of a roadside hedge, a little curve like the mihrab in Mahommedan mosques, receding a bit from the road between two clumps of wild roses. There in this sheltered place on a warm still day I saw the stir of a breeze. It only moved across that little curve, never passing either pillar of wild roses, and as I watched it moving the green tendril of a convolvulus, it fell to rest as quietly as it had arisen, and spoke to me. I think it had noticed my interest in the wild roses, or in a cluster of scabious that grew below them; for it said, "I know all the flowers along this hedge. Know them for miles. It's full of wild roses now."

"What are you?" I asked.

"I'm a breeze," it said, "the breeze that runs along beside the buses, all down this side of the road. I have a lot of work to do. Sometimes I come to a gap where there is a gate, or another road runs in. I have nothing to do there. But most of the way I have a great deal to do."

"More than I'd think, I suppose," I said to encourage it.

"A lot more," it answered.

"And what do you do mostly?" I asked.

"I run along the hedge beside the buses," it said. "Sometimes I shake down dead leaves, sometimes I shake off frost; but just at present I shake the wild roses and float away the petals that they don't want, and wave the heads of the foxgloves and all kinds of flowers, and loosen the seeds of the grasses and scatter them under the hedge. Of course at the moment I'm resting, but all kinds of work waits for me."

"I should think you've a lot to do," I said, "looking after the things you mentioned." And my remark had the effect I intended, of egging him on to say more.

"Oh, that's nothing," it answered. "Nothing to what I have to do. I have to wave the willowherb, and the big blue borage, and valerian and evening primrose. There are big flowers for you, and all waiting for me to come by. And sometimes I cool the Canterbury bells, which they want in this hot weather more than you'd think. And I run along and whisper to the elms, the little elms in the hedges, and brush the dust from the leaves of the hedge-maple, that have small red spots on them, you know. And the foxgloves and mulleins lean over as I come: they all know me. And there's the wild clematis all the way: I set their tendrils dancing with the convolvulus all in and out of the hazels. And there are sycamore, thorn and yew, all watching for the bus to come by, and waiting for me to come running along beside it."

"I expect you do a great deal for them," I said.

"Well, yes," it answered, "I blow the scent of the elder all along them, and the sweet heavy odour of privet; and sometimes when we come near cottage gardens I scent the air with syringa. And I wave big flowers that look over garden walls, and stir bunches of roses. The Madonna lilies sway when I come by, and I carry their scent away far down the road. I often rest in this hollow between wild roses; but never for long. There'll be another bus soon, and then I shall have to be off again. I have a great deal to do."

"The flowers must be waiting for you," I said.

"They are," it answered, "and the leaves of the hazels and elms, and the small moths. If it wasn't for me to blow them, there'd be only the big winds; cousins of mine, but very lazy: sometimes they don't come this way for a week."

"What about bus-strikes?" I asked.

"If there were a bus-strike," it answered, "I would run along without them."

"At the same hours?" I asked.

"O, certainly," it said. "I am never late."

And I heard just then the hoot of a distant bus; and I thought that the dim grey form of the little breeze grew slightly more visible. Then the bus appeared round a curve, and the breeze jumped up and ran out between the wild roses, elbowing each as it ran, and scampered away along the left-hand hedge.

A Channel Rescue

The senior clerk of the branch of Cobblar's Bank at Shellsea was walking one Saturday afternoon in July along the sand as the tide was running out, meaning to go to a cinema, when he saw a swimmer nearly half a mile from the shore. It seemed dangerous to be so far out, especially as the turn of the tide had set up a current that was drifting the swimmer along the coast to the right. He pulled out a small pair of opera glasses which he always took to the cinema, and he had not watched the swimmer's slow and slanting headway for long, when he saw that it was a woman. A woman half a mile out, with the tide against her, and that current that always ran with the outgoing tide! William Ablit was not a strong swimmer, but he had a strong sense of romance, and he pulled off his shoes at once and then his jacket and threw them down anywhere, and went into the sea without even taking his watch out of his pocket. Then he noticed a little launch not very far from the lady, and he stood in the water and shouted, but no one on board seemed to notice. There were only two men on board, and he realized that little waves could easily hide the head of the swimmer from them. So he stopped and shouted again. But there must have been more wind than he thought, for they did not seem to hear him. It was a long walk at first, and it was some while before the water was over his knees. He did not go straight out, because of the current that was all the while slanting the swimmer away to the right; so William Ablit slanted to his right too. Once more he stopped and shouted to the men in the boat; but a rock or two began to show their green heads over the tide, and the boat came no nearer. Yet still the swimmer was obviously in deep water, and presently Ablit was out of his depth too. The lady was swimming strongly in spite of the current, but she was too far out for safety, and with that current running there was no saying how far down the coast she would go, or whether she could ever get ashore without help. But help was coming and, with the aid of the same current, Ablit drew near to her faster than he expected. Then she saw him. She swam on for a few strokes more, then gave a glance round at the launch and began to fail all of a sudden. He reached her just in time. How to hold up drowning people was not a thing that he knew much about, but his presence appeared to encourage her and she swam with stronger strokes, which helped them both. How dangerous it had been for her to be so far out he realized now more clearly than ever, for he himself felt weak in the grip of that current. But, just as he felt he could do no more for either himself or the lady, he felt a rock with one foot, and, far from where they started, the current had drifted them to where his feet were soon upon good firm sand, and for the next two hundred yards he carried the lady, till he put her down on the shore. Her thanks were profuse, in a strong French accent. She turned and waved twice at the men in the launch, with what Ablit supposed to be gestures of contempt because they had not tried to save her, and the launch went away. She was young, barely more than twenty, Ablit thought, and had that clear profile which in England we associate with Norman descent, but which across the Channel is common, and curls of chestnut brown strayed here and there from her bathing-cap. Ablit interrupted her thanks to say, "Have you been long in the water?"

"Not very long," said the lady, with a look in her lovely brown eyes that seemed too childishly innocent for any exact estimate of the passing of time.

"Was it far from here?" he asked her.

"Not very," she said.

"Then we must get there quickly," he told her, "before you get cold."

"That is the difficulty," she said.

"But what?" he asked.

"I cannot now remember exactly where it was," she replied.

"You cannot remember?" he asked.

"Not exactly," she said.

"But where do you think it was?" he insisted.

She puckered her forehead in thought. "It must have been one of those bathing-huts," she said. "But I can't remember the number."

And she pointed to where the little canvas huts stood in two long rows on the shore away to the left.

"Perhaps you will remember when you see it," said he.

"Yes, yes," she said. "I will remember then."

And she started away towards the row of huts. And he was coming with her, but she said, "No. I am all right now. I must get to my clothes and we will meet later. Tell me your name and where you live, and I will come back."

He told her, and she told her name, Marguerite Estelles, but not where she lived, and as he began to ask her that she ran off alone to the bathing-huts, calling over her shoulder, "At tea-time tomorrow. That is 5 o'clock. No?" Then she was gone.

Ablit stood there on the sand for a while in his wet clothes, wondering. He had never seen her in the town before, though of course there were many others in that big resort whom he had never seen. He lived with his mother in a house in a little square, three sides of which were all houses, and the fourth side a view of the sea. It was not like any London square, because no road came through the corners, and one of those corners, with the downs rising behind it, sheltered his small home. There he went and told the story to his mother, who was stirred by the romance of the rescue and a little wistful at the thought that from such a romance might come the loss to her of her son. And then she asked questions. William only wanted to talk of the girl's beauty; but his mother wanted to know what she did, and why, if she was French, she lived in Shellsea, and where in Shellsea she lived. To all this her son could only reply that she was coming to tea tomorrow, when she would tell them everything. And tomorrow came, as it does, and just before 5 o'clock as they both looked out of the window of Mrs. Ablit's front room along the pavement towards the sea, they saw a very neatly dressed girl walking alone towards them. And it was Marguerite. She walked up the steps of Mrs. Ablit's house, as it seemed rather shyly, and then rang the bell. The parlourmaid let her in and then she was in the drawing-room before Mrs. Ablit and her son, dressed in very well-fitting French clothes and looking wonderfully unlike the weary swimmer he rescued. But it was the same lovely face lit by changing smiles, which had so charmed William yesterday; and the chestnut hair that had only peeped from her bathing-cap shone now in profusion around her neat hat and her forehead. William introduced her, and his mother greeted her and welcomed her to Shellsea, but her greetings soon turned to questions. Did she like Shellsea? "Very much," said Marguerite Estelles. Had she lived there long? "Not very." Where was she living? "In the Grand Hotel," said Marguerite.

"The Grand!" exclaimed Mrs. Ablit. "I am sure you are very comfortable there."

"Very."

"And do your father and mother live at the Grand?"

"Not at the Grand."

"You are French, are you not?" said Mrs. Ablit.

"O, yes," replied Marguerite.

"And do your father and mother live in England?"

"No. In France."

"I see."

But Mrs. Ablit did not see. There was nothing to see. And politely, and even talkatively, Marguerite Estelles gave no information whatever. There it was. And there it remained over the teacups till the dregs of the tea were cold. Mrs. Ablit's questions continued as much as politeness would allow, and the rapier of Marguerite's tongue parried them all. Then she rose to go. William and Mrs. Ablit looked at each other. What was to be done? William was in love with the girl: they both knew that. But who was she? Where were her parents? One could not marry a mermaid.

Marguerite had left them so gaily, full of thanks to William for her rescue, and to Mrs. Ablit for kind hospitality. But she left them puzzled and glum. Mrs. Ablit asked more questions of her son; but they were all of no avail, for he knew no more of the girl than she did. William knew her beauty with a different knowledge from that of his mother, knowing it with the sure eyes of youth; but his mother saw the same beauty reflected, as it were, in her experience of life, and knew just what that beauty seemed to the eyes of William. But there was no more to be said; nothing but guesses; but they were all idle.

Next morning William Ablit walked early into the town before he went to the bank, walking with no particular purpose along the seafront, though some magnet drew his feet all the while to the Grand Hotel. And then as he walked he saw suddenly under the lee of the pier the launch that had turned away as Marguerite landed. He recognized it at once and saw two men on board her. A drowning man can hardly expect straws to support him, and yet it is said that he clutches at them, and in all this mystery William Ablit clutched at those two men, who at least had seen Marguerite, although at a distance; and he knew nobody else, beside himself and his mother, who had. He could ask about her at the hotel, but what did hotels know of anybody? They were only numbers there. He would ask those two men. So he turned on to the pier and walked till he was alongside the little launch and only a few yards away, and hailed one of the men. The man looked up at once and seemed ready to talk; but when he asked about Marguerite Estelles they could not understand English. So Ablit spoke in such French as he knew; but the man's answers were vague and he turned to the other man, but could get no more information from him. So he went to the Grand Hotel and asked about her there; but they only referred to a book and said that Mademoiselle Estelles was staying there and gave the number of her room. Then he went back to the bank, and at four o'clock returned to the Grand, at which he and Marguerite had arranged to have tea. As he approached it he saw the two men from the launch coming out of the hotel. It was not the kind of coincidence that could be without meaning, and he felt sure that they had come to see Marguerite. So they knew her. And William Ablit stopped them and questioned them further in French. But their answers were vague at first and, when he pressed them for more information, they spoke rapidly and then dropped into patois. After all, he had no right to question them, and they evidently did not mean him to understand them. In the lounge he found Marguerite with tea all ready for him and she was charming; but, although her evasions were more delicate than those of the men in the boat, he got no more information about herself from her than he had from them. Her shining eyes and all her fascination lured him towards her all the time and towards happiness, and all the while there came down between him and her that mystery darker and darker, shutting him off from happiness. Sometimes she checked his questions by profuse thanks to him for having rescued her from the sea, and he left her that afternoon knowing nothing more about her.

That evening he and his mother talked it all over again. But all they knew of the girl was that she was French and on a visit to Shellsea, and that she was beautiful. Again next day William Ablit had tea at the Grand with Marguerite Estelles and walked in the garden afterwards.

And that day among the myrtles they got engaged. For, mystery or no mystery, he was going to marry her. When he told all this to his mother she was sad, even though she had seen it coming, for though she liked the girl very much, she definitely declared that her son could not marry a mystery, and that far more must be known about how Marguerite came to Shellsea and why, before she could give her consent. Her William was downcast and puzzled and, odd though it seems, some hours passed before it occurred to him to go to the girl and tell her exactly what the difficulty was. And this he did the next day, instead of having his lunch when the lunch-hour came at the bank. He went to the Grand and found her, and began to put the question before her with clumsy sentences; and he had not got far when Marguerite told him suddenly the whole story. She had not really swum from the bathing-huts; but she had said she had because she was so touched and grateful when she saw William swimming out to save her, that she had not the heart to tell him any other story. She had been taught that it was wrong to tell a lie, and she knew it well, and she would never tell one again. But surely the heart came first, and she could not make a brave young man feel ridiculous. No, she had come from the other side really. From France; not from the bathing-huts. And her manager in the launch said she had made excellent time. But she had told him to go away and had not allowed him to publish it; because what would William have thought if he had learned that he had not rescued her, when all the credit in the world was due to him for his brave desire to do so? So she had given up her credit for the Channel swim, for the credit that he deserved so much more. Was it wrong? After all, she could swim the Channel one day again. It was only La Manche.

IN THE GOVERNOR'S PALACE

It is years since I heard this story. Yet I still clearly remember it. I don't know why I remember this one so clearly, when I have forgotten so many others, many of them probably more startling and more dramatic; but I cannot say, having forgotten them. I think it was the Professor's grave face, and the contrast between that and his story, which left it shining so vividly in my memory, when more exciting things, as I have said, were forgotten. It was one evening at a university where he lectured on law, that I heard the story, where twenty or so undergraduates, members of some society in the University, were gathered together after supper to debate the merits of one of those lesser poets who lived like lonely stars in the dark of the space between the death of Milton and birth of Keats; and Professor Horbin and I were guests. I arrived before the Professor and heard something about him. There was whiskey and soda, and one thing and another, and the intention of the young men was to press drinks on the Professor with the object of getting him to talk about far parts of the world, in which he had travelled. For he was one of those Englishmen, of whom one hears every now and then, and sometimes even sees, that look as if Southall or Sydenham were about as far as they had travelled from London, who at one time or another have known Africa better than most of us know Hyde Park after dark. Of course there are mysteries in both these places, but Africa seems to us more romantic, and that is what these undergraduates wanted to hear about; for the Professor was one of those men. Well, that was the intention of a few of them, to give him several drinks and so get his story; but others, and they turned out to be right, said that you might lead a horse to water, and you might even make him drink, but it was no use trying that game with Professor Horbin. And so it turned out, and the evening seemed about to fall a little flat, when, feeling sorry for the young fools, who had so cheerfully planned to bait their trap with whiskey, I asked the Professor myself if he didn't sometimes feel that a little alcohol in the evening,—and whatever one does say of it on such occasions.

"No," he said. "No. I don't say I always avoided a drink as an absolute rule. But I got a great shock once, and it left me with the idea that we, or perhaps I should say I, have no way of computing the exact effect of alcohol. I used to think that one glass of champagne had no effect whatever, except to quench one's thirst, and that another did one no harm, or even a third; and then one day I found out that there is no exact measure by which one can calculate any invariable effect. There are so many other influences affecting the case, you see; and so . . ."

"What was the shock, sir?" asked a young undergraduate near him.

"Well, I will tell you," said the Professor. "I was in Africa, more or less in the middle of it; and airships, of the Zeppelin type, were new in those days, and I was given a journey in one of them, of course as a passenger, across most of Africa, going in from the North. We were stopping at a number of places, and I had letters of introduction everywhere, and it promised to be a most interesting trip, even apart from the fact that we crossed the Sahara, a land so romantic and mythical that the Arabs that live in it do not believe it has any other side, but hold that it goes on for ever and ever. Well, of course we did not contradict them, but left their brown tents and flew southwards. Had we come down in it in those days through any defect in our engines, there would have been no possibility of ever drinking water again, but we crossed it in perfect safety. We did however come down in the sudd, that is to say a marsh of enormous magnitude, and no more travelled than the Sahara. Africa has some extraordinary contrasts, a fringe of cultivated land, then the enormous desert, then that vast desolation of reeds, and sometimes floating islands, that goes by the name of the sudd; then a couple of thousand miles of forest; then something very like the desert again, the Karoo with its little dry bushes and rocky kopjes; then finally Table Mountain, and no more land after that until the Antarctic. We came down in the sudd because the engine stopped working."

"And what happened, sir?" asked one of undergraduates.

"Oh, nothing much," said the Professor, "nothing much. We were only two miles from the dry land, and there was a good clay bottom to the water, which made perfectly good walking, although we were up to our waists."

The undergraduate gave a kind of a shiver, but the Professor laughed.

"It wasn't cold, I can assure you. Very much the reverse. In fact without the water I doubt if I could have done those two miles. The heat was quite indescribable, to me who was not used to it, and coming to it straight out of the cool air. Two things alone made the walk possible, the cool water up to one's waist, and the sight of the Governor's palace barely three miles away; less than a mile, that is to say, from the edge of the marshes in front of us. We could see its gilded spires before us, and its oriental domes. For the nation that had grabbed that part of Africa held a very fanciful people, and they loved building like that and outorienting the Orient; or it may have been mere policy, trying to show that they were as eastern at heart as any follower of Mahomet in Africa. I knew that in that splendid and rather Arabian palace I should be given a good dinner and something to drink, and a change of clothes and a bed. When I call it Arabian I don't mean so much the Arabia of desert and rock and mirage, that we may sometimes see in our travels, as the Arabia of Sinbad the Sailor, of which we may read. Sometimes we came on invisible streams called khors, and that took us up to our necks, with our faces among the blue waterlilies; but that only cooled us, and we needed cooling. And at last we got to the shore. It was good dry land at once, with trees on it with red trunks, and white fish-eagles sitting upon their branches, and scarlet birds and bright blue birds all darting about, and the spires of the Governor's palace gleaming close in the evening.

"The mud at the edge of the marshes was all dried in the sun, and through it here and there ran rows of little pits, like the craters of small bombs, the tracks of elephants that had gone by when the mud was wet. The walking of that last three quarters of a mile was quite easy, but it didn't seem so to me. I had come straight from London into the climate of Equatoria. We must have looked awful sights when we arrived, drenched with two miles of the marshes and covered with sweat besides, and exhausted and muddy and stooping. But the Governor was expecting us, and that may have helped him to guess who we really were, and not to think we were a party of savages who had somehow stolen the clothes of some English scarecrows. For he came down his marble steps with some of his staff when we were more than a hundred yards away, and came out to meet us and spoke to us in English, with fine flowery phrases that sounded a little lost for not being dressed in the gracious garb of the language of his country. I apologized for my appearance, but he would hear nothing derogatory said of the clothes we were wearing, though he said that, purely for the sake of dryness, he would provide us with other suits. And we were taken to bedrooms and given white trousers and jackets, brightened along the seams and over the pockets and shoulders with patches of gold lace. It was now coming near the time, which in those lands is about 6 o'clock all the year round, when the sun goes below the horizon and all the daylight suddenly rushes down with it, and a coolness comes, like a strange guest into Africa, and the hyenas begin to howl.

"We were given less than one hour to have a bath and to dress. And then I should have liked to have gone to bed; but there was to be a banquet at seven, and of course I never for an instant thought seriously of going to bed at seven and rejecting the hospitality of the representative of a friendly country. I only hoped that there were not going to be speeches. But there were. The suits they gave us fitted us very well, and the gold lace didn't look in the least absurd, compared with the splendour of the Governor. In fact I was rather glad of it, since I sat next to him, and somehow it helped. Of course I had to keep awake through the dinner, and a glass of champagne helped there. On a second glass I made the little speech that I had to make, and it sounded a good deal grander than it was, because I made it, so far as I could, in the Governor's own language, and there is something about the pronunciation of its vowels alone that seems to me to bring it nearer to music than anything that we talk. I don't know if my pronunciation was clear enough to be understood, or even if I used quite the right words. Certainly the applause when I sat down was immense. But I knew that that was merely their hospitality, and the courtesy that has been an attribute of their people for ages. I determined to have no more than two glasses of champagne, thirsty and tired though I was, and I believe that I kept to my determination. Well, I can't say; but I believe I did. Perhaps not. Well, I don't know. Walking two miles through an equatorial marsh may not seem much, and probably is not much; but it seemed so to me. To people who live by the sudd it must seem nothing; but I was straight out from London. It was that walk that did it. And now I come to think of it, I had a small glass of a thing called Vino del Valdes, or something like that, a liqueur that I had never tasted before, but a wonderful thing on which to make a speech in a language you don't know, if ever you have to do it. Two glasses of champagne and this queer liqueur; I think that was all. And then the Governor stood up and made a speech. And after that a band broke out with a roar, playing the anthem of the Governor's country. And I realized an awful thing at that moment, the terrible shock that I spoke of. I realized that I couldn't walk two miles in the equatorial sun through a marsh. You may say I had done it. May be. But I realized that I couldn't. Without the champagne I should have completely collapsed. With it I was, there is no use in mincing words, with it I was drunk. Not drunk in a gutter, where I should have liked to have been, but the senior member of our party from England drunk in the presence of the chief representative in Africa of that respected and friendly power, drunk while he was doing all he could to show me the hospitality for which his people are famous, and drunk at a moment when there was a dilemma before me demanding the exercise of the soundest judgement, such as only goes with sobriety. It is little wonder that I decided wrong. The dilemma was simply this: whether to sit discourteously while everyone else stood, and to ignore the national anthem of my distinguished host beside me, or whether to stand up when a properly reasoned judgement would have told me I was unable to do so. It was the champagne in me that decided, and of course wrong, wrong as always. That's why I have given it up. The champagne said: Of course you can do it. Be a sportsman at least, and try. So I tried. I stood right up as straight as the Governor. I saw his great gold sash below me sweeping down from his shoulder and slanting across his chest. For one instant I stood beside him as straight as he. And then fatigue came over me with a rush. Well, call it what you will; I will not mince words. And I made things worse by a desperate effort to save myself, to save the whole situation when it was too late to be saved. I clutched at the table, and everything came away. Silver dishes and fruit and a gold dessert-plate and a length of the table-cloth and I, were all lying there on the floor. And while my tired wits were fumbling to find words for some kind of apology I heard the melodious words of the Governor's language saying, 'The honorable gentleman has been smitten slightly by the rays of the sun. Assist him to the chamber of his sleeping.'

"Still I had found no words to say. Words came abundantly a little later, all alone in the night; but not a word came then. And two great Nubians in white suits with gold lace lifted me gently up and half led me and half carried me out of the banquet hall, and across a courtyard walled with thatch, and strewn with broken white granite, to the room that I had been given. Their strong arms were round me on each side like the arms of giant nurses; and there was something very restful in being moved thus through the open air without any effort being required of my exhausted limbs, were it not for the tumult in my mind calling out one thing to me again and again, telling me that I had insulted the Governor of the land of a friendly power and lowered in his eyes the reputation of my own country. And awful variations of this thought rambled on and on after I had gone, or been put, to bed. For though you might think that in my exhausted state I would have fallen asleep, it was not so. My mind, that awhile ago had seemed so fuddled, had become lucidly clear and turned out phrase after phrase, whose polished perfection surprised me even at the time; and all to do with one subject, and all no good. They were all of them explanations of what could not be explained, and apologies for behaviour for which no mere words could ever avail to atone. And not only that part of the mind that plans such phrases was clear, but every other perception. I heard the Nubians walk away when they left me. For long I heard each step of their sandalled feet. So well I remembered them that I could tell the step of one from the other, for there haunted me with a more than natural clearness the memory of the sound of their great feet, and the dragging sound of my own as they pulled me along between them. That was indeed the most dreadful memory that troubled the next two hours, the memory of the sound of my feet dragging over the court that was gravelled with broken granite, and the great slow strides of the Nubians patiently walking beside me. Those were the sounds that in my troubled mind, unnaturally alert and hopelessly wakeful, intruded themselves into every phrase and every circumlocution of my apology that I prepared for the following morning, as though words could in any way alter what had occurred. They were fine apologies, might I say even brilliant? But perfectly useless, as I recognized while I composed them. And all the while the memory of the footfall of the taller of the two Nubians, and the sound of the other stepping out to keep up with him, and the double shuffle of my own dragging feet, were echoing in my memory, sometimes faintly and sometimes louder, but all the time reminding me that I had been hospitably greeted by the Governor of that land, and had returned his kindness by behaviour for which I was swiftly inventing phrases to minimize it, which of course no phrases could do. And that they could never do it I recognized at last, but recognized that, though unavailing, an apology was still necessary. That was the most sensible thing I had thought of, and I settled down to compose the right sort of apology, something without excuses, bluntly expressing the most profound regret, and yet not too bluntly, for that would not go so well with the flowery language into which I hoped to translate it. I was getting it clear at last, and even translating it as I went along; and would have got what I wanted to say, were it not for that awful memory, with the everlasting repetition and echo of those sounds, about which I told you, the slow strides of the Nubians, recognizable from each other, and the dragging shuffle between them. So unnaturally clear were those three vivid sounds, that after a while the fear began to come to me that my mind would hold them for ever, and that what had happened might leave in my brain this horrible permanent echo. And this thought so greatly alarmed me that I even gave up my work upon my apology and listened for the thing that I feared, as though it were actually there. And it was. I heard the steps of the Nubians, the gigantic one and the smaller one, the same two Nubians undoubtedly; and not only that, but the dragging shuffle between them. Louder and louder grew the dreadful sound, like madness coming upon me in the night under the strange constellations that look on the centre of Africa. I sprang to the window and looked out, in the glow of those southern stars. And the Nubians were really there; and, the starlight twinkling along his golden sash and gleaming on his white tunic, the Governor was going to bed exactly as I had gone."

HARd HORSES

It was a tough horse, a tough hard horse, and as Charlie mounted it he felt that he was a tough hard man. He mounted and paused a few moments looking at the long grasses of the waste land around him: then he galloped. He did not hear the beat of hooves as he galloped, but, rather, a wild music. Looking down at the tall sere grasses, he saw them wave in the wind that was always in his face, sere grass that seemed never to change, so that it was easy for Charlie's imagination to picture a prairie that went on for ever and ever, over every horizon to the very end of the world. Behind him came more horses, hard and tough like his own, their hoof-beats drowned by the strange wild music that was never to stop while he galloped, but he little heeded them. Whether they pursued him or whether he led them was all one to him, caring for nothing in all the world but that swift gallop over unlimited plains, or plains that, if they had any limit whatever, stretched far beyond his imagination or knowledge. A few weeds raised their heads through the sunlight on the sere grass; a poppy flared beneath him an instant, and was left far behind. On on he rode over the prairies, on on galloped the herd of hard horses behind him, and still the strong wind rang with the strange music that haunted it. Far on before him he saw again the flare of a poppy; again it fell behind him. He listened, wondering whether the howl of wolves would come over the levels of that unending plain; but nothing lurked in those grasses, and there seemed no life as far as the eye could reach, except the horses behind him; and no sound, if wolves there were, rose above the wild sound of the music. Where the music came from he no more enquired than he enquired of the source of the wind: both shrilled on and on, and both seemed eternal.

Again a poppy lighted the pale bright glare of the grasses: again it was left behind. Charlie calculated the passing of many hours, and still his steed did not tire. Once more a poppy flared at him and the herd of those hard horses; once more it dropped behind them. He began to number horizons by that gleam of occasional poppies. Each poppy he passed, a horizon fell behind him and new prairie lay before, yet a prairie not one of whose grasses ever changed, and Charlie came to know the meaning of a phrase, little heeded before, but very real to him now, the boundless steppes. Still his horse pounded on, fresh as when they started their journey. The wild music seemed to inspire it, as it galloped over those dead and flashing grasses, passing horizons as it passed the glow of the poppies; and its tough companions tirelessly paced behind it. Again Charlie looked for wolves, but saw nothing in the long grasses. Once he thought he heard a long quavering howl; but it was only a note of the music. For a moment he wondered then what the music was; but it was only one of the mysteries of the plain, where all was mysterious. Not a sound disturbed his horse or the herd that followed, as they all galloped straight on. It was as though those tough horses knew what the music was, and where, if anywhere, was the boundary of that prairie; and even if there was no boundary at all, they seemed to have the strength to gallop for ever and ever. Again a poppy; again it fell behind them almost as soon as it flashed.

More hours, as Charlie calculated, went by.

The illimitable prairie, the boundless steppes: those phrases suddenly came to him full of meaning. Shining sere grasses and an occasional poppy went on in their endless monotony: not a grass varied. Surely in such a prairie there must be wolves. And as this thought came to Charlie, he heard in the wild music a shrill high quavering note. But was it the music or was it the opening cry of a pack that at last pursued him? Might it not be that the wolves had got the scent of the horses, carried far by the wind that was so strong in his face? Neither his horse nor the herd that galloped behind him swerved from their steady course. Yet what could that high note have been? Again it arose behind them. Charlie carried a light switch, that he had pulled from a willow, and with which as yet he had not touched his horse. But as that ominous hungry note arose he used his switch now, and brought it down on the animal's tough flank. It neither swerved nor quickened, but galloped steadily on. And the herd behind it followed in a straight line, with no rhythm changed in the thundering beat of their hooves, as Charlie was sure although he could not hear it, for it was drowned in the sound of the strange music through which only the cry of the wolves could be heard behind him. Charlie struck again with his switch. He knew that his horse was hard and tough; so he struck even more strongly. But still the pace did not quicken, not even by the beat of one hoof in a hundred. That note intruded through the music again, and now the lonely rider was sure that he was pursued.

Why would the herd behind him not quicken their pace? Why would his own horse not answer the blows of his whip? If he had not heard that note before, but heard it now, the wolves must be gaining. Did the whole herd know they were doomed? Was that the fatal reason why they would not increase their speed? Again he struck his horse, and with frantic blows; and the hungry quavering note behind him was nearer.

Sere grasses that never changed, flashing in sunlight, a poppy appearing again and falling behind, and a horizon falling back with it. A boundless prairie, and the endless pursuit of the wolves. And yet that pursuit must end; for it was clear that the prairie went on for ever and ever, and as clear that the wolves were gaining. He hit his horse harder and harder, always with no effect, and shouted to the herd that galloped behind. But, like a hare that knows that a stoat is following close, they would never increase their pace. On and on they went through the bright dead grasses, with the gleam of a poppy flashing again and again, all through that strange music; and through the wild notes of that music the wilder cry of the wolves. A piercing note wailed close and his horse slackened, and all the wild hard herd slackened behind him, flog his own horse as he would. He dared not look round. And then the whole herd stopped, and he felt that the wolves were upon him. He clung to his horse tightly, his arms flung out round its neck, in the fond hope that there was some safety there that there could not be on the ground. The music had ceased when that wild gallop ceased, so that he heard every word of the woman that came through the withered grasses and trod on the poppy beside the hooves of that hard horse. "Come off it, Charlie," she said. "You've had your five minutes."

Above the roundabouts as they came away they saw a placard with big letters, that said: THE RIDE OF THE CENTURY. Well, Charlie felt that it was.

The Blundering Curate

"You write stories, don't you?" a friend said to me one day.

"Sometimes," I said.

"Why don't you write true ones?" he said. "I don't mean you in particular, but everyone who invents stories. Why don't you write true ones? There are more interesting things that actually happen than anyone can invent."

"Tell me one," I said.

"Well, I will," he replied. "I'll tell you one that I came across only last year. Perhaps I'd better not give you the actual name or the place. But they don't matter, do they?"

"No," I said. "Better not. I don't know what your story's going to be; but if it's about a real man and you take a view of him that's different to his own view, he might protest. And difficult to answer him if he does, as he probably knows a lot more about the local colour of his life than what you do. What is your story?"

"It's about a clergyman," he said. "And I've nothing but praise for him. But I won't tell you his name, for all that. He did a rather foolish thing, and might not like to see it discussed in print."

"No," I said. "He probably wouldn't."

"I don't say he wouldn't," said my friend. "But he might not. Well, I'll tell you about him. He was an old man, probably past 70 by the look of him, and he was a curate at Exham. If there really is such a parish, then that is not the parish I mean. So far as I know, I invented the name myself. Well, I went there one day last year to stay with some friends for a week-end, and I went to church with them on Sunday and the curate preached, and he preached the finest sermon I ever heard; and nobody to whom I spoke about it said they had ever heard anything better anywhere else, though they had often heard sermons as good as that from him, and, as they said, much better. 'Then why is he still a curate?' I asked. And the man and the woman that I was staying with told me between them all about that. He had been unwise when he was young, and hadn't stuck to his job, which was looking after that parish, but had said things in little speeches, at things like church bazaars, practically attacking a body of men living outside the parish, and they had got to hear of it. Journalists in the ordinary way had reported his little speeches. He did not attack anybody by name, but he attacked an organization, which was worse. And, as he never apologized for what he had said of it, one day that organization hit back."

"But whom did he attack?" I asked.

"That was just the trouble," he said. "He picked the very worst people to attack that he could possibly pick. If he wanted to attack anybody when he happened to feel pugnacious, he should have attacked bishops or their wives. They are all good Christian people, and they would never have hit back at him. Besides, if he had said that bishops' wives were immoral, the thing would have been so absurd that it would have scarcely annoyed them: any way they would have taken no notice of it. That's the mistake he made. There's no harm in attacking the good; they are not afraid that anyone will believe you if you do; they are not revengeful, and above all they are not frightened. Besides which, they are not organized, but evil has to be organized. It wouldn't stand a chance without organization, and a complete and perfect and silent one. You never heard of any organization to protect bishops' wives from calumny; but evil must organize, as I said. You don't hear of that either, but it's there. And like a fool he attacked an organization; the most silent one in the world, and therefore the best run. And one of the richest investments known to man."

"Look here," I said, "if you really mean what you say, could you tell me what that investment is? Not that I have anything to invest, but one is naturally curious to know."

"The white-slave traffic," he said.

"The white-slave traffic!" I repeated.

"Yes," he said. "And the blundering fool rammed his silly head at it and tried to knock it over. Something must have happened to some girl from his parish, and he must have got to hear of it, as you very seldom do."

"And what do you think did happen?" I asked.

"That I can't tell you," he said. "I can tell you what I was told, and perhaps you can make head or tale of it. The story I heard was this:

there was a farmer in Exham who had a young daughter, and she had gone as a housemaid to a place in Ireland, where according to this story they have fairies that come out and dance in the evenings, on mounds that they call raths. And one evening this girl went out and saw them dancing, and singing as they danced. And what they sang as they danced was Monday, Tuesday, Monday, Tuesday. Nothing else all the evening. And when it got too dark to see them any more, the girl could still hear them singing Monday, Tuesday. And a day or two later she got away from the house in the gloaming and went to the rath again, and there were the fairies. And they were still at it, dancing round and round a ring with their hands joined, singing Monday, Tuesday, Monday, Tuesday. And this time she spoke to them, and they all stopped dancing. And she said to them, 'You know, there is more than that. There is Wednesday. Why don't you sing Monday, Tuesday, Wednesday?' And the fairies said to her, 'It's the word we've been wanting, the very word we've been waiting for.' And then they sang Monday, Tuesday, Wednesday, and were delighted with the new song. And one day she went to the rath at evening again. And there were the fairies dancing, and singing the new song, Monday, Tuesday, Wednesday, all the time. And she wouldn't leave well alone. And she said to them, 'There's still more than that. Why don't you sing Monday, Tuesday, Wednesday, Thursday?' And they did. They stopped their dancing and suddenly looked very grave. And then they danced one round, singing the words in the new way, Monday, Tuesday, Wednesday, Thursday, as she had told them. But it didn't go the same way at all. And they said 'Now you've destroyed the rhythm, and we'll destroy you.' And she was never heard of again.

"That's the story that drifted back from Ireland. And many people were interested in it, though they were sorry for the girl. Some believed that it happened just as I told it you. Some thought that the story was told to cover something else, whatever it was that had happened. I offer no opinion myself. I don't know everything that goes on in the world, and so I don't like to say what is impossible. But that curate got some idea about it, and started that prejudice which has never left him, against those people I told you about. Fancy one man alone, and a not very clever one, trying to smash a business, any business, that was worth many millions a year. Why! There are houses in which they make hundreds of pounds in a single night, and keep it up regularly all the year round. And this poor fool set out to attack that. Think of hundreds of pounds a night in more than one house in every large city in Europe and South America, and pretty well everywhere else, and try to think of where all the money goes. I don't care where it goes; it must go somewhere; and the men to whom it goes, who are so perfectly organized that you never hear the name of a single one, are not all of them so sound asleep that they are going to let a silly curate take all that money out of their pockets and dry up the source of it and leave them penniless for the rest of their lives. Not likely. His rather aggressive remarks were only reported in the local papers; but you needn't suppose that that organization in Paris or Port Said or Rio didn't read them. Every paper is read by every big organization in the world. So they soon saw that he was after them, and they very soon hit back."

"How could they do that," I asked, "if they keep as much in the dark as you say? And I fancy they do. But how could they protest against an attack on them, and at the same time hush themselves up?"

"The white-slave-owners didn't protest against that curate," he said. "But the Mothers' Union of Exham did, and several similar societies throughout the diocese."

"The Mothers' Union!" said I.

"Certainly," he said. "I told you that they were organized. And I told you they had an income of millions a year. Well, money like that runs like a river going the wrong way, in every sense; and it runs up tributaries into valleys you wouldn't dream of, among hills that aren't marked on the map. When a big organization wants to put its foot down it can put it down heavily anywhere; and the wickeder it may be, the more it has to be organized, as I told you. A man like that might have been all kinds of things, if he hadn't been such a fool. But he has just stayed a curate."

"But who promotes curates?" I asked.

"The bishop," he said.

"So I thought," said I. "But you don't mean his bishop took orders from white-slave-owners."

"Of course I don't mean any such thing," he said. "The bishop was only influenced by the reports that he got about this man from all kinds of societies in his diocese that were interested in the well-being of all his parishes. They were the people that the organization got quietly in touch with. I don't know what they said. All I know is that their language, their manners and everything about them, would have been attuned to the ears of religious, respectable people. Probably what they said to them was suaver and milder than the reports that these societies themselves passed on to the bishop. But they knew the kind of thing to say; and, whatever it was, they said it. That's where an organization comes in; it employs men who will tell them what to say, and how to say it; what kind of charges to suggest, and how to indicate them. And in extreme cases, where they met pig-headed reluctance to help them, there was always their subscription-list and the hint of a threat of withdrawal. All organizations subscribe very widely. A hint was enough; they were always extremely polite. And so this man stayed a curate, and is one yet. Don't think, if you hear a curate preach a good sermon, that he is the one I am talking about. It wasn't merely a good sermon. It was a transcendent sermon; something quite out of the way."

"But can nothing be done for him?" I asked.

"Nothing," he said. "I was so stirred by his sermon that I tried to help him myself. I was introduced and I spoke to him."

"What did you say?" I asked.

"I spoke to him," said my friend, "and urged him to give up goading those people. I implored him to leave them alone. 'They've got to live, like other people,' I said. 'Live and let live, and leave them alone.'

"But he wouldn't. 'Not while I live!' he said. Well, when a man talks like that one knows he is hopeless. But there is a story for you; a preacher such as you may not find equalled anywhere in the country, obscure in an obscure parish, only a curate. You could write it up into a tale, and I doubt your being able to invent one as good."

"I see what you mean," I said. "But a tale has to be palatable and light; and the truth can be rather heavy."

"But if you can tell your readers that you are giving them sheer truth, won't you beat all the writers of fiction in the world?" he said.

"It's rather the other way about," I said. "Fiction is lighter and more easily handled. And there's one thing you've overlooked."

"What is that?" he asked.

"Simply," I said, "that if I claimed that my story was true, and if the white-slave-owners are as well organized as you say, won't they use their power and influence to deny what I write? And which of us will people believe?"

"Well, couldn't you say," he said, "that no reference whatever was intended to any person or persons?"

"But that is asking them to disbelieve me," I said.

"What does that matter," he said, "if they're not going to believe you in any case?"

A Tale of the Irish Countryside

Going one day down the white street of Ahravagh, under its dark thatches, to buy tobacco, I met with Jimmy Mullins coming the other way, and he called out to me with a loud greeting, and I said to him, "Has winter come yet, Jimmy?"

And he said, "It has not."

"Isn't it time it was here?" I asked.

"Ah, sure, you've been reading your books and almanacs again," he said. "But they won't tell you when God pleases to send the winter, which is not till the geese are come to Carricknahinch. And they're not yet come."

"It's very late this year," I said.

"Sure, it's not for us to say whether it's late or early," said Jimmy Mullins. "It comes when it will."

"Will it come soon now?" I asked him.

"God knows," said Jimmy.

We came to the thick white wall of the shop where they sold tobacco, and I bought a few ounces, while Jimmy waited outside, observing the sky and the wind, and whatever else he studied in order to come by his knowledge, which he acquires from such things as these, much as we get ours from books.

"And what were you wanting the winter for?" he said to me as I came out.

Just beyond Ahravagh the bog lay sleeping for miles, and I wanted to be out again with that eternal thing, among its reeds and dead heather.

"I want to go shooting again," I said.

"Aye," said Jimmy, "and you only have to wait. Sure the North wind will bring everything."

"Is there nothing on the bog yet?" I asked.

"Ah, sure, you might walk five miles," said Jimmy Mullins, "and get five snipe. But only wait for the North wind and everything will be there."

"When will it blow?" I asked.

"God knows," said Jimmy. And then he added, "Maybe tomorrow."

And sure enough, on the morrow the North wind came. I saw it in the morning by the brilliant pale-blue of the sky. And away I went to Ahravagh with my gun and my dog. And there was Jimmy Mullins standing in the white street, as though he had waited for me ever since. And the North wind was blowing along the street.

"Well, the winter has come," I said.

"Sure it has," said Jimmy. "The wind came out of the North last night, and the geese with it."

"Then we'll go to Carricknahinch," I said.

"And so we might," said Jimmy.

We started off at once, and walked in silence over the slanting fields that went gently down to the red bog. And in comparison with that wild land of withered heather and moss towards which we were walking, the orderly fields of grass seemed tame and dull; so that I turned to Jimmy Mullins to ask for some of that information which in Ireland is always at hand to spice events and to avert the dulness that seems to hang like a mist so close to all that is ordinary. "I suppose you've seen odd things hereabouts in your time," I said.

"Ah, I wouldn't say odd," said Jimmy. "Only sometimes may be they was a little out of the way."

"What kind of things?" I asked.

"Ah well," said Jimmy, "all kinds of things. Once Satan came, and was seen on Carricknahinch."

"Satan?" I said.

"Aye," said Jimmy. "The Devil himself."

"Who saw him?" I asked.

"Mickey Mulgraby saw him," said Jimmy Mullins, "one winter's evening when he was looking for geese. A great lad was Mickey. Sure, you never knew what he would be up to, never at all. And the Devil himself didn't know either."

"What was the Devil doing in Carricknahinch?" I asked.

"What was he doing?" said Jimmy. "Sure, what do you think he was doing? Did you never read any story that ever was told of him?"

"I did at times," I said.

"Then what was he always doing," said Jimmy, "if he wasn't buying souls? Sure, what else does he do?"

"Yes," I said, "of course, he does."

"Then that's what he was doing," said Jimmy. "But he wasn't sharp enough for Mickey. And he got the surprise of his life. For no sooner did that old lad begin to talk about prices and how they fluctuated and what a lot you could do with money, out there on the bog where Mickey met him, when Mickey turns round and offers to buy Satan's own soul. Aye, that's what he done, and it's likely it had never been done before, which may be said of most of the things that Mickey turns his hand to, for there's a queer twist in Mickey; and, sure, he surprises the Devil, and he hums and haws for a bit. And Mickey says to him, 'Sure, I always heard it said of you that you never refused to do business; but it's likely the lads that said that didn't know what they were talking about.'

"'I wouldn't say they were wrong,' says the dark lad.

"'Then what do you want for it in ready money?' says Mickey.

"So Satan names a price, and I never heard what it was. Of course it was some huge great sum. And Mickey accepts at once. Of course Mickey hadn't any money at all. Not a penny. But never mind that: he accepts. His idea was to form a syndicate and to raise the money. And he'd have done it too. And it's the way it was that the Devil saw that he meant to. You can sometimes tell what a man means to do, without his saying a word. And the Devil can tell always. So he takes out his soul and hands it to Mickey Mulgraby. And, do you know, it was quite a little soul, no bigger nor one of those balls that the gentry have to play tennis. And there it was gleaming in his hand. And Mickey takes it. And, mind you, this isn't idle gossip that I am telling you. It was told in Court and on oath, and was all taken down in writing; and anyone that can get a permit can go and read it for himself. Mickey takes his soul from the Devil, and drops it at once, for it was hotter nor anything Mickey had ever touched or gone near. And it falls on the old heather and it sets the turf alight and the whole bog is on fire, and Mickey has to run for his life, and the Devil rises up and flaps away. It was night by now, and Mickey sees him going off like an old heron, all black in the firelight. And a charge is brought against Mickey for maliciously burning the bog, and naturally when he's brought into Court he tells the truth and explains to the magistrate how it all happened, and that is the story I'm telling you."

"And did the magistrate believe him?" I asked.

"I wouldn't say he did that," said Jimmy. "And I wouldn't say that he didn't. For that soul had gone right down through the turf and burned its way home. So there was no way of telling. But from the way he looked at Mickey, I should say he did not. For I was there at the time. But that magistrate was a man that never mixed himself up with religion or politics; so he made no comment on what Mickey had said, except to ask what he paid for the soul. And Mickey said, 'Paid for it, is it? Sure, I never got the soul. And isn't this a court of justice? Is there any justice in the world if I can be asked such a question here? Sure, if you'll go and get it from where it is, won't I pay for it at once. But I never properly laid any hand on it.'

"And the magistrate could see from a single glance round the court that Mickey had the sympathy of the people, and doesn't continue the argument, but puts an end to it by discharging Mickey. That's how it was."

The Price of the World

For me the beginning of this tale was what I suppose is really the end
of it. I knew a country doctor for many years, and then one day he was
given a good job in one of the finest asylums in England, and the following year he asked me to come to a dance that was being given at
the asylum. I went, and was astonished by the magnificence of it. One
forgot two wars and two financial crises, and was looking at the kind of
festivity one remembered when King Edward VII was on the throne
and champagne was ten shillings a bottle, and the very best could be had
for a pound, and suppers at balls were banquets. From what market they
got the food I did not enquire, for it was no business of mine; but, black
or white, it was up to the standards of the days that know nothing of
coupons. And there was a magnificent band, playing good music. I
naturally supposed that the ball was given by the doctors and nurses of
the asylum, however they raised the money, until I got this astonishing
story from my friend the country doctor. It happened like this.

Men have swum the channel, gone in a barrel over Niagara, walked
across it on a tight-rope, and discovered both of the poles; there seems
nothing they have not done: and one day a man totally unknown to the
doorkeeper and everybody else in the street, walked into one of the of-
fices in Whitehall and obtained an interview with an Under-secretary
of State. How such things are done I don't know; it is all, I imagine, a
matter of manner; but at any rate he did it. He passed the doorkeeper
almost without noticing him, and just a nod of the head. His manner
was light and easy in the hall, but from then on his gravity deepened,
and he was somehow able to impress on every secretary he saw that he
came upon business that was portentous. Luck must have aided him as
well as his own wit, and his visit must have coincided with a period of
leisure during which time hung heavily on the hands of the Under-
secretary and he allowed the visitor to be shown up. Alone with the
Under-secretary and his private secretary he pulled out a bunch of papers, and with a few words that put both men at their ease, handed it

to the chief. A glance at the papers showed that the man knew something of what he had been writing about. They were about atomic fission. And there too luck favoured him. For the Under-secretary chanced to be something of an authority on that grim subject, and the private secretary knew nothing about it. Suddenly the Under-secretary looked up from the papers. "Where did you get your uranium?" he asked.

"I don't use uranium," replied the visitor. "I have a method by which I can liberate the power of all atoms, the atoms composing grass or soil, for instance, just as easily as those of uranium."

The Under-secretary looked down at the bundle of papers again.

"You will find it all there," said the visitor.

"Yes," said the Under-secretary. "Yes. I have not time to read it all now. But you realize, do you not, that such a widespread release of the atom could be very dangerous. It is, as I see you understand, of the nature of the atom to affect adjacent atoms whenever its power is liberated. The explosion might spread to wide areas and be very dangerous indeed."

"That is my point," said the stranger.

"Your point?" said the private secretary.

"Ah," said the Under-secretary of State. "Let me introduce you. This is Mr. Harper. I don't think you told us your name."

"Arnett," the stranger said.

"Exactly," said the Under-secretary. "Well, now we know who each of us is. I, as perhaps you know, am Meglum. You were saying that was your point; the spread of the explosion, I think."

"Yes," said Arnett. "Liberated as I should do it, the atom in blades of grass or a lump of clay would liberate adjacent atoms, as it does in a lump of uranium."

"Exactly," said Sir Chortney Meglum.

"And the resultant explosion," continued Arnett, "would spread instantaneously, or as near instantaneously as we are able to calculate, over the whole earth."

"The whole earth!" said Sir Chortney.

"You mean . . ." exclaimed Harper.

"Precisely," said Arnett. "It would blow up the planet."

"But, but," said Harper. And his chief said much the same.

"You see," said Arnett, "if I may explain my motive to you, without taking up too much of your very valuable time, I have seen all kinds of expensive festivities all my life from the outside, without ever having had any opportunity of taking a part in them, or in any festivities at all; nor was I ever likely to have. And at last this power is put into my hand, and by my own industry. No power of such magnitude can be without its commercial value, and the power to wreck the world must be of incredible value, something far beyond what I can possibly calculate; and I am only asking a million for it."

"A what?" said the private secretary.

"Only a million," said Arnett. "It would be worth that to any one industry alone. The soap-boilers, the cloth-manufacturers, the motor-car-makers, any one of them would subscribe that to save the world. I don't know any large public body that wouldn't. I am only asking a million." No word came from either of the officials. "But perhaps," he said to Sir Chortney, "you would like to study those papers a little longer, so as to see, as I think you will, that the whole thing is perfectly feasible. Briefly, as you will see from my plans, the solid lump of this planet will be made to act and react with all its atoms as does a lump of uranium when detonated by the ordinary method. I am no pioneer. I have merely improved an existing invention, as all inventions are improved. Artillery could not always remain as it was at the battle of Crécy; and atomic research was not likely to stay as it was over Nagasaki, even without my efforts. As you will see, we can now do a very great deal with it."

"But, but," said Sir Chortney, "you would not blow up the whole earth!"

"Why not?" said Arnett. "I've never had a good time on it. And I'm not going to, should you refuse me my million. I've had disappointments, considerable ones, and no money. The world does not mean to me what it means to a very successful man like yourself. It's probably worth a million to you alone, even if you were to consider nobody else."

"But what would you gain," said Sir Chortney, "by blowing up everybody?"

"Yes, what would you gain?" said his secretary.

"Why, nothing," said Arnett. "And I hope not to have to. But I am quite ready to risk it. It has never meant much to me. It means more to you and to others, and you may think it worth the million I ask for, in order to save it. But, if not, I blow it up."

Sir Chortney turned to his secretary and spoke in a low voice.

"And if I may interrupt for a moment," said Arnett; "it would be of no use to kill me; in fact very much the reverse. It would mean the end of the world. You see, I have set in motion all the machinery already."

"We do not commit murder," said Sir Chortney.

"I quite realize that," said Arnett. "At the same time, in a case like this, I recognize that a quiet assassination, hushed up by all the clerks in your office, would be the obvious step; indeed, I admit, the correct one. But I have set the machinery in motion already: you can read in those papers, page 12, what it is; and unless I go home to stop it, that is what must happen."

"Let me read a little more of your invention," said Sir Chortney.

"Certainly," said Arnett.

And Sir Chortney read. Meanwhile the private secretary tried some of the arts of persuasion.

"But have you no relations?" he asked.

"None that I care about," replied Arnett.

"And no friends?" Harper continued.

"None that have ever helped me when I was hard up," said Arnett, "as I am now, and shall be till I get that million."

"And do you care nothing for your home, or your country, or the world?" Harper continued.

"The world is nothing to me without the means of enjoying myself, which I have never had," said Arnett. "With a million it would be very different. I shouldn't want to harm it then."

"No. I see," said the private secretary, and said no more.

Sir Chortney looked up from his reading. "Actually a million," he said, "is a sum that at the moment the Treasury would be unable to lay its hands on."

"I am sorry," said Arnett. And in his voice there seemed to sound some note of a real regret for the human race and its old home.

"I wonder," said the private secretary, "if you have fully considered what a million is. I wonder if, say, a hundred thousand pounds would not amply provide you with all that you hoped for from a million."

Arnett thought for a moment. "Very well," he said. "I'll take a hundred thousand."

"That is really very considerate of you," said Harper.

"Actually," said Sir Chortney, "the Treasury would not be able at present to sanction the payment of even a hundred thousand."

"To save the world?" said Arnett.

"Not as things are at present," said Sir Chortney.

"They can't set much store by it," said Arnett.

"As things are at present it would be impossible," said Sir Chortney, "without American aid. And we cannot possibly ask them for any more. There are limits, even to their generosity."

"Not to save the world?" Arnett repeated.

"They've been saving it all they can," said Sir Chortney. "We can't possibly ask them to do any more."

"Then if the Treasury can't find a million . . ."

"Impossible," said Sir Chortney.

"Or a hundred thousand . . ."

"Out of the question," said Sir Chortney.

"In order to save the world . . ."

"Not for any purpose," Sir Chortney said.

"Then what will they pay?"

"Perhaps a quarter of what you ask," said Sir Chortney. "Perhaps twenty-five thousand."

"It's not much," said Arnett.

"You can do a great deal with twenty-five thousand," Sir Chortney said.

"It's not much for saving the world," said Arnett.

"Any more is impossible," said Sir Chortney, "as I happen to know."

In business deals all, of course, depends on the real intentions of the men who are doing the deal. When those are known, the rest is easy. Somehow Arnett shrewdly knew that Sir Chortney meant what he said. How he knew this I can't explain. To know it was just a part of business acumen, a very subtle thing, which Arnett evidently possessed. And so he knew by some tone in Sir Chortney's voice that he would get no more from him than twenty-five thousand pounds, even to save the world, and he opened his mouth to accept. But as he opened it the private secretary made one more appeal, sketching hurriedly but poetically some of the better known beauties of our planet, only to be met by an emphatic statement that in his present circumstances, and those in which he had always lived, the world meant nothing to him. Then Harper dropped that argument at once, and turned to the other way out, to the twenty-five thousand pounds; for the less he knew of atomic fission, which was indeed nothing, the more he relied on the judgement of his chief, who was known to have made a very considerable study of it, and seeing that the man's figures had satisfied Sir Chortney, he had no doubt that, what is after all a quite reasonable supposition, the destruction of the world by the force of its atoms was a problem already solved. So he just said, "Sir Chortney has offered you twenty-five thousand pounds."

And Arnett accepted. He accepted with a pleasant smile and a wave of his hand.

"Well, I am glad we are agreed about that," said Sir Chortney quite sincerely.

"Shall I telephone to the Treasury, sir?" said Harper.

"Yes, do," said his chief. And then he turned to Arnett. "Of course we rely on you to be as straight and aboveboard as we shall be ourselves. We both give you our word to hand you the cheque as soon as ever we get it round from the Treasury; and you will, I am sure, give us your word that as soon as you have the cheque you will destroy these notes and all other notes you have made and all your appliances, and to do no further work on the atom whatever."

And all this Arnett promised, in an easy graceful way that ensured complete belief, a product of that very manner which had got him into that inner room at Whitehall, to which access is not usually obtained without applications upon the appropriate forms, and not always then.

"Well," said Sir Chortney, "that will be all right. And you can rely on us to post the cheque to you by tomorrow evening at the latest. Twenty-five thousand pounds. What is your address?"

The inventor was giving his address in the North of London, when there was a loud knock on the door and two men entered hastily, while another stood on the threshold.

"Ah, so we've found you," said one. And to Sir Chortney Meglum he added, "I beg your pardon, sir, but this gentleman has escaped from Croutchley Asylum."

"Dear me," said Sir Chortney, "I shouldn't have thought it."

His secretary said nothing, but looked concerned that his chief should have been so duped and that such a thing could occur in his room as was now occurring.

"Yes," said Mr. Arnett, "that is so. I certainly escaped from these gentlemen."

"Well, come along," said his principal captor.

And quietly and wonderfully quickly, and with only a hurried apology to the Under-secretary of State, the two men were gone through the door with their polite lunatic arm-in-arm between them, and that calm was restored to the room that there was before he had managed to enter it, and that had been, before that, for ages. And the first words that broke in on the silence of that calm came from the private secretary. "Well, that was lucky, sir. They've just saved us twenty-five thousand pounds."

Sir Chortney thought for a moment. "I'm not sure of that," he said then. "You see we promised to send him the cheque tomorrow. Of course he fooled us; but, apart from that, he seemed a man of his word. I mean, if he had had any such invention I feel sure he would have destroyed it as he said. I think we ought to keep to our promise too."

"Send him the twenty-five thousand, sir?" said the secretary.

"I think so," said Sir Chortney.

"It's a lot of money, sir," his secretary said.

"I know," said Sir Chortney. "But a principle is involved; the principle of trusting a government department. The public must be able to do that. An eighth of a farthing per head of the population is all that the public lose by it. But the principle . . ."

"Yes, I see, sir," said the secretary, who never required more argument than that to persuade him to agree with his chief. "Then, shall I send the cheque to the asylum when we get it round from the Treasury, or to the address that he gave us?"

"The asylum, I think," said his chief. "You see, he was inventing a lot of queer things while he talked to us, and he may have invented the address too. Better send it round to the asylum."

And this was done. And with the consent of the patient, and indeed at his own suggestion, the doctors arranged this splendid ball. And all the nurses came to it, and all the patients that could be trusted, and many friends of the doctors and nurses, and it was the greatest possible success. And Mr. Arnett is seeing, from the inside, some of that revelry of which he had been so starved in his life. They tell me that it cost about five thousand pounds and they are going to have it annually for at least five years.

WHEN MRS. FYNN WAS YOUNG

In the townland of Runshannoch they are nearly all Fynns, Ryans, Byrnes, Murraghs and Careys. The few that have other names are only men that have strayed in from Dublin or anywhere, to do odd jobs, and have no real business in the townland at all. Old Mrs. Fynn, who lives in a white cottage under a black thatch on which house-leeks grow, is great-grandmother of the five families that I have mentioned. I've seen as many as forty children playing there, and very noisy they are when they are all playing on the white road that runs through the village. For the road is white whenever the dust is dry, as it has been since times out of mind, and the pleas to tar it have never materialized, and motors avoid it because of its bumps and dust, and the children play. And when they make too much noise old Mrs. Fynn comes out of her cottage, walking with her old stick, and the children scatter. They have never known her as other than an old woman with a stick, and do not know that she once was young. When old Mrs. Fynn was young she was Eileen Carey, and at a little past 17 a marriage had been arranged for her with a fine farmer who had sixteen cows, and ample land to support them. They were not the kind of thin grey cows that you often see grazing coarse land by the edges of bogs, but good fine cows, as good as any for more than five miles around. It is thought by many that things are wholly altered from the days when Eileen was young, and that the Ireland she knew is gone. It has certainly gone from the towns; but of Runshannoch it is hard to say, for the old are slow to talk, and the young are not ready to listen, so that the comparison is not easily made. But, be that as it may, Eileen, who was engaged to be married, was as much in love as any young girl today, though not with the farmer to whom she had been engaged. Michael Carey, her father, had only one cow, and that cow was giving milk that, however well it had once satisfied the Careys, was less than what was usually given by any one of Geogehan's sixteen cows, the farmer to whom Eileen had been engaged by her father with the help of a go-between.

One day it occurred to Carey that the only thing to do to attain the level of Geogehan, though with only one cow, was to get a charm from a Fairy Man. There was one in Athroonagh, nearly 14 miles away, well known for his magic, a man who could read your thoughts with a glance of his eye, and give you a charm that might save a man even from death, when the doctors had given him over. So Carey, one evening at supper in his house by the forge, for he was a blacksmith as all the Careys had been before him for generations beyond counting, said to his son Pat, who was 15, "Let you go for me to Athroonagh tomorrow and see the Fairy Man, and tell him how it is with our cow, and that the cows of Timothy Geogehan give three gallons a day, and ask him for a charm that will give us the same. And start before it is light, the way that no-one will see you, for Father Horan puts a terrible penance on anyone that has dealings with Fairy Men."

And the boy said he would go. But suddenly Eileen spoke up, and said, "Let me go, father. For Paddy is over young for the long journey, 21 miles there and back." But it was Irish miles she meant, and the whole journey was nearly 28. And Pat complained that the journey was nothing to him, and that he should go. But he complained too hard, and his father silenced him and said that Eileen should go instead.

So Eileen started in the dark night before the next morning, and no-one saw her go from Runshannoch, for she went quietly by starlight and was well away from Runshannoch before the first bleak light had widened along the sky to make its chilly prophecy of the dawn, and away from it Eileen walked, for she was going westwards, with darkness all before her, till dawn came up and shone from behind her and slowly lit the fields and a bird sang. In little more than three hours she was in Athroonagh, just as the village was waking, and asked of the first she saw for the house of the Fairy Man. And he lived a mile further on; and there she went. And when she came to the thick wall of his whitewashed cottage and knocked at the door, the door was opened at once, and there in the dark of the cottage was standing the Fairy Man. He was wearing a long black coat, and there was a tall hat on his head, and he asked her to come in. And Eileen went in and found the wife of the Fairy Man sitting before her fire. She offered Eileen a chair, but said nothing; and Eileen sat down on the chair before the wide fireplace, where great logs were burning and a cauldron hung from a hook. And the wife of the Fairy Man sat silent beside her. Some thought there was magic in her that she feared would get out if she spoke and that would form spells and do harm, while others said that there was no magic in her and that she kept silent so that it would not be known that she understood nothing of magic. But Eileen had told her story about the cow. And, when she had ended, the Fairy Man said to her, "It was not only about a cow that you came to see me."

And she said, "It was not."

For it is no use trying to keep secrets from a Fairy Man. And he said, "There's a young man in it."

And she, forgetting for a moment whom it was that she spoke to, said, "How did you know that?"

And he said, "Amn't I a Fairy Man?"

And she said, "Indeed you are, and I need say no more, for you know everything."

"That is so," said the Fairy Man. "At the same time you may tell me your trouble in your own words, so that I may see if they fully accord with what is known to my wisdom, and that I may know you are speaking the truth."

So she told him how she was engaged to be married to an old man, as she called Timothy Geogehan though he was only 40, but that there was a young man whom she would rather marry, a young lad named Patsy. And while she was telling her story the Fairy Man was packing his pipe with some black tobacco; and when she had finished he lit it and said no word until it was well alight, and then he said to her, "Is there any stump or bole of an old tree in front of the window of your house?"

And Eileen said, "There's the bole of an old willow that is all white and decayed away and is no more now than the height of a man, and it is close in front of our window." And he said, "It is as I thought. And it will do well. And let you now watch for a night on which it is sure to rain, and take this packet in the evening before the rain has fallen, and put it on the top of the bole of the old willow, and rake a few bits of decayed wood over it and leave it there with this side uppermost just as I show you." And he showed her the paper packet, which felt as though it had a few little hard crystals on top and was all powder below. So Eileen took the packet, and the Fairy Man went on. "And be-

fore you do that," he said, "you will put the other powder into the
cow's mouth and tell no one that you have done it. And as the things
to be and the things that were are as one to the Fairy Men, I see that
your cow will be taken terrible ill. But on the night that the rain falls
there will be a green flame rise from the top of the old willow, as a sign
that the cow will recover, if you do the things that I say. And it will be
a great sign for all of you, for fires do not burn in the rain. And it will
be a sign that the cow will live, if the third powder that I now give to
you be put into the cow's mouth by the man that is to marry the eldest
daughter of the master of the cow, which would be yourself. And if
the powder is not given to the cow, or is given by any other hand, she
will die."

"And how will the fire burn in the rain?" asked Eileen.

"That is only known to the Fairy Men," said he.

"And how will I know what man is the man I will marry?" asked
she. "For my father says he is Timothy Geogehan."

"The knowledge of the future is not for him or for you or for the
go-between," said the Fairy Man; "but for only the Fairy Men. But the
man you will marry is he who will come to your father's house by
night, and after the usual greeting will say to him these words, 'Did you
see e'er a black hen coming this way? For it's the way it is, we have lost
one.' Those words and no others. And he who says those words by
night is the man you will marry, and you will put this packet into his
right hand, and bid him put the powder into the mouth of the cow.
And she shall live, and give as much milk as any of Geogehan's cows.
And if you do not do as I said, she will die. And you may tell your father this and do as I said and pay me with a gold coin, and the cow will
recover from the sickness that is to come on her."

So Eileen gave the Fairy Man a half-sovereign, and said farewell to
himself and the silent woman, and went home with her three packets
all the way to Runshannoch, for such a walk was nothing to any young
girl in those days. And by dinner-time she was home, and she told her
father all that she was to tell him of the sickness that was to come on
the cow, and how she would be cured when the green flame shone on
the willow and give more milk than ever, if the powder were given her
by the hand of the right man. And all that evening Eileen watched the
sky, and all the next evening, and they waited and watched the cow,

and she seemed as well as ever. But on the third evening thick low clouds blew up from the West, and Eileen slipped out and put the packet, that had little crystals on one side, on the top of the old white bole of the dead willow that stood in the field in front of her father's window; and put another powder into the cow's mouth. And the cow sickened, and Eileen's father and mother heard her bellowing, and went to see what was the matter. And Eileen reminded them of the sickness of which she had told them that was to come on the cow, and the green flame that was to burn in the rain from the top of the willow as a sign that she should recover if the commands of the Fairy Man were carried out. And her father had said that they should watch for the flame. "And after that," he went on, "we shall have Timothy Geogehan looking in for his hen. And, please God, he will save the cow." And a little while after nightfall the rain came down. And they all sat watching the window. And in no longer time than it takes for rain to soak through a sprinkling of rotten wood and a piece of thin paper, a green flame rose up in the night from the top of the old willow. And a queer light glowed all round, such as they had not seen, and bushes and hedges and trees came out of the night and shone with a green they had never known before. "It is the sign," said they all. "And doesn't it show you what Fairy Men can do?" said old Carey. "To make a fire burn in the rain!"

And indeed in that light the power of Fairy Men seemed something more than it does as you read of it in cold print, for it was not like night around them nor yet like any day, and the Careys' bit of a garden and shrubs and paling, and all they could see in that light, was unlike the world they knew, and seemed by all accounts to be more like fairyland, though none of them ever had been there; and in such a land as it now appeared, and in such a light, it seemed that anything might be walking abroad, though they dared not think what. And just as their fears had nearly seen shapes moving, the green flame suddenly went out, and the night came back blacker than ever. For some moments they all sat silent. And then Eileen's father spoke. "And all we have to do now," he said, "is to wait for Timothy Geogehan, whom we are glad to see at all times, and he will save our cow. Have the packet ready, Eileen."

Eileen had the packet ready, the last of the three. And very soon there came a knock at the door. And out of the dark and the rain came, not Timothy Geogehan, but a young fellow named Patsy Fynn, whose father was still alive and who had no cows of his own, or any land as yet upon which to graze them. They looked at him in silence as he said, "God save all here." And then in that silence and with the night behind him he said carefully and slowly the words, "Did you see e'er a black hen coming this way? For it's the way it is, we have lost one."

For a while no-one spoke. And then old Carey said, "It's a mistake." Though I don't know what he meant. But Eileen went up to Patsy and put the packet into his right hand. And Carey opened his mouth, intending to say that this was all nonsense and the Fairy Man had fooled them. But he thought of the terrible penance that Father Horan would put on him, if it got out that he had had dealings with one of the Fairy Men, and he closed his lips and said nothing. And Patsy went into the cow-shed, as Eileen told him, and put the powder into the mouth of the cow. Certainly the cow recovered. Whether she ever improved her supply of milk I was never told. I don't think anyone bothered. For they were all more interested in Eileen's marriage to young Patsy, and no details of the cow's milk have been handed down. And what she said to Patsy before he came to the door in the night, nobody knows. Of course one may have one's suspicions. But no-one seeing the venerable white-haired figure of the matriarchal Mrs. Fynn could readily believe she would ever have got up to tricks like that.

At the Scene of the Crime

On a bright November morning with the first frost on the ground, and the elms still shining in their dresses of pale gold when all other trees were bare, a man was riding a bicycle along a road through Kent with his back to London. He was enjoying the beauty of the morning as he went, the white rime on the grass, the glow of the elms, the clear bright pale-blue sky, and the chalk hills gleaming under it. Sometimes he passed a garden and noted a rose, blooming still in November among ragged tendrils and dying geraniums, and sometimes he passed by chrysanthemums in their full glory, triumphing in their season. The countryside was so fresh and fair that morning that, in spite of being a little tired, he delighted in his journey. And then he came to a point at which the roads forked, and had to think which way to go. And from wondering which road to take, he began to wonder why he should choose one more than another. And out of that rose the question, what was he doing? And the further question, who was he?

None of these things he remembered. Nor did he remember at first what he had been doing five minutes ago. But from then on, and at a snail's pace, his memory began to return. He remembered cottage gardens that he had seen ten minutes ago, and then a dark wood on the crest of a gleaming hill that he had passed a quarter of an hour back, and then a house that glowed with the last brilliant leaves of a Virginia creeper, which must have been twenty minutes back. And slowly, but very slowly, his memory reached on backward still. But dim and paralyzed though his memory was, his reason was clear and active; and so were all his nerves, except that one controlling memory. For he was very clearly aware of a pain on the left side of his head, where a big lump had formed round a jagged cut that had stopped bleeding. And it seemed to him only reasonable to suppose that he had been fighting with someone, whose right hand, or whatever the right hand held, had hit him there, and that the blow had been the cause of the loss of his memory.

How then had that fight gone? And why was he running away? For that he had been going very fast for a long time was clear, since he was covered in perspiration, and not recent perspiration either, for it had gone cold. He had been going for some time. Was it likely, he reasoned, that he was running away all that distance merely from a man who had hit him? England was not a country in which one had to do that, where there were plenty of police to protect one. And he knew that he was in England. From what, then, was he fleeing? And a dark thought came to him then. There was nothing to harm him in all this peaceful countryside. Had he been harming it? It was only men who had done something dreadful that had to flee in England. And he was fleeing: there was every indication of that. What had he done? Could it be . . . could it be . . .? No. He must not let his imagination run away with him. It could not be as bad as that. But what was it? Certainly he had been fighting. What had he done? How could he find out?

The bruise on his head was throbbing. Certainly it must have been that that had shattered his memory. But, however little his thoughts could enter the past further back than twenty-five minutes, they could deal with the present all right; and he soon realized that the thing to do was to buy a newspaper. Such a fight as he had had, with such a flight as the consequence, must have got into the papers, unless the whole thing were more trivial than what his increasing fears were imagining. If so, then so much the better, and he would not grudge the threepence that he would spend on the paper.

Presently the gables and the smoke and the spire of a village rose before him against the pale blue of the sky; and he stopped at a shop and bought a morning paper and went on, leading his bicycle and reading through all the headings as he went. And there was nothing about any fight, or about any criminal escaping. For a while his fears were lulled and he mounted his bicycle and rode more slowly now, but still rode away from London. At the next village he came to he stopped at its inn, and his feelings of guilt and flight, and even terror, had faded away enough for him to dare to go in and ask for lunch. Nobody questioned him as to where he had come from, and he was given a good meal. He avoided beer, which was offered, because he knew alcohol was bad for concussion and had decided that that was what he must have been suffering from. Still his memories went backward slowly, not nearly as far as the beginning of his journey, but far enough back to tell him that he must have been going for most of the night. He had a pound-note and a few shillings in his pocket. At any rate he had not been guilty of robbery, if he had no more on him than that. But what had he been guilty of? And his fears began to return. He paid for his meal then rather hurriedly, and went out and mounted his bicycle and rode away. He was tired certainly. But it was not a time to rest, until he knew what he had done and for what reason his flight had started. And then it struck him that, if he had fled by night, the deed on account of which he had fled might have been committed at night, and the morning papers might not yet have got it. Then he would not be safe till he saw an evening paper. And his fears all rose again.

The days were drawing in and there came in the sky a hint of evening, and a long white lovely plume passed through a valley from a train coming from London. The evening papers would be on that train, and he avoided any turns that led away from the railway, so that in the next village he came to he could expect to find an evening paper. As he went forward his memory still ran backward. And now at the other end of the night he began to see a dim scene in which two men had fought in the darkness. One of them was himself. He had a memory of fierce anger felt against that other man. But how utterly that had faded now! And he felt only an immense regret. Then he reached another village; and there at a little shop that sold the odds and ends that the village needed he bought an evening paper. And it was on the front page. MAN MISSING. NO BODY FOUND, was the dreadful heading. It told of the very fight that his memory saw, though the paper told far more vividly. Witnesses had heard a heated quarrel, then a scuffle between two men in the dark, and one of them, Frederick Mingle, missing from his home and seen by nobody since. It had been a dark night, said the newspaper: he remembered that: and there had been time and opportunity to conceal a body. And the police would like to interview Albert Pornick, as they believed that he might be able to help them with certain enquiries that they were making. And they invited Albert Pornick to call.

So he must be Albert Pornick. He could easily find out for certain, for he had read that there were two small dints on the back mudguard of the missing man's stolen bicycle, one an inch from the end, and the other three inches. But he did not dare to look. He assumed he was

Albert Pornick and went on.

All this had happened on the outskirts of Lee, and its name became more and more familiar to him as his memory went back further. How far he was from Lee now he did not know. He should be a long way, if he had gone at that pace all night. If the bicycle had the two dints in the back mudguard, it was Frederick Mingle's bicycle. And still he would not look. It would do no harm, he argued, to go further and further into the deeps of the country, even if he were innocent; and, if it were the stolen bicycle, the further away he was from the scene of the crime the better. And so he kept on hard, tired though he was, riding away, as he supposed, from Lee. But before sunset he came to a signpost pointing to Lee; and it was only five miles away. Had he gone all night in a circle, as lost travellers do? Or was that attraction of which he had read, pulling him back to the scene of the crime, to which all murderers are said to return?

He took the road towards Lee. Was that old pull drawing him now, or was it reason? For reason was guiding him to the scene of the crime also. Reason said that when he returned to that familiar scene which his inner eye could see dimly, and less and less dimly as the hours went by, his memory of what happened there would return. And it was of the utmost importance that it should. He saw that. A matter of life and death. For he did not know how well he had hidden the body. And, whatever the law may be, he was sure that no-one had been hanged for murder in England, at any rate for over a hundred years, without the body or some part of it having been found. Reason told him that he must find out all about that, and hide the body better, if in the heat of the moment and in the dark it had not been perfectly hidden; and that strange gravitational pull that is said to pull murderers was dragging him there too. But it would not do to go there by daylight. He knew that. So at last he could let himself have a little rest, and he took an hour over the last five miles.

And when he got there, to that hamlet on the outskirts of Lee, it all came flooding back to him; the quarrel, the fight in the dark, and not with fists either, but with heavy and jagged things that they picked up as they fought from the untidiness that strews the feet of a city. The other man had picked up a brick: he remembered it now; and he had found a piece of a jagged stake. And then he had had a blow on his head from the brick, after which he had struck blindly, and did not know what he had done. That was his only defence, that he did not know for certain. But he had read too often of that defence before, and knew that it was a poor one. That stake had been heavy and sharp, and he had hit hard. And then, and then he had fled. But what had he done with the body? Had he hidden it carefully? And where? He could not remember. He did not think that he had stayed there long, after the fight had suddenly ceased, hardly long enough for the care needed. He must find his hiding-place and make sure. He felt that his life depended on it. Certainly he had not burned the body. But where could he have put it? Those were his thoughts; but he could not start searching yet, as there was the risk of there being too many people about. He must look for that hiding-place in the dead of night, in the small hours when there would be nobody up, except one policeman, whom he would have to wait for and watch, and do his work when he had gone by. The hiding-place: where could it be? But till his search began, he must hide. And then there was his bicycle. The time had come when he must know for certain whether it had the incriminating marks that, if found, would hang him. He stopped at a lamp-post when nobody was in sight, and examined his rear mudguard, and it had. The two small dints were there, an inch from the end and three inches from the end, exactly as described in the paper. It was Frederick Mingle's bicycle. So he would have to hide it as carefully as himself.

Then he went a little way from the houses, till he came where hedges began and pavement ceased; and behind a straggling hedge all dark in the night he lay down and hid himself and the bicycle. It was very cold lying there in clothes that sweat had damped on his long journey, but the rest was very welcome. Shining through the hedge that hid him, he saw the lights of the windows ornamenting the night with their orange glow, and more and more were lit. Voices, dogs barking, the drone of motors, came to his ears so clearly that it seemed to him strange that no-one knew he was there: he seemed so near to them all, and, indeed, he was. And now, lying there in the dark so close to where it all happened, he could remember vividly the man he had fought. That is to say, he saw his face and all his features clearly, as clear as if the man had been close to him, and as if it were not dark. He could not remember his name; but names were the last of the things that his searching memory found in the dark of the past; and, indeed, not one name of any human being had yet come back to him, and only one name of any place, and that was Lee, the scene of the crime, or near it, for the name of the actual hamlet upon its outskirts he had forgotten with so much else. Vividly he could see the vision of that man's face; and the fight came back to him from the very beginning, right up to the moment when he had been hit on the head, and had hit out blindly after that, not even knowing what he was doing at the time, still less remembering it. And he remembered the trivial cause for which they had fought; something about a dog. How he wished now the wish that sooner or later all murderers wish, that what they had done had not happened. On this vain wish, and upon all the worries on which it throve, sleep mercifully descended. And the tired man must have slept for a long time. For, when some sound suddenly woke him, he saw that the glowing lights had moved to upper storeys and that all lower windows were dark, except only one or two, where some late worker sat long at a desk alone.

It was cold and late and still; and nothing stirred the hush but the murmur of a far train and, when that was gone, a breeze that whispered along the hedgerow, and which also was lost in the silence. Then the returned fugitive rose and, leaving the bicycle where it was hidden under the hedge, he walked to the scene of the crime. A glance in one direction and then in another showed him, even in the darkness which a setting moon lighted dimly, that there was no possible place in which to hide a body in either of these directions. For the backs of the houses were before him and on his right, while on his left was a wall that he could not have climbed holding a heavy body, and the body of the red-headed man he had fought must have been, as he clearly remembered, much heavier than himself. There was only one direction in which to look, the open country, if those ragged lands that lay at the skirts of a town could have been so described. And so he began his search in fields that were near to where he had fought, looking in the dark for any sign of soil recently dug, and finding none. And then he came to a sagging, blackened haystack, that must have been left for more than a year in the corner of a field, where now it looked like a monster crouching. It looked like the one place. Where else could he have hidden the body?

And what now? He would look carefully so as to see where the haystack had been disturbed; and, if he found any mark of that, surely the best thing would be to set fire to the haystack. Would the fire utterly consume a body? Would anyone look for remains of a body there, when the fire was over? Would they be able to identify it if they should find it? These were only a few of the thoughts that a sense of guilt sent racing through his mind, as he walked round the old dark haystack. And suddenly there rose from sleep under a side of the haystack, and almost under his feet, the figure of a man. And that sense of guilt alone told him whose shape it would be, even had the moon not peered from the edge of a cloud to light up with its full ghastliness the features of the man he had murdered. A wild scream broke from the lips of the ghostly figure, which turned and fled, and a cock awakened by the scream crowed at that moment, and the faintest hint of dawn shone on one cloud in the East, and to the fugitive it seemed like a ghost returning to Hell. Haunted by those features, more awful than he had seen them before, but quite unmistakable, without further search he put a match to the haystack, certain now that it must be there he had hidden the body, and fled back to Frederick Mingle's dinted bicycle, and found a road and raced away once more towards open country.

All through the dawn he fled and all through the chilly morning; for it seemed to him, now, that his guilt was a scandal in two worlds. He fled from the scene where he felt that a ghost was reproaching him, and from the police whom he pictured even now adding to the charge of murder another of arson. How a few miles on a bicycle would outdistance ghosts or police he did not stop to reflect, but only fled on.

The morning papers had nothing new about his crime; but when after a day of weary flight, he bought the earliest evening paper, another shock awaited him, a shock of astonishment that fell on him from the front page. For a heading said LEE MURDERER CONFESSES. And then he read: Albert Pornick confessed early this morning to the murder of Frederick Mingle by striking him on the head with a brick in the course of a fight over a dog, which had snapped at Pornick and is understood to have been owned by the murdered man.

Yes, he remembered his dog. It had snapped at the red-headed man, and they had fought over it. Then, if Albert Pornick had been at the police-station that morning confessing to murder, he himself was not Albert Pornick. But the other man, Frederick Mingle, was dead. Then who was he? He could not be Frederick Mingle. Yet the name seemed familiar. And the more he thought of it, the more familiar it seemed.

He got off his bicycle and rested then. If another Albert Pornick had been charged with murder, then he was safe and could sit and rest anywhere. And he needed rest. Yes, it came back to him now: he *was* Frederick Mingle. And, names being the hardest things of all to re-member, when he remembered that, his memory was restored, all but the part of it that still could not exactly recall what had happened after that blow on the side of his head. Sitting there by the road he felt the greatest relief that he had ever known, relief from pursuit from two worlds, for not only had he committed no murder, but the red-headed man was no ghost. Neither police nor spirits would be able to harm him now, or even wish to.

As for the true Albert Pornick, he was all that day in prison and all the next. And it was no malice in the heart of Frederick Mingle that kept him there that long, for all anger had completely disappeared from him, and he realized how trivial the cause of it all had been: it was only negligence that held frayed nerves and weary muscles inert. So the day after that he went round early to the police-station, of which the evening papers had given him ample details, and argued to the inspector that he had not been murdered. I say argued, because his mere statement that he was not dead seemed a little weak against a considerable pile of official documents, involving not only the police but the Home Office itself, and statements that had been officially is-sued to the Press. But in the end he made his point. So the real Albert Pornick was released. And, when the two men met, so far was Freder-ick Mingle from wishing to avenge the blow on his head, that his whole attention was occupied in breaking gently to the true Albert Pornick that no ghost was standing before him.

A Tale of Bad Luck

The prison chaplain had come into Ernest Smeeger's cell, and was sitting talking to him, and the convict was quietly listening; but, when he made some regretful reference to Smeeger's criminal past, for the man had been in prison before, Smeeger broke out with the words, "It isn't that, sir. It's just that I'm a victim of persistent bad luck. Other people makes mistakes besides me, lots of them. But they don't have the bad luck I've had."

"Tell me about it," said the chaplain.

"It was like this, sir," said Smeeger. "There's a friend of mine called Jim Morson. Very clever he is. He made a very clever plan once before. But no plan can hold out against persistent bad luck. That's how I got caught that time, just bad luck: Jim Morson's plan was all right. Well, I got three years over that. So did Jim Morson. And when we comes out we naturally looks round for something to do. One can't sit and starve. You wouldn't have me do that, sir?"

The chaplain muttered something, and the convict went on.

"Well, then, we looked round for something to do, to put a little bread into our mouths, so as not to starve. And one day Jim Morson comes to me and says he has got a plan. And I says, 'Glad to hear it. But it's got to work this time. You remember the last one. That didn't work.'

"'The exception proves the rule,' says Jim Morson."

"That is pure nonsense," said the chaplain.

"I am sorry to hear that, sir," said Smeeger. "For I have often heard people say it. Clever people too. And it convinced me. So I said to Jim Morson, 'All right. Go ahead. Tell me the plan.'

"And Jim Morson says, 'It's like this. There's a lady what goes up to London once a week, from Ketteringham Station in Surrey, nearly always on Fridays; and whenever she goes up to London she wears a tortoiseshell comb, and it has an arty design on it with a bunch of grapes hanging down from a stalk; and the whole bunch is sapphires and emeralds, nice little stones varying from the size of the head of a tin-tack to that of a big pin's head. And the big stalk that they hangs from is all emeralds, and you only have to lift it out.'"

"You weren't thinking of doing that!" said the chaplain.

"*I* wasn't, sir," said Smeeger. "It was Jim Morson's idea, and he says, 'You only have to lift it out. And she goes in one of those long carriages that hold thirty or forty people, and I have found a way of getting at the wire that lights all the globes in the carriage, and there's a long tunnel to go through and it will be dark. And, if she doesn't get into the right carriage, or if I can't manage the lights, then it's off and you do nothing. And if everything goes right, all you have to do is to lift out her comb in the dark and sit down again, and wear rubber-soled shoes. It's perfectly safe.'

"'What if we are searched?' I asks.

"'Searched?' he says. 'Who is to search thirty people? Who will have any authority to do it, or the time?'"

"Why didn't this wicked man do the deed himself," asked the chaplain, "instead of making a catspaw of you?"

"He was directing the entire operation, sir," said Smeeger. "I carried out his orders. And then he was going to see that the suspicion fell where he wanted it, instead of on him or me. He was going to arrange everything, if it hadn't been for my persistent bad luck. It's bad luck that has been dogging me, sir. No man can hold up against that."

"What happened?" asked the chaplain.

"Well, sir, I got into the train on that Friday at the next station after Ketteringham on the way to London, and the lady was there. And Jim Morson was there, taking no notice of me. And there was the comb sticking up with the emeralds and sapphires in it, a little bunch of grapes hanging down from a stalk, only waiting to be lifted out. And I wouldn't never have done it if Jim Morson hadn't told me she didn't really want it. I wouldn't indeed, sir."

"He said that to you, did he?" said the chaplain.

"He proved it, sir," said Smeeger. "He told me she always wore it behind, where she couldn't see it. And sure enough I saw that she did. So what use could it be to her, sir?"

"Well, go on," said the chaplain.

And Smeeger went on. "There were quite thirty people in the carriage, as Jim Morson had said, and of course the lady was perfectly safe, or thought she was. Nobody could walk up and lift out the comb without being seen by lots of people. She was sitting well forward. And then we gets near the tunnel. I knows the line, and that's where the lights always go on. And, sure enough, they didn't. Jim Morson is sitting there reading a paper, a little in front of me, and level with the lady on the opposite side of the carriage. Another mile and we comes to the tunnel, and all is pitch dark. 'Tch, tch,' says Jim Morson, and puts his paper down with a rustle. I waits a few seconds, gets up quietly, leans over the back of the lady's seat and lifts the comb out quite easily and turns round to walk back. And that's the moment when my bad luck comes down on me, sir, through no fault of my own. You can't hold out against bad luck, sir; not when it follows you like that. You couldn't yourself, sir. Nobody could. I am just singled out for misfortune. I do my best to bear it. But it's hard."

"What happened?" asked the chaplain.

"What you would never have counted on, sir," said the convict. "Jim Morson had cut the wire all right, the whole carriage was in pitch darkness, and I had just started walking back to my seat, when suddenly the place was all lit up, dimly, but bright enough to see everyone in the carriage, and there was I walking back to my seat away from the lady."

"But what lit it up?" asked the chaplain.

"Exactly, sir," said Smeeger. "You would never have thought of it. Nobody would, and it might have happened to anyone. But it has to happen to me, because I am dogged by bad luck. There was another train in the tunnel, and it came by, with all its lights flashing from every carriage, and it lit up ours. It's very hard, sir, such luck as that. It is indeed."

In a Hotel Lounge

I met him by one of those chances of which all life is made up, a bank-clerk just too young for Hitler's war, whose expression seemed marked by no romantic event; and yet he told me this story. He might, even he, have led a romantic life, or what seemed romantic to him from its far remoteness from all he was doing or had done all his life, except for a few weeks. It was of those few weeks that he told me, weeks of extravagance on a sunny coast, of a lawless love, of intrigue with a beautiful woman: that was to him the romantic life; and romantic it was while it lasted. He had saved up a little money, enough for a cheap fare to and back from the South of France, and three days in a big hotel. And there he had seen her sitting in the lounge, with eyebrows like the antennae of a moth, and a dark complexion she brought from some southern land, and ripples in her hat that followed the waves of her hair. She must have been most expensively dressed; but Rillet, the little bank-clerk, as he told me his story, only said that she was dressed beautifully. Her figure he said was perfection. Even there in France she was so much what the French call chic, that, in little Rillet's opinion, all the people that passed her by as they went through the crowded lounge were merely people; but she was something apart, something like a creature of another fauna that he had never seen before.

He was on one side of the central carpet running right through the lounge, she just on the other. Common people in common dresses, he said, continually passed between her and him, and common people in magnificent dresses, that would not fit their figures, while she sat there talking with her lips to another woman, and talking with her hands and her sinuous arms, and giving expression to what she said with her whole body, slight though her movements were, so slight, indeed, that at first he did not even detect them, but was only aware of her radiating expression. It was on his first day that he saw her, and he watched her for as long as he sat in the lounge, taking considerable pains to prevent her, as he supposed, from seeing that he was watching her. Altogether he seems, that day, to have watched her with shy adoring glances for several hours. And then he had two days left.

Again he saw her in the lounge next day, sitting in the same place, and he walked carelessly up to a chair not far away and sat down in it as if by chance. All that morning he watched her and again at tea-time, and was by then so fascinated by her graceful ways, her slender figure, her clear profile and her radiant expression, that he quite forgot his funny little pretence of not looking her way, and the more he looked at her the more unhappy he was, till unhappiness began to border upon despair, because of one question that troubled his thoughts, looming darker and darker: could she be married? Of course it stood to reason she must be married; the rings of her jewelled fingers that he saw as she lifted her cup, her gold cigarette-case, the gold clasp of her little bag, her gold watch and chain and all the gold things about her, all told the same story: somebody must have poured out wealth on her in profusion. But where was he? Not in the hotel. Might she not be a widow? That was his hope, and he clung to it all that day as though he had no other. Among the mass of her rings he could not see, from the distance at which he sat, whether there was any wedding ring. But what did that matter, so long as her husband was dead? That was the one essential thing. He must ask her. But all that day he did not dare to approach her. He had not hesitated to fall in love with a woman to whom he had not been introduced and whom he had never seen before; yet seemed unable to tell her so. I suppose he had learned when young never to speak to ladies without introduction and never to pat strange dogs, and abided by what he was taught when he had the power to do so, but falling in love was involuntary. And so that day went by, and he had one day left. Again next morning she was sitting there in the lounge, an object of grace and beauty that, in Rillet's opinion, was too lovely for any words. She was utterly strange to him, and her strangeness enchanted him as much as her grace and her beauty. Never to pat strange women: the words of his early training got all jumbled something like that. He was to go that evening, his three days of luxury ended, the only three he expected ever to have. It was his last chance, and he took it. He walked across the long strip of carpet that divided the lounge, down which mere people walked between him and her, and asked her if it wasn't a fine day. Her answer was wonderful: there had been sunlight upon the flowers, and hawkmoths hovering over them, and the songs of strange birds, and the sea full of beautiful colours, all of which he had never noticed, and her voice describing them made all these things immensely more beautiful still; so that all the land that lay around that hotel, and the sea that glimmered before it, became, as Rillet assured me, not unlike what Eden must have appeared to Adam, the day that he first saw Eve. He sat entranced, not liking to interrupt her. But one question burned in his mind, one question upon which all depended for him, and it must be asked. Was she still married? And soon he asked it. She saw him there adoring before her feet, like some suppliant in an old temple before the statue of Venus. "Are you married?" he blurted out, with a look in his eyes that flickered between hope and despair.

"Well, yes," she said to him. "But what of that?"

"But it is everything, everything," he answered. "I could love you for ever."

"O, very well," she said, the trivial sentence illuminated by a most lovely smile.

It was a rapid courtship.

"But your husband," he said.

She waved a beautiful hand with a graceful curve through the air, and rubies and emeralds and sapphires flashed as she waved it; and at the end of that graceful curve like a bird dipping over a skyline, all thoughts that had troubled the bank-clerk seemed utterly waved away.

"Together!" he said.

"Yes, yes," she smiled.

"For ever," he said.

"Yes, yes," she said again. "For your forever."

He did not understand.

"Your forever will be for a few weeks," she explained. "We shall be happy. No?"

"For ever and ever," he repeated.

"Yes, yes," she said. "For a few weeks."

And again he blurted out, "For ever and ever."

"Yes, yes," she said. "A few weeks and you will tire."

He could not argue with her, any more than he could have argued with the goddess Venus herself, if she had come up there to him out of the sea, speaking a strange language.

And for a few weeks they were happy with a bliss beyond what he had ever dreamed of finding either in Heaven or earth. His three little days of luxury, that were to have been for him the memory of a life-time, were extended to twenty or thirty; for she had money to do whatever they wanted. Everything about her was gold; her hairbrushes, her mirrors, her shoehorn, and even the handles of her nail-files and tweezers, and her inkpot and paperknife too.

And those blissful days drew to an end in the smile of the Mediterranean, beaming upon a coast whose flowers all smiled back. And one day, after some trivial disagreement of which he told me nothing, she had said, "Well? Your forever is nearly up. No? Do we part now? Or do you really wish for marriage?"

"Yes, yes," he said. "Divorce him immediately."

"We don't divorce," she said, "in Capricornia." That was her love-ly land. "We all belong to Holy Church, which does not permit divorce."

"But, but," he began.

"We may sometimes err," she went on; "sin, if you will. But we obey."

"You never divorce?" he said in despair, at which she only smiled with her lovely smile.

"No, no," she said. "We always shoot."

"You shoot?" he muttered.

"O, yes," she said. "I always carry this."

And she drew out from under her heart a little neat pistol with a handle of solid gold like that of her nail-file. The short small barrel of course was straight, but the thin gold handle was slightly curved to fit the delicate curve of her neat figure.

That was all that Rillet definitely told me. The rest was vague and rather incoherent. I think he was a little ashamed of leaving his lady and going back to his bank, one of the safest in the City. But he realized that he had had his few weeks of perfect bliss, and estimated quite reasonably that there would be very few more for him, before the gold-handled pistol flashed out upon some petulant day. "And it was a very small bore, you know," he said. "I shouldn't have so much minded a sudden end coming from a four fifty."

The Chambermaid of the Splendide

The day began with the chirping of numberless sparrows, and the sun peeping brilliantly in through chinks of curtains, and waking between them the visitors and the staff of the Splendide. Margaret Allen woke with the chirp of the first sparrow, as wide awake as she had ever been. She was a chambermaid at the hotel, and on this day, after she had called a dozen visitors and brought them their tea, she had the whole day off, and the whole of the next day. Nor were they two ordinary days off, for by then her savings had reached an amount that would enable her to make an old dream a reality, which was to be herself what she had so long seen, a visitor in a luxurious hotel. There were in the town the Splendide, in which she had worked for ten years, and the Magnifique, its great rival. There were several other hotels there too, but no others with any pretensions to compete with either of those two, or to compare, as they did, with the great hotels of the continent. The commodity in which they dealt was luxury, and no luxurious food came into any shop in that town without being at once snapped up by one of these two, and usually it was a race to see which got it first. And for the matter of that they often competed with each other at Covent Garden to get the best fruit in the morning. And to the most luxurious food came the most luxurious people, like flies with golden wings in bright sunlight to honey. It was of being among these people that Margaret Allen had dreamed, as a nun may dream of Heaven, and on this bright morning to which the sparrows woke her, and the sun flashing over the sea, the dream was to be fulfilled.

Mrs. Van Delft lived in hotels. Whatever her nationality, they were her home. She liked southern coasts, preferably those of France; but in summer England would do very well. She was one of the ladies that Margaret Allen called that bright morning, although the work of waking her had been actually done by the sparrows.

"You have your day off today, haven't you?" said Mrs. Van Delft.

"Yes. And tomorrow," said Margaret.

"What are you going to do?" asked Mrs. Van Delft. For she saw the light of that bright morning flashing in Margaret's eyes with a brilliance that seemed a little more than its own. And shyly at first, but warming to it as she went on, the chambermaid revealed the dream of her life; to be for once waited upon, hand and foot, to sit in a sunny garden all the morning in perfect idleness, and afterwards in the lounge among all those jewelled women.

"And you'll enjoy that?" said Mrs. Van Delft.

"It will make up for ten years of hard work," said the chambermaid.

How lost she will be in that smart crowd, thought Mrs. Van Delft. "But have you the clothes for it?" was all she said.

"I've bought a frock," said the chambermaid. "I've been saving for it for years."

"But you'll have to have another for dinner, too, you know," said the lady.

"I've bought that too," said Margaret.

"And where are you going to stay?" asked Mrs. Van Delft.

"I'm going to the Magnifique," announced Margaret, with a pride in her voice not unworthy of the Magnifique's pretensions.

"The Magnifique!" said Mrs. Van Delft. "You'll be quite out of it there without jewelry."

"Jewelry!" gasped the chambermaid.

"But I'll give you all mine for those two days," said that most expensive lady. "It will be safe enough in the Magnifique. But you must take a taxi through the streets."

Through all this amazing speech Margaret Allen had remained silent, with her mouth open wide enough to take big breaths.

"But you wouldn't trust me with all that!" she got out at last.

"Don't talk to me," said Mrs. Van Delft, "at my age, about whom I can trust and whom I cannot. Though I haven't found I can trust very many."

And so that was decided. The jewelry was all diamonds; not worth a king's ransom, but worth the ransom of a man from a lifetime of any work, which those diamonds could have exchanged for ease for the rest of his days. Idly they had lain in the mines for ages, then for a little while many men had worked at them, and now hidden among their rays they had this great gift of leisure. Mrs. Van Delft was accustomed to be obeyed and Margaret Allen to obeying, and so the diamonds were thrust into her hands and she was ordered to pack them at once and to get a taxi.

Margaret Allen's two days at the Hotel Magnifique cannot be told of in ordinary language. Things that could bring no joy to us, such as the bowing to her of many waiters, things that to us are no higher than mere comfort, such as deep and soft armchairs, little idlenesses such as tea in bed, and conveniences such as a bathroom of her own, were fulfilments of a long dream, so that to tell of them adequately I should have to clothe my words with something of that enchantment with which dreams are haunted, something far from our life, like queer weeds waving in illuminated water in which swim tropical fish all shining with brilliant colours. To understand those two days as she saw them, and it is about her that I write, one should picture some palace of Asia in the days of Haroun al Raschid, or whatever one may have imagined of life on a planet nearer than ours to the sun. Therefore no mere facts as I could tell them, describing the luxuries of a modern hotel, could ever tell Margaret Allen's story of those two days. Nor did she tell it herself with any coherence, when she came on the third morning to Mrs. Van Delft's room to give her back her jewelry and to pour out thanks that got all mixed up with tears that fell glittering on to the diamonds. Yet Mrs. Van Delft understood her, she understood that the waiters had been polite to her with the politeness that they show to the very rich, she realized that her last penny had gone in paying for the two taxis, for which Mrs. Van Delft had forgotten to pay, and that she did not mind, and that as she had sat in the lounge before an early dinner, with all her diamonds on, a gentleman with a splendid moustache and beautifully dressed had introduced himself to her; and they had dined together, and they had sat and talked together for most of the following day; and that night she had worn all Mrs. Van Delft's diamonds again, and they had made her look like something out of a fairytale, or a queen, or she didn't know what.

"You must have had a fine time," said Mrs. Van Delft.

"Oh, but that wasn't all, mum," said the chambermaid of the Splendide. "He proposed to me only this morning, and he was a baronet."

"Oh, but was he really?" exclaimed Mrs. Delft. "Are you sure?"

"Oh yes," said Margaret Allen. "He was genuine. I made quite sure of that."

"Why, then, that is wonderful," said Mrs. Van Delft. "Wonderful. My most hearty congratulations. I'm so glad my diamonds helped, if they did."

She was looking in Margaret's eyes and, though they were shining, something made her wonder if they were shining at the marvellous future that promised, or at what? And she added, "Of course you accepted him."

"No, I didn't," said Margaret.

"No?" repeated the astonished Mrs. Van Delft.

"No, mum," Margaret Allen said. "I've been here ten years, and I've seen more people than you would ever think. And I've watched them. So I know what people are doing. And I knew that he was only after my money. But I had a wonderful two days. Wonderful."

THE MOTIVE

"My first case," said the old detective, "my first case was an infringement of the licensing laws. A man had neglected to take out a license for his Sealyham puppy. But my first interesting case, my first big one, was a case of murder. Mind you, murder is not a word to be thrown about lightly, but that's what it was all about. A lady had died suddenly in a rectory in East Anglia, of a very violent form of food-poisoning. You can poison with food just as well as with chemicals, and it looked very like murder. But the difficulty was that there was no motive for anybody to have done it, and that's what I was sent down to find out, and not a motive could I discover. Plenty of people had had access to the rectory; so I had to examine them all. And that took a long time, working in the dark without any guiding light. Give me a motive, and I usually know who's done it, which sometimes is nearly half way, all the rest of the way being proof. But without a motive I was in the dark. Well, I went to the Rectory, and the Rector quietly shook hands with me, a tall man in the late thirties, with a grave, solemn face; which of course it would be: I don't know if he ever smiled at other times. He very kindly gave me the run of his study, and there I sat at his oak desk with thirty sheets of foolscap and made out a thorough dossier of twenty-five people who had had access to the Rectory during the week of the murder, if murder it was, which it is not for either you or me to say. But she had eaten that deadly food, which nobody else had eaten, and died within twenty-four hours. The Rector was most helpful; he came into his study where I was, and sat in an armchair smoking his pipe, which, indeed, he did all day, for he was obviously under a great stress, and he gave me all the details for which I asked. Among others he showed me his whole financial position. He had a small stipend, little more than three hundred a year, and a private income of two hundred. But his wife had an income of £800, which when she died went back to her family, so that he suffered a double loss by her death. None of that family had had any access to the house for a long time.

Indeed the only motive that I could see in the whole case could have been with a relative of the poisoned woman who had come into her fortune. But motive without opportunity can of course get one no-where. And there was no opportunity whatever, except where there was no motive.

"Greed had not done it, for no one gained except this relative who was two hundred miles away, nor was there any place in this sad story for any other of the usual motives, a jealous lover being out of the question, for she had been of a saintly type, nor could she have ever invited any other form of jealousy. Under his clouds of tobacco the Rector told me everything I asked, and was perfectly open. About him the opinion of the whole parish, as I collected it bit by bit, was practi-cally unanimous, and before I had done I had enquired of pretty nearly all of them about him and his visitors and his servants. And he was a man about whom it was easy to get information. For he preached re-markable sermons and managed pretty well to fill his church every Sunday, and the evidence was that there was a moral in those sermons that was uplifting to all. What particularly struck me was that to a cer-tain proportion of his parishioners he appeared to be too high-church, and they criticized some of his genuflections etc., being low church themselves; but even from them I got the same story, that his sermons were moving and powerful.

"I was a week in that parish, spending day after day in that study over my sheets of foolscap, and wherever I found opportunity I came upon obstacles like that, a man not only a clergyman but a very re-markable one, suffering grievous loss by that death and without any trace of vice. I stopped at the inn of the village, the Green Dragon, and every afternoon I had a glass of beer at the bar, and I would get into conversation and perhaps stand a glass or two to others and talk to them a little myself, and then sit in a chair and listen for an hour or so when conversation had got going. I collected a lot of information in that way, but none of it that pointed in any direction that a detective wants to go. In fact every bit of it pointed the other way, which was to prove that everyone in the Rectory, and all who had gone there, were innocent. And yet I could not go back to London with the story that the whole thing was an accident, for that had all been gone into, and the fact that nobody else in the house had suffered in any way, and the suddenness and the violence of the poison, did not point that way at all.

"I went from the Green Dragon every day to the Rectory, and the Rector was always most helpful; and still he smoked on and on, trying to numb his sorrow or soothe his nerves. I wondered which of the two it was, and whether all that smoking could do either, or only make matters worse. That his sorrow was overwhelming, or that his nerves were all on edge, he did not actually show; but only that he needed this constant soothing. The time came when there was no more information that I could get out of anybody, and all that I had collected was the very opposite of what I had been sent down to find. I felt like a prospector who had burdened himself with heavy sacks of gold-bearing quartz in which no particle of gold could be found. Reluctantly I had to admit that my work down there was concluded, and that meant that I must return to London and hand in my report. I knew how the Chief Inspector would look at me when I did that, and I knew what he would imply, though I didn't expect him to say anything. It would be easier for me to put up a case if he did. But he wouldn't. He would look at my report of a week's work and then look at me. And that is pretty much what happened at first, when I stood in front of his desk. And then there came a change all of a sudden. He was a man who could read you. I think he always knew when a suspected person was guilty. Proving it was another matter, other men's job. And he read me then. I was young, with my career all before me, and he must have seen how hopeless I looked. For he suddenly came out with advice.

"'Look here,' he said, 'all the people at the Rectory are too good. I have read your report, and there's no vice or fault in the lot of them. Yet a murder has been committed. You go back and find some flaw among them. Men without any flaw in their character don't commit murder, and a pretty big flaw too.'

"So he was giving me another chance, which was wonderful. I could have blessed him. I somehow saw from the way he glanced at the part of my report that told in glowing terms of the Rector, that my chief suspected him.

"'It couldn't have been the Rector,' I blurted out.

"'It couldn't have been you,' he said. 'Because I didn't send you down there in time for you to have done it. And it wasn't me. Because I can prove I was here. But you can't leave out anyone else without proofs as good as that, when there has been a murder. Someone has done it. I suspect the greatest motive first, and then the greatest opportunity, and I tell no one whom I suspect. But don't wear blinkers. Don't say of anyone "He couldn't have done it." Prove he couldn't, by all means.'

"'But a clergyman of the Church of England, sir,' I said. 'And a man who they all say preaches the finest sermons in all the diocese.'

"'Most unlikely,' said the Inspector. 'And it's unlikely that I did it. But I can prove that I didn't. Can he?'

"'It's a dreadful suspicion,' I said.

"'Not a word about that,' said the Chief. 'Suspect nobody. Prove it. That's all. And, to begin with, find some fault among your spotless innocents. And follow that up.'

"It was very kind of him to give me all that advice. He didn't usually. And I saw that I was not going to get any more. So back I went to Reedham, and back to the Rectory, and the Rector came to the door when I rang the bell and greeted me cheerily, his cheeriness overcast, as it should have been, with something of the solemnity becoming a mourner. And I told him that I had been sent back there to question certain of his parishioners, which was quite true so far as it went. I did not tell him that it was about himself that I was going to ask the questions. He asked me to come into his study, and we went in. And I noticed that he had not been smoking so much since I left. Various little trifles showed me that. But as soon as I sat down in his study he began smoking again, and had the pipe smoking away for as long as I was there. I talked to him about his parish and his parishioners, but I was looking all the time for the fault or flaw that the Chief Inspector wanted, whatever the flaw might be. I did not mention any names to him, saying that I did not want to cast any suspicion, but that I had to make further enquiries in certain quarters. And he quite understood, or appeared to, though both of us may have been quietly playing a game: certainly I was. And I had the feeling that one sometimes has at draughts, when one is playing a better player, that all the while I was getting nowhere. Everything that he said to me was just what he should have said; and beyond the clouds of his smoke and the veil of his conversation that fault for which I was searching lay hidden away. I never got it from him. I stood up after a long time and said that I must now go and make those enquiries in certain quarters, that I had been sent to make. And he gave me a friendly farewell, and asked me to come back whenever I liked, and to use the study whenever it suited me.

"I went to a man whom I had met when I was in Reedham before, an artist who had rented a cottage in the village. I am giving no names of anybody. He was only a very occasional churchgoer, and I chose him for that reason, because an artist who had come to that village from London and who seldom went to church was a bit outside the massed feeling and opinion of the village, a thing that I cannot define, but as much a part of Reedham as the mists that on autumn evenings hung over the little stream which ran through the village. From this massed opinion I already had a verdict, and as it was not one that suited my chief or that got anyone any further, I obviously had to tap another source. He only had a sitting-room and a kitchen downstairs, and a shed in the garden that he used as a studio. He asked me into his sitting-room and offered me a cigarette, and lit a pipe himself and we sat down and talked. We talked of all manner of things, things far beyond any horizon that bounded the village, and I gradually narrowed the conversation till it closed in on the Rector. And then I made all the running. I said what a perfect example he was of what a rector of a parish should be, what a saintly character he had, untouched by any one of the faults some of which are to be found in all other men.

"'Well, yes,' said the artist and went on puffing his pipe. And, when he said that, I knew I had got what I wanted. I mean, I saw as it were the glint of an end of the nugget that only needed digging out from the earth. So I verbally dug.

"'I shouldn't say that he had any fault whatever,' I said.

"'I wouldn't say that,' said the artist.

"'No?' I said.

"'No,' he went on. 'I wouldn't say he was entirely without any fault.'

"'And what fault could he possibly have?' I asked.

"'Ambition,' he answered, 'if you call that a fault.'

"At last! At last I had it.

"One fault among all that innocence of which Reedham seemed only too full. The fault I had been sent down to find. No good, of course, as far as I could see: it got one no further. One didn't murder one's wife out of ambition. One had heard of passionate murders, but not of ambitious ones, short of murdering emperors. No, it got one no further. But it was a fault. And I had been sent to find one. I should not come back quite empty-handed, and be told that the profession to which I have devoted my life was not quite my vocation.

"'I shouldn't have thought he was ambitious,' I said.

"'Yes, definitely,' said the artist.

"'But, after all, why not?' I said.

"'Yes, why not?' he answered.

"'He preaches beautiful sermons,' I said, 'and has every right to ambition.'

"'Quite so,' he replied.

"'I don't blame him,' I said.

"'Nor do I,' said he.

"'I suppose any clergyman would like to be a bishop,' I said.

"'More than that,' said the artist.

"'More?' I exclaimed.

"'Yes, more than that in his case,' he said.

"'Does he want to be an archbishop?' I asked.

"'I don't think that's quite the line his ambition takes,' he replied. 'The field is too limited there, owing to the Church of England having only two archbishops.'

"'What then?' I asked.

"'Rome has more gorgeous prizes to offer,' he said. 'I painted a cardinal once in his full regalia, and I assure you it was a joy to paint him. The picture shone at me. I was never able to get so much colour into a portrait before or after.'

"'A cardinal!' I exclaimed.

"'It's not beyond the bounds of possibility,' said my host, 'and certainly not beyond the scope of ambition. A man who can preach as he does would be welcomed by Rome, if he left the great heresy that has always been a thorn in her flesh.'

"'But has he ever shown any leanings towards Rome?' I asked.

"'I think so,' he said.

"'But a married man can't . . .' I began, and I caught my breath.

"The motive! The motive! I could hardly keep silent. The thing came in a flash. Here was a man with motive and opportunity and one fault. What more could headquarters want? Let them put the story together: that was no business of mine.

"I got out a few dull words to the artist, and hurried back to London with my valuable information. I say valuable, because it was what they wanted and what they asked for. And that I brought them, and it saved my career. It was no use to them and it never came to anything, because the whole case was much too slender to bring against a clergyman of the Church of England, with not a flaw in his character, except the very slight one alleged by one artist, and one that judge and jury and most of us might very well share.

"I went into my chief's office, and I think he saw in my face as I entered the room that I had not failed in my mission. He didn't say a word, and I started speaking and told him all that the artist had told to me.

"'I see,' said my chief thoughtfully."

The Quiet Laugh

One afternoon of the Eton-and-Harrow match I was walking round the ground at Lord's, while a great number of other people were doing the same, when I heard a lady in the crowd beside me say to her husband, which I took him to be, "Look out. There are those tiresome Brent-Harritys just behind us."

A glance that I had seen her throw over her shoulder showed me which the Brent-Harritys were, and the woman who had spoken slightly increased her pace, taking her husband with her, while the couple they were avoiding continued at the same pace. And presently something, I do not know what, seemed to tell Mrs. Brent-Harrity that the other two were avoiding her, and she stopped for an instant and gave a little laugh, a quiet laugh that I could not hear, but I saw her teeth shining, and then she said something to her husband, and they walked slower, while the others continued their pace, so that soon the four of them were out of my sight, two of them in front of me and two far behind. There is of course some story connected with every action of men and women, though it isn't often you find it, nor did I for two years. And then one day at a party I happened to be introduced to Mrs. Brent-Harrity, and I remembered the name. And as we talked she brought to me over the pavements of London, and among the noise of the motors and the talk of passing things, something of the unchanging things of the hills of the heart of Ireland, something that turned me from the thought of cocktails and bridge to thoughts of curlews and heather and white cottages and the odour of turf-smoke, and we spoke of Ireland and of happy days and of troubles. And I liked her so much that I asked her if we might meet again, and she kindly arranged another meeting. And we often met after that, and one day she told me a story that was evidently about those two people that I had seen before her at Lord's; and at different times we talked of them a good deal, and so I got their story. They were relations of hers, but superior to her in wealth, and indeed to all their neighbours, so that, though they lived in

Ireland, their friends were all where they had a wider choice, chiefly in London. Their neighbours were all friendly enough to them, rather too friendly; and these two, the Frayne-Eagans, found them a bit too demonstrative for their taste. But they found it very easy to put the countrypeople in their place, and with a few tactful rebuffs where they seemed to be needed they checked any undue familiarity from the small neighbouring landowners.

And then the trouble came. All this was many years before my chance sight of those four at the cricket-match. The troubles came and, right or wrong, or whatever their politics, those whom the people liked were spared, and those whom they hated were in deadly peril. The loyalists had all been disarmed with everyone else, and there was nothing to protect any man now but the affection of the people. The Brent-Harritys had it, and the Frayne-Eagans had not. Both the Brent-Harritys had had it all their lives, neither of the Frayne-Eagans. Mrs. Frayne-Eagan was an Englishwoman and wealthy: it was her money that ran Eagan Towers, as their little house was called. They and the Brent-Harritys lived nowhere near each other; but news, or rather the knowledge of men and women, travels today about Ireland as quickly as ever it did, and the invention of trains and motors has never quickened its pace, for it goes faster than either of them. But surely, it may be urged, the telegraph can beat it. No, not even the telegraph. For a telegram has to be translated from morse to English, and then written down and put in an envelope, and addressed and sent off on a bicycle, and delivered; and long before that the postmistress will have discussed the contents with whomever she considers worthy of confidence, and the gist of it will be the talk of the little village before it is read by the man to whom it has been addressed. And so where Mrs. Brent-Harrity lived in the next county but one, everything was known about Mr. and Mrs. Frayne-Eagan that was necessary for an estimate of their characters, and for an exact knowledge of what they would always do. And what the people knew in any county of Ireland Bran Pheely knew, and on the information he had of what the people knew of the Frayne-Eagans in the hilly county that they inhabited, he decided to kill them both. He never let out his plans, but the information on which he had based these plans was common knowledge in Munster, and the people of the county in which Mrs. Brent-Harrity lived knew what he would be sure to be doing about this case. And one of them went to Mrs. Brent-Harrity one night and knocked at her door, because she had been kind to him, as indeed she had been to everybody, and said, "I only called, Mam, to ask how you were." And she waited for him to go on; and he went on, and said, "And to ask if it mightn't be a good thing to warn your cousin over in Borrisadair, and that wife that he has, to get out of the country till the trouble blows over and while they are still alive, which they mightn't be if they were to wait too long, which might happen to anybody."

And she said, "Thank you, Mickey. But it might be too late for that, with things as they are. But if you would tell Bran Pheely that I would like a word with him, I would ask him if he wouldn't let them live."

And Mickey had said, "Sure, I don't know Bran Pheely at all."

"I know that," said Mrs. Brent-Harrity. "I know that. And I am not saying you do. But if ever you met anyone who knew him, ask him to tell him that. And try and meet him quickly, for there might not be too much time."

"Sure, I will, Mam," said Mickey, stepping out of the glow of the house, and the dark night covered him up.

And late the following night there was another knock on the door, and Mrs. Brent-Harrity went to open it and her husband came with her. She opened the door a crack, then wider and wider until it was wide open, and saw nobody, but stood there looking out into the night beyond the glow on the gravel that shone from the open door. And then Bran Pheely stepped into the midst of the light, and pointed to Brent-Harrity and looked at his wife and said to her, "Tell him to go back into the house."

And she turned her head and nodded to Brent-Harrity, and he walked away into an inner room. And then Bran Pheely said, "I heard it said over beyond the hills that it's the way it was that you wanted to see me."

And she said, "I did, General."

"And what is it I can do for you, Mam?" he asked.

And she said, "Didn't you have a good enough time when you were here in the stables?"

And he said, "Sure, I had the grandest time, and I loved all your horses. Sure they were great, every one of them, and it was a pleasure to groom them."

"Well, now," said Mrs. Brent-Harrity, "didn't I always give you good advice whenever you asked for it?"

"And indeed you did, Mam," said Bran Pheely.

"Didn't I advise you to stick to your religion," she said, "when you wanted to change to ours because you had quarrelled with your priest?"

"You did so, Mam," he said.

"And aren't you the better for it?" she asked.

"By all the Saints I am, Mam," he answered.

"Well, then," she said, "I have a bit of advice for you now. And that's all I wanted to give you."

"And what would that be, Mam?" he enquired.

"You know," she said, "how the English have different ideas from what we have. They look at things in a different way. And I didn't want you to do anything that might tell against you in the end. And that's why I have this bit of advice for you."

"And what is that, Mam?" he repeated.

"It wouldn't be a good thing to shoot the Frayne-Eagans," she answered.

Bran Pheely looked very thoughtful at that.

"They wouldn't like the shooting of a woman," she said.

"She's the worst of the two of them," he answered.

"I know," she said. "And they are both bad. But hasn't my advice to you always been good?"

"It has indeed, Mam," he said again.

"Then don't shoot the Frayne-Eagans, General," she said to him.

"It mightn't be too easy to take that advice, Mam," he told her, "considering the orders I have higher up."

"Then do it for my sake," she said.

And he looked at her and nodded and stepped aside, and there was nothing there but the night and the glow on the gravel. And Mrs. Brent-Harrity closed the door, and even the glow was gone.

That was all a long time ago, and Mrs. Frayne-Eagan had been to many matches at Lord's since then, where she met a good many people who were worth knowing. "But one has a certain position to keep up," she used to say, "after all; which one cannot very well do if one hobnobs with everyone."

And then came that day when I saw the four in the crowd that was drifting round at Lord's, the Frayne-Eagans ahead of me and the Brent-Harritys dropping behind; and Mrs. Brent-Harrity's story lighted the incident up, so that I saw what had been happening, as one so rarely does, and I even knew the thoughts of Mrs. Brent-Harrity as she gave that quiet laugh. She was thinking of the night when she talked with Bran Pheely on the little patch of gravel that shone in the dark.

BIBLIOGRAPHY

Advance Regulations. *Punch* No. 5496 (8 May 1946): 405 (unsigned). Text derived from the manuscript at Dunsany Castle.

As It Seems to the Blackbird. *Evening News* (London) No. 21,009 (13 June 1949): 2. Text derived from the manuscript at Dunsany Castle.

At the Scene of the Crime. Unpublished.

The Awakening. *Poetry Review* 44, No. 5 (July–September 1953): 375–77. Text derived from the manuscript at Dunsany Castle.

The Blundering Curate. Unpublished.

A Breeze at Rest. *Time and Tide* 35, No. 35 (28 August 1954): 1136. Text derived from the manuscript at Dunsany Castle.

The Burrahoola. *Evening News* (London) No. 21,248 (21 March 1950): 7. Text derived from the manuscript at Dunsany Castle.

The Chambermaid of the Splendide. *Homes and Gardens* (August 1953): 30–32 (as "The Chambermaid at the Splendide"). Text derived from the manuscript at Dunsany Castle.

A Channel Rescue. *Illustrated London News* No. 6030A (Christmas Number 1954): 15–16. Text derived from the manuscript at Dunsany Castle.

The Cook of Santamaria. *Everybody's Weekly* (16 May 1953): 27–28 (as "The Cook of Santa Maria"). Text derived from the manuscript at Dunsany Castle.

The Dance at Weirdmoor Castle. *Homes and Gardens* 32, No. 6 (December 1950): 26–27. Text derived from the manuscript at Dunsany Castle.

A Day on the Bog. *Punch* No. 5580 (3 December 1947): 544–45 (unsigned). Text derived from the manuscript at Dunsany Castle.

The Dwarf Holóbolos and the Sword Hogbiter. *Collins for Boys and Girls* No. 1 ([July] 1949): 9–16. Text derived from the manuscript at Dunsany Castle.

The Ghost in the Corner. *Punch* No. 5175 (29 May 1940): 588 (unsigned). Text derived from the manuscript at Dunsany Castle.

A Goat in Trousers. *Everybody's Weekly* (11 July 1953): 24–25. Text derived from the manuscript at Dunsany Castle.

Hard Horses. Unpublished.

The Haunting of Whitebeams. *John Bull* No. 2347 (23 June 1951): 21–22. Text derived from the manuscript at Dunsany Castle.

Helping the Fairies. *Strand Magazine* 113, No. 2 (May–June 1947): 28–31. Text derived from the manuscript at Dunsany Castle.

How Mickey Paid His Debt. *Evening News* (London) No. 21,271 (18 April 1950): 7. Text derived from the manuscript at Dunsany Castle.

In a Hotel Lounge. Unpublished.

In the Governor's Palace. Unpublished.

Kind Pagan Lights. *Evening News* (London) No. 21,586 (24 April 1951): 5. Text derived from the manuscript at Dunsany Castle.

Little Tim Brannehan. *Punch* No. 5631 (10 November 1948): 431 (as by "D."). Text derived from the manuscript at Dunsany Castle.

Lost Lyrics. *Homes and Gardens* 32, No. 3 (September 1950): 22–23. Text derived from the manuscript at Dunsany Castle.

The Lucky Escape. *John O'London's Weekly* No. 1386 (14 April 1950): 221–22 (as "The Short Story of 1950"). Text derived from the manuscript at Dunsany Castle.

Mid Snow and Ice. *Modern Reading* No. 20 (Winter 1951–52): 40–43. Text derived from the manuscript at Dunsany Castle.

A Modern Portrait. *Punch* No. 5497 (15 May 1946): 413 (unsigned). Text derived from the manuscript at Dunsany Castle.

The Motive. Unpublished.

The Old Detective's Story. *Ellery Queen's Mystery Magazine* 34, No. 2 (August 1959): 86–89 (as "Three Men in a Garden"). Text derived from the manuscript at Dunsany Castle.

One Night in Eldorado. *Homes and Gardens* 31, No. 9 (March 1950): 22–24. Text derived from the manuscript at Dunsany Castle.

The Price of the World. Unpublished.

Progress. *Evening News* (London) No. 21,189 (11 January 1950): 2. Text derived from the manuscript at Dunsany Castle.

The Quiet Laugh. Unpublished.

The Rations of Murdoch Finucan. *Punch* No. 5571 (8 October 1947): 340–41 (unsigned). Text derived from the manuscript at Dunsany Castle.

The Romance of His Life. *Harper's Bazaar* No. 2884 (March 1952): 170, 229. Text derived from the manuscript at Dunsany Castle.

The Stolen Power. *Prediction* 18, No. 12 (December 1952): 7, 11 (as "Stolen Power"). Text derived from the manuscript at Dunsany Castle.

The Story of Tse Gah. *Tomorrow* 7, No. 4 (December 1947): 19–20. Text derived from the manuscript at Dunsany Castle.

A Tale of Bad Luck. *Evening News* (London) No. 22,048 (17 October 1952): 7 (as "Just His Luck"). Text derived from the manuscript at Dunsany Castle.

A Tale of the Irish Countryside. Unpublished.

Tales for the Dark Continent. *Punch* No. 5391 (24 May 1944): 452 (unsigned). Text derived from the manuscript at Dunsany Castle.

A Talk in the Dark. *Tomorrow* 10, No. 11 (July 1951): 19. Text derived from the manuscript at Dunsany Castle.

A Theory of Evolution. *Spectator* No. 6484 (3 October 1952): 420–21 (as "Darwin Superseded"). Text derived from the manuscript at Dunsany Castle.

The Traveller to Thundercliff. *Colophon* (London) 1, No. 1 (March 1950): 16. Text derived from the manuscript at Dunsany Castle.

A Treasure of India. *Singapore Free Press* (27 January 1956): 14. Text derived from the manuscript at Dunsany Castle.

Two Young Officers. Unpublished.

The Unforgivable Choice. *Sphere* No. 3006a (8 November 1957): 19–21. Text derived from the manuscript at Dunsany Castle.

The Use of Man. *Harper's Bazaar* No. 2626 (August 1931): 85, 108. *Harper's Bazaar* (London) 4, No. 5 (September 1931): 60–61, 80–81 (as "What Is the Use of Man?"). Text derived from the manuscript at Dunsany Castle.

Very Secret. *Punch* No. 5330 (14 April 1943): 305 (unsigned). Text derived from the manuscript at Dunsany Castle.

When Mrs. Fynn Was Young. *Sunday Chronicle* (London) (23 April 1950): 2. Text derived from the manuscript at Dunsany Castle.

A Witch in the Balkans. *Everybody's Weekly* (2 June 1951): 21–22. Text derived from the manuscript at Dunsany Castle.

CPSIA information can be obtained
at www.ICGtesting.com
Printed in the USA
BVOW11s1042210517
484712BV00009B/23/P